BY STRUTHERS BURT

THE INTERPRETER'S HOUSE

CHANCE ENCOUNTERS

SONGS AND PORTRAITS

JOHN O'MAY AND OTHER STORIES

CHARLES SCRIBNER'S SONS

THE
INTERPRETER'S HOUSE

" Then he went on till he came at the house of the Interpreter, where he knocked over and over; at last one came to the door, and asked Who was there?"

PILGRIM'S PROGRESS, BOOK I.

THE
INTERPRETER'S HOUSE

By

STRUTHERS BURT

CHARLES SCRIBNER'S SONS

NEW YORK : : : : : : : 1924

TO HORACE LEEDOM CARNCROSS, M.D.

DEAR HORACE:

Neither you nor I especially like great cities and we both agree that some day a more intelligent race will find means of getting along without them. But meanwhile, and in the curious age in which we are living, we are forced to admit that these labyrinthian "interpreters' houses" are the most typical expression of the unconscious and baffled desires of the human race as it now exists. Like the old Chinese vases in which they used to grow the dwarfs of the seventeenth century, cities form those who live in them to their convexities and concavities— usually malform them. And when the latter is the case, it is a pity, for both you and I have lived together too long in lonely countries not to have achieved a respect for human nature in itself, and a vast contempt for what circumstances can do to it.

As one of the most acute investigators of the phenomena one finds in the various "interpreters' houses" of the world, as one of the few persons more or less properly "compensating"— to use, or possibly misuse, one of your own psychoanalytical terms—I dedicate this book to you. As to the affection and admiration and friendship back of the act, we have ridden too many nights together, worked too much side by side, hungered and worried and thirsted too much, to dwell upon such obvious commonplaces. I wish you luck in your patient researches into the old paradox of why, with beauty all about them and beauty in their hearts, men and women still let evil and ugliness conquer them.

Affectionately.

STRUTHERS BURT.

BAR B. C. RANCH,
September 15, 1922.

BOOK I

"Sir, here is a traveller." — PILGRIM'S PROGRESS, BOOK I.

* * *

"Then he took him by the hand and led him into a very large parlor that was full of dust, because never swept."—PILGRIM'S PROGRESS, BOOK I.

		PAGE
I.	15 MADISON PLACE	3
II.	GULIAN RETURNS	14
III.	MRS. PRENDEGAST IS LATE	29
IV.	THE BIRTH OF A DETERMINATION—PERHAPS TWO	38
V.	"HE WENT FORTH WITH THE LOVELY ODALISQUES"	55
VI.	AUNT VIRGINIA CONTINUES HER ADVICE	78
VII.	PHILIP BUYS THEATRE TICKETS	88
VIII.	"Only they were premature, only they believed that they could make their contemporaries, who had scarcely outgrown their childhood, without enlightenment, without preparation, men worthy of their Third Age."—*Lessing*	102
IX.	SOMEWHAT OF A RELIEF	116

PAGE

X. "The older I grow the more convinced I become that scandal is at the bottom of half
the evil in the world, and that more people
have been driven to desperation through
the loose tongues of others than by any
other one cause.   But there is some consolation, although not a very satisfactory
one, in the veracity of the old Spanish
proverb that eventually 'a fish dies through
its own mouth.'"—*From a letter of Mr.
Eyre's to his friend and classmate, Professor
Hartlemas of Princeton University* . . . 124

XI. THE GATES OF BEWILDERMENT 145

XII. "There is but one truth, outside science, the
truth that comes of an earnest smiling survey of mankind."—*New Letters: Stevenson* 155

XIII. MAY NIGHT 168

BOOK II

*"I saw moreover in my dream, that the interpreter took him by
the hand, and led him into a little room, where sat two
children, each one in a chair.   And the name of the eldest was
Passion, and the name of the other was Patience."*—PILGRIM'S
PROGRESS, BOOK I.

I. WISTERIA 187

II. "THE DEEP, DEEP COUNTRY" 205

III. VANNYA BECOMES ARTICULATE 227

IV. HEAT AND COOLNESS 244

V. DRUSILLA ENTERTAINS 253

VI. "A LITTLE LOVELY MOONY NIGHT" . . . 265

VII.   THE NECESSITY FOR A USE OF INTRIGUE .   .   277

VIII.   But there it is, as we said, a man joins a sect
            and becomes one-eyed. — *New Letters:*
            Stevenson   292

IX.   THE LAYING OF A GHOST   307

X.   JUNE DUSK   317

BOOK III

*"So he had him around to the backside of the wall, where he saw a
man with a vessel of oil in his hand, of the which he did also
cast (but secretly) in the Fire, . . . by the means of which
notwithstanding what the devil can do the souls of the people
prove gracious still."*—PILGRIM'S PROGRESS, BOOK I.

I.   AN INTERLUDE AND A MEETING   341

II.   A man is never better than when he has the
            humblest sense of himself; he is never so
            unlike the spirit of Evil as when his pride
            is utterly vanished. — *Donald Mitchell:*
            Dream Life   356

III.   PHILIP RETIRES   376

IV.   DAWN AND NOON   395

V.   AND VARIOUS DAYS AFTER   413

OCTOBER EVENING

OCTOBER EVENING   433

THE
INTERPRETER'S HOUSE

BOOK I

"Sir, here is a traveller."

    *   *   *

"Then he took him by the hand and led him into a very large parlor that was full of dust, because never swept."

PILGRIM'S PROGRESS, BOOK I.

CHAPTER I

15 MADISON PLACE

GULIAN EYRE was coming home and his aunt, Mrs. Dorrance, recognizing the importance of the occasion, had forsaken her accustomed seclusion to lunch with her brother Henry, Gulian's father. Mrs. Dorrance's first name was Virginia, a name that had been given her seven decades before as a subtle rebuke on the part of her parents to the growing importunities of the Abolitionists; otherwise, she was completely of New York and the Hudson river valley.

At this moment, half past two of a pleasant late April day of the year 1921, she was smoothing out the silken folds which encircled her ample but politely controlled waist—a gesture habitual to her and based upon the assumption that crumbs on the floor were better than crumbs on the lap—and was gazing across the shining little table at her brother who was finishing his after-luncheon coffee. Those who knew Mrs. Dorrance would have been aware that she was on the point of saying something unpleasant.

The little table was set in an alcove of the dining-room where three long windows, leaded and diamond-paned, two of them open, formed a square bay giving upon an oblong garden. It was the custom of Mr. Eyre to have his breakfast and luncheon at this table, for the rest of the room was dark, as the dining-rooms of old New York houses are likely to be, whereas the bay, added by a mid-Victorian architect more cunningly than he knew, was flooded by an eastern sun in the morning and by a delicate less direct sun in the afternoon. Mr. Eyre, moreover, was proud of his garden and liked to look at it.

There was something about a city garden hidden and astonishing; something secret and intimately beautiful. Mr. Eyre was even more attached to this bit of urban verdure than he was to the spreading box-bordered paths and beds of 'Hibernia,' where in the summer he looked down from the hills of the Hudson on the shining river, as his father and grandfather and great-grandfather had looked before him. At 'Hibernia' anything would grow; it had always grown; whereas in Madison Place there was a fine yeoman-like unconquerability about the way tulips and crocuses and hyacinths raised their unperturbed faces despite high buildings and gusts of dirty air.

Mrs. Dorrance spoke suddenly. Her thin little mouth opened with a startling precision in the midst of the indeterminate pink folds of her chin and cheeks, and out of the thin little mouth issued a voice mellow and coiling, with occasional metallic notes in it; a voice not unlike her hair; beautiful silver hair, a trace of saffron still left in it, and arranged in the way Mrs. Dorrance had always worn it; parted, caught up over the ears in heavy braids like twisted mint candy.

"You're not listening to me," she said.

Mr. Eyre for many years had been in the habit of pitying Mrs. Dorrance's maid. There is no greater torture than having to be a professional listener. He wished that his sister would see more of her mental equals. However, he supposed he should never forget what she never did, and that was that she was his only sister and three years his senior, a double superiority that accounted partly, he imagined, for the manner in which invariably she addressed him. Poor Virginia!

He withdrew faintly amused grey eyes from a contemplation, over his coffee cup, of the garden. A slanting nebulous light was falling into the garden from the west of the house, and at one end, beyond a strip of soft grass outlined with tulips and hyacinths, red and yellow, and purple and white, a small fountain was let into the high brick wall. The meditative trickle of water as the little bronze boy of the fountain poured it out from the conch shell he was holding, reached Mr. Eyre.

It was all very nice and placid and sunny and reflective. Spring to old people was a time of whispering memory—no not altogether! There was anticipation as well! Gulian was coming home! Mr. Eyre raised his eyes.

"I didn't know you had said anything, my dear," he apologized gently.

His sister's broad bosom rose and fell as it always did when she foresaw any discussion, even of the mildest.

"I was merely going to say," she resumed, "that it is a pity—on a day like this—that Gulian—as usual—is late."

Mr. Eyre's eyes twinkled.

"That's hardly fair," he asked. "Is it? It's scarcely his fault this time. He couldn't very well have jumped overboard and swum ashore."

"Don't be absurd," begged Mrs. Dorrance. "Of course I know it isn't his fault, but fate has a way of keeping the late late and making the prompt prompt."

The twinkle in Mr. Eyre's eyes amplified itself.

"If I understand you, my dear," he said, "to suggest that I should have let you know, I only learned myself two hours ago that his steamer was delayed and wouldn't dock until this afternoon." He pushed his coffee cup away from him. "But after all—" His smile was ingratiating—"we've had a very nice time, haven't we? It's been very pleasant having you. . . . I don't get you here half enough, Virginia. We ought to see more of each other.

Mrs. Dorrance brushed aside the implied compliment. It was not often that she left her own home for family visits—expeditions should be saved for the adventurous gossip of friends—and she had no intention of wasting effort on frivolous amenities. There were always a great many consanguineous questions to be asked when she was with her brother Henry; gloomy consanguineous questions, and as usual she had been considerate enough not to ask them until he had finished his meal.

Her relatives mismanaged their lives frightfully; even Philip, her oldest nephew and her favorite. Philip was a fine man; a big, upstanding, blond haired, successful man, who to the fact that he practically ran the famous old bank of Eyre & Co.—and he must be a good business man, for he had charge of most of Mrs. Dorrance's business as well—added the nowadays exceptional virtue of being a Christian man too. A Christian man, an active church member; a reformer in city politics. Very different from most of those other Wall Street brokers of whom Mrs. Dorrance had heard. And Mrs. Dorrance, being a Christian herself, was not easily deceived by meretricious manifestations of that faith. But look at Philip's wife, Margaret! A silly gadabout. A hot-headed follower of all sorts of nonsensical newfangled schemes. And look at Drusilla and her husband. And finally, look at this father, or father-in-law, of them all, her own brother Henry! Incredibly weak. Absurdly weak. No firmness at all. Why, the rice pudding he had just given her hadn't a bit of sugar in it! She'd like to see a cook play a trick like that on her!

She gathered herself together and spoke a trifle breathlessly.

"The point is," she said; "the point—now that luncheon is over . . . I really do think it is always better not to—that is, discuss things at table; don't you? The point is—now that you've made him come home where he ought to be—what are you going to do with Gulian?

She snapped shut impatiently the clasp of a gold bangle that had become loosened, having very little patience with inferiors and other inanimate things.

Mr. Eyre's expression was polite but not ardent. In the momentary silence that followed, Mrs. Dorrance raised unexpectedly a small plump hand, white and jeweled and slightly enlarged at the knuckles with gout.

"And I must beg of you," she added, hastily, "not to lose your temper!" She sighed deeply. "I cannot understand anger. It makes me cold."

Mr. Eyre spoke under his breath and earnestly.

"I am not losing my temper!" he remarked. Out— loud he said: "Go on, Virginia."

"Then why adopt that tone of voice?"

For a moment Mr. Eyre's eyes were troubled. He stroked his white, well-kept moustache. Silently he was saying, "Dear me! . . . Dear . . ." And then he said, "Oh, well . . .!" The twinkle had returned to his eyes.

"My dear Virginia," he proceeded quietly, "I used no tone of voice whatsoever; none, I assure you. I seldom do use a tone of voice. To the contrary, I welcome your suggestions as always. It is very kind of you to take this interest in Gulian—like your usual kindly self—but as to my having brought him home, and as to what he is going to do, once he's here, in the first place he is coming home entirely of his own accord, and in the second, he is completely a free agent. Advice, yes—if he is good enough to ask for it. But not too much advice. More people have been damned by advice than by anything I know of."

"After all," he met her misty, perpetually affronted gaze more directly, "we must remember that he is a man of some experience, thirty-five years old, and at one time something of an explorer. He has also written some creditable verse. Recently, for the past four and a quarter years, he has been serving his country not notoriously inefficiently as a captain of artillery and as a member of the embassy at Tokyo. It is not a record to be ashamed of, is it?"

Mrs. Dorrance took her courage in both hands.

"And during all his holidays," she interjected crisply, "getting tipsy when he wasn't making a fool of himself about some girl."

Mr. Eyre's mild eyes lost their twinkle and his thin cheeks, with their small patches of permanent color near the cheek-bones, showed suddenly white. His words, however, were still patient. "Not very tipsy," he objected. "And as every young man of spirit has done since the world began. But no matter;" his voice expressed distaste, "he has outgrown it, as we all know. And as for the rest—why, that'll be as he thinks fit. A crime in which I'm afraid I'm going to aid and abet him, Virginia. You mustn't forget he has a streak in him that we haven't—his mother's Dutch obstinacy. It doesn't do a bit of good to bully him. . . . By the way," he announced with subtle irrelevancy, "he's bringing home a young Russian with him."

Mrs. Dorrance gasped.

"Russian!"

Her brother nodded.

"Woman?"

For the first time Mr. Eyre laughed outright.

"Neither a woman, nor a Bolshevik, nor a starving child. A young artist. He picked him up somewhere in Japan."

"And you are going . . ." asked Mrs. Dorrance with tremulous incredulity . . . "to permit a Russian in your house?"

Once, years before, a friend of hers had entertained two Russians, and they had spent all day in bed and all night smoking cigarettes on the drawing-room floor when they weren't making love haphazardly to any woman who happened to be about. The horror of this memory had burned deep into Mrs. Dorrance's consciousness.

"I cannot conceive of it," she concluded sombrely.

"No more can I," agreed Mr. Eyre cheerfully; "but it's about to happen. It's happened before, you know. And it will be only for a little while. Gulian's going to get him into an art school, or something, and find him lodgings."

Mrs. Dorrance arose slowly.

"Then I am to understand," she said, "since you have changed the subject, that the discussion is closed . . . even before it is opened . . . It always is closed, where I am concerned, before it is opened."

She took her plaintive way towards the door. "Every year," she added, "I find that what I have to say seems to be of less and less value. I don't see the slightest use in getting old; I really don't. I only wish that we could at least have conducted the conversation more amicably. My heart is beating violently." For a moment she was silent and then she remarked gently, "And there is not the slightest sense, Henry, in being insulting."

Mr. Eyre, his hand outstretched towards the door, was struck dumb.

"An obdurate silence," explained Mrs. Dorrance, "is always more insulting than speech."

Mr. Eyre's good humor returned; fortified, almost bubbling. Fortunately his guest could not see him.

At the door of the dining-room she faced about again. "Of course," she said rapidly, and as if someone were trying to stop her, "if you want my advice . . . which you have already shown you do not . . . I would suggest that you put Gulian immediately into your bank, and, when he shows any signs of real seriousness, marry him off. In New York, no doubt, it will be difficult to find a suitable girl, but we have relatives in Boston. Philadelphia, of course, is out of the question; they tell me it is the worst of the lot. However, it is your own business. Absolutely. I admit it. It is entirely your affair whether the name of Eyre is perpetuated or not. I have frequently told Margaret that any moment Philip and her boy might die. Then where would we be? No one left but yourself and Gulian."

For a moment she was lost in reflection.

"I cannot understand," she concluded helplessly, as if this was a problem for younger and stronger shoulders, as undoubtedly it was, "this modern custom of having but one child, or, at the most, two."

Mr. Eyre did not think it necessary to remind his sister that she herself, so tradition reported, had been wilfully childless, and had, by a ferocious virginity, so alarmed her late husband, dead these twenty years, that he had transferred with frightened haste all his paternal instincts to the upbuilding of the quiet club to which he belonged and to the breeding and showing of wire-haired fox-terriers. Mr. Eyre recalled how dog-like Spencer's own face had become in later years, especially after he had taken to wearing a curious straggly beard expressive of well-bred dejection.

"I'll ring for Prescott," he said, "and see if your car is waiting."

"Influenza," continued Mrs. Dorrance, unshaken in her train of thought, "might wipe out the whole family in the twinkling of an eye, even you and Gulian."

She proceeded down the hall, followed by Prescott and her brother, in the manner of a meek but dignified Luther who has flung a final decision in the face of an unsympathetic judge. Her short, anhelose figure gave the impression that she would pant were she not a woman of the strictest upbringing. "I'm sorry I can't dine with you tonight," she said, "but I never go out more than once in a day, as you know. Tell Gulian I shall expect him for tea at five o'clock tomorrow afternoon. Of course, he won't come."

At the door she halted her attendants.

"No!" she said sweetly; "no, both of you are much too old to be exposed needlessly."

Without meeting Prescott's eye, Mr. Eyre was conscious of a mutual masculine indignation at this too frequent feminine insult. . . .

On the steps outside, Mrs. Dorrance paused for a moment and looked down upon the vernal activities of Madison Place. Her hand rested on the shoulder of a uniformed young man who regarded life as a series of

humiliations designed to affront a first-class chauffeur.
He was not a lady's-maid! No, he wasn't!

Madison Place was caught up by spring. Its narrow,
four-sided formality had abandoned itself to the in-
roads of vagrant winds that drifted down from the
cornices of the tall buildings lining the main thorough-
fares just beyond, or crept stealthily up the mean
streets that debouched into the small island of respectability still holding its own against encroaching slums
and warehouses. The winds smelled of dust and new
warmth and asphalt newly watered and of damp cool
corners where the sun could not strike. There was
something flowing and wantonly deliberate about them,
like the gesture of an elderly banker who unbuttons
his waistcoat in a country lane.

Towards the east, the scarred façade and short squat
tower of St. Jude's raised themselves against the blue
sky. St. Jude's was no longer a fashionable church as
it had once been, although Mr. Eyre and the survivors
of Madison Place continued to frequent it; a lack of
theological enterprise discouraging to Mrs. Dorrance,
who herself went every Sunday up town to Philip's
more fashionable church, Holy Trinity.

Before the closed iron doors of St. Jude's, in the
small park Madison Place reserved for its own progeny
by means of a bolted gate and special keys, numerous
pleasantly dressed children played—with the conscious
unconcern soon learned by the pleasantly dressed for
the unpleasantly dressed—beneath the envious glances
of other children who peered through the railings.
About the nursemaids of the former, however, there
was no lack of concern, instead, a something that fluttered with their skirts and the sparrows and the new,
moving leaves. The nursemaids were old enough to

feel the stirrings of spring and yet young enough not to realize that life held nothing for them.

But Mrs. Dorrance was not interested in nursemaids and not much more so in children, except when unruly enough to prove useful as examples; what really interested her was the theory back of the park in Madison Place, and it pleased her to see that the theory was being perpetuated. The age in which unwillingly she found herself was skirting the abysses of destruction—there were no Christian men left, except possibly her nephew, Philip, and certainly no Christian women except a few tried friends, and these were very old, but so long as there remained in New York a park where selected little children could play and other little children couldn't, there was, undoubtedly, hope. . . .

The young man upon whom Mrs. Dorrance was leaning, shifted his weight with ill-concealed boredom.

CHAPTER II

GULIAN RETURNS

GULIAN EYRE having seen his family only half a dozen times in twelve years, and then only for intervals of a few weeks each time, entertained towards them a lively admiration not uncommon to the sympathetic person frequently away from home. This was accentuated in his case by the fact that he was the youngest; two years younger than his sister Drusilla and five years younger than his brother Philip; and so, having all through his teens and twenties been granted the privilege of irresponsibility usually accorded the Benjamin of a household, especially a Benjamin as disarming as Gulian, had built up in his mind an exaggerated respect for the stabilities and capabilities of relatives in general and of his sister and brother in particular.

To his mind, particularly when later on it was mellowed by distance, Drusilla and Philip were exceptional persons, representing all the specific virtues that his own usually humble opinion of himself reported impossible of personal achievement.

They were prominent and self-contained and marvelously stationary; spending their winters in one chosen place and their summers in another, and moving, when they did move, to judge from the photographs Gulian saw in occasional illustrated papers and the letters he received, with a dignity truly cosmical. 'Mrs. Perry Shipman, one of New York's loveliest younger matrons,

14

in company with Mr. Henry Battercup, the well-known
financier (all financiers being well known) on the
strand at Palm Beach,' or, 'Mrs. Perry Shipman, with
her son, Pendleton (10), and her daughter, Millicent
(15), on the point of braving the sea at Bradley's
Beach,' or, 'Mr. Philip Onderdonk Eyre, the active
head of the famous old banking house of Eyre & Co.,
together with Mrs. Eyre and some friends (reading
from left to right) enjoying the sunshine of Santa
Barbara.' . . .

That they ever did anything but 'enjoy' sunshine,
were at times infinitely bored with it, or suffered any
of the other ills and sullennesses commmon to human
nature was not apparent from the pages of 'La Mode
Moderne' or 'Country Gossip'—journals which, incidentally, turned the more or less conservative Gulian
—he thought of himself as a conservative-radical, most
men of thirty-five do—temporarily into the bitterest
of communists. . . . It is possible to endure with
patience the superior wealth of others, but it is not
possible to endure with patience the thought that they
are perpetually happy.

And yet, despite this admiration for his family, until
recently Gulian never had had the slightest desire to
be either like them or one of them; nor had he, even at
this moment of his return, any very formal desires in
these directions. He had always detested the thousand and one unnecessary relationships and demands
that were the lot of Drusilla and Philip, and his father,
and even his aunt Virginia, and of every cousin and
friend and stranger you met on the streets of New
York; he had run away from just such things. He
remembered certain relatives who had always seemed
unable even to break an egg gallantly lest it disclose
unexpected life. In the more complicated centers of

civilization, there was merely the choice, as far as he could make out, between a self-protective stuffy conservatism, or a gangling loose-witted liberalism. Just as with machinery, man in his social relationships had built up a Frankenstein's monster that controlled him instead of being controlled. Gulian had always so much preferred exotic countries and the men and women, blessedly devoid of tradition and rigidities, who inhabited them. It destroyed your sense of adventure to know that an attractive stranger was after all nothing more than the granddaughter of an ugly old man whom you had hated as a boy.

Gulian regretted the pleasant days of his past when, with just enough to do to keep him busy, he had been content to let time go by as it would and await, without hurrying events, the possible advent of an ambition stirring woman, or a not-to-be-denied career, or a commanding determination. But that these days were over, there was no longer any doubt in his mind—unless (he still secretly cherished this hope) a short experience of ordinary business and his native land would so disgust him that he would be able to return to the life that really pleased him with a conscience proof against any further possibilities of moral agonizing. He would not forget this chance of a homeopathetic cure—it would cheer him in his bleaker moments.

In short, Gulian was coming home not because he wanted to, and not because he had the slightest desire to imitate the chastened heroes of the more popular magazines; certainly not because he was seeking a bride; not because he wished to make money, or because, 'after all, America was the best country in which to live'—he knew perfectly well that it was probably the most uncomfortable and expensive of all civilized nations—but because he could think of nothing else that might quiet the vague restlessness that had recently overtaken him. Other expedients had been tried and had failed.

Immediately following the war, for instance, six months had been spent in Paris writing verse. An experiment that had begun gloriously and had ended unsatisfactorily. Not that there was anything the matter with Paris or anything the matter with poetry. Assuredly not. Here was the most beautiful city in the world and the one pursuit for which Gulian had hungered, but, granted for the first time in his life complete freedom, a sort of metrical paralysis had set in. Instead of writing poetry, Gulian had made discoveries about the universal and misunderstood law of human perversity.

Until the will of the poet is hardened by maturity and habit, a beautiful city is by no means the best of places in which to write beautiful verse. Poetry—all fine human endeavor—being merely an attempt to mould the world nearer to the heart's desire, in the beginning at least is much more likely to result as a protest against the ugliness of Akron, Ohio, than as a glorification of loveliness already perfected.

Rather desperately Gulian had turned to diplomacy as a profession that would occupy part of his time but still leave enough over for more personal dreams. Diplomacy had proven even more disappointing than Paris. To be sure it did not occupy all of his time, but it irritated him so much that it occupied most of his thoughts. He suspected that he had come across merely an anachronistic and clumsy method of giving dull dinners and not saying what you meant. Absurdly solemn young men, portentous over unimportant details and curiously light-hearted about such matters as wars and massacres and the subjugation of nations, parceled-out human destinies like cigarette-smoking gods. One saw too near at hand and too depressingly one of the contributing causes of the world's idiocy. Besides, any man who had served two years in any army had had enough for life of the lack of the ordinary frankness and common sense that makes civilian intercourse possible.

Meanwhile, an eternity of youthful nonchalance was growing more and more questionable. Experience for the sake of experience was losing its piquancy. Gulian was alarmed to find how many of the things that had once pleased him no longer pleased him at all. He was being forced gloomily to the conclusion that after all the maxims of stupid people concerning the necessity of a man limiting his field of action as he grew older might have a germ of truth in them. Certainly the one murder you did not seem to be able to commit without at the same time killing yourself was to kill time. Some way or other, time, to the contrary, had to be distilled, so that each moment became important because it was utterly forgotten in the passion and importance of the thing you were doing. Otherwise, joy slipped away from you down a long lane of unimportant hours.

The idea was not a comforting one, it was opposed to all of Gulian's principles, it contained in it something of surrender, and his greatest dread was that it might be no more than the indefinite ghosts of Puritan ancestors pulling at his coat-tails.

He was inclined to blame the war for a good deal of his uneasiness. Its vast absurdity and lack of definition had made suddenly imperative the necessity for each survivor to define the tiny limits of opportunity granted him personally. Society as a mass having failed, a new responsibility had devolved upon the individual. Furthermore, Gulian's time-sense had been destroyed, as had been the time-sense of all men past their first youth. He felt hurried. He had an impression of ages spent and of comparatively little time left. His two years of warfare appeared now as a misty aeon of effort that had got nowheres in particular and had blotted out all the years that had gone before and made ridiculously short those that were to follow. For one thing, he had gone into the war a young man and had come out a man approaching middle-age.

His Aunt Virginia, therefore, was right—on the surface—in her conclusions regarding her nephew's future. More right—and that is saying a good deal—than even she imagined. Marriage, and furthermore a fairly disagreeable marriage, seemed the only thing at the moment likely to save him; save him, that is, according to what Mrs. Dorrance thought was salvation. A marriage, in other words, sufficiently disagreeable to keep him anchored to one spot and occupied with bothersome details, but, naturally, not so disagreeable as to reach a breaking point. A sympathetic and cordial love-match would merely result in Gulian making the unfortunate girl part of his own vague and erratic wanderings.

It was the height of bad luck for any such plans that Gulian at this particular time should be so little preoccupied with thoughts of romance, disagreeable or otherwise, and so much preoccupied with thoughts about himself.

. . . You will have recognized, of course, that in this exaggerated respect for his family and this equally exaggerated conviction that he couldn't in the least be like them (in fact, didn't want to be like them); in this disinclination to follow a traditional

career, and yet this nagging misgiving that possibly
he should, Gulian was suffering from what the im-
passioned Freudian would call a "family-complex."
But since everybody suffers from a "family-complex"
in one direction or another, and since those who suffer
from any but the inferiority side of it seem to be people one avoids as much as possible, the complex, as is
frequently the case, need not be regarded as fatal.
Indeed, as to thinking yourself quite the best of your
period and race, or thinking yourself quite the worst,
there is no choice. . . .

As a matter of fact, with the best intentions in the
world, Gulian, like most Americans of his generation,
had been trained to have no definite ideas at all,
the ones he had being merely the result of experience
and his own fairly intelligent mind. Mr. Eyre had
brought his children up on the theory, and fundamentally it is an excellent one, that, within reason, they
were to do exactly what they pleased. He belonged to
the more broad-minded parents of the nineties, exhibiting in this respect a radicalism that shocked his relatives and frequently, in the secrecy of his own closet,
alarmed himself, but he stuck it out. He had seen far
too much of the misery, and even horror, that comes
from trying to force a square peg into a round hole.
He believed, and not altogether wrongly, that most of
the evil in the world arises from just such Procrustean
carpentering.

Unfortunately, however, like most explorers, he had
stumbled upon the right river, but had chosen the
wrong channel. It was not until later that partial
freedom was discovered to lie, not in whimsicality of
choice, but in an early selection and concentration upon
the things done best.

Philip had been easy to account for. He had shown

from an early age, from the time when, with a placid
blond self-possession, he had annexed Gulian's services
and belongings, that he was destined to be a successful
banker or broker. And he had continued uninterrupt-
edly upon his way.

Christianity seemed to come to him as naturally and
blandly as adroitness in games, and he went to a university where, at that time—the early years of the
twentieth century, probably as selfish and ungodly a
period as could be found—piety won a man almost
as much recognition as a team letter. Philip had
triumphed doubly. He had not only played guard on
a championship eleven but he had missed the presi-
dency of the Y. M. C. A. by—and a very dirty bit of
politics it was—one vote. However, he had gained a
moral victory. He became a synonym for strength
and sanctity; the sort of undergraduate about whom
other undergraduates, knowing themselves less perfect, repeated lovingly bits of gossip, despairingly hope-
ful that these bits of gossip might be true and thus
connect them and the paragon in a common humanity.
Usually these bits of gossip had something to do with
swearing in a foot-ball game; or the inadvertent drinking of too much champagne.

As for Drusilla, she had been equally satisfactory.
Having been born at the end of a generation in which
only the most homely women demanded any unwom-
anly privileges, or else, having been born so early in a
generation which expected everything that she had
escaped the contagion, she was inalterably and charmingly feminine, and had done very well by herself by
means of a fashionable boarding-school, where she
learned nothing, and Europe, where she learned much.

She was tall and snowy shouldered, and golden
haired—crinkly; real gold hair—and had humorous

gray eyes. It is not difficult to understand why she was one of the most distinguished girls of her day, nor why, after two years and many suitors, when she finally selected the equally young Perry Shipman, everyone, even her Aunt Virginia, was for the moment satisfied. The marriage seemed a perfect one, although, as Mrs. Dorrance afterwards pointed out, life is a dangerous thing and beauty even more so, and the chances are that no good will ever come of either.

So much for Philip and Drusilla. Gulian, slight, dark, and passionate, given to fits of temper in which he banged the floor with his head, and excessive rages during which his one desire was to bite his brother and sister, was not so readily disposed of; Gulian had given his father more concern, despite the latter's laissez faire principles. And even when Gulian went away to boarding-school and university—a different university from Philip's, chosen with a vague conviction that what had made Philip popular would not do the same by Gulian—and had come back much subdued and outwardly conventional, he was still mysterious and disconcerting.

A capacity for complete withdrawal into himself, an ability for long stretches of absent-minded concentration, broken by observations unexpectedly apt, for moments of disinterest and moments of rapt attention, distinguished him.

In his more puzzled intervals Mr. Eyre was tempted to believe that these idiosyncrasies could be explained only by some remote Iberian adventurer who, during the time of the Spanish occupation, in the days when both Dutch pigment and Dutch morals broke down together, had made himself too comfortable in the household of one of Gulian's maternal ancestors.

There was nothing in Mr. Eyre's own sanguine, fair-headed race to account for them.

Mr. Eyre, sitting in his library one story down, before a pleasant small fire, the evening having turned cool, was thinking, the night of the pleasant late April day on which he had had lunch with his sister Virginia, of many of these things, while Gulian, a story above, in his old rooms which had been kept just as he had left them, had given up thinking about them for the moment, and was thinking of nothing but the tying of a white tie. Of this he was thinking with all the restrained passion of his nature.

With his usual absorption in everything but the matter of importance, he had got himself into the uncomfortable position of having after his bath only twenty minutes left in which to dress—his steamer had not docked until five that afternoon. Dinner was at eight; and he did not want to be late, because his family had always laughed at his lateness, and in recent years, so he assured himself, he hadn't been late at all or . . . not very much. From the next room he heard Vannya singing, and that increased his haste and his irritation. No doubt by this time, Vannya, dressed in an old evening suit of his host's which fitted him perfectly, was completely attired and merely putting the finishing touches to a faultless, pink-cheeked appearance. Vannya never hurried and he was never anything but on time. When you yourself arrived breathless upon the scene of an engagement, Vannya was invariably there to welcome you with a smile.

The high, sweet, rather wild monotone ceased, and the singer came from the sitting-room, which had been turned for his convenience into a temporary bedroom, and leaned against the doorway.

For a moment Gulian paid no attention to this intrusion, and then, "Why do you stare at me that way?" he asked darkly and in French.

"I was wondering," said Vannya, "what you call trousers in your language—in English?"

"Nothing."

Vannya was unabashed. He strolled over to the bureau and leaning one elbow upon it, withdrew his cigarette from his mouth and regarded Gulian affectionately.

"Then I cannot get them back," he said gently, "if I should happen to lose them in the street, can I?"

Gulian pointed over his shoulder to a large chintz-covered chair. "Sit down!" he commanded. "Ever since we left Japan I've been telling you the names of things in English. You ought to know English thoroughly by now—I half believe you do."

Vannya sighed regretfully. He went over to the chair and stretched himself out in it. "It is impossible," he said, "to master it, unless my friends are more patient. It is a language in which there are ten words for each thing and many of them indecent."

With a dexterity habitual only to the dilatory, Gulian had by this time slipped into his trousers and with practically the same motion had drawn his suspenders over his shoulders. There was nothing now left to be done except to put on his waistcoat and coat. He heaved a sigh of relief. "Three minutes!" he said to himself.

Vannya looked at him thoughtfully and took his cigarette out of his mouth.

"Three min-utes!" he repeated slowly, as if this was a priceless phrase. "Three min-utes! Four, fife,

seex, seven min-utes! Quarter to an hour!" "Ah,"
this in French, "that is very pretty! I am learning."

The gay cretonne background accentuated the
brown blondness of his short crisp hair and tiny
moustache and the pinkness of his cheeks and brought
into relief the ease of his medium-heighted burly figure.
He was a very good-looking and ingenuous-looking
young man, Ivan Polienoff—and half a dozen other
names—despite the scar acquired on the Western
Front, which ran in a jagged half-moon from the left-
hand corner of his lip to the point of his chin. When
he was excited the scar turned white.

Gulian was not quite certain how he had got hold
of Vannya, or why Vannya happened to be with him
at the moment, staying in his house and sitting in his
chair and wearing his clothes. He would probably
never be altogether certain, but he had made a vow to
himself to set Vannya on his feet. The vow was not
altogether altruistic, for Vannya in some sort of way
added to Gulian's life and amplified it; proved a
vicarious release. Vannya did not know of this vow
and since he was by nature, concerning himself, unin-
quisitive, although gluttonously inquisitive about the
world at large, probably never would. The exigencies
of a precarious existence had produced in him the
qualities of a sagacious and comfortable dog. He
fitted into wherever he happened to be with a minimum
amount of disturbance to himself and others.

Suggesting nothing, but open to suggestion, he had
drifted into the ken of the embassy at Tokyo, and suggesting nothing, but open to suggestion, he had drifted
to America with Gulian.

Back of this drifting, however, was an intense purpose; and his life had not been a drifting one until
circumstances had made nothing else possible.

He wanted to be an illustrator; he had always wanted to be an illustrator; and despite practically no training in the art, he possessed already an oddly accurate cunning of line. Life, however, being itself frequently the most sardonic of caricaturists, had seen to it that, in company with numerous other sensitive young men, Vannya's talents heretofore had been applied largely to the purposes of slaughter. From the age of eighteen to the age of twenty-four he had spent his entire time trying to kill somebody.

Vannya's calmness was a constant source of wonder and admiration to Gulian. Here was a young man who had lost everything; a father, two sisters, a brother, his position in the world, his country, and yet who went about the business of the moment with an unfailing cheerfulness and expectancy.

Somehow such calmness gave a new value and dignity to life; made the individual seem unbeatable beneath the assaults of a fate whose petulance made it appear rather like a cruel and elderly tease. There was a racial quality as well, an acceptance of a fact as a fact that was still many centuries away from the average American mind. Back of such acceptance were generations of discipline and disaster.

Gulian pulled his coat down around his shoulders and gave a final tug to the ends of his tie and turned out the lights above the bureau.

He found himself suddenly, unexpectedly liking these lights as he had found himself suddenly, unexpectedly liking everything else about the house to which he had returned. The lights were old gas brackets fitted to electricity, just as the bureau, of ancient design and long use, was yet newly polished and provided with modern conveniences. He looked about the room in the dim radiance cast by a shaded lamp on the reading-table; at the gay chintz coverings—blue parrots whose scarlet heads rose up against a sand-colored background—at the mahogany furniture, the white curtains, the glistening bed. On the walls, of a faint yellow paper, were a couple of watercolor landscapes, deep-distanced and meditative.

The room was redolent with the atmosphere that old rooms alone possess; of having been lived in, thought in, prayed in, smiled in. Its corners were shadowy with restfulness.

Gulian switched out all the lights and passed through the sitting-room followed by Vannya. The sitting-room looked down upon the garden at the back of the house. The windows were open and creamcolored curtains drew themselves back and forth with a faint breathing sound. Here even the rare night noises of Madison Place were absent. There was almost a country silence and fragrance and desire to lean out.

In the hall beyond there came up the well of the stairs a faint illumination and the warm perfume of the house.

A feeling of security and relaxation and gay anticipation seized upon Gulian. Yes, he was infinitely glad to be home . . . for awhile, anyway. He had never thought that he would be, but he was. There was something after all in being surrounded by one's own kin; by people bound to one in a way no others could be.

A vision of New York out beyond the quiet backwater in which his father's house stood appeared to him. The great buildings would be lighted up by now; the electric signs would be leaping and twinkling, the streets would be filled with crowds. And they were his crowds—at least, most of them were. At all events, they were living under the magnificence and power and good nature of his countrymen. By God, it was, say what you would, a great city—a great people!

And then Vannya's voice interrupted him, murmuring as if to himself, some disconnected phrases of how all over the world the houses of gentlefolk smelled alike.

CHAPTER III

MRS. PRENDEGAST IS LATE

GULIAN remembered this smell; a blend of burning wood, of old but clean rugs, of the gentle memories of good food, of tobacco smoke and books in leather bindings; all this penetrated by the warm essence of the roses which were sent twice a week from 'Hibernia,' and accentuated, held in solution, by a faint cool overatmosphere, the result of windows constantly opened. A delicate, exciting, yet robust smell; thoughtful and masculine.

He turned the corner of the rail where, before the final flight of a dozen steps to the ground floor, there was a small landing, holding, in a wall niche, a little bronze figure of Artemis—naked, exquisite—and so came from the semi-obscurity of the upper floors into the soft radiance of the front hall.

At the end of the hall, two sidelights behind vizors of silk cast a mellow reflection across a tri-parted mirror that was hung between them and pooled themselves in an Italian table below, and opposite these lights, a door opened into the drawing-room and an oblong of brighter light showed itself. The hum of voices and the winged sound of laughter penetrated the quiet.

For a moment the brilliance of the narrow primrose-colored room, with its girandoles above the mantelpiece shining back into the big tawny edged glass behind in a thousand marshalled reflections, blurred

29

Gulian's vision. He had merely an impression of several people, their heads turned in his direction, and of a cessation of talk. Then he saw his father standing with his back to a gentle blaze of logs; a small, fresh-colored, silvery-toned figure, his firm chin set deep in a high collar and his white moustache standing out against the clean curves of his cheeks; and, to one side, from a big chair, the crisp golden hair and glimmering shoulders of Drusilla emerging.

Somewhere in the background was Perry, and the blond bulk of Philip, and the dark shadow of Margaret.

Mr. Eyre waved his hand. He had no modern habit of making an occasion as little noticeable as possible. "Here he is!" he exclaimed. "Ulysses!" Gulian's heart beat rapidly.

He turned towards Drusilla, but halfway across the room she met him and flung her shining arms, bare save for narrow strips across the shoulders, around him. They were warm arms, and yet cool, and smelled faintly of violets and the sweetness of warm flesh.

Good old Drusilla! Warm, glimmering, lovely Drusilla; with her red lips and her mother-of-pearl skin! Still giving one the impression of a girl running away from the misty pursuing aura of womanhood; would have none of it!

She gave Gulian an extra little squeeze and then held him off at arm's length, her flower-like head cocked on one side, and her long, gray, humorous eyes peering into his. "Not very old," she decided, as Gulian greeted Philip and Margaret abstractedly. "Still ridiculously young, aren't you? A little gray at the temples, but that's distinguished. . . . Gilly, your eyes are just as outrageously hare-bell as ever. They're indecent! How have you helped getting married? Oh yes; speak to Perry."

She laughed and indicated her husband, who had joined the group, a look of careful unconcern upon his face.

It was a principle with Perry never to admit by any gesture of his that anyone had been out of New York longer than a night. His obliviousness made him an object of search whenever there was a particularly rude foreigner to be shown about, but otherwise, except with those who for financial or social reasons were forced to be cordial to him, he was unpopular. Perry did not bother about such matters as popularity, however; he could purchase things outright. Purchase avoided any entangling of the emotions. Possibly it was for this reason that he was always so careful to avoid intimacy with women of his own class.

"Hello!" he said, and laughed his meaningless little laugh. A small, unexpected, explosive exclamation of two notes.

"Hello!" retorted Gulian with equal casualness, and turned to Vannya. "This is Major Polienoff, Drusilla. He speaks only French . . . at least, he says he does, but I don't believe him. . . . I'm going to turn him over to you for the evening. You're the possessor of the Eyre French."

Vannya's incredibly long, bronze eyelashes closed and opened again. His expression was that of a contented cat. He had found himself without warning in the presence of a charming woman.

Gulian was aware that Vannya in that lowered and raised glance had encompassed Drusilla as completely as she had encompassed him, although by a different method; had made her, from the crown of her head down through her peach-bloom brocaded dress to the tips of her silver shoes, completely part of his memory; each gracious line and lineament of her. It was a trick

foreign men had; all—Englishmen, too. They were
cognizant of a woman in a way no American was. And
Gulian was aware that women liked the cognizance
even when they protested against it.

He wasn't sure whether he liked it or not. He rather
envied it. Despite his cosmopolitan training, he had
long ago realized that his own eyes possessed the trick
of being at the same time both too dreamy and too
bright and that absent-mindedness frequently caused
him to fix them too rigidly upon random portions of
a lady's anatomy. This had caused him embarrassment. He regretted that it had been impossible in the
majority of cases to tell the flurried ladies that the
cause was boredom and not a too eager attention. . . .

Perry broke in upon these thoughts.

"I don't speak French," he announced briefly. He
said it simply and gravely.

Perry had a way of announcing his predilections in
this manner, usually without any apparent connection
with what had gone before or what was to follow. It
was his idea of conversation, and would have been a
fairly interesting game—matching tastes—if the
listener had had a chance as well. Perry detested des-
serts, except rice pudding, and he disliked little dark
women (God knows why!) and music, and the income-
tax, and the English (possibly because they were the
only people he had ever met more rude than himself);
and H. G. Wells (although he had never read him);
and all writers and artists, and anyone who wasn't a
New Yorker, and Woodrow Wilson, and Theodore
Roosevelt, and every other great American since the
time of Grant, except Mr. Morgan; and bow ties, and
anyone who talked about God. . . . 'God being an
accomplished fact and that was all there was about it.'
You went about your business and forgot him. . . .

And he was fond of polo and golf and burgundy and pigeon shooting and nice, good-looking girls, 'without any damn nonsense about them,' a cryptic phrase . . . 'and he didn't want to hear any rot about women, anyhow.'

Following his present admission of manly ignorance, he thrust his hands into his trouser pockets and strolled off in the direction of Prescott, who had appeared with cocktails and sandwiches.

"He thinks it undignified to speak French," explained Drusilla. "Lots of men do, you know. Verdun was rather a shock to them, but they're recovering, due to France's present attitude. Talk to Philip, Gulian. He's worried about himself because he's getting lines under his eyes. You'll cheer him up." She sighed. "We've needed you to cheer us up. I tell him it's because he thinks too much about bonds and heaven and not enough about exercise. After all, heaven more or less did run itself for years before he was born, didn't it?"

She turned to Vannya, leaving Gulian in a circle composed of his father and Philip and Margaret.

"He's been working too hard," commented Mr. Eyre. "He really runs the whole show now. I never get down. I'm a lazy old man. I know nothing about the bank, and old Prendegast is merely a figurehead."

Gulian peered up at the bulk—not fat, but wide and tall—of his brother. He wondered if in five years he too would so obviously show the passage of time. But forty wasn't old. Yet under the blue eyes of Philip there were tiny puckers, and the eyes themselves were tired. You received, moreover, the subtle impression, perhaps too imaginative, that the carefully restrained gestures and speech were the very essence of restlessness; were those of a man telling himself that he wasn't restless. But, none the less, Philip was a splendid-looking fellow. Solid; dependable. An epitome of those virtues. It was this damned city; the absurd life most business men allowed themselves to lead!

"Why—I think you're looking pretty fit," he said. He believed in telling people that they looked 'fit,' if you possibly could.

"And Margaret, too," he added. He smiled at his slow-smiling sister-in-law.

But he didn't mean the latter; not in the least. Here, unlike his vague uneasiness concerning Philip, he was as always definitely oppressed and definitely irritated. What was the matter with Margaret, anyway. What had always been the matter with her? Hers was a real beauty, or, at least, the foundations of a real beauty; a much more complete beauty, for instance, than Drusilla's; and yet the spark that should inform beauty and make it valuable was lacking. The annoyance that the normally interested, healthy person finds in the person who is not interested, who is subtly out of gear, made his blood run quicker.

He looked about helplessly for his father, but Mr. Eyre had gone back to the fireplace.

"Don't you take any exercise at all, Phil," he asked, "down there at that place of yours?"

"Exercise!" Philip shrugged his big shoulders and smiled under his drooping yellow moustache. "I've no time for exercise. Some squash, every now and then. . . . But real exercise! Why, even in the summer I only get down to Westbury late Saturdays. It's getting worse all the time."

"What's the use, then, in being head of a big firm?"

"None—if you mean getting time to play in. You're worse off than a clerk. Besides, everything has gone

to pot now. You'd hear more about it if it wasn't for
modern business methods."

Gulian grinned painfully. "And I was thinking,"
he said slowly, "of going into business myself. That's
why I'm here. Did you know that?"

For an instant Philip raised his head and looked at
his brother more directly. "So I heard," he said, "but
not into a bank, I hope! This is a poor time to go
into a bank." His eyes lingered upon Gulian's face
uncertainly.

For a moment color crept into Gulian's dark cheeks
and then receded. He was slightly taken aback at this
lack of cordiality. There wasn't much encouragement
here for sober intentions, was there, nor for any very
public declarations concerning one's plans and perplexities? But then he remembered from the past
Philip's Christian pessimism, and felt relieved. Philip
didn't believe in allowing God to think you were too
happy in your business affairs, or anything else, lest
Providence become jealous. In this respect, like most
fervent believers, Philip was a pagan.

"Let's get a cocktail," suggested Gulian cheerfully.

Philip shook his head. "I've given them up," he
explained gravely. "I can't very well go and talk to
workingmen about drunkenness and take a drink myself, can I?"

Philip always had had a trick of adding a further
disconcerting sentence just as you were re-establish-
ing cordial relations with him once more in your mind.
He was like a large white sea washing away the little
sand forts of good feeling you tried to build up along
his edge.

Now what in the world had taking a cocktail got to
do with drunkenness? A perfect analogy would be to
say that eating a bun inextricably involved one in

gluttony. Why, anyhow, should Philip be talking to workingmen? There was a breath-taking absurdity about such a large bland person addressing passionate mechanics. Probably he told them to 'save their pennies.'

Gulian, greatly sobered, strolled over to his father.

The sparkling room, with its crackling wood fire, its roses in bowls, its heavy curtains shutting out whatever of threat the night might contain; its mellow Constable, of a rain storm coming up a valley of elms, facing, on the wall opposite, an Eyre of the eighteen-thirties, was infinitely secure; the people in it—More secure than anyone, three years before in France, had ever thought anything in the world would be again. Curious how life went on! Always would! A few million people had had the light suddenly shut off from them; dark shutters before cameras—or was it really darkness? Maybe they had merely been flung from light into a greater brilliance; stones thrown from a window into high noon. . . . And meanwhile, life dragged itself along and pretty soon the wounded end healed and no one knew where the wound had been. In that lay most of the splendor and most of the tragedy of life; all of its bravery and half its cruelty.

Drusilla had gone back to her chair; Vannya had drawn a little stool up to her side, and they were laughing and chatting; getting along together famously. At the other end of the mantelpiece, Perry, an elbow on the black veined marble, was drinking, with an air of alert detachment, what must have been—allowing for time—his third cocktail. There seemed to be little ground for Philip's atmosphere of apprehensiveness.

Mr. Eyre looked at his watch rather helplessly as Gulian joined him. "It's a quarter past eight," he said, "but no one seems to care for good food any more, do they?   Dining has become merely a necessary excuse for a cigarette and a dance."   He sighed.   "I'm hungry."

"Whom are we waiting for?" asked Gulian.

Prescott answered him; he re-entered the room.

"Mrs. Prendegast!" he announced.

CHAPTER IV

THE BIRTH OF A DETERMINATION—
PERHAPS TWO

IT WAS not, Gulian assured an inner voice, that he wanted especially to talk about himself. As a matter of fact, direct questions on that subject numbed his brain, but it did seem to him that it would have been more polite if Margaret, on this his first night at home in two years, had shown a trifle more interest in him as a man and a brother-in-law.

He cast a discontented eye, grown vague, become the color of March water, about the table, shimmering beneath its weight of roses and silver. Beyond the radiance of the candles under tawny shades, the outer shadows occasionally gathered themselves into columns of greater opacity where Prescott and a parlor-maid moved like attentive genii. One of the leaden-paned windows was open, and from the garden stray breaths of air touched with the scent of early spring, made their way into the room.

The dinner was progressing slowly. Mr. Eyre entertained no newfangled ideas concerning a virginal paucity of food or decoration. His tastes in those directions were Christian and Victorian rather than agnostic and modern. In his library was a book published by a chef at Delmonico's in 1889—Alessandro Filippini—a charming and chef-like name—which contained this modest menu for New Year:

Blue Point Oysters

Cream of Asparagus   Consommé Royale   Haut Sauterne
      Radishes   Timbales a l'Ecossaise   Olives
            Bass a la Régence

Potatoes a la Windsor   Rauenthaler Berg
      Fillet of Beef, larded a la Parisienne
Saddle of Mutton, currant jelly   Pommery Sec
      Sweetbreads, larded a la Colbert
Terrapin a la Maryland   Chateau Latour
            Kirsch Punch
      Canvas-back Ducks   Chambertin
Artichoke Bottoms   String Beans   French Peas
            Plum Pudding a l'Anglaise
Vanilla Ice   Pistache Ice
Fruit   Cakes
                  Coffee
                  Cordial

And although Mr. Eyre would have deprecated any
such strain on the digestion, he did not at the same time
believe in letting oneself be starved by neurasthenic
hosts or equally neurasthenic footmen.

Gulian's reflective eye . . . not in reality reflective, merely resentful . . . dwelt for a moment upon
Drusilla and Vannya, still immensely pleased with
each other, and passed on to Philip and Perry, who,
there being a paucity of ladies, were sitting next to each
other. Philip ate with a quiet disregard of Perry;
Perry ate with what was manifestly a nervous fear
lest Philip draw him into conversation. He swallowed
his food with a hunted obliviousness. He hadn't very
nice table-manners anyway; he had gone to a boarding-school too early.

Gulian's reflective eye grew amused before it focused
once more upon Margaret.

"Every paper I've picked up lately has had your
name or picture in it," he remarked. "You're as important as Lady Astor, aren't you?" Yes, and as

wrong-headed and hot-headed and generally ornithological.

Margaret was not to be trapped into any particular show of interest. "As soon as we get the next Amendment passed," she said with her usual tumbling vagueness, "I hope to be able to turn my attention to other things. We're working on a new Amendment now. It will clinch the Nineteenth."

Gulian sighed. "Good God, another Amendment!"

"Yes. Why not?"

"Nothing—except one wonders if the original admirers would recognize their classic virgin in the present harridan."

"You still object to all change?"

Gulian flushed. That was just like Margaret! Never in all his life had he objected to change. As a matter of fact, he had welcomed it too joyfully and in his youth, like all heaven-fearing, imaginative young men, had been given to Socialism.

His voice was absent-minded. "I don't see the sense of curing indigestion with dynamite," he murmured. He faced his sister-in-law more squarely. He wondered what Margaret would look like if she let her hair down and rolled down a green bank? Rolled over and over. . . . In the spring, of course, when it was warm. Did she ever have such impulses? All the nice people he had ever known had. . . . The idea fascinated him. He even began to imagine Philip following Margaret's example.

"I am so glad," he ventured, thoughtfully but irrelevantly, "that I've come back to warm weather and light clothes. People are so much nicer when they have on light clothes, aren't they?"

Margaret frowned. "I don't think I exactly understand," she said with amazed annoyance.

She wouldn't.

The vague low-pitched voice carried the same sub-arid convinced tones that had always depressed Gulian in the past. Margaret, he realized, looked upon him as too lightminded even for argument. If she would only copy the despised male for awhile and, out of business hours anyway, exercise whatever feeble social charm mankind had managed to build up since the days of his prehistoric revels! Even Philip, after six o'clock, forgot for the most part God and finance. But Margaret in reality, like most feminists, secretly loathed her sex and mistook sex advantages for sex humiliations, using the former only when there seemed a chance of making a prominent proselyte or, unconsciously, when she was worshipping at some frenetically modern shrine. Then she became almost lasciviously feminine; Aphrodite embattled; absorbed, flushed, disingenuous, dangerous; a member of a 'Flying Squadron'; like one of the young ladies of Catharine de Medici, or a Babylonian priestess, or a mediaeval abbess; pursuing votes and changing opinions, or adoring new ideas, with the ardor and, in the first two instances, the methods of an unwearied courtesan.

Mushrooms were before him, and Gulian ate them soberly, his mood softening at the touch of their benign flavor. Pleasant mushrooms! A lot more important in the real economy of the world than all the Margarets created! Out of the corner of one eye he noted with relief that Vannya, shaken by politeness and temerity, was on the point of provoking Margaret's Farmington French, and it did not decrease his satisfaction with this interruption that an immediate deadlock over the names of various foods occurred.

There seemed no common ground of linguistic meeting. Alarmingly, startlingly, and desperately, Vannya broke into lyric English. The subject was still food, but to the unaccustomed ear the rhythm suggested deep-toned and passionate love.

A voice at his left interrupted Gulian's invidious meditations. He had heard the voice before, talking to his father. He had also noticed a youthful dazzling back and shoulders, and a slim hand with a single sapphire upon it; dusky hair, too, lustrous and blue-black, parted at one side, and a faint perfume—violets, he thought it was. But he had purposely made no attempt to turn the voice in his direction. At the moment he was weary of women.

The voice was cool and slow, almost insolently slow, with occasional warm slightly blurred notes in it, as if its owner's mind stumbled upon thoughts too unsmooth and too exciting for the ordinary restrained pace. "Are you always so very thoughtful?" it asked.

Gulian, gathering his wits together hastily, faced half way around in his chair.

"Never, when I meet a person worth——" he began, without interest; and then he ended: "Oh, and so you're Mrs. Prendegast?"

He found himself smiling into a pair of dark eyes, level, shadowy, under two half-moons of ebony. They returned his smile squarely; indeed, they held him with a slight widening of the irises that seemed to him at first astonishing and then altogether childlike and delicious. He had an instantaneous impression, very unusual, very rare of recent years where women were concerned, of meeting personality, of meeting texture, glamor. Already he had an impression physically of slimness—rather tall—of an exquisite smoothness of lines and of a shining inner whiteness uncommon with northern brunettes.

"And so that's all you remember of me, is it? I met you in the drawing-room."

Gulian became eagerly contradictory.

"I remember everything about you," he insisted, "and will continue to do so. For the last fifteen minutes I've been trying to overhear every word you've been saying—I missed some of the nicest ones, but, you see, I've been having a horribly serious conversation, and . . . like most serious conversations . . . it was pure nonsense."

"Don't you like serious conversations?"

"No, of course not."

"Don't you?"

"No. The more seriously a man works, the more likely he is to be amusing when he talks; the more he wants to be amused and amusing. Distrust the fundamentalists. Besides, witticisms change history, not information. I've always imagined it was some practical joker who wrote 'Mene, mene, tekel upharsin' upon the wall."

"And you really believe that?" She sighed and the smile faded from her eyes. "Life is so short. Possibly it's all right for a man to think that, but women so seldom meet anyone who can tell them things. It's stupid for them to waste the opportunity. You've no idea how dull most talk is. . . . Or perhaps you have. Some day I want you to tell me all about Japan! You've just come back, haven't you? I've been there myself but my experiences weren't like yours. Like all women, the only reality—the only adventures—I have are as a rule inside myself."

"As a matter of fact, that's true of all people, man or woman," said Gulian. "The more you hunt objective adventure the more you realize it."

Despite warnings to himself that such gestures were

a clever woman's stock in trade, he was finding himself unreservedly elated that someone was at last showing some interest in what he had been doing. Nobody else had, up to the present, except his father. This dark haired girl . . . woman . . . whatever she was . . . she could not be more than thirty . . . was unaware that she was healing the wounds Margaret had inflicted. And never is a man in such a dangerous position as when he is smarting from feminine indifference. That the indifferent one is despised does not lessen the hurt. Too many centuries of masculine pride are involved.

Gulian hoped this woman had a sense of humor. He wasn't quite sure. She had a sense of play—he met her eyes again and reflected that, after all, he wasn't sure that it mattered very much about her humor. He was growing a trifle tired of indiscriminate humor, especially where women were concerned. They so seldom got the heart of it. Derision or fantasy, perhaps, but not the tender, coarse, beautiful reality. Maybe it would be cool and restful to see something of somebody again who still found life eagerly mysterious and thrilling.

Mrs. Prendegast stared at him without smiling.

"You are blushing under your sunburn," she said musingly. "Why are you blushing? Have I said anything?"

Gulian laughed. "No, not a thing. I seem to be acquiring the habit. That is twice I've blushed tonight. The first time, I know why—I was angry . . . this time . . . To tell you the truth, I haven't the vaguest idea."

"I think I know. It's because you're still so young. You are young, aren't you? Most people nowadays can't even blush at their speeches, let alone blushing at their thoughts. What were your thoughts? Frighteningly young?"

Gulian shook his head and frowned. Curious that he did not resent this remark about his age. He would have resented it if Margaret had made it. "You can't imagine how old I am," he retorted, "in sin, sorrow, and experience. Since I have been in Japan my thoughts have become oriental and ancient."

"Oh, no." Mrs. Prendegast shook her head. "Age isn't what you do, it's what you think. You're young. . . . I like it."

She had, it seemed, the trick of isolating from the surroundings herself and the person to whom she was talking. Ordinarily Gulian hated this trick; it was like being tickled by a comparative stranger, but he could find no hatred in his heart at present. There were occasions, after all, when the trick had its constructive side; when it bridged the gap between acquaintanceship and intimacy.

"I need immediately," he said, with deliberate malice, "a guide—I'm a stranger in this city. A guide for my feet, and my head—and my heart. Would you like to take on the job? It would be very charitable."

To his surprise the flicker of mischief died out of his partner's face as suddenly as it had come and the fingers of her hand lying upon the table drew themselves together. He even suspected her of giving a little gasp. She raised her eyes and he was struck by their singular width and stariness.

"I am afraid I would be a poor guide," she said hurriedly. "No—I'm afraid I would be a very poor guide."

Good Lord! She hadn't much humor, had she? But for the second time that night Gulian experienced a momentary slurred tightening of his heart, and he had not had that feeling for years. It was an innocent enough feeling in itself . . . rather pleasant . . . but it was much too capable of expansion. And he had no desire for expansion. This was a married woman. Long ago he had segregated certain follies and put them behind him, finding them unprofitable. At present he was searching—if he was seaching at all—for something more enduring and satisfying. But he wasn't even searching for that. He wanted to be left alone. Left free to discover unimpeded whatever there was to discover about this new and hostile world it was his intention to enter.

"I'm not at all a dangerous person to guide," he said gently, with the purpose of removing the personal emphasis from his former words.

He couldn't quite make this woman out. She was a disturbing person; reserved, and yet giving signs of being extraordinarily candid; ingenuous, and yet obviously not unsubtle. Possibly she used ingenuousness as a weapon. It was a modern habit to do so, like the wide, completely unchildlike childish stare. Certainly her appearance was not artless. He gave it up. He remembered that he was talking to an American woman, and he hadn't talked to an American woman for a long time. That might explain a good deal. But secretly he knew it explained nothing at all.

He plunged into an objective conversation—he strove to keep it objective. It proved to be equally unfolding and — intrinsically — equally undisclosing. Mrs. Prendegast . . . he remembered that news of her marriage to young Sydney Prendegast, son of old Mr. Prendegast of the bank, had reached him eight years before in Africa, and he learned now with a little twinge of regret what he already knew, and that was that young Sydney was still alive—Mrs. Prendegast wasn't happy. But then most young married women weren't happy or, for social purposes, implied that they weren't. He tried to recall young Sydney to his mind. Not much good, as he recollected him. A pale, rather unhealthy, overdressed, talkative person, always terrifying you lest you be sprayed, literally, by his pallid, insincere enthusiasm . . . No, Mrs. Prendegast wasn't happy. . . . Gulian found himself annoyed by the fact that she wasn't happy. People ought to be happy, especially young and beautiful people. . . . Moreover, she was too calm about her unhappiness; too willing to accept it as final and proceed upon that basis. Why should a woman expect happiness, she asked. There was lots for a woman to do in the world, wasn't there, except to marry or pursue romance? She was busy with her friends, with her mother, with charity. She no longer looked for happiness in personal relationships.

"But in friendships?" protested Gulian.

"Oh, yes, possibly in friendships."

She danced for charity—she hadn't any money to give. Her husband didn't really work, although he thought he did. He was some sort of a broker, but he spent most of his time playing bridge. She wished she were a man ——! Oh, very fiercely she wished she were a man! Like Gulian, for instance, to have done the things he had done and to have similar things to do. Adventure and romance, as she had said, were outside a woman's grasp. New York was stupid; modern life, modern women, modern men, hard, unsympathetic.

Gulian thought he peceived here a confused ideal of completeness, of consummation; a misty feminine Holy Grail; an idea, touching, pathetic, absurd; perhaps fortunately no longer very much met with. This woman was curiously old-fashioned and new-fashioned at the same time. The duality increased his growing interest; sharpened the edge of the friendly tenderness he was beginning to feel.

"I remember now," he said thoughtfully. "Your name is Vida, isn't it? And it used to be Vida Blair. I think I met you years ago when you were still a little girl, and I was quite grown up. I think soon I ought to call you Vida. We're really sort of relations, you know, if your father-in-law is my father's partner."

Her wide, scarlet, serious lips, the lower lip caught a trifle away from the upper, so that there was to that part of her face a hint of questioning, a hint possibly of petulance, parted in a smile.

"You are even younger than I thought," she observed musingly. "Why won't you let me talk seriously? It's a relief—at least for me, you know— to talk seriously."

Gulian noticed the marvelous curve of her chin. "I think," he said, "perhaps one of the most important things in the world is the fact that I remember you were Vida Blair. It's like picking up an old friendship. I need old friendships just at present."

Mrs. Prendegast studied him for a thoughtful moment of silence before she replied, "So do I."

The remainder of the dinner seemed to Gulian to pass with brutal rapidity. Astonishingly soon he was left alone with his father and Philip and Vannya and Perry, smoking a cigar and sipping a cordial, and with Mrs. Prendegast's last words in his mind—"You have something of the father-confessor in you. Do you like to hear nonsense? . . . Well, I will tell you a lot; I'm a Catholic." He kept his place across the table from Perry and studied with ruminative distaste that debonair person's crisp little moustache and crisp, well-cut hair, and crisp, sparkling eyes; young eyes except for the forked lines that surrounded them. Perry, to judge by his eyes, cherished always the same small unpleasant joke audible in his laugh.

"That little Vida what's-her-name . . . that little Prendegast woman's damned good-looking, isn't she?" said Perry, a trifle too lingeringly.

No one seemed anxious to pick up the conversational gage.

"Have some more coffee, Perry," urged Mr. Eyre hastily.

Philip removed his cigar from his mouth and studied its end.

"I hope they're getting along better," he remarked thoughtfully.

"Who?" asked Gulian ruthlessly.

Mr. Eyre chuckled. "No one, my dear fellow," he observed soothingly. "No one, at all. Perry and Philip are always anxious to find something wrong with everyone, although they approach their researches from different angles. It's astonishing to me how fine most women and young girls are, considering the circumstances."

"It's astonishing to me what damned rascals they are," chuckled Perry. He turned to Gulian—"I hear you're going into business?"

Gulian wondered if all his relatives were determined to find his more serious intentions so funny.

"I am going to if you and Philip will let me," he answered briefly.

Perry's comment was to laugh shortly—twice.

"Try it!" advised Mr. Eyre heartily. "Try it! There's nothing very hard about it. And don't let Philip or Perry discourage you. What their idea is,

I don't know. Banking has its percentage of fools like everything else—about ninety per cent. There's not much competition. These fellows who are in it try to make you believe it's an esoteric priestcraft. Bunkum! You've done lots of harder jobs."

"Times have changed since you were in business, father," remarked Philip gravely.

"Want to play squash tomorrow?" asked Perry suddenly, as if the conversation was too absurd or too burdensome for him to take further part in it.

"No!" retorted Gulian shortly.

"Well, you'd better get your muscles in shape if you're going into business with Philip."

Mr. Eyre stood up.

"Shall we join the ladies?" he asked.

Philip and Perry and Vannya followed him, but Gulian lingered behind for a moment. He went over to the fireplace and peered thoughtfully down at the mild fire of soft-coal, placing both hands on the mantelpiece before him and tapping meditatively with his foot the shining fender. Suddenly he straightened his shoulders, faced about, and set off after the others. He had been thinking about Philip's reluctance and Perry's sneers. "By thunder," he said to himself, "nothing in God's world will stop me from being a banker now! Nothing at all! . . ."

Afterwards, in the drawing-room, he found no further opportunity to speak to Mrs. Prendegast, Drusilla commandeered him.

"I think he's charming, your Major Polienoff," she began, with a gray eye a trifle too reminiscent. ". . . And now tell me all about yourself, Gilly."

Gulian discovered an illogical annoyance in the burning interest women and men took in each other. Here they were at it again—in his own home—just as they had been in Japan and France and Central Africa and Guatemala and all up and down the Andes. He saw the world as a large unkempt place where everywhere at the moment male and female conversationalists were permitting childish inflections to creep into their voices because they had just overtaken attractive persons of the opposite sex. Drusilla had been married seventeen years. Of course, if he had been Drusilla he would have left Perry ages ago, but since she hadn't, by now she should be habituated. At all events, compared to Drusilla, Vannya was a mere child.

At half past ten, Drusilla arose and embraced her father. "I'm to meet some people at a restaurant for dancing," she announced. "I loved your party, Daddy. . . . Your cheeks are as pink as peonies. . . . Why don't you and Major Polienoff come along, Gilly? It will interest you. New York has changed. You can play Rip Van Winkle. You'll make a fascinating Rip Van Winkle."

Gulian hesitated. "I've had a long day," he said. ". . . Is Perry going?" He wouldn't go if Perry was going. He had seen enough of Perry for one night.

"Good God, no!" said that gentleman suddenly, arousing himself from where, upon a sofa, he was engaged in a desultory but, as far as he was concerned, secretive conversation with Mrs. Prendegast. "It isn't public enough, if I want to dance publicly; and it isn't private enough, if I want to dance privately."

"Get your hat and things, Gilly, and I'll take you in my car," suggested Drusilla.

Gulian bade Mrs. Prendegast good-by. He thought her hand—cool and yet warm—lingered in his for a friendly instant. "Aren't you coming with us?" he asked.

She shook her head smilingly. "I don't know your sister very well," she said. And then, as if she was penitent, "And I haven't asked you any of the interesting things I meant to, have I? I did nothing but talk about myself. That comes from being stupid and living in New York."

"Drusilla?" . . . expostulated Perry. "Don't know Drusilla? Damned easy to know! . . . Why don't you know her? I'll take you both out to tea some afternoon if you'll let me."

Gulian regarded the speaker with a jaundiced eye.

In her taxicab, an unpleasant taxicab that smelled of stale leather, Mrs. Prendegast sped northward until the car turned into Forty-fifth street, where she had her apartment. She sat with her blue velvet cloak about her, staring out of the window. She hated taxicabs. The smell of stale leather made her thoughts even more bitter. Why should she be forced to ride in taxicabs? She had made a bargain eight years before when she married and the bargain hadn't been kept. She felt cheated. She always felt that way when she left gayety and wealth behind her and rode home in taxicabs. The act somehow discounted her beauty. If Sydney wouldn't play cards so much she might possibly have a car of her own.

At the door of the converted brownstone house, rather charming with its French windows and balconies, she let herself in with her night-key and walked gravely up to the second story with the pretty, slow steps of a graceful woman deep in thought.

When she opened the door of her hallway, she saw a light in the library beyond, and focused in the light

the brown, sparsely covered head of her husband showing above the back of a big chair in which he was reading a newspaper. He looked at her over the edge of
the paper as she came in. His eyes did not change
their expression.

"Had a big day," he said. "Made a lot of money.
Cleaned up Grayson and a couple of other fellows.
Have a good time?"

"Better than I thought," returned Mrs. Prendegast
languidly. "I expected to be bored. . . . I usually
am bored when I go to the parties you ought to go to
. . . but I wasn't."

She went to a table where there were some roses in
a tall vase and stooping over, smelled them.

"He's very good-looking, the youngest Eyre," she
said musingly. "He seems to be a real man, too.
There aren't very many. Did you ever meet him?"

"Yes. I thought he was blamed conceited."

Mrs. Prendegast smiled into the roses.

"He isn't conceited at all. I think he's really a little
shy. I think I scared him."

Her husband suddenly stood up and threw his paper
down with a gesture of impatience. "I suppose," he
said, "most of this is meant for me? Well, let me tell
you something—leave him alone. There're too many
business connections there. Leave him alone. Most
of the money you live on comes from my father. Don't
you try any of your silly tricks." He thrust his hands
in his pockets and stared at her truculently, his long
sallow equine face wrinkled and sneering. "And by
the way, your friend Rannie Sedgewick called you
up a little while ago. It's none of my business what
you do—if you don't do too much—and I don't care,
so long as you don't interfere with me, but I do think
you should tell your playmates what your schedule

is so that they won't bother me. Otherwise, some day, you might get into trouble."

Mrs. Prendegast left the roses and walked slowly towards her husband, her eyes widening as she did so. She paused when her face was within a few inches of his, and his eyes, attempting to meet hers, fell.

"I think," she said softly, "you're the cheapest man I've ever met. I don't know why I go on living with you, except that I'm a Catholic and a coward, and because you're a habit. And the most curious thing to me is why you should want me to go on living with you, although I suppose I'm a habit too. But you're a habit that comes too high where I am concerned. Some day I'll leave you out of sheer weariness. What you can't hinder you spoil. Whatever there is of beauty in my life I snatch behind your back, for even if I'm not afraid of your tongue, it soils whatever you talk about. I believe if you knew how much I loved the things I've saved my own money for to put into this apartment, you'd chuck them out the window." She paused for a moment and her eyes became reflective. "I wish to God I had a profession," she said.

"You have," said her husband; "getting things from men without paying for them—that includes me. . . . I hope," he continued thoughtfully, still staring at the floor, "I hope, by gad, I hope you do make a fool of yourself with Eyre—the damned conceited pup! . . . The only times I ever saw him I hated him. I'd like to catch him out in something." He seemed completely absorbed in this cheering prospect.

"If I had been going to make a fool of myself," returned his wife, "I would have done so long ago."

She went into the room beyond.

CHAPTER V

"HE WENT FORTH WITH THE LOVELY
ODALISQUES"

MEANWHILE, in the soft corduroyed obscurity of Drusilla's car, Drusilla and Gulian and Vannya had turned from the comparative darkness of Twenty-first street into the long illumination of Fifth Avenue. To the east of them lay Madison Square and a great tower that rose like a mortal exclamation point marking amazement at the aloofness of the upper night. Against the stars there was a hint of the arabesque foliage of spring about to expand into a solidity of bloom, and through the glass front of the limousine, the traffic towers glimmered in a long line, as if a martial glow-worm had brought his fellows into single file. Both the side windows of the car were lowered, and the soft heavy April air, restless, amorous, hinting of the fortuitous, smelling of rain and loosened earth, fanned into a breeze by the forward motion, touched the faces of the woman and the two men.

Gulian spoke from the shadows of his corner. "It's exciting . . ." he said. "Too exciting."

Drusilla had been searching in a little bag she carried, and now she drew out a gold case that twinkled in the reflections from the street lamps they were passing, and extracted a cigarette.

"Have you a match, Gilly?" she asked.

He struck one and held it towards her, and she leaned forward, her long lashes veiling her eyes, and

55

her mouth, in the act of drawing in the first breath of smoke, drooping and pathetic.

The light went out and she settled back against the cushions.

"And what did Vida Prendegast say?" she asked, with a laugh.

"Mrs. Prendegast? Why . . . What made you think of her?"

"I couldn't help overhearing her remark about subjective adventure and your answer—that it was the only fundamental adventure. It's an old aphorism; I wonder how true it is? It's rather easy for men like you to talk that way—you don't have to depend upon subjective adventure."

"Eventually we do. It's the only dependable thing there is."

"But you've had the other thing, and most women —at least, most American women, haven't."

"What are you driving at?"

"I don't know," said Drusilla hastily. "I haven't time to think. . . . I'm too busy." Her voice became more reflective. "But I see the women about me and I hear them talk."

"What do they say?"

"They're restless. I should say that at present they are finding too much subjective adventure and, at the same time, too little."

"What do you mean?"

"I mean they've lost the ability to find adventure in the subjective things that used to be adventurous to them and are reaching out blindly towards subjective adventure they know nothing about."

"Hasn't that always been the case?"

"No, not always, and not for a long time in the same way. The trouble is they don't know where to begin;

they haven't any starting point any more; no taking-off place; no premises. They no longer know what adventures they have a right to and what they haven't a right to. . . . The world's too big and too small at the same time. . . . There're too many possible adventures. The mountains look little because we suddenly find ourselves living in them."

"Then the field has really been limited?"

Drusilla gestured with the hand holding the cigarette. "No," she said fiercely, "it's been expanded; tragically expanded. It is only limited by a complete lack of limitation—the most confusing limitation there is. A nun in a convent is better off—that is, she's happier—than a nun with the universe before her and no knowledge as yet of which road to take. . . ."

Her cigarette glowed in the darkness. She took it from her mouth and leaned forward. "Gilly," she said, with a hurried gravity, as if she suddenly remembered that here was a man to whom she could speak with complete frankness, "of all the generations of the war, our generation—yours and mine—suffered, I think, the most. We were in it, as the older generation wasn't, and yet we can't get over it the way the youngsters can. It's made a division right in the middle of our lives. Our fathers and mothers still go on thinking as they've always done, and the boys and girls were on a fresh track anyway. But we began one way and now we've got to end another. It's not so easy to be good, in the old-fashioned way, and it's twice as hard—if you're decent at all—to be bad, for now you're responsible to yourself alone, and that's the most exacting responsibility of all. You haven't even the satisfaction any longer of thinking yourself, as progressive women used to think themselves, a martyr to new causes. For thirty years or so we believed

certain things were true only to find now that we're
not a bit sure that they are true; and we're just as
much in doubt about the new things—we're not sure
they're true either. We have neither the sublime arrogance of the young nor the unshakable although
shrunken confidence of the old. And we can't keep
off the dark any longer by telling ourselves fairy tales
in the old way."

"But these problems aren't new," protested Gulian,
"they've been troubling the world ever since it began."

Drusilla shook her head in the darkness.

"Not in exactly the same way——" she reiterated,
"Never in America. And in Europe they had their
own oblique way of getting around them. But the war
has changed all that—or hastened the change. It's
unsettled most moral axioms, but at the same time it's
made people more honest—and that's a trying combination. You may think lots of things right you used
to think wrong, but you can't go ahead with them until
you've settled accounts with yourself. You no longer
can think one thing and do another, all the while lying
comfortably to yourself . . . at least, you can't and
get much fun out of it."

"You mean sophistry is becoming a lost art?"

"It's been badly damaged—at least, with thinking
people. And yet what is one to do? Time flies, and
life slips away from one . . ." She paused abruptly,
interrupting herself with another laugh. "Poor Gilly!"
she said. "This is a dreadful way to treat you on the
night of your fatted calf, isn't it? You'll think that all
women do nothing but talk about subjective or objective adventures. And please don't imagine I'm referring to myself, for I'm not. As things go, I'm getting
along famously. Tell me more about yourself."

Gulian considered this latter statement. "I think

perhaps you are," he said slowly, "getting along famously, but also, because you're fine and good, that
maybe you're exaggerating the difficulties of others.
I imagine, despite the upset, the wicked are settling
down as usual to their accustomed wickedness and the
righteous are returning to their habitual thorny self-
bedevilments. I'd forgotten what a translucently good
woman you are, Drusilla. You think straighter than
most of your sex."

In the semi-darkness Drusilla's hand stole out and
touched his.

"Thank you, Gilly, my dear," she said, "I hope I'll
stay that way—translucent—— But I'm afraid I'm
not—very translucent." She laughed uncertainly.
"It's a little difficult to remain translucent. Those
who try to be honest are having a hard time of it at
present. They're confused."

Gulian was flattered by the intimacy this sister of
his, after so long an absence on his part, was offering
him—as if she had picked up as a matter of course
something that had been merely temporarily put aside.
His heart warmed towards Drusilla, and for the first
time in his life he began to wonder just how happy or
unhappy she really was. He had always imagined her
contented—if, to his mind, rather oddly—with her more
than ordinary lot in life; properly oblivious to the
limitations inherent in it, as in everything else, but
also well aware of the advantages, although, of course,
at the back of his brain there had always been an
uneasy suspicion that complete sympathy between her
and Perry was out of the question. But now it looked
as if Drusilla too was beginning to shake her own
small spear at the leaden skies of Fate, adding another
to the multitude of spears already being shaken.

The thought depressed him. He was depressed

at the possibility of Drusilla being unhappy, and, in a
large quasi-philosophical way, he was depressed because, like most men, outside of the particular woman
in whom at any given time he happened to be interested, he could not help being vaguely distressed, although he knew it to be wrong, by any kind of feminine discontent or rebellious intellectual groping.
Where the woman he happened to be interested in was
concerned it was just the other way about. He would
have been equally distressed, but not vaguely, had she
failed to companion his own questionings and insur-
gency. He could not abide unintelligent women—
intimately, that is. The average woman, however,
was different. The average woman should be the only
static thing in a world of change; a lighthouse—although, like lighthouses, to be more or less avoided.
This was peculiarly true of sisters. In a perfect world
sisters would be especially static.

He stared through the glass front of the car to
where, above the dark shoulders of Vannya who was
sitting on the folding chair at his knees, the traffic
towers blinked in the tawny dusk.

Vannya, oblivious to the winds of conversation blowing about him, was occupied solely in the difficult task
of trying to see at one and the same time the right and
left of the strange street upon which he found himself.

"What do you do with yourself mostly?" Gulian
asked.

"Dance," Drusilla answered, "and laugh too much,
and go to boring parties, and flirt with an inclination
towards mischief. That's a complete history of the
average wealthy woman's life, isn't it? I'm supposed,
also, to be very much occupied with good works."

Her voice carried an undercurrent half wheedling,
half chuckling, as if she was sardonically amused at

herself but at the same time asking for commiseration.

Vannya, without turning around from his chair, spoke in French.

"It is like a beautiful woman in a hall of mirrors, this avenue of yours," he observed thoughtfully.

You wondered what memories of other avenues, avenues lined with great square palaces; of open places beneath frosty northern stars; what memories of rooms with mirrors, were in his mind at the moment.

Gulian chuckled. "Vannya is not troubled with our doubts," he said. "He regards women as being solely ornamental . . . whether they are moral or not, is merely a question where their especial talents happen to lie. The unornamental woman and those who have to work for a living, he looks upon as insoluble problems, outside his province of thought—like drink, or crime, or vice. . . . Is New York very different?"

He imagined that Drusilla would welcome a change of subject. Possibly she was already beginning to regret the emphasis of what she had said.

"I understand," said Vannya, still without turning his head . . . "practically everything you are saying. I am beginning to understand English dangerously well."

"We have said nothing," Gulian assured him, "you shouldn't hear."

"I know, but you will," concluded Vannya comfortably.

"He is sweet," murmured Drusilla. "I adore him." She addressed Gulian. "But you saw it two years ago."

"I heard that," said Vannya. "You said you adored me."

"After I got back from France?" asked Gulian. "I

was here only three weeks, and then I was too tired to notice."

"Yes, it has changed a lot. It's more cosmopolitan and heartless and—although I suppose that would follow—more polite. At least, it is ruder in the streets, except for the policemen and the motorbus-men and the various officials, but it is politer in the places that have had time to settle down—the hotels, the shops, the restaurants. The politeness comes from the head instead of the heart, and as a rule that's the more certain way for it to come."

"More polite?"

"Infinitely. You'll notice it. We've grown up and have the good manners of self-assurance. We leave cockiness to the unconquered rest of the country. But it isn't the old New York . . . the place is swarming with little black beady Mediterraneans. And there're large ungrammatical persons about now you wouldn't have met fifteen years ago. I've collected two for tonight. I'm devoted to them. In England they'd be coronetted."

"And that's a sign of growing up?"

"Of course it's a sign of growing up. The ungrammatical ones don't get in unless they're amusing or generous or useful. The stupidest society in the world is the society based on birth alone. Look at what Vienna was, or what the Faubourg Saint Germain is. Nasty children matching idiot ancestors. And then, you should see the sons and daughters of the ungrammatical ones after they've been to Groton or St. Paul's.

Gulian leaned forward smilingly intent. He wanted very much to ask a final question.

"And are they as good as they are beautiful?" he asked. "The young ones, I mean. They seem to be occupying the limelight. I hope to meet a few. One of my reasons for coming home—although don't tell anyone—is to conduct a philosophical research in that direction. Philosophical, or anthropological, or psychological, or whatever it is. You see, all over the world I've been hearing how magnificently wicked they are. I imagine the only good young people left must be the Japanese. . . . At least, that is the impression I've gained from ladies who have dragged me off into dark corners to tell me about it, and from books, and from shocked but pleased elderly gentlemen."

"Did the ladies show a tendency towards personal advances themselves?" Drusilla queried.

"Why . . . why . . . I don't know. Perhaps they did, only I'm no longer by way of being very encouraging in that respect. . . . Why? What do you mean?"

Drusilla laughed. "Nothing. A little private investigation of my own. I think the more timid of my sex and generation are getting a left-handed sort of enjoyment out of talking about supposed wickedness, while the bolder are being led to try experiments themselves. After all, it isn't quite fair, is it, that we should have been suppressed so long and the ones right after us should be having their fling?"

"But are they having their fling? That's what I'm asking."

"I don't know, and after all I'm not especially interested. By the time Millicent comes out, three years or so from now, there'll be something new. It's the women between thirty and fifty that bother me. I believe most of them think they've been cheated. Look out for the woman between thirty and fifty, Gilly. This isn't a second-blooming, it's a first-blooming such as the world has never before seen. I wouldn't bother about the young ones, no matter what their theories. They're always comparatively harmless."

Gulian chuckled.

"As usual," he said, "the younger generation, with the theories it doesn't put into operation, is doing infinitely more harm to the generation just above it than it is doing to itself."

Drusilla was lost in thought. "I wonder," she said, "if the American girl and woman is going to lose her position as the one demi-virgin of the world?"

The car had turned from Fifth Avenue into a side street and was coming to a halt on Madison Avenue where from a lighted entrance a striped awning stretched to the curb. A huge commissionaire in a uniform covered with gold cord, the last surviving romantic uniform, outside of the Balkans, in an age that has come to hate uniforms, stepped forward and twisted the handle of the door nearest Drusilla. Gulian descending, still in full cry upon the trail of the discussion, barked in his astonished and unintelligent face.

"Thank God!" he exclaimed. "I'm glad of it! That was the rottenest compliment that could be paid us. The most shameless. It implied that we were a nation of titillators . . . and we were. I'm for vice . . . or else virtue. Nothing hypocritical and in between."

He turned about and helped Drusilla to the street.

The commissionaire's eyes expressed bewilderment that anyone talking in this manner could still be in such apparent control of his body.

"Of course," Gulian continued, walking beside Drusilla towards the doorway, "I don't believe half these tales. Each generation has always told them about the one following. People are about the same as they've always been—some good, some bad—mostly good. But the one thing I do believe, is that there has been an accession of frankness, and that is admirable. If nothing else, it will enable one to separate the goats from the sheep. Men will be able to do what women have always been able to do; instantly, that is, tell the rake from the ordinary citizen. Think of the blindfold marriages that will be saved. I rather believe I'm for the younger generation."

"I trust," said Drusilla, dryly, "you won't be disappointed."

Vannya, who seemed to be devoting his night to the making of aphorisms, caught up to them and spoke over their shoulders.

"There is nothing," he said, "so charming, is there, as the entrance to a smart restaurant in spring . . . women . . . their cloaks fluttering behind them? . . . like swans in a fairy-tale."

Gulian's first impressions were of noise and smell; then of arms—dozens of excessively bare arms; arms everywhere, some gesticulating, some poised gracefully, some cutting like shining scimitars the black coats of the dancing men— and then of legs. But the last was not until he had seated himself at the table where Drusilla's party was and had had time to look about him.

The first two impressions, the auricular and olfactory, were strange, for there was, as a matter of fact, very little noise and, save for the faint smell of flowers on the table and a trace of mingled and expensive perfumes, nothing on which the nose could lay hold. The room was perfectly aired. Even the cigarette smoke did not hang too long.

It was an eminently discreet room, as well-bred as a public dancing-restaurant could be; the walls a subdued rose color, the shades of the electric candles rose, the waiters lined and secretive men, or young men infinitely suave; the orchestra playing with the soft weary abandon recently become the fashion amongst ultra-modern orchestras. To its not too broken rhythms the dancers moved with a languid grace; a velvet ripple of the long muscles of a race recently acquiring once more, through dancing and exercise, long muscles. Their steps were the apotheosis of jazz; its qualification on the part of the highly trained; the initial signs of a revolt against a barbarism that had for a few years overwhelmed the blond nations with the darkness of tom-toms and shuffling feet. Those few who copied the intuitional agility of the world at large, who shook their shoulders or waggled their hips, seemed out of place and comic. No gesture was allowed to go beyond the subtle primary undulations of the beginnings of undulation.

But there were too many arms and too many legs . . . and too many women. The philosophic observer was forced to admit that there was some truth in the saying that 'woman' is a beautiful word and 'women' by no means so beautiful; that a plurality of loveliness has a tendency to become unlovely. One reason, no doubt, why no truly artistic nation has ever gone in for polygamy, even the most liberal of the sensitive-minded being unable to imagine living synchronistically with a sewing-circle.

Drusilla threaded her way through the crowd until she came to a table where a very red-faced man and woman, a tall, uninterested, beautifully dressed blond young man, a small bright-haired discontented-looking young woman, and a fat man with convex eye glasses were sitting. The men sprang to their feet and made room for her and bowed to Vannya and Gulian.

As a wind ripples a wheat field and is gone, boredom died out of the face of the blond young man and he turned to Drusilla. You felt that until then he had not spoken for ages.

Pemberton was his name, so Gulian discovered, and his first name was DeWitt, and Drusilla called him 'Divvy.' The discontented pretty woman was his wife. She looked at Vannya and Gulian appraisingly as at one time the discontented matrons of Alexandria must have looked at the most recent importation of slaves, but the way in which the eagerness of appraisal made place for a smile of subdued conventional greeting indicated that there would be no immediate purchase at the moment, that is, unless the merchandise possessed tricks and qualifications as yet undisclosed. There was a certain type of woman that did not like Gulian. He was, as most emotional people are, on the surface too self-contained.

Pemberton's manner towards Drusilla was gently possessive, a manner that Gulian resented. He told himself that this wearied young man mentally rested his arm on Drusilla's shoulder. Weeks later when he mentioned this to Drusilla she laughed delightedly.

"People don't have affairs with Divvy," she explained, "except possibly Follies girls and people like that. Divvy's a preface; not a history. He's always that way with women he dances a lot with—he seems to consider it a form of marriage. He thinks of me as nothing more than a hundred and thirty-five pounds of agility. As long as I'm agile, he'll be tender. At present, he's my dancing young man."

He was—decidedly. For the sake of manners he asked his wife and Mrs. Hurd—that was the red-faced woman's name—if they would accept his skilled guidance, but he was palpably relieved when they both refused. The rest of the time he circled the room with Drusilla in his arms.

Every now and then they lounged up, like swimmers leaving a lazy surf, to puff once or twice at a cigarette or sip an iced drink, and then slowly, abstractedly, they would find their way back to the dancing floor, to be swallowed up again in the weaving mass. Glimpses of their faces showed them rapt and ecstatic. There was no emotion visible save the holy one of rhythm. They were very beautiful, in reality; utterly matched in that one direction; devotees practicing an absorbing, transforming rite.

Gulian found himself between Mrs. Pemberton and Mrs. Hurd, disliking the former and liking the latter. He realized that to get on with Mrs. Pemberton oblations were necessary, and since he wasn't in love with her, and wasn't going to be, he saw no reason why he should pretend that he was. Nor was he anxious to praise her beauty. Mediocre beauty was a common enough thing when you came to think of it. He had seen too much of it to find it exciting unless illumined by the small inner lamp of personality. An ugly nose, showing a trace of understanding, was infinitely more entrancing than a perfect nose taut with complacency. Powder had made all women's noses alike, anyway.

"I'm sorry I don't dance," he said. "At least, I haven't for years. I daresay I'll have to take it up again."

"Don't dance? Oh, but you must dance! Everybody dances. What in the world do you do with yourself?"

She looked Gulian over with wide corn-flower eyes and seemed annoyed that he withdrew his own so hastily. He sat with his sunburned chin sunk forward on his shirt bosom and a thin brown hand twisting the stem of his glass. "Nothing!" he said. "Not a thing! . . ." His eyes apparently tried to focus for a moment upon the end of his long nose and this gave him a cross-eyed appearance. "Not for four years. Absolutely nothing!" He turned to his questioner and opened his eyes upon her. "I really must learn to dance, mustn't I? Try Major Polienoff." He nodded towards Vannya, who was talking to the man with the eye-glasses. "He's part Russian and part Pole. His reactions are simple and sensuous and almost instantaneous."

Mrs. Pemberton's plucked eyebrows expressed a slight bewilderment. She didn't like men who tried to be funny. She looked across the table at Vannya.

"Do you dance, Major Polienoff?" she asked in halting French.

Vannya abruptly ended his conversation.

"Magnificently," he replied enthusiastically; "with a variety that is amazing. The schottische, the polka, the old-fashioned waltz, with reverse, and several native dances. But the modern dance . . . that, I regret to say, I have had but little opportunity to master. With you as instructress, however, I have no fear but that I shall speedily learn."

It was doubtful if Mrs. Pemberton understood very much of this rapidly spoken lyric, but to Gulian's relief she accepted Vannya's challenge, and from that time on, they too were non-existent.

"He's a handsome young man," said Mrs. Hurd comfortably. "Beautiful eyes." You felt it would have been a great relaxation to her if she could have crossed her hands over her matronly but gorgeously decorated stomach.

Here, no doubt, was one of Drusilla's 'large ungram-

matical persons.' Not that Mrs. Hurd was actually
ungrammatical, but you were never quite sure when
she was saying 'come' and when she was saying 'came,'
and her 'wases' and 'weres' were doubtful, moreover
her eyes grew very large and she breathed heavily
whenever she used fashionable and abstract adjectives
such as 'abominable' or 'heavenly' or 'splendid.'

But Gulian liked her. Beneath her careful exterior
he believed she was direct and kindly, possible to
inveigle, if the conversation in other quarters became
too subtle or disingenuous, into quite homely simple
talk, about children, and dentists and early life, and
illnesses and digestion. She was not, however, as
much of a person as her husband. The up-rooted
female seldom is. The feminine mind is too barnacu-
lar; neither has it the masculine intuition for
simple dress, nor the masculine tradition of minding
its own business.

At some period Mrs. Hurd's figure had been arrested
half-way between the happy expansion of the unfash-
ionable and the obliteration nowadays desired. The
obliteration did not seem to be progressing. Over
certain areas there remained undue concentrations of
flesh that might have been useful if used somewhere
else.

She seemed sensitive on this subject for she con-
fessed to Gulian that she was 'rolling.' Having been
out of the country for a long while, he was not sure
just what she meant. He had always heard the parti-
ciple used in connection with wealth.

"Rolling?"

"Yes—Professor Tarantous. We meet Tuesdays
and Thursdays." She sighed. "But I'm rather disappointed. It seems to take it off one place and put it
on another. I've tried so many things . . . stretch-

ing and running and baths and dieting and New Thought and aesthetic dancing and head-standing."

"Head-standing?"

"That was last year under a man named Bergen. It was supposed to be good for your aura as well. The class took their clothes off and stood on their heads. Someone played Beethoven."

"Took their clothes off?" Gulian had a horrid vision of what Professor Bergen had been forced to endure in the course of his profession.

"Oh, with thick nightgowns, of course."

"Tied at the ankles?"

"Naturally."

"Thank God!" said Gulian softly.

"It was hard," said Mrs. Hurd, mistaking the syllables, "but I think I'll go back to it—or New Thought. New Thought may not really take off any flesh but it makes you feel thin, and that's the principal thing. And then you can eat candy. You see, it's all the way you look at candy, or anything else. If you say to yourself, 'It's not fattening! It's not fattening! It's not fattening!' why then it isn't. . . . Charley, I wish you'd take New Thought. . . . He gets so excited over things," she added; "and I notice it is always after a heavy meal."

Mr. Hurd drifted smilingly into the conversation. He was a heavy man, with a florid clean-shaven face and wiry iron-gray hair. His eyes were fine and intelligent; his lips thick and generous; his hands worn and fastidious.

Gulian warmed towards him. Here was one of the élite of the much misunderstood—blindly worshiped, blindly damned—world of business; a world at its worst, childish, at its best, composed of poets, adventurers, buccaneers, pontiffs. A world that was passing with the narrowing of opportunity. Hurd was a survivor. He was of the same race as the exploring merchants of Carthage, the Doges of Venice, the traders of the Free Cities. Old and wise in his texture, young in his impulses and imagination. And that is the stuff of which great things are built—paintings and ships and warehouses.

"I can't undertake New Thought, my dear," he said, "there is so much old thought I haven't even touched on yet. Did you meet van Zeeland in Tokyo, Mr. Eyre? He's with his embassy."

Gulian remembered with a smile the dextrous, slim, exquisite Frenchman.

"Yes," he said.

"He's a great friend of mine."

Well, it was altogether natural he should be. These two men would meet, coming around from different sides of the circle. Good taste was a matter of being at one end or the other of things, never in the middle.

The eye-glassed man had by this time brought out a little curved flask and was pouring some whiskey into his own glass and the glasses of the others.

"Since my government has become so childish," he observed, "it is necessary for me to become childish too. We're all children together. I am nothing if not patriotic. This is Haig and Haig. The country is growing charmingly pastoral. Like the shepherds, we take our simple pleasures by hook or by crook—usually crook. If I had a son I should bring him up as a bootlegger. There's a career for you, and not without its worldly compensations, either. A great picaresque novel is yet to be written on the subject. Are you for Prohibition, Mr. Eyre? No, of course not. Your expression is not dazed."

His pale eyes glared from behind his convex glasses

with the complete lack of emotion characteristic of the very shy, very gregarious man. "My name," he explained to Gulian, "since your sister did not mention it, is Cyprian Bland. I chose Cyprian myself in the height of the Oscar Wilde enthusiasm, but now, I regret to say, it is both bizarre and antedated. However, I can't change it since in a small way it is known. . . . My name originally was Amaziah, which means 'the Lord is strong,' and it was very popular in the small Ohio village where I was born. That shows you that the country has progressed, at least a little, in fifty years."

"I had an uncle," said Mrs. Hurd, off her guard, "named Athanasius."

"I trust," said Bland gravely, "he did not make the same mistake I did."

He was quite unsmiling; apparently he never smiled. Above his white full-moon face his fluffy, cherubic hair rose like a slightly mussed halo. Only his mouth exhibited any expression; it was both mobile and humorous. Gulian liked him immediately, as he had liked Hurd. Evidently he was that pleasant and, in America, rare creature who, to much experience and an overwhelming interest in life, adds an entire lack of all but aesthetic prejudices. As a result he would be sympathetic and unmoral, clear-sighted and just, witty, and, in his private life, probably above reproach.

Before the night was over he asked Gulian to call upon him.

"You probably won't have much to do for awhile," he said. "I have an apartment on Thirty-second street. I work in fits and starts—mostly starts. I'm a writer. Come around, and we'll damn everything we can think about."

Later on he asked Gulian if he didn't dance.

"Neither do I," he remarked. "My figure is built for the kindlinesses of acquaintanceship, not the convexities of intimacy."

Drusilla and Pemberton returned for one of their brief periods of relaxation.

"Your friend, Major Polienoff," Drusilla informed Gulian, "is dancing with a graceful abandon which I think is frightening but delighting Gertrude Pemberton to the point of unconsciousness." She suddenly looked up and over her shoulder. "Oh, hello!" she said. "Where did you come from?" and Gulian, following her backward glance, saw a slim girl in white standing at her shoulder. . . .

A very gold and white girl; rather like one of the swans of Vannya's simile. Of medium height, possibly, but made to look taller by youthful slenderness and the straight-lined dress she was wearing. She was very young, for she had the lustrous quality, the lambency, that as a rule does not outlast the middle twenties, no matter what more solid beauties may take its place—a little lovely peach-blossom flame; an irradiation.

"This," said Drusilla to Gulian, "is Lael Satori, and this—" she turned to the girl "—is my brother you've heard me talk so much about."

Gulian struggled half-way to his feet; always an awkward gesture; and then sat down again. He wished Drusilla hadn't introduced him. But the next moment she explained herself.

"Lael's rather a distinguished specimen of what we were talking about, Gilly," she said.

The girl twisted her painted lips into a button.

"Specimen? That sounds horrid."

"It isn't—merely amusing."

"What kind of a specimen? . . ." Then her in-

terest as abruptly flagged as it had arisen and flicking
Gulian with uncurious smoky gray eyes, she bent over
Drusilla again. "I wanted to find out," she said, "if
you were going tomorrow." Apparently an entirely
feminine question about a feminine engagement.
Gulian caught only scraps of the talk, for at that
moment Mrs. Hurd cut him out like a huge man-of-
war capturing an unresisting neutral and led him into
a little conversational harbor where she described to
him the horrors of modern motherhood.

He heard the girl say, "Good. . . . I must be getting back," and looked up to see her turn away.

She did not include him in her smile, not purposely,
of course, but with an entire forgetfulness. He watched
her as she walked back through the wilderness of little
tables.

She walked with the curious, tripping, hastily demure gait that young women nowadays affect. She
was remote and self-contained in the presence of the
people she passed; oblivious of the stares of the men
and women who, ten years before, would not have
stared, but then, ten years before a girl would not have
walked through a restaurant in just that way.

Gulian, considering her, found her suddenly annoying. If this was the younger generation he didn't like
it. The girl, when you came to think of it, was more
startling than beautiful anyway; her hair, parted in
the middle, too golden, too much of a contrast to the
darkness of her eyebrows; and her lips were a mere
impressionistic blotch of red. In this respect she had
gone even beyond her impulsive sisters, and as a result
—the increased size of her eyes and the diminished
length of her mouth—there was about her a puzzling
impression of youth and age; an effect cynical and
infantile; a childish worldliness.

"What do you think of her?" asked Drusilla.

"My thoughts are confused," murmured Gulian.

"She's rather a sweet little thing, really. At all events, she displays an interest in me that most of them don't. Poor little devils! They're like small birds beating against a net. So wise and so ignorant. I think they're even more pathetic than we used to be."

"Pathetic?" Gulian's voice had in it a note of anger.

Drusilla—before she laughed—looked at him with a startled expression.

"Why, Gilly!" she exclaimed. "Why, Gilly! I believe she's hurt your feelings! The stupid little wretch!"

Gulian and Vannya got home shortly after midnight. Mr. Eyre was still up, reading, with quaint horn-rimmed spectacles, in his library. He put down his book—it was Henry Adams' autobiography—as Vannya and Gulian, subtly redolent of the world, the flesh, and the devil, who is supposed to accompany the two former misunderstood allurements, entered.

"Poor Puritans," he sighed, slipping a thin finger between the bleak pages of Henry Adams. "Poor modern Puritans. Too thin-skinned for life; not gorgeous enough for heaven. Not like the old fellows with their sense of bacchic salvation; a heaven as colorful as Mahomet's. Of course they could put up with sixty years of a slab-sided psalm-singing wife if they were going to have an eternity of houris. But these modern fellows . . .!"

Gulian lit a cigarette and sat down opposite the fireplace, where embers still glowed.

"Who's Mrs. Prendegast, father?" he asked, "and what's her trouble?"

Mr. Eyre smiled. "Nothing essentially important, that I know of," he replied.

"Is she very poor?"

"No, I wouldn't say that. She was before she married—She was James Blair's daughter and he lost everything he had about twenty years ago. But, although I can't make out that her husband does anything much, I imagine his father gives him a handsome allowance. He's an only child."

"She thinks she's very poor."

Mr. Eyre's smile broadened.

"It takes a great deal of money to be really comfortable nowadays in New York," he observed. "Most of my friends are poor, if poverty means spending more than you should and worrying about it. We exceed our incomes spiritually, financially and physically. The one thing we cannot abide is the sweet spaciousness of frugality."

Gulian stretched his long legs out in front of him and inspected the tips of his pumps.

"Oh, well, damn women, anyhow," he observed sombrely; "they're never busy except when they're unhappy, and then they're too busy. They're the ones who are raising hell, and then, they're the ones who are trying to reform the ones who are raising hell, and that's about all there is to them. . . . So you know Vida Prendegast well?"

"Oh, no, not at all well."

Mr. Eyre got to his feet and banked the embers of the fire.

"Your Aunt Virginia expects you to call upon her for tea tomorrow," he said.

CHAPTER VI

AUNT VIRGINIA CONTINUES HER ADVICE

But Gulian did not call upon his Aunt Virginia the next afternoon, nor the next, nor the afternoon after that; in fact, he did not find time for this pressing but uncomfortable engagement until five days later—a Friday which began with a cold spring rain and ended in some blue and white hours, high-keyed, virginal—little clouds flying above the city—that took the imagination away from streets to an ocean horizon, cross-waved, with a schooner on it. He did not find time for this engagement, although, like a great many other relatively unimportant people, Mrs. Dorrance, because of her character and the manner in which it furnished inciting motives for her relatives and friends, occupied a position of spiritual prominence not at all deserved.

Gulian had found his first three days well occupied with getting Vannya settled in an art school and in rooms, and with redeeming, from the Custom House, his own and Vannya's baggage, a task that caused him to question Drusilla's cheerful assurance that New York was growing more polite. But the unpleasantness of the Custom House was to a large extent made up for by the interest attached to getting Vannya started upon his career and in finding him a studio, the former being illumined by a moment when, under Vannya's prolonged and tenderly impersonal glance, the charming near-sighted eyes of the bob-haired young lady secretary flickered behind her horn-rimmed spectacles and her steel-like business voice softened; and the latter taking Gulian into parts of the city he had not visited for years and introducing him to numerous landladies in various states of suspicion and dishabille.

Finally a large room with an excellent north light, and a small bedroom and dilapidated bathroom attached, was found in Washington Place. The single dirty window of the bedroom looked out upon a disarray of chimney-pots and streaked roofs sufficiently ugly to cause even the laziest artist to set about a search for beauty, and in the studio the previous occupant had left traces of himself in the shape of a broken easel and several scurrilous limericks, having to do with the private lives of his friends, scrawled in charcoal upon the walls.

"I meant to wash 'em off," said the landlady damply.

Vannya was warmly and placidly and immediately content with his new home. He pointed to a cot of an intricate folding description which had been shoved back into a corner of the studio.

"I shall have that made up for you," he informed Gulian graciously, "in case you want to get drunk."

"Have you ever seen me drunk?" demanded Gulian indignantly.

Vannya lit a cigarette and smiled.

"No," he said slowly, "but that is no sign. It comes upon a man in the night. I had an uncle who was a general in the army and a great authority on bridges and engineering; he never drank. . . . Yes, there are Russians who don't . . . but when he was sixty he fell in love with a little milliner, and since she was virtuous and married, he took to vodka and in three months saw elephants and blew his brains out." He sighed. "Why should he have picked a virtuous milliner when there're so many who aren't?"

"The moral of the story being," remarked Gulian, "that safety consists only in knowing the unrighteous?"

Vannya opened his eyes very wide. "I have never yet," he replied, "seen a little milliner worth the blowing off of a head full of cosines and tangents. That's the trouble with your country—you think otherwise. Virtue, which is a matter of chance, is more respected than knowledge, which is a matter of character. You applaud little milliners when they kill useful men."

That was at three o'clock, and the final arrangements having been completed, Gulian, unable to think of any further excuses for delay, returned to Madison Place to make himself presentable for his visit to his aunt. Vannya, enlisted unwittingly in the role of a shock-battalion, went along.

An hour and a half later he and Gulian arrayed in morning-coats, for Mrs. Dorrance liked formality, rang the doorbell of her house with a shining eagerness which in Gulian's case was not ingenuous.

Mrs. Dorrance lived in Twelfth Street just off Fifth Avenue, in the house she had always lived in and from which, as she cheerfully informed her relatives—whenever other conversation languished—she expected to be buried.

It was a double brick house with a cornice of white stone cut into jigsaws and flutings and with extremely white marble steps and square small-paned windows, placed at such regular intervals and so exactly alike that they gave the impression of a number of innocent eyes gazing with astonishment upon the passing wickedness of the world.

On the day in question, Aunt Virginia had had a 'good day.' She had spent her morning dispatching checks—accompanied by letters of suggestion; querulous suggestion—to the innumerable charitable organ-

izations to which she belonged and, from eleven to
one, she had sat upon the board of a society for helping delinquent women of which she was a directress.
This latter duty had necessitated a sharp reprimand
to one wayward girl, the separation of another from
the young criminal to whom she was attached, and
the forcing of a third into an immediate and undesired
marriage. All in all, Aunt Virginia had experienced
vicariously the excitements of prostitution coupled
with a sense of sanctity; an ideal towards which many
of her sex consecrate their most earnest endeavors.
Coming home for lunch, she had found Octavia Hiatt
awaiting her and that had meant another hour of
delicious bullying

Octavia Hiatt was the last representative of an
ancient and penniless race. For years she had been
a protégé of Aunt Virginia's buoyed up, one suspected,
and with one of the few determinations left her, by the
thought that Aunt Virginia might die first and leave
her some money; a supposition not at all likely of ful-
fillment. She was not, however, without cleverness.
Her intercourse with her patron consisted largely of
allowing herself to make innocent and egregious statements upon which Mrs. Dorrance could pounce like a
sleek cat.

At half past two, having crushed Octavia, and
Octavia having succumbed with a deliberate collapse
known only to the poor and dependent, Aunt Virginia
had retired for a nap, and it was while she was arising
from this, shortly after four, that Gulian's name was
brought up to her.

A recrudescence of her annoyance with Gulian for
not calling when he had been told to flared up in Mrs.
Dorrance's mind. It was very queer that a young man
with nothing whatsoever to do in the world couldn't

find time to keep an engagement with a devoted aunt; an aunt he hadn't seen in years; an aunt who took such an interest in his future. Very queer. She had half a mind not to go down at all. That would be a rebuke.

She stared gloomily at herself in the large mirror before which she was sitting, where, to one side, upon a bracket, a Dresden china shepherd and shepherdess strolled with linked arms through a miniature and troubled sea of painted china daisies. Somehow this had always reminded Aunt Virginia of Spencer's and her married life.

"He has brought that dreadful Russian with him," she said brokenly to Octavia and her maid Ella who were standing near. She knew nothing about Vannya, but the adjective seemed nationally apt. "Will you go down, Octavia? You speak French. I understand he only speaks French."

Miss Hiatt did not speak French beyond the simplest words of appearance and departure, but Mrs. Dorrance, who had always disliked the language, never having been able to learn it, considered that enough.

The two ladies descended to the lower floor with dignified slowness and Aunt Virginia had more than enough time thoroughly to regurgitate her displeasure with Gulian. It was, therefore, a very cold cheek she turned up to his kiss. "You are looking very thin," she said.

For some reason a mysterious incompetence that annoyed him excessively always took possession of Gulian in the presence of his Aunt Virginia; an obscure fear; a relic of childhood, deep down in his consciousness. He watched her warily as she sank, with a rustle of unnecessary skirts, into a chair, the tall back of which rose behind her like the stall of an irate abbot.

She smiled wanly. "I still have a little sentiment, you see, regarding the meeting of close relatives after long absence," she began. "I realize it is old-fashioned. You modern young people are so cruel."

Gulian protested bitterly. "I've really been trying to get here, I really have. I told you over the telephone how busy I was."

Mrs. Dorrance raised her hand in the pontifical gesture common to her. "We will not mention it," she said graciously. "We will forget it. Now that you are here we shall try to think only of pleasant things." She looked at Vannya inimically. "Does he speak English?" she asked in a hoarse undertone.

Gulian moved his lips warningly. "Enough so that one has to be careful what one says," he whispered.

"Good!" Mrs. Dorrance spoke with a relieved loudness. "Then, since he understands so little, we can be quite frank, can't we?"

Tea was brought in. It was the sort of tea Gulian particularly disliked; small tasteless cakes and sullen strawberry jam. He ate a cake despondently. It tasted like sawdust.

"And now," said Aunt Virginia, putting her cup down and brushing imaginary crumbs from her lap, "we have wasted enough time already. We can really begin to talk. Tell me what you intend doing?"

Gulian reddened. Life became arid. He had faced death, he had commanded men, he had written poetry, he had loved women, but to what end? He was back again in the nursery.

"I—I'm not sure," he stammered uncertainly; "I've been thinking of . . . The first thing I'm going to do is to take dancing lessons," he concluded brightly, his stifled brain darting back to Mrs. Pemberton,

"You can't get on in New York without dancing, can you?"

For a moment his aunt stared at him and then her tight lips relaxed into a smile. She prided herself on being able to take a joke as well as anyone. "Of course!" she said, "I understand perfectly." She nodded her head. "Naturally you don't wish to discuss your private affairs before so many people, do you? That is quite right. But you must come soon again. There are so many things, Gulian; so many things. You have no idea." She leaned over and laid a plump little hand on his knee. "It is only our affection and anxiety for you." Her tones were mellow. "The city has altered so. It is so dangerous for the inexperienced."

Gulian saw a loophole and made for it. "It has changed, hasn't it?" he adventured earnestly. His manner was subtly deprecating; this, he believed, was the attitude Aunt Virginia expected.

"Changed?" Mrs. Dorrance's heavy lids opened wide. She waved her hands with a strangled gesture. "Changed? That is not the term for it! I do not like to speak of Sodom and Gomorrah, Gulian, but with you I can be frank." Words seemed to fail her. "Ask Octavia," she continued weakly. "She knows. She is younger than I am."

"Is that so, Miss Hiatt?" inquired Gulian briskly, much cheered by the success of the diversion.

Octavia turned her seaweed eyes in Gulian's direction to the obvious relief of Vannya, who saw in this attracting of her attention a temporary release from the contemplation of a homeliness that was incomprehensible. "No words," she said sibilantly, "can describe it."

Vannya sighed. "Are you talking about the younger

generation again?" he asked gently in French. "They
must be much worse here than anywhere else. . . .
Since I have been in this country I have heard nothing
discussed but juvenile wickedness and Prohibition."

"A dreadful language!" commented Aunt Virginia
in an aside that was intended to be inaudible.

She settled herself more comfortably in her chair.
"And now," she said to Gulian, "tell us all about your
adventures."

She said it in the simple manner of one who asks
how you have spent the last twenty minutes.

Gulian's mind floundered back to its former state
of terrified childishness. He wondered where he was
expected to begin. With a history of the late war, or
with a detailed account of American-Japanese relations beginning with Commodore Perry? In his desperation he could think of nothing except a rather
disgraceful dinner he had attended just before he left
Tokyo. Octavia's attentive face seemed fantastically
bony to his hunted sidelong glance. He found himself talking in a dreary, disconnected way about
Yokohama.

A maid appeared and turned on the lights. She
seemed an angel dressed in black to Gulian and an
opportunity for departure.

"I have a lot of things to do before dinner," he
began, springing to his feet.

His aunt's mouth withdrew itself into protesting
folds.

"I will come again very soon!" he assured her
hastily. "Very soon, indeed. I have loads to tell you."

He aroused Vannya from his happy apathy and
shook hands with Octavia. The seaweed eyes somehow struck him as infinitely pathetic. His hand lingered warmly in the slack fingers. " . . . How well

you look, Miss Hiatt!" he exclaimed. "Yes, you do.
. . . I never saw you look so well!" A trace of pink
crept into Octavia's dim cheeks. . . . He and Vannya
repeated their adieus and departed.

Mrs. Dorrance waited until she heard the front door
close, then she arose and went to one of the windows
and pulled aside the heavy curtains of crimson satin
and lace. Outside a blue dusk was beginning to inlay
the blue and white of the afternoon. The street lamps
were blurred rotundities of topaz.

"He is a lovable boy, despite his faults," she said.
She gasped, and the plump little hand holding the
curtains tightened.

"Octavia!" she called.

"Yes?"

"Come here!"

Miss Hiatt joined Mrs. Dorrance and her seaweed
eyes searched the emptiness of Twelfth Street and
paused where that retiring thoroughfare joined the, by
now, occasional traffic of Fifth Avenue, eddying past
like a dark and broken river lit by the flaring torches
of a quay. At the corner she made out the shc lowy
figures of two men talking to a shadowy woman in
black. Presently one of the men lifted his hat and
turned eastward, while the other man, the woman close
beside him, crossed Twelfth Street and disappeared in
the direction of Washington Square.

There was something about the two figures, the tall
one and the smaller one at its elbow; something about
the iridescent violet of the approaching April night,
that seemed to Miss Hiatt to epitomize romance. She
wondered who the two people could be. She wished
that some time in her own life she could have walked
like that near a man, looking up at him.

"Well?" she asked slowly.

"Tch!" said Mrs. Dorrance impatiently. "You are more of a fool than I thought."

She sighed and let the curtain drop. On her pink carefully folded face was the look of an executive person aroused.

CHAPTER VII

PHILIP BUYS THEATRE TICKETS

As for Mrs. Prendegast, she had been unaffectedly delighted at the unexpected meeting with Gulian. She had been crossing Twelfth Street, her head lowered under her black broad-brimmed hat, and it was not until she had almost collided with the two men that she recognized them.

"Hello!" she exclaimed, her dark eyes smiling. "How nice! I knew it was going to be a night for adventure. Haven't you an aunt living around here somewhere?"

"Yes," Gulian assented grimly. "I've just left her."

Gulian found himself liking Mrs. Prendegast even better in street clothes, immersed in this indistinct light, than he had in an evening gown. She was even more appealing, more glamorous and uncharted, as if she had cut herself entirely loose from her environment and he and she were alone together in a darkening and delightful, an uncertain world. She looked younger, smaller, slimmer, and there was a touch of the gamin about her he had not noticed before . . . a little charming casual swagger. Beneath her hat her eyes peered out with the gay scrutiny of youth.

"Where are you going?" he asked.

"Home."

"Is that Forty-fifth Street?"

"Yes. But I like to walk at this time of day, so I'm walking to Twentieth before I take a bus. I've just been to see my sister."

For a moment Gulian considered asking if he might join in this walk, and then he changed his mind. He had found the accompanying of a woman along a street, especially when she was in a hurry, a poor substitute for enjoyment; a compound of broken conversation and anxiety lest his companion fail to survive each intersecting thoroughfare. Like most men, he failed to credit the opposite sex with any urban self-protectiveness. How they managed when they were alone he had never stopped to think.

"Let's go somewheres for tea?" he suggested.

Mrs. Prendegast laughed. "At this hour? Why it's almost six o'clock."

"That doesn't make any difference—I'm dining out. I'm not due until half past eight."

"So am I."

"Dining out?"

"Yes."

"Well, then. . . ." Gulian smiled down at her. . . . She had the most extraordinary wide level eyes and red lips. . . . "Come along. We won't have tea—we'll just order it as an excuse to sit somewheres. Except, maybe I'll eat it; I'm hungry. Aunt Virginia's ideas of tea and mine are not the same." He waved his stick. "There used to be a Lafayette . . . or a Brevoort, or something, in this neighborhood. Is it still in existence?"

"Both. Very much so."

"Very well, let's go. Afterwards you can take a taxicab—one of those fast ones that advertise every driver a married man, and therefore reckless."

Vannya raised his hat and made sudden unintelligible excuses. He was by now accustomed to hovering, with a smile he tried to keep from becoming set, upon the outskirts of conversations only partially understood, but in this case, and in the interests of society generally, the procedure seemed simple and clearly outlined. It always was to his mind when a man met a woman and both seemed pleased at the encounter. He raised his hat and set off across Fifth Avenue before the protests of the other two could stop him.

"He has the foreigner's insistence upon making everything a rendezvous, hasn't he?" said Mrs. Prendegast. She laughed and looked up at Gulian with her carefully inexpressive eyes. "I am unexpectedly happy," she confided. "I always am when I do things I hadn't planned to do. I think if I were a young girl and had to do it over again, I would elaborately plan to marry one man and then run away with another at the church steps. I had planned, you see, a little exercise, and a little rest, and a great deal of hair fixing and dressing—and . . . well, here I am."

"Yes," agreed Gulian thoughtfully, "here we are." He walked beside her in silence.

He was wishing that she had not said just exactly what she had said. It embarassed him, laid undue emphasis upon Vannya's desertion. Nor could you excuse the remark on the grounds of the average woman's lack of verbal foresight. Mrs. Prendegast gave no impression of fortuitous rashness. To the contrary, you were sure her most disturbing speeches were the ones most carefully calculated—little darting, charming tentacles, stretching out to feel what would happen, and then withdrawing themselves to a safe retreat.

Gulian found himself a prey to conflicting emotions; irritated with Vannya and yet grateful to him; a trifle afraid of being so abruptly left alone with Mrs. Prendegast, and yet overjoyed that he was. At all events, disturbed that what had been intended for a casual

half hour, a fleeting contemplation of unusual good-
looks, an obliteration of time that might otherwise
have passed slowly, had been turned into something
more personal; something that had, possibly, a prick-
ling sensation of intrigue about it. Gulian was discovering that fundamentally he was mildly afraid of Mrs.
Prendegast. There had been moments, five nights
before, when he had felt that such a thing might be
possible.

Despite the reserve in her dark eyes, perhaps partly
because of it, despite the cool, slightly insolent slowness of her manner, there had been from the beginning
between this girl . . . this woman . . . whatever she
was . . . and himself too much initial clearance. It
was very flattering; but it was too flattering. The most
temperate development of such an implication would
constitute a lien upon his time and imagination that he
wasn't in the least prepared to give. Ten years before
it might have been different; even five; but his values
had altered. He was well aware of the demands even
the most platonic friendship with an attractive woman
makes upon a man, provided the woman has nothing
to do except be attractive. And Mrs. Prendegast was
no Egeria. She was not the stuff of which kindly
unselfish promoters of careers are made. She was, to
the contrary, perilously feminine. One suspected
that friendship with her would be a profession. When
you were with her, there was an impression of a torch
handed down from obscure generation to generation
of feminine hands. You were, for one thing, so completely aware of her as she walked beside you, of
something softly alert and undulating. Gulian had
met Spanish women like that; women whose minds
were undiverted by by-paths.

He didn't believe in imperturbable friendships between the sexes anyhow. He didn't see how anyone could. It was like believing in spiritualism. You postulated a flattering premise because you were really so much afraid of hell. One day everything was pleasant and accustomed and casual, and the next, —and you couldn't see the reason for it—there was that indescribable mixture of torture and blessedness that may attach itself to the mere turning of a wrist.

And yet, Gulian asked himself, what, after all, did he know about Mrs. Prendegast? What over-subtle and, to himself, over-complimentary impression might he not be forming. He was too prone to trust to his intuitions, anyhow. But, then, when you came down to it, what else in a mysterious world was there so trustworthy? In the past whenever he had condemned his intuitions, he had found them disconcertingly correct. One thing alone was certain, and that was that life became a damnably complicated matter whenever a woman entered it. The pleasant things suddenly grew dangerous, the safe things suddenly seemed dull.

Upon his thoughts Mrs. Prendegast intruded with a complaint. "I don't think this is going to be such a nice party, after all," she remarked mournfully.

Gulian looked down at her. "Why?"

"Because I like to talk, and I don't like grimness. I think grimness ought to be saved for the home circle. . . . Why are you so grim?"

"I?" Gulian laughed. "I'm not grim. . . . You're wrong," he concluded, with an abrupt note of determination in his voice; "it's going to be a lovely party. I'll make it so. My . . . my aunt depresses me."

"She depresses me, too," admitted Mrs. Prendegast; "but then I'm not your aunt. . . . Look! Those lights in the Square are exactly like illumined kites, aren't they?"

"You've been in China?"

"Oh, yes, I've been everywhere. I'm married to a man who thinks everything holds him down but himself."

They had come to an awning that led out from one of the side entrances of the hotel and for an imperceptible moment they paused. Mrs. Prendegast touched Gulian's arm lightly and smiled up at him. "Let's forget your aunt," she urged, "and I'll forget the things I don't want to think about. Is it a bargain? We'll pretend for a while we're at the ends of the world . . . in a nice place. . . . I'm still rather happy, aren't you?"

Both the accent and the words gave the instant a sudden, unexpected emphasis, a breathless quality that stirred Gulian's heart again, uncomfortably but with a fluttering delight. He thought he was more than ever aware of hidden depths of misfortune and discontent in this woman's life and he believed that she really did find a relief and pleasure in his society. He saw her obliquely, without turning his head. The lingering smile drew her lips back and her eyes had temporarily lost their deliberate inexpressiveness. For the first time she seemed childlike and appealing in a new, ingenuous fashion. The touch of her withdrawn fingers clung to him.

"Come on!" he said abruptly. "We'll have to hurry."

They discovered a small room, deserted except for a few couples like themselves and some waiters intent upon resting before the dinner hour. Gulian's disarranging order for tea met with but little gratitude. "And quickly!" he added with the Anglo-Saxon's savage irritation with anything but the height of Gallic courtesy.

The table they had chosen was beside an open window that looked into the empty obscurity of a cross street given over to the milky orange of lamps and the quiet going of the day. High up in a tall building opposite, two lighted windows stared blankly across the city towards the newly repopulated suburbs. They were like mournful office-workers left with an uncompleted task.

Mrs. Prendegast rested her chin on her interlocked hands and regarded Gulian speculatively.

"You're a very stern man," she said sagely, with one of those quick plunges into intimacy that he had come to expect, "aren't you? But you're a gay one as well. I daresay, however, that's a much more common combination than one would suspect. Why are you stern? You lead a singularly pleasant life."

Gulian frowned at her smilingly. "I'm not so very stern," he retorted. "I merely like people to do what they do with some enthusiasm. Nobody forces a man to be a waiter. So long as he is one, why doesn't he keep to the technique of his job? People despise too much nowadays the technique of the particular position in which they happen to find themselves . . . that applies to millionaires as well as doormen."

Mrs. Prendegast shrugged her shoulders. "Oh, the waiter! I'd forgotten him. I was talking about you. Aren't you happy?"

Gulian's smile became thoughtful. "Not particularly. Why should I be? But what makes you think I'm not happy?"

"Your expression. Yet you've everything most people want. Freedom, money, good health, good looks."

"Thanks. Everything but a knowledge of where I'm going."

"Oh, that's it, is it? Is that important? Why do you want to know where you're going? It's lots more fun just to go . . . when the time comes."

Gulian shook his head. "That's what I used to think. But I don't any more."

Mrs. Prendegast sighed and her eyes widened. "Then you too are troubled with an American conscience despite a cosmopolitan experience?" she inquired.

"Possibly."

"Surely you are not so stupid as to think that what is called worthiness constitutes virtue? . . . All the nice men I meet are so much in earnest—and all the horrid men are—well, so much in earnest, too."

"No, I don't in the least think worthiness constitutes virtue. I believe with Chesterton that virtue is flame-colored, not white. But when a man reaches my age he should have an inkling of certain finalities, shouldn't he; certain simple fundamental truths concerning himself? He must make up his mind about something, you know. Until a man is thirty he is learning to live with the world; after he is thirty he is learning to live with himself. It's a much more difficult job. He has to discover, for instance, whether he is content to be an amateur all his life or whether he'll never be happy unless he has the trained mind of a professional."

"Oh."

"Every position definitely taken means some sort of loss, of course, but if you don't eliminate, you'll find neither salvation nor sanity."

"You're a Puritan, too, then?"

Gulian protested hastily. "Good God, no!—if anything I'm an artist. But they both start with the same desire to concentrate and to simplify, the only difference being that one thinks life is worthless, while the other thinks it is the only thing worth while. The Puritan eliminates because he despises life, the artist because he wants to taste its essence." He smiled down at his lighted cigarette. "I'm lecturing," he interjected, "aren't I? Do I lecture well?"

"I like it."

Mrs. Prendegast lowered her eyes as if she was meditating. "The trouble with you," she decided, "is that you're not fused. I wonder what will fuse you? In a way it's a misfortune to be born a Gulian Eyre, isn't it? And you're still curiously young, as I told you the other night. Your ruthlessness is still too tender, and your tenderness still too ruthless. You want to eliminate, to simplify your life, but you're not cruel enough. You're not quite ready to give things up either for heaven or damnation."

"That's what I'm talking about, and the bother is one doesn't know beforehand which is heaven and which is damnation."

Gulian paused and stared out of the window.

"And what are you?" he asked abruptly, turning about. "Are you fused?"

Mrs. Prendegast's hands paused among the tea things. "I'm a woman," she said musingly, "and so I don't suppose it makes very much difference whether I'm fused or not, particularly as I haven't fulfilled any of a woman's functions. . . . I've no children, and my husband is disinterested." She poured a cup of tea. "How do you like it? . . . But I'm eliminating, if you mean that."

"Strong, sugary, with milk. I've lived too long in

England to have any taste left in tea drinking. . . . How do you mean, eliminating?"

Mrs. Prendegast handed him the cup. Her eyelashes fell once more over her eyes.

"I suppose," she said, "I mean that I've found out what I like and I stick to it, only what I like isn't definite and doesn't amount to anything. It's no theory, it's the simplest rule of thumb. And I don't in the least care whether it's ethical or not. I've discovered the limitations of my life, and I've made a fairly amusing exercising ground within those limits. I'm not even sure any more I'd like the limitations taken away. It's exciting to have them."

"You're very hard, aren't you?" sighed Gulian quizzically. "The other night I thought you were very gentle."

"No, I'm not very hard. I'm not hard enough. I'm like you—I wish I were harder. . . . And I'm very serious, too, please. I wonder why men do that? They take a woman who ordinarily detests serious conversation and make her talk seriously, and then suddenly they're funny."

"But you said the other night you liked serious conversation?"

"Did I?" She stared at him thoughtfully. "It depends on the person."

"I'm sorry!" said Gulian. "What have you eliminated?"

"A great many things. The people I used to know bore me for one thing. I'm rather a derelict. . . ." She paused abruptly, her eyes questioning his. "You will hear a great many odd things about me," she announced quietly. "I wonder if you'll believe them?"

Gulian stiffened. She silenced him with a protesting smile. "I know what you were going to say. I don't believe you do make your friends by what you hear of them, but . . ." her smile deepened . . . "possibly you make them by what you hear against them. That would be like you." Her eyes became inscrutable. "Perhaps they are true,—the things people say about me. Suppose they were?"

Gulian leaned forward across the table, but she looked down at her wrist-watch. "Gracious! No— don't flatter me—you don't know enough about me. Drink your tea! I must go! Instantly! Pay the bill and find me a taxi, please."

She hurried ahead of him through the corridor and into the street. For a moment he felt her soft texture brushing against him as he helped her into the cab. From where he stood by the door he could see the whiteness of her face in the streaked shadows, above her sombre dress, beneath her sombre hat.

"Tea is like everything else in the world," he said, "it's over too soon." And then he suddenly said to himself. "You poor, silly fool!"

Mrs. Prendegast held out her hand. "You must come to see me very soon." She laughed. "Oh, yes, don't be afraid . . ., that is, if you don't mind a little harmless talk. If I had no men friends I'd see no one at all—Sydney and I only meet by accident. The only people who will seriously object will be your family. They regard me, I think, as a poor and rather disreputable relation. I shall ask you to dinner, too. I want you to meet some of my queer playmates. Goodbye; you're exciting. After you've been in New York awhile you won't be. Tell him to hurry, please."

Gulian slammed the door.

As the cab turned the corner, Mrs. Prendegast looked back.

She saw Gulian standing where she had left him, his tall figure focused by the lights from the hotel. He *was* exciting. She wondered why. It couldn't be because he had lived in so many different places. Sydney had lived in a good many different places and she had lived with him. Her memories of those places were composed mainly of cigarette smoke and cards. Nor was it because Gulian had done romantic things. That was a young girl's point of view. She had lived long enough to know that most men had done romantic things—the most unexpected men did romantic things. The war had proved that if nothing else. Nor was it because Gulian was good-looking; although he was exceptionally that.

Perhaps it was his naïveté; a naïveté that persisted despite his cynicisms and his knowledge. He wasn't bored; that was the principal thing. She believed he still found glamor, even in women; that women still actually delighted and hurt and even mystified him. He was eager and she was not used to eager men. . . . Sydney certainly wasn't eager; nor were the actors and half-artists and the wives and husbands of actors and half-artists, who made up her more intimate circle. They were not in the least eager—except about themselves. Nor was Randall Sedgewick eager. She thought about Randall Sedgewick.

She thought about his plump white face and bristling short moustache and dull blue eyes; about his faultless clothes and faultless ties. She thought especially about his hands. He had horrid hands; short and too well manicured and with little hillocks of fat along the knuckles. Gulian had beautiful hands, lean and brown. They took hold of things with a delicious directness.

No, Randall Sedgewick certainly wasn't beautiful, but then he was very useful. He supplied everything that Sydney wouldn't or couldn't supply—well, not everything, but almost everything. She wondered, however, how long he could be kept in his present state of harmlessness. There had been signs lately that he was growing impatient. He was not an altruistic man. And what would she do then? She couldn't get along without him, and yet she did not want to marry him, rich as he was, even if her religious beliefs did not put divorce practically out of the question—one unattractive husband was enough. But . . . the other thing!

She didn't know. Of one thing only was she sure, and that was that life was going to keep on giving her what she wanted. She had not had a poverty-stricken girlhood and a disappointing marriage for nothing. A little shudder ran along her shoulders.

"I wish to God," she thought, closing her eyes, "women weren't like that!   I wish they didn't always have to care so much!"

Gulian, stepping back from the curb, had stepped into the large bulk of Philip, dressed in evening-clothes and apparently just descending from a waiting car. Or possibly, not just descending, for Gulian had a disagreeable impression that his brother had not altered his position for several rather long minutes.

"Hello," said Philip blandly. "Margaret and I are dining with Aunt Virginia, and I stopped in here to get some theatre tickets for tomorrow. Margaret's in the car. Speak to her."

Back of his casual words, however, there was a carefulness that suggested that they were not altogether casual after all.

"I was having tea," explained Gulian brusquely.

"Were you? With Vida Prendegast? Yes, I thought so. I saw her just as we drew up."

For some unaccountable reason Gulian suddenly found himself excessively angry.

CHAPTER VIII

"Only they were premature, only they believed that they could make their contemporaries, who had scarcely outgrown their childhood, without enlightenment, without preparation, men worthy of their Third Age."—LESSING.

MR. EYRE had no intention of bothering Gulian about his plans for the future—that would have been contrary to all his theories—nor had Gulian, on the other hand, any intention of being bothered; that would have been contrary to his theories as well. Mr. Eyre respected Gulian and Gulian respected Mr. Eyre; an exceptional enough circumstance, when you come to think of it, in family relationships. But Mr. Eyre none the less cherished certain very definite opinions— the results of a long life; and from these opinions arose certain very definite wishes where Gulian was concerned, and he thought, moreover, that Gulian was singularly fortunately placed for the carrying out of any heart's desires he might have—if he had any. Therefore, although he would rather have remained silent forever than have forced directly these opinions or wishes upon Gulian—or anyone else—he thought it possible perhaps to express them inoffensively by means of occasional moods of gentle reflectiveness.

One such mood took possession of him at breakfast upon a mid-May morning three weeks or so after Gulian's return.

It was a lovely, soft, sparrow-noisy morning, with the tulips in the little garden still growing bravely, although the more humble early varieties had by now given place to the flaunting gorgeousness of their later brethren; the multi-colored parrots; the emblazoned Bizarres. In a distant corner, sheltered by a brick wall, a group of peonies were beginning to open to their flocculent, ant-haunted bloom, and the small bronze boy of the fountain glistened in the sun, his slender chest seeming to rise and fall with the cadence of the water.

Mr. Eyre sat facing his garden, the tolerant light of nine o'clock, compounded of blue sky and fleecy clouds, with a trace of the green of grass and the crimson of flowers underlying it, shining into his gray, a trifle faded eyes and upon his cheeks with their patches of permanent color. Opposite him sat Gulian, very dark and sunburned, and very sleek from his bath; well clothed and refreshingly in a new suit of blue; altogether, it seemed, in the luminous matutinal mood that comes not too regularly after thirty and seldom survives beyond the earliest quarter of the day.

But Gulian was by no means in a luminous matutinal mood, his appearance to the contrary. He was, in fact, rather worried; flattered but worried; somewhat prickly all over as a man is whose arms and legs have gone to sleep. In his mail he had discovered a square, delicately colored envelope, addressed to him in the upright childish hand the modern woman affects, and recently the arrival of these square envelopes had become almost a daily occurrence. Gulian was not sure what to think about this, and whether he ought to take steps to prevent it or not. Vanity prompted him to believe that he was merely indulging in a fine, adventurous, helpful friendship; common sense and experience assured him that he was doing no such thing. He sighed and slit the envelope open. The missive it contained was neither important nor exciting, merely an invitation to go to the theatre the following night with Mrs. Prendegast.

He put the envelope down.

His father noticed the sigh and looked across the table and pushed aside his own pile of mail. Mr. Eyre never looked at his mail until he had breakfasted, dilatoriness in this respect being due to a theory of his that more than half the satisfaction of life depended upon an intelligent handling of the, as a rule, unconsidered details. Any mail might contain disagreeable news, so why spoil your eggs and coffee by precipitousness? At the same time that he had noticed Gulian's sigh, however, he had noticed the square envelope in Gulian's hand, and as he had noticed several of these square envelopes in the past few days, he had begun to put two and two together and wonder who the woman was who was writing Gulian so regularly and what she was doing to make him so unhappy, or, at least, so restless. He resented the woman, but he felt that her present lack of kindliness, or her over-kindliness, or whatever it was, undoubtedly made the moment a propitious one for what he wanted to say. Perhaps he was too imaginative, but he fancied that he could detect even from where he sat a faint odor of violets. . . . Quaint, the various perfumes, wistful, desirous, self-assured that meet hourly in a city letter-box!

He helped himself to another cup of coffee and hot milk from the tray at his elbow, and stirred the mixture with a sudden grave attentiveness. "I don't suppose," he said, without looking up, "you've ever thought of going back to 'Hibernia,' have you? The

place really needs someone to actually live upon it."
He raised his head. "Affection is always necessary
for successful crops. There are over six hundred
acres. . . . And afterwards, you know, you might go
into politics. I'd back you."

He couldn't tell Gulian exactly how he felt. It is a
fault of the English tongue that it dare not express
itself deeply except in writing, and that this fault in-
creases with the sensitiveness of the speaker. Those
most capable of emotion find themselves only with into-
nations, and silences, and occasional gestures, and ex-
pletives. . . . Perhaps, however, that is the reason
why English poetry is so much nobler than the poetry
of nations where pen and tongue run close together;
poetry being the release of passion endured in silence.

To live upon the land, to go into politics, had been
Mr. Eyre's own early dream put aside by the pressure
of circumstances. But he still believed, had come back
to believing, after many excursions into fields radical or
otherwise, that no matter what you might say or what
elaborate theories you might invent, the health of a
nation depended upon how close its citizens were to
the countryside and how close the educated man, also
close to the countryside, was to his government.

Not that the trained always remembered their training. By no means. But much observation had led
Mr. Eyre to the opinion that, laying aside cant, the
virtues necessary for good government were not part
of the natural man. Loyalty, for instance; a sense of
obligation; lonely courage as opposed to mass courage;
fairness; urbanity; adherence to unpopular principles.
Say what you will, these were the results of a certain
amount of instruction, of leisure and, above all, contemplation. Therefore, when it came to a question of
leadership, both the workingman and the man of

meagre education, except in rare instances, were eliminated.

As for the workingman—and he knew him well—Mr. Eyre admired the workingman, but not for those virtues usually the subject of admiration. With all his magnificent qualities, he was the least fitted of all men to govern. Socially, he was infinitely more pleasant, but ethically he was considerably less dependable than the man of wider contacts. He was more humorous, simpler, more poignant; but, living just one jump ahead of bankruptcy, he was also uncertain, egotistical and unmoral. He was not to be blamed for this. It was not his fault. The cultivation of the finer self-denials requires an income. Saints are made not by sackcloth and ashes; those come later; but by a weariness of opportunities. Mr. Eyre was a little tired of the lies told about the workingman and the hypocrisy concerning him. Both had been going on now for almost two centuries.

But even more than he mistrusted the workingman did he mistrust the great amorphous, glutinous town-dwelling, not city-dwelling, but town-dwelling, and remote country-dwelling mass between the workingman and the educated man. It was impossible to have many clear ideas about this mass because it had no clear ideas about itself. Between it and the other two classes there was entire lack of sympathy. The educated man and the workingman more or less liked each other and more or less understood each other. Shoulder to shoulder they had fostered every revolution in the world. But the gray ambergris of the mediocre slid from between one's hands. Fear ruled these people and fear in the end defeated them. Their timid obstinacies and their scurrying flights were responsible for most of the bedevilments that arose. And at the moment the nation was in their hands. The great land-owning classes, the men weathered and tried and hardened by the individualism of fields, the hardy common sense of hills and valleys, but endowed too with knowledge and vision, had been sucked into the cities, or had lost their interest in government, or had been transformed into narrow and petty farmers.

Mr. Eyre was not a Democrat, if democracy meant, as it seemed to him it was coming to mean, the lowest common denominator of ugliness and cowardice.

. . . Systems amounted to very little anyway—provided that once a system sufficiently elastic had been obtained. A system was worth merely the sum total of the individuals composing it. Modern thought, particularly American thought, was besotted by the delusion that systems in themselves implied something; could of themselves accomplish results. The country was honeycombed with the idea of system and the intention to cure further ills by further systems. Life died at the root; individuality was strangled by a parasite.

Gulian, looking somewhat troubled, had been buttering a roll, now he raised his head. "That's the very difficulty," he said slowly. "The very difficulty. I'd like to go back to 'Hibernia' too much. It's too much the thing I should want to do—if I were to consult my inclination alone."

"How is that possible?" asked Mr. Eyre, perplexed. "It doesn't make sense. Why shouldn't you consult your inclination alone?"

Gulian sighed.

"I can't explain it," he said evasively. "An internal madness, I suppose." He arose to his feet. "Anyway, I must be off. I've an engagement this morning. Can you imagine what it is?"

"No," said Mr. Eyre, "I can't."

"I'm going to beard the lions of Wall Street. I'm going to see Philip. I'm going into banking. And I wish you hadn't mentioned 'Hibernia'; it's unsettling."

Mr. Eyre shrugged his shoulders. "I'd hoped you had forgotten all that," he sighed. "I think you are very silly. It's a stupid thing to try to make money unless you have to. Anybody can, if he's willing to give up everything else. It's one of the simplest things in the world to do. Money is as important as food and sleep, no more and no less. It's only the crudest washing in of a background. . . . I'd rather hoped that young America was getting over the frontier formula under which I was brought up. What's more, I think it has, with the exception of a few like yourself. It's not immoral, you know, to go into something besides a money-making pursuit. See here. . . ." he looked up with a quick determination, ". . . Won't you go down, anyhow, and get things ready for me? Delay any decision until then? I leave the first of June."

Gulian hesitated.

"When would you want me to go? . . . You are very subtle. You hope to trap me by country sounds and country scents, don't you?"

Mr. Eyre smiled.

"Tomorrow. . . . The day after."

Gulian lit a cigarette and blew the smoke into the sun-flecked air. For a moment his eyes were reflective.

"I can't, my dear parent," he said finally. "I wish I could, but I can't." His eyes, which had sought the opposite side of the room, returned to his father, the smile in them relit. "I haven't seen 'Hibernia' in May for ten years, and I should love dearly to see it, but first it is necessary for me to mortify the flesh before

I seek self-indulgence. Don't ask me why; accept it
as a fact. Remember, I've got lots of Scotch-Presby-
terian blood in me."

Mr. Eyre, definitely laying aside his theories of non-
interference, began to speak quietly and at length;
began to amplify his unspoken thoughts of a few moments before. He was trying to express the results
of six decades of experience; the essence of his eagerly
inquiring mind and his cool processes of reflection. He
wanted so much to save Gulian some of the needless
waste of time that he himself had suffered . . . a
pathetic desire that has troubled each generation of
parents since the world began.

And so, since what Mr. Eyre thought was Mr. Eyre
himself, and since it was very much what Gulian, after
years of turmoil, was beginning to think too, it is
worth further enlargement perhaps even at the risk
of seeming to emphasize the platitudinous. The platitudinous, moreover, having a way of getting itself so
buried that all of a sudden it pops up above ground
like the newest sort of radicalism.

Mr. Eyre had many thoughts about his country
besides these that had to do with the political trust-
worthiness of the workingman and the man of limited
education, although all these thoughts converged upon
the central insistence that the country could not survive without the trained man, or the trained man without the country. He had watched his country pass
from the perhaps necessary huckstering following the
Civil War, through the complete materialism of the
early twentieth century, when drunken millionaires
travelled about the land in private trains, accompanied
by orchestras, and their sons made of New York a
Babylonian midden . . . juvenile beastliness; father
and son . . . backwoodsmen suddenly became rich

. . . until this luridness of intention had faded with the beginning of the next decade into something that for a while at least had promised a future more distilled and selective and disinterested, and he had seen this, in turn, brushed aside by the war. As a result, despite the brushing aside, he had been encouraged.

Subsequently, it is true, into the vacuum thus created, materialism had swept back again with a sound of many winds; but it was a different kind of materialism; a more sophisticated materialism. And it was in this self-consciousness that Mr. Eyre, unlike most of his contemporaries, saw grounds for a survival and an increase of hope.

After all, self-complacency and ignorance were the only irredeemable sins, and whatever one might say of this distressed post-war period, it was neither self-complacent nor ignorant. It was reckless, hard-bitten, lustful, but it was not contented. People still Gadarened down steep places to the sea, but they did it with a new self-realization.

Incidentally, but unduly important and necessitating comment because impeding progress and because mistaken by many for paramount issues, two released forces were at work, both of them mercenary and calculatedly rash. Between them the mass of sensible people stood, their cloaks drawn about them, waiting for the adventitious hurricanes to subside. On the one hand, paid reformers made a gigantic trust of reforming; on the other, sinners made a spectacular trust of sin. And the churches, driven by the derisive devil of ineptitude usually present in their councils, and imagining that the pure teaching of love was no longer profitable (if they ever had) were turning themselves, particularly in the cases of two of the more active and less well-balanced sects, into grotesque pseudo-ethical corporations, capitalizing for their own benefit the supposed vices (or graces) they knew themselves socially unfitted for, or didn't happen to like.

It amused Mr. Eyre sardonically to see, going on behind the back of the ordinary, non-observant citizen, the very alliance of church and state so feared by the founders of the country.

But these indigestions were incidental, and life has a mysterious way of eventually refusing to allow itself to be killed, and intolerance of all kinds is necessarily sporadic because it is opposed to the tolerant principle of survival, contains within itself the seeds of its own death, so Mr. Eyre did not permit himself to be turned aside from the main trend of his observations by temporary distractions. The only immediate tragedy was that a very real and awakened question in the hearts of men—a question that some day would have to be met—was going unanswered, and that the less thoughtful were in their disgust confusing Christianity with the Christian.

These general deductions concerning his country were based upon Mr. Eyre's completely stark views concerning religion and government. He had begun life with a simple philosophy—fundamentally simple—and he saw no reason why, after many excursions into the by-paths of radicalism and reaction already mentioned, and despite the blind alleys of recent construction, he should not end life with a philosophy equally disencumbered. He was a republican and a Protestant, with a clear understanding of what those seldom defined terms mean; the loneliness and the distinction. And neither of them had in the least to do with any political party or any sect.

A republican was a man who believed in a complete

reaction between every citizen and his state; a Protestant was a man who believed that between himself and what he chose to call his God there should be no obscuring medium. This was strong wine; this was the top of a high mountain; but it was the only possible practical ideal for the individualist the mind of man had as yet conceived; an ideal as far away from the mincing weaknesses of an hereditary aristocracy as it was from the thick-lipped sottishness of a plutocracy, or the vague cruelties of a commune. It was a personal and political pledge open to all those who qualified; it had much to do with the words of Micah: "And what doth the Lord require of thee, but to do justly, and to love mercy, and to walk humbly with thy God?" It required imagination, but then what thing worth doing didn't require imagination?

In short, if you believed, as Mr. Eyre did, that the nation was balancing upon the edge of a great step forward—or else eventual destruction—and if you were, as he was, an individualist—it was quite possible, of course, and proper to belong to the other great school of thought and allow yourself to be ruled politically and religiously—then it was not only necessary but obligatory for you to do three things in order to save your soul.

First, to strive constantly for some approximate conception of the age in which you lived, the land in which you lived, your own position in that land; second, to achieve some central passion so that you could fuse and make forcible your own otherwise diffused personality; and thirdly, whatever your passion might be, to relate it as nearly as you could to your conception of your age, your land, and your own position in both. In short, to become a self-conscious citizen.

"And so you see," said Mr. Eyre, "that's more or less the way things seem to me. Probably its old-fashioned and no good, but if it's any good to you, or any part of it, use what you want. You understand now, however, why I want you to go back to 'Hibernia.' We're more alike, Gulian, you and myself, than you think. I'm trying to use you as a delayed substitute for my own unfulfilled desires."

Gulian had not thought it worth while to interrupt his father long enough to tell him that his own central passion happened still to be the writing of verse, and probably always would be; nor acquaint him with the reasons why he no longer mentioned this passion even humorously. Had he done so, Mr. Eyre undoubtedly would have replied that in all the world there was no passion that could be so self-conscious nationally and so important as the passion for writing verse. But Gulian did not interrupt his father at all, merely listened attentively and smiled at him. Beneath his agreement with what his father was saying there was something more powerful than intellect, an obscure black devil of obstinacy driving him on.

"We'll see," he said, and arose from his seat.

"We'll see!" groaned Mr. Eyre. "That's what I always kept saying. That's the reason nations are the spectacles they are. If the young only knew what fools they'll think themselves when they get older!"

"The country has got on quite a while without me," smiled Gulian, and waved his hand at his father and departed.

He envied his father. He carried a vision of the quiet room and the quiet old man it contained out into the hall and into the freshly washed greenness of Madison Place. The vision sent him on his way elated because such quiet was to be his daily companion, and depressed because it was not his own.

He scurried down the steps of a subway station.

Good God! . . . Rabbits! . . . Smells! . . . There it was, always coming up against you! The irreconcilable, the disconcerting, and the overwhelming! You settled existence neatly and commonsensibly only to find that the arrangement was a million miles away from the practices of man. People should take up this question of smells and ugliness more, and leave men's souls and minds alone a bit. An abolition of smells and ugliness would bring God a good deal nearer than an indefinite series of prayer-meetings; would be a better herald for equality than all the social tracts printed. How could a man respect either God or himself if on every side he saw man-made ugliness, God-permitted? If he couldn't even see the spring from a railway-train for the signs telling you how to worship God or what kind of tobacco to smoke . . . ?

Left to himself, Mr. Eyre gazed out into his garden. The blue haze of his cigar melted into the blue patch of sky visible from where he sat. The trickle of water, now distinctly heard, reminded him of the little stream that ran close to the house at 'Hibernia.' The stream would be bordered thick with forget-me-nots and cresses would be beginning to grow. He wished Gulian had considered his proposal more seriously. When you were sixty-seven, little streams and forget-me-nots and cresses were infinitely more important than Wall Street and its doings, or even the square envelopes that young women addressed to you.

That reminded him. He would have to call Ellis up and get him to make an examination. He hadn't been feeling himself lately. Queer stuffy moments. Doctors

were a nuisance. Once you got into their hands you
never got out. He was glad he hadn't had to see Ellis
for over two years.

He opened his mail. The third letter from the top
attracted his attention and he unfolded the single sheet
with a frown. It was from his sister Virginia.

"MY DEAR HENRY," it began. "With extreme hesitancy I
take up my pen to write you (if Mrs. Dorrance had allowed
the 'extreme hesitancy' with which she set out to write most of
her letters to overcome her natural courage her correspondence
would have been limited), but I can wait no longer. I had
hoped to see you personally; this, however, seems to be a
difficult thing to do. No doubt you are aware of what everybody else is talking about, and that is Gulian's infatuation for
Vida Prendegast. I warn you so that you can take whatever
steps you see fit. Do not say, then, that I have not told you
should disaster occur.

Your devoted sister,

VIRGINIA.

P. S. I am sleeping badly and as usual my rheumatism is
none too good. You have the queerest servants. I telephoned
yesterday for five minutes before one of them told me you
were not in."

CHAPTER IX

SOMEWHAT OF A RELIEF

EYRE & Co. were on a side street that led off at right angles from Wall Street. You plunged down the latter canyon more convinced every moment that men were by nature troglodytic and deserving of nothing better, and then you came to a corner and the top of a crooked thoroughfare that ended in a glimpse of ships and blue sky and the unseen presence of the harbor. If you liked such things you were overcome with sudden relief that in a topsy-turvy world there were sailors as well as brokers.

Had Eyre & Co. been more enterprising they could have occupied a building the top stories of which would have afforded an unobstructed view of this strange outer world, troubling, atmospheric, of different manners, customs and braveries, that lapped up almost to their doorsteps. But this probably would have been bad for office-boys and stenographers. As it was, when they built their new home in the early nineteen-hundreds, they had chosen a double-decked Grecian temple of a chaste and attenuated design, which satisfied everyone concerned. The attenuation implied the immense value of the land preempted; the smallness and lack of convenience, tradition as opposed to the flamboyancy of newer houses; while the architecture nourished some misconception on the part of the architect that modern business resembled the philosophic activities of ancient Athens.

A well-dressed young official met Gulian at the door and referred him without interest to offices in the back, where he was again interviewed by a pretty girl, who was evidently impressed by his name, and in turn passed on to an elderly eye-glassed female who wasn't impressed at all. Eyres apparently were common in her life. Undoubtedly she stood very close to Philip and, bringing to business a misplaced maternal instinct, regarded the bank as her child and achievement. This made her disagreeable and motherly.

She kept Gulian waiting twenty minutes before she admitted him to Philip's presence.

Gulian, it has not been concealed, admired Philip in much the same way that a man admires an alligator pear—he found him mysterious and provocative, but not easy to love. In his presence he was as a rule seized with a desire to argue incitingly about danger-ous topics and only subdued this desire with difficulty. But Philip in his office was a different man from Philip anywhere else. Here his blandness and blondness and alertness became quietly formidable. He should have been painted by Holbein . . . a gold chain, a green velvet vest, a fur-trimmed tunic.

As Gulian entered, Philip was sitting behind an immense polished desk on which stood a silver vase filled with crimson roses. The light from a long win-dow powdered him with tawny iridescence and fell warmly across the rich rugs. Back of the desk was an open fireplace, with logs neatly arranged, and over the fireplace a full-length painting of Mr. Eyre.

Gulian plucked up heart when he saw his father's portrait. The room seemed to become a trifle more familiar. Mr. Eyre was smiling gently, as if Philip and the financial district amused him.

"It isn't bad," said Philip, getting to his feet, "is it?

I had Borie do it a couple of years ago." It was, as a matter of fact, an exceptionally fine portrait, but Philip cultivated a kindly condescension toward all the arts. The winter before, when Margaret had been giving Sunday night musicales, it had been his habit to refer to distinguished violinists as 'little Wienerpacki of the Symphony,' or 'Gadinski—you know—the—er—little soprano who sings at the opera.' Artists of any kind invariably were 'little' to Philip. "Sit down," he added in his fine voice.

Gulian subsided into a mahogany chair. He wished he could overcome the trick of talking between partially clenched teeth during moments of excitement.

Philip smiled ingratiatingly, the tips of his fingers joined together under his nose.

"So you've really made up your mind?" he asked.

"Yes. I told you I had."

"Determined to go into business?"

"Why not?"

"Nothing, only. . . . Has father spoken to you about 'Hibernia'?"

"He spoke to me about it this morning."

"And you won't consider it?"

"I'd like to—but. . . . No, I won't."

"Umph!" Philip removed the tips of his fingers from under his nose and sighed. "I'm sorry," he said. "It was I who suggested it to him." Gulian's gray eyes suddenly grew dark. "Oh, was it?" he commented; and then "There's no use talking about it," he concluded brusquely. "I'm here for a job."

Philip picked up a pencil—beautifully sharpened; the work, Gulian imagined, of the disagreeable woman —and placing the point on the desk in front of him, studied the rubber end with a half smile. The smile deepened and became almost a grimace.

"I've been thinking over your situation," he said slowly, "and I'm afraid I'll have to take back a little some of the things I said. Frankly, I don't think it would be a bit good for you to start in here. . . . No, not a bit. Too much family. I . . . well, for one thing, I couldn't exactly fire you, could I, Gulian?"

"Why couldn't you fire me?"

Philip shrugged his shoulders and raised his head for a fleeting added smile, a smile that became almost too deprecatingly affectionate. He returned to the pencil.

"You started here, didn't you?" asked Gulian.

"That was different."

"Why?"

Philip allowed the question to go unanswered but his silence was filled with meaning, the implication of which was that the answer was too obvious to be put into words.

For a long moment Gulian gazed reflectively at his father's portrait, and then, with a sudden determination, picked up his stick and soft gray hat.

"All right," he said quietly, but with a red face, "I wouldn't have bothered you at all, if I had known this. I won't waste any more of your time. Why didn't you tell me, without making me come down here? Of course"—he hesitated—"I can force you to take me in.

"You can?" Philip's question was a challenge. His under jaw shot slightly forward. Then the smile returned. "Oh, no, you can't," he concluded good-humoredly. "I took this business over from father on condition I should do with it what I wanted. He wouldn't think of interfering. Besides, he agrees with me. It is very foolish of you to try banking." He got to his feet and stretched out his hand. "Come on, let's be reasonable. Sit down again. It's for your own good. Let's discuss it amicably. It's only because you're my brother that I'm objecting, you know. Don't be an ass. Heaven knows why you should want to get into this grind, anyway; but if you're really obstinate, why, I'll give you any kind of a start you want. Of course I will. There're half a dozen houses I'll see. They'll be glad to have you. You know very well it isn't my personal feelings I'm consulting. It's this way—you've the thing to learn and a family concern isn't the place to learn it in. Everybody'll tell you that. Later on—when you know something. . . . You won't have a bit of trouble getting a job, even though business is rotten. Have you tried Perry?"

He was very smiling and cordial. He seemed to be asking for understanding and agreement.

"Perry . . . ?"

Philip nodded sympathetically. "Yes, yes, I know," he agreed hastily. "I shouldn't like it myself. But sit down, do." He pointed to a chair. "I'll write you a couple of notes."

Gulian had been studying the point of his stick with which he was digging into the heavy pile of the rug; now he looked up with a smile that was disarming, but his eyes did not altogether keep his lips company.

"Philip, my friend," he said slowly, "in the words of the ancient story, 'you can take your Jamaicy rum' and your letters, and, if you weren't a highly religious man, I'd tell you 'go to the devil with them.' You're frightfully keen not to have me in the bank, aren't you? What's the matter with the bank, my son? Oh, well, never mind. In about five years I'll come around and help you out. Until then, the poor but ambitious boy is through. Goodbye, Cosimo d'Medeci." He turned towards the door.

"Won't you come back for lunch?"

"No, I won't come back for lunch—I have an engagement with Cyprian Bland."

Philip sighed and replacing the pencil carefully on the desk, overtook Gulian. "Your disposition," he said, "hasn't improved, has it?"

"It is frequently sorely tried."

"I'll go along with you to the entrance. I want you to speak to old Mr. Prendegast. But we'll have to look for him. He's seldom where he ought to be. I can't quite make out whether he thinks himself a janitor or a watchman."

Near the glass-encased, circular enclosure of the outer offices they came across a small, gray-bearded man, dusty-looking despite the neatness of his black morning coat and carefully creased striped trousers. In his buttonhole, surviving memory of what might have been an imaginative thin-boned youth, was a white carnation. His eyes were absent-minded and hastily cordial.

"Mr. Prendegast," said Philip, "you remember my brother?"

Mr. Prendegast hesitated as if the demand for recollection was asking a good deal of a man born before the age of card-indexes. Then he sucked his lower lip and the upper edge of his beard in between his teeth and released them with a small curious explosive sound.

"Oh, yes," he said ruminatively. "Yes—yes. Umn! . . ." He repeated his hirsute meal. . . . "Yes. . . . Umn. Of course. When did you get back from the West Indies, William?"

"Japan."

"Oh, yes. . . . Umn. Japan. Queer country. Good

business men. Do you know Sydney? He's about your age. Does he know Sydney? . . . Does William know Sydney?" he shrilled at Philip with startling loudness and as if Gulian was deaf and an imbecile.

Philip's eyes narrowed as he turned them for a moment upon his brother. "I don't think you do, do you, Gulian?" he said. "But he knows Vera. . . . His name is Gulian," he added.

"Well, he's a good boy—Sydney," continued Mr. Prendegast. "No business man—no business man. But a good boy." He chuckled. "Damn extravagant, though. Maybe it's just as well I've only got one of them. Well. . . . Umn. . . . Goodbye . . . er . . . William. Glad to have seen you. Come in again"; and he waddled away like a dusty black spider.

"A ghost!" commented Gulian. "Altogether; isn't he?"

"Completely. We would have retired him long ago if it wouldn't have broken his heart." Philip held out his hand. "Call on me for anything, Gilly," he said warmly; "and let me know when you want some letters. Don't bear me any hard feeling. When you think it over you'll know I'm right. You understand, don't you?" There was something about his manner suddenly humble; almost pathetic.

Gulian grinned sardonically and sought the street. He didn't understand in the least.

Poor old Philip! What a solemn thing he made out of life!

This first direct assault upon the citadels of finance had been hardly successful. Gulian wondered if his quest was to continue to be unsuccessful in a period that was beginning to be characterized by a multitude of applicants and a minimum of positions. However, Philip always made what he himself did well appear hard to the inquiring amateur; made it appear so suavely, convincingly. Probably this served a double purpose; narrowed the field and nourished a spring of egotism in Philip's soul.

But it was discouraging. The eager young applicant felt abashed.

Gulian smiled wryly at this picture of himself. Yet even the sturdy soul of Benjamin Franklin would have been crestfallen.

CHAPTER X

"The older I grow the more convinced I become that scandal is at the bottom of half the evil in the world, and that more people have been driven to desperation through the loose tongues of others than by any other one cause. But there is some consolation, although not a very satisfactory one, in the veracity of the old Spanish proverb that eventually 'a fish dies through its own mouth.'"

From a letter of Mr. Eyre's to his friend and classmate, Professor Hartlemas of Princeton University.

If Gulian, however, considered the preceding interview with Philip humiliating and depressing, before many days were over he was to look back upon it as merely the initial light slap of a fate that, after a peaceful interlude—except subjectively—of many months, seemed to be bent upon challenging him to a final knock-down combat.

Fate usually does behave in this way, having a fine sense of climax. A man seldom, for instance, returns home to find that his wife has left him except at the end of a day that has begun with premonitory symptoms such as burst plumbing or half-cooked toast.

It had been Gulian's intention to call that afternoon upon his sister-in-law Margaret, and on his way up to Bland's club where he was to meet Bland and Bland's two guests, this intention had hardened into a fixed decision. The day had begun inauspiciously, it had continued inauspiciously, and it might just as well be completely ruined by going to see Margaret as by anything else. You had to be fairly polite to Margaret or you got into trouble.

124

Gulian was innocently unaware what, politeness on his part or not, Margaret at that moment, in what she considered to be the routine of her duty, was preparing for him.

But he did not go to see Margaret after all. Two and a half hours after he had met Bland, and Bland's guests, Mr. Dadum and H. F. W. Dawlish, at half-past three, to be exact, he and Bland had stood on the outer steps of Bland's club, leading down to Thirtieth Street, and with somewhat fatigued faces, clearly outlined in the spring sunshine, had decided that they would devote the remainder of the day to simple pleasures.

"Thanks, very much," Bland had retorted to Gulian's invitation to join him, "but I don't think I'll go up to see Mrs. Eyre; I suggest, instead, that you go with me to have tea with a delightful Danish dancer who has just landed. Her name is Olga Leiven, and she is pretty, and ignorant, and kind. Afterwards, we will take her out to dinner, as she is not working as yet." His near-sighted eyes interrogated Gulian. "You need a rest after Dadum and H. F. W. Dawlish."

Gulian felt that he did. He hesitated and weakened.

"Come along," said Bland, and slipped his arm through Gulian's.

It is in this manner that most complications are given opportunity to grow. Events do not stand still. Had Gulian called upon Margaret that afternoon instead of the next afternoon, he might have prevented many things from happening. . . . And then again, he mightn't; a train of events, after all, seeking its climax as a river seeks its outlet. One may build dams, but the water eventually finds its way around.

Mr. Dadum, the well-known critic, and H. F. W.

Dawlish, the visiting English novelist—one of the
eighty-odd English literary men then touring the country—had put Gulian into an excessively bad humor,
even a worse humor than he had been in before, and
he judged, from Bland's reddened face and slight
tendency to puff when he talked, that this humor had
been shared from the moment that all four men had
sat down to lunch. Gulian had never met two people
whom he disliked as much as he did Mr. Dadum and
H. F. W. Dawlish. They were convinced and condescending and insensible, wallowing in the opaque
waters of their own opinions like complacent hippo-
potami. One saw a huge slimy back emerging; an
occasional staring insolent eye. They weren't even
polite to each other; when Dawlish was talking,
Dadum drummed on the table and whistled absent-
mindedly, and when Dadum was talking, Dawlish ele-
vated his immaterial moustache and looked superior.

Once Bland had lost his temper and had interrupted
in a choked but daring voice. "Why?" he had demanded. "Why? . . . What's the idea? If life's as
ugly and confused and malformed as you say it is—
fundamentally so comically not worth while—why
bother to write about it at all? Why force the dogs
back to their own vomit? I know life is mishandled
and abused, but if I didn't think there was such a thing
as underlying beauty, I wouldn't write a line."

Mr. Dadum turned upon him as if he was going to
bite him, an injury that might have been serious, as
Mr. Dadum had long ago given up caring for his
teeth. "Beauty!" he asked peevishly. "What d'you
mean by beauty? It's a word used vaguely by minor
poets—Masefield revived it. What is beauty?"

"God knows," Bland had retorted weakly.

Mr. Dadum was a large critic, physically, and apparently in his extreme youth—before the modern taste for disillusion and secretive self-containment had set in—had attempted to model himself after Dr. Johnson and Gilbert Chesterton and was now finding it difficult to tone down a robust, ex cathedra manner to the sly destructiveness of the present. He ate very selfishly. Dawlish, on the other hand, was sleek and rapier-like and possessed with the weary disbelief of the clever Englishman who has been born outside the frequently silly but to some extent, where they are concerned, necessary traditions of his countrymen. Life was a small thing to him; easily dissected; frankly understood. A disorderly jungle in which the amorous monkeys of his acquaintance sprang lightly from branch to branch. Never having seen the jungle and having no real knowledge of monkeys, he was unaware that the former, despite its confusion, is hotly mysterious, and that the latter, despite their lack of plan, are pathetic and humorous and charming; even aspiring maybe—if one watches their little eyes.

He had a vast reputation for his knowledge of women—except amongst women. He was about done with women now, however, and was going to take up men.

Gulian grew more and more convinced that the trouble with the world wasn't that it was growing urban but suburban—everybody living on little separate plots of ground with their windows open to everybody else who cared to look in.

Now, as he and Bland walked along Thirtieth Street, Bland announced his plans for the future. "I am never any more," he said, "going to entertain literary men, or near-literary men. I'm going to entertain inquiring-minded plumbers and bricklayers.

Conviction is the root of all evil. . . .   If Dadum and Dawlish insist upon stripping men and women of their pretensions, they won't leave the women a thing to wear, will they?   About all they're wearing now are their pretensions. . . . No, you don't!"   This, as Gulian made a further half-hearted attempt to leave him.   "Your afternoon and evening are decided—you shall not call upon your sister-in-law."

And this, as has been said before, gave opportunity the very chance for which she was looking—probably *she*, since opportunity is exceedingly active-minded and has little to do.

Margaret, being a propagandist, labored under the delusion that if you mentioned a thing often enough and mentioned it loud enough, what you wished concerning it would in the course of time take place. Argument to her mind consisted of a series of trip-hammer blows, delivered with breath-taking monotony, and it meant nothing to her whether the victim actually experienced a conviction or simply succumbed through weariness.   Moreover, being a very busy woman, and a very unimaginative one, she had adopted, in order to save time, a manner she called 'frankness.' Politically this method had been fairly successful, since the politician, the lowest form of reflex action known, responds to almost any stimulus sufficiently repeated, but personally it had gained Margaret not a few enemies. The people who admired her most and dwelt most upon her candor were not, as a rule, those who knew her best.

Ever since the dinner two weeks before with Aunt Virginia and the accidental sight a little earlier on the same evening of Mrs. Prendegast and Gulian leaving the hotel together, she had considered it her duty to turn over in her mind—whenever she found time for it—this family problem. There was no problem too small or too great to attract to some extent her attention, especially if it contained an opportunity for moral rebuke. Besides, in the present instance, Mrs. Dorrance had made a direct appeal to her, incidentally designating her, with unconscious flattery, as the very kind of person Margaret most thought herself to be.

"I am too old," Aunt Virginia had said. "Too old. Nobody pays any attention to me. But with you it is different. They respect you. Also, you are the only one of the family who will act. Henry is out of the question, and Drusilla is too easy-going and too infatuated with Gulian; and Philip, as a brother. . . . Well, you know . . . as a brother."

Margaret did not know 'as a brother,' but the phrase seemed to contain an element of misty truth in it; brothers did have some sort of code of non-interferences between themselves; also she secretly suspected that Philip, curiously enough, was just a little bit afraid of Gulian. Why, she couldn't imagine. She, to the contrary, had neither a code nor the least timidity. In fact, it rather increased her eagerness that Gulian was to be the brand snatched from the burning by her fireproof fingers. Gulian annoyed her.

"He's hardly worth bothering about," she murmured, with the intention of being provocative; "he's always in some sort of trouble. Now he's in for real trouble, and it will serve him right."

Her provocativeness had occasioned a more passionate response than she had anticipated.

Aunt Virginia's veiled eyes had lost their veiling and for a moment had been shot with little flakes of light. She opened them very wide upon her offending niece-in-law.

"He's my nephew," she remarked quietly, "and is therefore always worth bothering about—at least, to me. He is also an Eyre—a family to which your husband belongs. I need not mention that I am very fond of him. . . . Of course, if you are not interested . . ."

"Oh, of course—of course I'm interested," Margaret interrupted hastily. "I was merely commenting. Naturally, I am interested. I will do what I can."

Under her inspection and the inspection of Aunt Virginia the circumstances were taking on an undue portentousness; were becoming bat-like and shuddering. Seen with a moment's complete and shocking clarity, and then lost with a creepy fluttering of wings in the mysteries of surrounding shadows.

Imagination could not fathom what Vida Prendegast and Gulian had already done; imagination failed to predict what they were proposing to do.

"She's a Catholic," reflected Margaret. This after a pause.

Mrs. Dorrance stirred from a similar reverie.

"Do you think that would prevent a woman like Vida Prendegast from getting a divorce if she wanted one?"

"I don't know. . . . It is always a very important question to them, no matter what else they may do."

But then divorce, after all, was no better than anything else. Perhaps worse. Neither Margaret nor Aunt Virginia wanted Vida Prendegast in the family. Like most respectable people, when it came to the point, they preferred a lack of respectability, well hidden, to an open respectability uncomplimentary to themselves.

They were sitting in Aunt Virginia's dark little

library after dinner. Their faces threw grotesque long-nosed shadows upon the wall. Philip, lost in bulky thought, stared at the floor. They seemed to be plotting against something. . . . Perhaps they were; against broadmindedness and common sense.

Margaret took the question home with her. She was especially busy at the time—there was the Twentieth Amendment; there were some local bills in the New York Legislature; two English poets and the English novelist Gulian had met to be looked after; her city house to close and the Westbury house to be got ready; and Philip, her son—commonly called 'June'—aged eight, was suffering from a slight attack of tonsilitis; but despite all this she managed at odd moments to tuck in a thought or two about Vida and Gulian . . . while she was brushing her teeth, or while she was dressing for dinner, or while she was taking a bath. Long ago Margaret had discovered that baths were especially convenient for the thinking out of remnantal family perplexities.

She considered it especially fortunate, therefore, when, two weeks later—the day after the one upon which Gulian had conducted his ineffectual assault upon the breastworks of the banking world—she came across Vida Prendegast at a woman's luncheon. This simplified matters, saved her the trouble of writing the letter she had intended writing—letter writing was always a dangerous and unsatisfactory device.

As she watched Vida Prendegast across the table, her determination hardened. She recaptured an earlier irritation. Vida Prendegast was too insolently good-looking and too insolently aware of the fact; and of the fact that she was at the age—just entering the thirties—when beauty is at its most insolent. Moreover she was openly contemptuous of women; had always been; had never liked women.

Margaret felt herself morally and physically insulted. Physically, by a superior beauty; morally, because she suspected that Vida Prendegast enjoyed a superior freedom of action; the two bases of most virtuous indignation.

She knew Vida Prendegast well—at least, she thought she did; she had gone to the same school with her, although there was a difference of five years in their ages; and this advantage, the absurd feeling of superiority and license for unsolicited advice seldom relinquished by the schoolmate or university-mate of greater maturity, appealed to her—had from the beginning appealed to her—as a final reason for what she was about to do.

The two women came out together into the warm May afternoon of three o'clock. The side street they were on seemed particularly spacious and quiet and unoccupied after the darkness of the house they had just left and the confusion of ten feminine voices. Just beyond where they were standing, Park Avenue swept past, cutting from the sunlight of the south to the sunlight of the north, like a great plaisance, bordered with ornamental hedges and strange next-century palaces.

Margaret hesitated beside her waiting motor.

"Why don't you let me drop you somewheres?" she asked.

"Oh no, thanks. . . . I've a little shopping to do."

"Please. I've been wanting to see you, anyhow."

"To see me?"

"Well, we've grown up together, haven't we? We never seem to see each other any more."

"No, not much."

"And besides, I wanted to ask you something."

Vida Prendegast's level eyes, surveying the other woman, were stirred for a moment by an amused question. Then her wide, rather pathetic mouth parted in a smile.

"All right," she agreed. "Take me to Tyson's, and wait for a second while I look at something, and then I'll go back with you."

She stepped into the car and sank back against the cushions with the languor that was characteristic of her when there was no occasion for effort. She hadn't the vaguest idea what Margaret Eyre wanted to see her about. To her own reserved, sinuous mind the real explanation would have seemed preposterous—it was not the sort of thing that people did; especially not the sort of thing women did. The simple explanation was never what occurred to her, anyway. But she had detected some sort of challenge in Margaret's voice and that had decided her. The unknown always appealed to her, and if Margaret wished to convince her of something—probably some 'silly woman stuff'— so much the better. She wouldn't be convinced. She would enjoy not being convinced. She had never liked Margaret, and she felt for her the contempt that the pretty, quick-witted woman feels for the mentally ponderous member of her sex who deliberately neglects what comeliness has been granted her.

She was quite sure that she could hold her own in whatever might arise. She felt herself completely mistress of the situation. As for the rest of it, she was enjoying this luxurious car; the warm sunshine that fell through the open windows and struck through her thin dress so that it felt like a caressing hand upon her shoulder; the passing, glittering traffic; the sudden uplifted glance of some man who from a distance became for an instant aware of her beauty. This last was exciting; was much more esoterically exhilarating than the compliments of friends.

She rather wished that it was always that way—that one would never know men well. That they would come to you strange and adventurous and with the beauty of strangeness upon them, and be with you for a little while, and then go away forever, before you had time to realize each small disfigurement of intimacy—the ugly gesture, the ugly wrinkle, the ugly mind. In ancient Greece they had known how to do things —blue moonlight, and ilex trees, and a horizon of cypresses, and white marble overhanging dark seas, and lovers like wandering winds, who enwrapped you for a night and were gone, leaving no disturbing memory.

Neither woman spoke very much on the way down town and little more when, Vida having completed her shopping, the car was headed back towards the Eyre house on Sixtieth Street.

"Are you leaving town soon?" Margaret asked.

"Not until very late—Not until about the end of June. Then I'm going on some visits."

"We close our house in about a week. I go down to Westbury and Philip will live here at his club and come down over week-ends. He seems to be increasingly depressed over business."

Vida's eyes flickered. The fools, if she only had one-half what they had!

Presently they came to a stop before the gray stone renaissance façade of Margaret's house.

The facade of Margaret's house was imposing; the interior was equally so. You entered a little vestibule and went upstairs in an electric lift and found yourself in a multitude of drawing-rooms and libraries and halls. A number of disconnected and disconsolate servants appeared at intervals. Margaret spoke to them as if they annoyed her. From the spiritual caesura where the decorators and architects had stopped no one had gone on. There had been no further attempt at rearrangement or reanimation. You lived among the forgotten thoughts of men whom you did not know and who were not there. It was like the palace of an enchanted beauty; not a sleeping beauty, but one who was seldom at home.

Not altogether, however, for there was a touch of Margaret's personality in the subtle hint of a neglect more suspected than actually seen and of a large, cold-blooded, vague sort of hospitality. As someone had once remarked you hesitated to look behind a chair or into a corner lest you come across a bemused East Indian philosopher, or an alien literary man, or a large, grossly material exponent of the latest immaterial school of dancing. The impression was that Margaret left them there when she went out, and found them there when she came back, and that at night they slept without plan in a large dormitory-like fourth story into which Margaret herself never penetrated.

On this occasion Margaret and her companion precipitated themselves, without warning, into the presence of an exceedingly impressive Bengalese pundit.

The pundit was sitting in the library at the back of the house, close to a window where, as he afterwards pathetically explained, he had placed himself in the hope of getting whatever sunshine there was—a hope in which he was doomed to disappointment. Sunshine was very important in his life. His straggly gray beard and sand-colored robes and slow, delicate, gesturing hands made him appear old and wise and burned-out; an impression which disappeared when he spoke, for he spoke—about Occidental customs in general—in a high fluting Oxford voice and with extreme querulousness. The perpetual smile that played about his thin lips was not to be mistaken in the least for humor. There were moments when his comments might have seemed to the inattentive listener profound, but not when the inattentive listener became attentive.

"Gracious!" whispered Margaret. "I thought he would be off delivering a lecture. Good afternoon, Mr. Chundra. . . . Never mind. We'll sit here on this sofa and I'll order tea. His being here won't bother us. He never hears anything except what he says himself. But sit in the shadow. If he sees you are beautiful he will never leave you alone."

She considered this last sentence a masterpiece of propagandial tact. It paved the way. For all her frankness, Margaret still believed at times in paving the way.

She continued the paving by leaning over and patting Vida's hand. "My dear," she said earnestly, and in a low voice, so that the philosopher could not hear, "I'm so glad I've got hold of you at last. I've been wanting to have a talk with you for ever so long. I had intended writing you, but this is much more satisfactory. I think what I have to say is very important for your own sake, as well as the sake of others."

She held with her eyes the dark, puzzled eyes confronting her.

"You won't be offended, will you?"

Her guest stirred uneasily. "That depends," she murmured. "Just what is it to be?"

Margaret overlooked this comment.

"Somehow I feel," she continued soberly, "as if I could talk with the utmost frankness to you. I've know you ever since you were a child, and then . . .

well, you're really almost a member of the family."
She smiled graciously. ". . . I'm so much older than
you, Vida. So very much older. I have a child. I
have been forced, my dear, to think problems out."

The puzzled frown on her listener's face deepened,
and the little restless movement was repeated; as if
there was a desire to escape, followed by a change of
mind.

"Just what do you want to say to me?" the wide
mouth asked softly.

Margaret, believing that enough paving had been
done for the day, attacked the question briskly. "It's
about Gulian," she said. "About you and Gulian.
Shall I say more? I don't want to. If you tell me to,
I'll drop the subject and talk about pleasanter things."

"About me and your . . . brother-in-law?"

Margaret nodded.

"What is there to be said about me and your brother-
in-law?"

Margaret sighed. Infinitely cleverer than men as
women were, they were sometimes extraordinarily obstinate. "I see you are forcing me to go on," she protested. "Very well then, but you must listen and you
mustn't be angry." She leaned forward again, hovering over the other woman, who had sunk back against
the cushions of the sofa and was watching her with
unwavering but darkening eyes.

"You don't realize," she proceeded, " . . . people
never do. But it is time you should. Vida—there is
dreadful talk about you and Gulian."

"Dreadful talk?"

"Dreadful."

There was no response.

"I ——" Margaret's concentration wandered a trifle
because of the lack of reciprocity. "I——" she began

again; and then, taking hold of herself, caught up breathlessly with her subject. "I can't," she said, "and won't tell you all that people are saying, and, remember, my dear, I haven't said that I believe it, but naturally, when two people are in the position of you and Gulian, there is bound to be gossip, isn't there?"

"What position?"

Margaret found herself becoming increasingly irritated by this repeated, senseless questioning, and to add to the irritation Vida had now turned away her eyes and was apparently completely apathetic.

She was staring up at the portrait of a Spanish dancer which hung above the library fireplace. The dancer held a red rose between her lips, and a red shawl was wrapped around her challenging breasts and hips. Margaret had never liked this painting; Philip had bought it against her protest. The artist had caught and put on canvas too much the ephemeral gorgeousness and power of unthinking womanhood; the fascination of the great white moths who live only for a night of warmth and efflorescence. In some vague way, the portrait made Margaret jealous.

"What position?" she repeated, the convinced arid tones that Gulian so disliked beginning to creep into her voice. "Why, the position of you as a married woman, of course, and the position of Gulian as a man just returned home. Can't you see what marked people you are, especially Gulian? It is necessary for him to make a good impression. He may be thirty-five actually, but to all intents and purposes he is merely a boy entering business for the first time. You wouldn't want to ruin his career, would you? Philip——" she invented this hastily—" is thinking of taking him into the bank. You see," she added, more casually, "people know nothing of Gulian except the tales of his foolish youth. And heavens knows they are wild enough." She thought this rather clever.

Vida's lips curled. "And Philip objects to Gulian . . . to your brother-in-law having women friends?"

Margaret realized that kindliness and diplomacy were getting her nowhere. Her face hardened. "I will not discuss it with you," she said acridly. "You know what I am talking about. Much as it has grown, New York is not yet Paris, nor ever will be—at least, amongst people I know. Besides, even in Paris some discretion is necessary."

"No," agreed Vida reflectively, "not yet Paris. . . . especially amongst the people you know."

The quiet absent-minded tones alleviated somewhat Margaret's growing annoyance and encouraged her to further demonstration. She patted again the small unresisting hand. "It's a disagreeable subject at best, my dear," she said consolingly, "and the less we go into it the better. I merely thought, in the words of the old saying, that a word to the wise would be sufficient, and that probably, when you came to think it over, you would be grateful to me."

Vida looked down at her hand as if it were no part of her and withdrew it from the stroking fingers.

"Is that all?" she asked.

Margaret made a gesture of assent.

"Well then, I do thank you," said Vida slowly and bitterly and thoughtfully, a curious disinterestedness in her voice, a trace of the submissive weakness, possibly, of a person who has heard such things before and finds it impossible to explain her own position; "I thank you immensely. You prove to me again that all vulgar people hate beauty and happiness—and a knowledge of that, I suppose, is a part of the process of growing up.

Had we been very wicked we would not have been so careless. You make me grow up. Goodbye. I shall not hurt your Gulian. It wasn't very nice to bring me to your house to tell me this, was it?"

She rose to her feet and looked down upon her hostess.

"Wait a moment!" commanded Margaret.

Vida stepped back and drew in her upper lip between her teeth. A little sinking feeling overtook her. She hated anger; she felt herself trembling as Margaret slowly stood up.

"Wait a moment," Margaret repeated breathlessly.

Vida remembered that this old schoolmate of hers was capable of passion; a dusky, dry sort of passion, like a desert storm. She stood stock still.

Margaret drew close to her. "You have called me vulgar," she said quietly, "and you had no right to call me vulgar." Her voice vibrated slightly. "But I shall not waste words with you—especially since you are in my house. I was foolish to do so in the first place. I might have known that with a woman like you even the dictates of common intelligence would have no weight. Now I shall tell you what I should have told you to begin with. You shall leave my family alone, utterly, completely—Do you understand? You had better, for if you don't I shall take the matter to your father-in-law and he will apply the only pressure you recognize, and that is one of money. I hope you hear me? I want you to hear me very distinctly."

She paused for a moment and looked down thoughtfully. "And I never fail," she added, looking up once more. "I have never failed in anything I have undertaken . . . especially when I've been insulted. . . . Now, if you will tell me where you want to go, I will ring for my car."

Vida shook her head without speaking. She continued for an instant to shake it with a curious automatic, absent-minded persistence, staring with wide eyes into the hard eyes surveying her; then she abruptly drew herself together and walked from the room.

Margaret watched her exit and as the shadows of the hall swallowed up the slight, deliberate figure, put her hand up to her throat. Her anger had turned upon Gulian. How she hated Gulian!

"Eeet — ess — ver-ee — curious — to — me," said the philosopher, arousing himself temporarily, "how — leetle — the — Ameer-i-can — cares — for — sunlight. You — have — no — sun — een — your — house. The — ladee — did — not — say — good-bye — to — me. She — ess — veree — beautiful."

Vida found her way down through the interminable halls and stairs and vestibules and out through the iron-grilled door to the street. She wished that she had on a veil. She wanted to cry. She hardly ever wanted to cry, but when she did, the effort to suppress her tears was an agony. She was sure people would notice her.

She bit her lips and pressed her hand against the knob of the closed door until the metal hurt her, and then, relinquishing her grip, paused in the shadow of the threshold and drew from a mesh bag a little powder puff and mirror. Her hand shook so she was hardly able to manipulate these quaint instruments of deception.

She felt as if her delicate soft body and fastidious brain had been actually bruised by outraging hands; as if the veils, actual and mental, she kept about herself had been torn away. And her humiliation was unfair; utterly and completely unfair. Her friendship with Gulian had been the most transparent interval that had marked her life for a long time; a reincarnation of something young and spring-like. And she had consciously kept it so. She was no fool; she knew better than most the dangers of such a friendship. But what was the use of all her self-denials and reticences if this was what people were thinking of her? What was the use of trying to be decent if you got no credit for it? God knows life would be infinitely simpler if you weren't decent.

The sunshine striking her eyes, accustomed to the dimness of the room she had just left, no longer seemed cool and sparkling. Instead, it had swept the street like a harsh broom, brushing away all color, leaving only whiteness and an unbending rigidity. It seemed to her that she was seeing below the thin surface beauty of life to the vacant dullness beneath; where not a breath of wind stirred; where in the level blinding stretches people walked aimlessly and spoke with soundless words.

A vision of her hampered childhood, her hampered youth, her pathetic (so she told herself) attempts to snatch a few moments of happiness and loveliness from the perplexing, obstructed tale of her days, rose up to her. In her self-commiseration she even forgot temporarily her anger that a woman whom she despised as much as she did Margaret should, by a trick, so have outwitted and defeated her.

A man and a woman, laughing, looking at one another, gay, well-dressed, walking with the slow, almost elbow-touching gait of a man and woman intimate and glad of the intimacy, passed her on their way eastward. She watched their retreating backs enviously. Why hadn't she with all her beauty—oh yes, she knew she was beautiful—in all the world one

single man who would look at her like that; who would
talk to her like that; gently, laughingly, passionately;
who would protect her from such people as Margaret?
Who would lift her up in his arms and dry her tears
with his kisses. Some one man who would clothe
her mind with his tenderness and strip her body
with his blind and trembling love. Yes, just that. She
meant it. She was weary of tautness.

And it was at this moment that Gulian, cool, sunburned, preoccupied, turned in from the street.

He, too, must have been deeply involved in his own
affairs, for he was almost beside her before he realized her presence. When he took off his hat, it was
with a flourish that expressed delight.

"Oh, hello!" he smiled. "What good luck! . . ."
And then, "What are you doing; coming or going?"
His shrewd eyes studied her face.

She made a desperate effort to regain control of herself and smiled back at him, but her smile was wan.

The question in his eyes deepened.

"Now what," he asked soberly, "in the name of
common sense is the matter with you?"

"Nothing."

"Nothing? That's strange. . . . Well, I'll ask you
another question. What are you doing with yourself?
I'm paying a call on Margaret. It is three weeks over-
due. I hope she isn't in. Have you rung?"

A little chuckle, by no means humorous, stirred the
surface of Vida's tragedy. "She is in," she gasped.
"I've just left her. And I wouldn't go to see her, if I
were you; she's angry."

Gulian laughed. "Margaret angry? Good! Did
you make her angry? That's an accomplishment.
She's never taken the trouble to be angry with me—
Well, I won't call on Margaret, then; I'll walk with you

instead, wherever you are going. . . . There's the sweetest smell of dust and new grass out here by the Park. Want to smell it?"

Vida put out her hand blindly. She couldn't stand kindliness just yet, especially from Gulian. She steadied herself.

"Oh no," she said, "no! And I want you to go away please. Go away at once. I must never see you again. . . . Never."

Gulian looked down at her for an amazed moment, before his smile twisted again his lips. "Don't talk nonsense," he said coolly. "Come along. I'll take you wherever you want me to and leave you there. Meanwhile, I'll tell you that this afternoon you're a distractingly pretty woman but an absurd one. What's all this talk about my never seeing you again?"

Suddenly his lips tightened and his eyes became narrow.

"You're crying!" he said accusingly. "Damn Margaret! Damn her! What's she been doing to you?"

CHAPTER XI

THE GATES OF BEWILDERMENT

VIDA and Gulian walked slowly back along Sixtieth
Street to Fifth Avenue, and then turned south.

The long glistening avenue, underneath the feet of
the people temporarily possessing it, held an echo of
the footsteps of Spring; a hint of fluttering draperies;
of something unseen that for a little while paused
in its swift flight across the city and with shy
and hesitant eyes followed men, and touched them upon
their shoulders, and gave them an invisible companionship, laughing and young. High above in the blue sky
an army balloon floated like a grotesque cloud. . . .

Out of the corner of his eye, Gulian watched his
companion. The drooping long lashes, the demure,
compressed lips, told him that something rather serious had happened. He had never seen Vida like this
before. He had always thought her fairly impervious
to the attacks of the world; cool under its comments;
daintily flippant. His heart turned over with pity.
Vida's spiritual isolation impressed itself upon him
more than ever. The world was not kind to rebels,
unless they were great and successful rebels. But if
Margaret, or any of his family, were inaugurating a
campaign of unkindness against this woman . . .!

"Would you rather take a taxi?" he asked.

"Oh no, thanks; I like walking."

And so, presently, in silence, they came to the Fifties
and the gray facade of the Cathedral. A sudden im-

pulse seemed to alter the current of Vida's sombre reflections. She touched Gulian's arm.

"Do you mind coming in for just a moment?" she asked hesitatingly. "Or you can leave me, if you want to."

"Oh no," he said, shaking his head determinedly. He had no intention of leaving her until he knew what all this was about.

He followed her up the steps and into the dim greatness of the interior. There were a few worshippers scattered about, small patches of blackness, whispering with bowed heads to the silence the four walls had captured from the noisy city. Or was it silence? Gulian did not know. Possibly it was the brooding quiet of an infinite pity. The afternoon sun, assuaging and moted, fell through the high windows.

It occurred to him that this was not America, nor Fifth Avenue, nor New York; but a republic that stretched across the world, and back through time, and indefinitely into the future; that had persisted from the beginning in many different shapes and despite all folly and mismanagement. . . . A republic founded by that proud, humble, contradictory creature, man, to meet his need of a place where, laying aside all pretense, he could confess his fear and abasement in the presence of a question he could not answer.

Vida paused half way up an aisle and turning into a pew, sank upon her knees, and Gulian found a place beside her. The nape of her neck, disclosed beneath her blue-black hair, was very touching, very childish, very appealing; a too delicately thin link it seemed between the busy brain and the body it controlled.

Gulian watched that ivory link for a while and then stared ahead of him, to where, far off, the high altar swam in a mist of shadow and incense.

His eyes came back once more to the kneeling figure, following down the white column of the neck until the whiteness of the neck was lost in the darkness of the dress; and along the dress, from the grace of the bowed shoulders and the litheness of the hips, now disclosed, to the small feet in their juvenile attitude and their incongruous sheer stockings. This woman had never seemed so remote and yet so near as she did just then. She was pathetically alone and defenceless. Fundamentally all women were pitiful. They did not know it; they hated you if you told them so; but nevertheless they were. . . . A wind of feeling so startling and unexpected that it left Gulian rigid and breathless; a hot rush of tenderness; blew along his veins. For a moment he was dizzy and bewildered. And then he knew definitely what he wanted; and the knowledge frightened him, yet stirred his heart with an old delight. He wanted to take this woman up in his arms and sweep away her prayers with his lips; to feel against him the soft yielding of her personality and her body.

The wave of feeling passed, and he discovered the church to be very quiet again, and he said to himself: "Gulian! Oh, Gulian! You fool! You utter fool!" . . . Once again he had lied to himself!

His hand, gripping the pew behind him, relaxed, and as if in answer to his return to self control, Vida looked around and smiled at him and got to her feet. "Come along," she whispered. "I feel better now. We'll go to my place and have tea."

In some mysterious way it was as if she had lifted a material pack from her shoulders and transferred it to someone else, and Gulian marvelled at a faith that could bring about a reaction so sure and yet one having so little to do with the actual events of life.

As for himself, he was by no means so well satisfied.

He was shaken, and alarmed, and abashed by the emotion that had recently overpowered him. The dim interior he had just left seemed to make even wider the breach between the desire for beauty—his own desire for beauty—and most of the other desires of mankind. And he was calling himself a hypocrite, as he had so often in the past called himself a hypocrite; a hypocrite awakened now to where all the past three weeks had been leading him; a sophist deliberately self-blinded. Even more soberly than before he walked beside Vida towards Forty-fifth Street.

It was a quarter past five when they came to the converted house, with its French windows and balconies, and turned in through the many-paned front door, and took the elevator, painted a dove gray and cared for by a sardonic-faced youth in a dove gray uniform.

Vida opened the door of her apartment with a key and crossing the narrow hall, hung with tapestry, rang a bell and ordered a maid to bring tea. Then she led Gulian into the big room beyond.

"I'm going to take off my hat," she said, "and make myself utterly comfortable. It's hot. I'm glad to be home. I've had a bad day." She sank with a sigh into the long blue-gray lounge that faced the empty fireplace; a table, with books and a piece of gold brocade and ivory and crystal trinkets and silver boxes scattered about its wine-colored surface, showing behind her head. "Come here," she commanded, "and be nice, and tell me interesting things. The first night you met me you were going to tell me interesting things, and you never did. Strange, isn't it?" She gave a little laugh. "We've had so much else to talk about, haven't we? I'm tired." She raised her hands to her hair and then let them drop with a sweeping gesture.

"Would you like a whiskey and soda?"

"Oh no, thanks," said Gulian, "tea'll do. Is Sydney off on that motor trip?"

"This morning. To Saratoga. Four large red-faced men and Sydney. Beside them even Sydney looked spirituelle. But don't let's talk about Sydney. Never —never again, . . . for two weeks anyhow. For two weeks, this apartment is mine, and don't let's talk about anything unpleasant." Her smile and voice faltered. "At the end of two weeks . . ."

"Well?"

"At the end of two weeks. . . ." She raised her eyes with a blank, deliberately careless expression in them. "I suppose I'll go back to prison again."

Gulian leaned forward and lifted one of her hands and held it in his.

"Look here," he said gravely, "you have absolutely and entirely got to explain what happened this afternoon. What did Margaret say to you, and what's wrong? If you don't tell me, I'll go to Margaret myself."

Vida looked down at her hand, clasped in his. "Don't, please!" she whispered and tried to draw it away.

Gulian tightened his clasp angrily. "I'm not trying to hold your hand sentimentally," he retorted with a sort of despairing exasperation in his voice. "I'm holding it as a friend. New York ruins women, doesn't it? And I want to help you. I insist upon helping you. I've a right to know. Margaret is my sister-in-law."

He was standing in the angle formed by the tea table and the lounge upon which Vida was sitting, and, as he frowned down at her, she raised her eyes slowly to his. He saw in them a sudden, timid, shining look that left him abruptly afraid and silent.

He moistened his lips and felt himself trembling. If he could only turn away his own eyes she would misunderstand him and everything would be all right, but somehow he couldn't turn them away, and she understood him completely.

"Well?" His lips formed the word but there was no sound. He stepped back abruptly, releasing her hand. "What was it Margaret said?" he asked harshly.

"Lean down," she whispered.

Very unwillingly he bent his head.

She stretched out her arms and drew him close to her.

"What do you care?" she asked stumblingly. "What do you care about Margaret? . . . Oh, Gilly! Gilly!"

It seemed to Gulian that the time from the moment when he had first seen Vida's eyes with this new look in them to the moment when he felt her lips against his face had been incredibly long and yet incredibly short, like the flight from a flat dusty August rock to the cool waters at its feet. Now the waters covered him completely, drowned him beneath them. And he did not struggle against them. He wanted to stay in their warm, mind-deadening embrace! a shadowy embrace shot with little flashes of broken thought like refracted sunlight. For an instant he was glad and liberated and elate.

He raised the slim yielding figure to its feet and bent its flexibility between his arms and kissed the wide, red, slightly open mouth. He didn't want to think. He wanted to smother his thoughts.

For a while Vida lay inert, her eyes closed, before

her lids opened and she smiled and lifted her head and kissed, with a strange little half-petulant, passionate eagerness, again and again the dark face bent down to her's.

"And I was going to send you away!" she murmured. "I was never going to see you again! Silly me! As if I could send you away!" She tugged at Gulian's coat impatiently.

"Put me down on the lounge," she said, "and sit close to me. I'm glad now. I was so afraid that this would happen, and . . ." She laughed softly ". . . so sure it would."

Gulian obeyed her, and for a while she lay silent in his arms. Finally she spoke without moving. "Oh Gilly," she said, "they've made me so unhappy."

"Who?" He was still confused; still trying not to think.

"All of them—Margaret. She said I was a bad woman and was ruining your career. That isn't true, is it?"

She nestled back against his coat with a small breath of contentment. He stroked the shimmering darkness of her hair and its perfume brushed his lips.

"I haven't any career," he said bitterly.

"But I wouldn't hurt it if you had, would I. . . . I'd help it?"

"Certainly you would."

Yet he was a trifle hurt that she had accepted his statement so unquestioningly. He was doing his best to make a career. He didn't like it being taken for granted that he wasn't. And he wished Vida hadn't returned so promptly to the grievances of the afternoon. Somehow her complaint intruded an incongruous note into the moment; was, under the circumstances, too self-conscious. It awakened, moreover, his own self-consciousness, never very far distant.

His hand continued its caressing movement, but he lifted his eyes and looked about the room.

He felt that he was seeing the room more clearly than ever before; its gray painted walls, its gray woodwork, the soft engravings and watercolors, the delicate blue-gray coverings of the furniture; the bowl of red roses on the mantelpiece; the late sun falling through one of the long open windows and cutting a swath of soft gold across the reticent blending of colors. It was a lovely room, restful and distinguished, and it had often caused him to smile at its owner's complaints of poverty, but it was on the whole a cold room, difficult to reconcile altogether with the occasional stumbling warm notes in Vida's voice and the occasional vividness of her looks and gestures. It was more like the cool indifference of her usual manner. Well, that manner was gone now, he reflected, as far as he was concerned; he had broken its surface forever.

"What are you thinking about?" Vida asked suddenly. "You mustn't think."

Gulian stared at the wall opposite him. "I'm afraid I'll have to," he said soberly . . . "at least, I'll have to begin to think presently."

He drew his arm gently away from her and kissing her lightly, got to his feet.

"I must be going now. I will come for you at your cousins' at quarter past eight; that is, if you still want to go to the theatre? Do you?"

"Yes, why not?"

She did not open her eyes and he rather hoped—and yet dreaded the hope, that she had noticed his sudden change of manner, but a quaint inspiration towards chivalry, none the less, made him bend down and kiss her relaxed hand. It was an apology too. An apology to himself and to Vida. Most men are overtaken with a desire to apologize obliquely when they have lost themselves in an indulgence.

"Goodbye," he said softly. Words of endearment did not as yet find his lips with any sort of ease. They seemed pretentious; artificial.

He paused at the table to light a cigarette and this task completed, started towards the hall. A swift stirring of feet made him turn about. Vida was at his side, her fingers on his arm.

"No!" she said earnestly between half opened lips. "I was right to begin with—Margaret was right. You must go away. You must never come back again. We have spoiled our friendship. Knowing me now will only hurt you—hurt you horribly. . . . You must go away."

Gulian experienced a sharp revulsion of feeling. It seemed to him that in some way or other his masculine intelligence had been challenged; his ability to take care of himself and of other people. He was still, after all, quite master of himself. He looked down at the wide eyes staring up at him and laughed and took Vida by the shoulders. "Stand still," he commanded. "You couldn't hurt me even if you weren't the sort of woman you are. Leave things to me. Don't be afraid. . . . Don't. . . ." He bent down and kissed her. "That's the last time, my dear," he said. "The very last! . . ."

Walking thoughtfully along Forty-fifth Street to Fifth Avenue, he decided that he would get a bite to eat at a nearby club and telephone his father he would not be home for dinner. He wanted to think and he could imagine no better place for that purpose than the deserted dining-room of the club to which he was bound.

He looked at his watch. It was half-past six. At the edge of the pavement and the basements of the houses an amethystine haze was beginning to gather into pools of indigo. The lights in the shop windows were dimmed and discreetly drowsy.

CHAPTER XII

"There is but one truth, outside science, the truth that comes of an earnest smiling survey of mankind."

New Letters: STEVENSON.

ABOUT an hour earlier, Mr. Eyre, coming out of a brownstone house, ten blocks further uptown, had arrived at the same decision as Gulian. He would not go home for dinner but would go to a club and dine quietly by himself. He did not want to see anyone. He would telephone Gulian that he would be out. For the same reasons that actuated Gulian he chose the same club.

He stood for a little while on the top step of the brownstone house he was leaving—narrow-shouldered steps with wrought-iron railings—his eyes absent-minded, his right hand pressed down upon the curved handle of his cane. He was very dapper, fresh colored, alert in his appearance; his white spats showed that he was still interested in dress; and he had just been introduced to death.

The brownstone house held the offices of his friend, Doctor Ellis, and Mr. Eyre had spent a curious, thoughtful, rather breath-taking hour with this friend. In an outer room a permanent-waved young woman had beaten upon a soundless typewriter, and a restless pallid girl patient had resented the time Mr. Eyre had taken up and had turned sullenly the pages of a magazine. In the inner room, the constant chatter of sparrows had drifted through the open windows and there had been a pleasant cool smell of disinfectants.

155

Doctor Ellis had been cordially impatient, politely anxious to complete his long afternoon.

The permanent-waved young woman smiled at Mr. Eyre as he left and bade him goodnight.

"Goodnight, Mr. Eyre," she had said, emphasizing the name a trifle to show respect for a distinguished client.

"Goodnight," Mr. Eyre had replied.

He wondered if she realized what a manicured Charon she was, or if she ever paused long enough in her soundless typewriting to reflect upon the thoughts of the people who all day long passed through her hands, some of them, like himself, to a stage set for a final tragedy. In a few minutes she would close her typewriter with a sigh of relief and go home to her family, and rather patronize them, he imagined, and probably, after supper, go to 'the movies' with her young man, and marvel, in the midst of make-believe emotions, why nothing dramatic ever occurred in her own life. Some day she would marry and bear children, and they would die, and she would, too. And her childrens' children. People who hadn't even been born would die. . . . Nothing would become something and then become nothing again. No, that was a physical absurdity. Nothing couldn't become something; and something couldn't become nothing. Something became another thing and then something else; or manifestations of the same thing. The last seemed more logical. . . . She would make a rather charming, casual, unconcerned ghost, this manicured Charon. Most young New York women would.

. . . Mr. Eyre slowly descended the steps and crept westward through the gathering shadows, rather like a shadow himself.

The club he was seeking hid itself behind a smoky exterior on one of the lower Forties and was of such a conservative description that few of its members used it except for lunch and a great many even forgot they belonged to it until their bills for annual dues arrived. Then they cursed it and swore they would resign, but seldom did because belonging to it vaguely reassured them that they were still not wholly contaminated by the modern spirit of vulgarity.

Mr. Eyre turned in through the front-door and nodded to the archaic doorman,—one of the few real snobs left in New York—and walked along the dim hall to the reading-room.

He seldom used clubs any more; he had an excellent library of his own, and feminine society was now such a rare thing in his life that he no longer felt the distracted masculine craving for wholly masculine seclusion. Besides, city clubs had changed greatly during his lifetime. They no longer had the slightest touch of gayety about them. The younger men preferred games or dancing for their leisure hours; sports and feminization having come in hand in hand in a rowdily Attic sort of companionship. And certain ill-advised sumptuary laws had added the final touch of dissolution to the tottering edifice of cheeriness.

Not that Mr. Eyre failed to recognize the fact that most clubs had their own methods of evading these ill-advised sumptuary laws, but he deprecated the methods. They seemed to him servile and unmanly. It annoyed him that men who wouldn't even discuss the subject, much less take steps to clarify it politically, none the less continued to disregard the edict stolidly. They were contemptible and un-citizen-like.

Meanwhile, as one palpable result, friendliness was

disappearing; not because of a lack of drink—there was no lack—but because the old and frank and beautiful gesture had been made secretive and criminal and a matter of small boys sticking out their tongues. Mr. Eyre hated Prohibition on all counts; morally and legally and historically and philosophically and as a matter of plain common sense and practicality, but he hated it especially because it was the most cowardly and coward-making law that had been passed in any so-called enlightened epoch.

He entered the reading-room and picked up an evening paper. Five old gentlemen, none of whom he knew or wanted to know, glared at him, and one of them coughed. Mr. Eyre avoided their acrimonious glances and sitting down, tried to appear as sullenly interested as his companions, but the attempt was a failure.

He himself was unsettled and the paper he had chosen, supposedly the most conservative in the city, annoyed him even more than usual. Conservatism was a much abused word. Real conservatism was as clean-cut and vigorous and youthful as real radicalism; it was full-bodied and alert; and had no more to do with the fussy dullnesses of senility than had radicalism to do with the frantic ineptitudes supposed to be attached to it. This journal, the pages of which he was turning, was not conservative, it was merely timorous and unillumined; trying to adapt its Victorian voice, which might have been dignified if used properly, to the broken falsetto rhythms of the present. It was like a bedizened old woman, eyes foggy from too much exercise, dancing in a modern restaurant. One had an impression of pantalettes peeping out from below a modern skirt. It's news columns, set in heavy type in order to give a false

appearance of solidity, presented a striking contrast
to the editorial pages. The former featured two prominent divorce cases, each—regrettably—distracting
attention from the other, a bishop who had announced
that women should not smoke—very important, of
course, and very convincing—a banking house that had
failed—Mr. Eyre knew the principals—seven or eight
unknown people who had been robbed or slain, a
chorus girl, evidently virtuous as the ceremonies
showed, who had divorced her third millionaire husband, and a Germany that was again refusing vaguely
to perform some vague obligation. Incidentally, Lenin
was dead and two days later had made a speech in
Moscow, and half a dozen wars were raging in various
parts of the world, and a Congressman had delivered
an address in which he had mentioned the extraordinary increase in knowledge and goodness as exempli-
fied by 'the great and fortunate republic' to which he
and his audience belonged. Several lynchings and the
tar-and-feathering activities of a secret society were
tucked away in one corner.

. . . The two innermost pages, the editorial pages,
did much, however, to save everybody's face and re-
store the balance of the mind by turning away from
this tarantella of death, destruction and libidinosity,
to concentrate upon late spring flowers and the nesting
habits of birds. Long editorials with hardly any para-
graphs, written in what might be called the 'tread-mill
school of thought,' discussed public questions with a
lack of constructiveness which, after much pro and
con, and yes and no, left the inquiring reader exactly
where he had started. A more passionate note was
struck by an irascible correspondence, evidently of
long duration and evidently between two gentlemen of

great age, as to whether one of them had seen a snowy-owl the winter before or not. . . .

Mr. Eyre sighed and put the paper down and left his easily disturbed companions, whose minds by this time must have resembled an unpleasantly frothy dessert, to seek the dining-room on the second floor back. As he had anticipated, it was deserted except for a couple of waiters. Beside an open window a table was set for two, a vase filled with white lilacs upon it, and at this table Mr. Eyre settled himself.

Between the silhouetted roofs of the houses whose back-buildings faced the window, a little moon, like a tulip leaf blown up from some garden, drifted in the sky. . . . Mr. Eyre studied the moon with a thoughtful tenderness, a trace of whimsicality in his smile, and as he did so he perceived a shadow falling across his table and looked up to find Gulian leaning over him. Gulian was smiling, too."

"I came here to be alone," he said, "and then, of all people, I discover you. The Eyres think alike."

"They do," agreed Mr. Eyre with a grim good humor. "I came here myself to be alone. But sit down. It would be rather silly for a father and son to dine at separate tables in an empty dining-room. And you don't have to talk, you know."

"No," said Gulian. "I know of no two people who can be more pleasantly silent than you and I. That shows you are still very young. Most old people talk too much."

The soup was brought. Mr. Eyre watched Gulian's face with meditative intentness.

Roast mutton succeeded the soup.

"Rather heavy fare for this time of year, isn't it?" commented Mr. Eyre.

"Rather," said Gulian.

"I'm not very hungry. Do you mind if I go on to the salad?"

"Certainly not. I think I'll do the same."

Mr. Eyre stirred restlessly. The most extraordinary heart-gripping little twinge of tenderness seized him for this dark, thoughtful son of his. After all, thirty-five was so young. Everyone was so young, even the oldest and wisest of men, once you put them up against the background of time. In all a man's life there was only one moment when he became completely wise and adept, and that was when he knew that shortly he would have to die, and that experiment, and struggle, and hope were no longer of any particular interest to him. When he gave up, that is, flinging about breathlessly beneath the concave, opaque shell of present existence that hemmed him in. Beating his wings against it like a captured bird. . . . But until that time . . . so very young, all of them; so very young!

He leaned forward.

"Gulian," he said with the haste of uncertainty, "at first I didn't think I would tell you—I don't believe in spreading apprehension—but I've been considering it, and I believe it is only right you should know. However, I don't want anyone else to hear of it, not even Drusilla or Philip. . . . I saw Ellis this afternoon."

"Ellis?"

"Yes. You remember John Ellis? You've met him at my house. He's a very famous specialist."

"Oh! What did you see Ellis about?" Gulian's eyebrows drew themselves together into a frown.

Mr. Eyre picked up a fork and drew diagrams on the cloth with it. He seemed embarrassed.

"I haven't been feeling very well lately," he said, raising his head. "Dizziness and stuffiness, and that sort of thing. I thought I would get him to look me over. . . . Of course," he added hastily, "a man of my age must expect something. . . ."

"Well?" Gulian's voice carried the accusing sharpness of apprehension.

"He told me," said Mr. Eyre, with an elaborate casualness, "that I would have to take rather good care of myself from now on. My heart and arteries, you see. . . ."

"Are what?"

"A little damaged." Mr. Eyre lied blandly.

The silence, pressing back on either side, left a narrow corridor of complete stillness, at the end of which Gulian saw his father, a small, shadowy shape, smiling deprecatingly.

"Are you sure of that?" he asked hesitatingly. "Sure —only a little?"

"Absolutely. Why should I tell you anything else?"

Gulian's eyes were not convinced. He remained rigidly thoughtful for a moment and then he leaned forward with an impulsive gesture. "Somehow," he said quickly and shyly, "—I don't know why; maybe it's always that way—but I can't tell you, I never can, just what I feel; but . . . you know, don't you?"

"Yes," said Mr. Eyre, "of course I know."

"Well—that's the way I feel. You do understand? I've been a rotten son, I suppose—often. I daresay I'm not much good, but it hasn't been because I wasn't fond of you. And you can tell me anything you want to. . . . I wish you would."

Mr. Eyre patted Gulian's hand lying outspread upon the table. "Of course I understand," he repeated a trifle impatiently. "And I have told you; and you haven't been a rotten son. There're a lot worse things than occasional aberrations; there's not caring, and you do care. I've always known that." His smile broadened. "It isn't so very bad, anyhow. I didn't mean to alarm you unnecessarily. There isn't the slightest immediate danger. I've been hanging on two or three years already without knowing anything about it, and I'll hang on a long time yet. All I have to do is to avoid shock and over-exertion and worry, and that shouldn't be so hard at my time of life. . . . And now push the matches my way, will you?"

"Worry?" Gulian repeated the word absent-mind-edly, as if it had some connection with thoughts of his own. "Yes," he resumed briskly, "you'll have to be kept away from worry. But then you mustn't be-lieve too much in doctors, anyway," he added, with a firmness he imagined reassuring, "particularly special-ists. They always scare people. It's part of their religion. You'll see somebody else too, won't you?"

"If you want me to," assented Mr. Eyre meekly.

Gulian laid his other hand over the thin hand that had patted his. "And you certainly will take damn good care of yourself," he resumed threateningly. "I'll see to that. If you don't, I'll tell Drusilla and Philip. Meanwhile, remember it's the people who have been warned that live the longest. I have you in my power now." This too—this last sentence—seemed to make him thoughtful, for he broke off abruptly and sat back and puffed at his cigarette, staring at his father.

"Of course," retorted Mr. Eyre cheerfully, "I'm going to live long—I'm going to live to be ninety. . . . Well, go about your business. You have an engage-ment, I'm sure. Don't stay on my account. I'm not going to keel over here. It would be too dreary to die in this club."

Gulian was reluctant. "I have got an engagement," he affirmed, regretfully. He looked at his watch. "It's at quarter past eight and it's that now; but . . . Let me call up and I'll break it."

Mr. Eyre waved a dissenting hand.

"Of course you won't break it," he protested indignantly. "What do you think I am, a valetudinarian? Whom is the engagement with? A lady? You ought to be ashamed of yourself! Be off with you! I want to go home and read. I've just reached another crisis in Henry Adams' life where he believes he's going to believe that he may someday believe something about something. It's quite thrilling. And don't you give me another thought. Now that I've told you, I feel much better. Moreover, I have a temperate nature: it won't be in the least hard for me to take care of myself. I always have, against the dictates of my better imagination." His eyes were troubled again. "I do so hope I haven't disturbed you too much, my dear boy," he added. "It really isn't a bit bad. All old people have high blood-pressure, and that sort of business. . . . I hope you're not worried."

Gulian drank the last of his coffee and put down the cup and got to his feet and crossed over to his father's side. "I hate . . ." he began. "I'm sorry to leave you. You will tell me if anything goes wrong, won't you?"

"Yes, I will," agreed Mr. Eyre decidedly. For a moment he was silent, and then he twisted around in his chair and looked up at Gulian lingeringly. His eyes were reflective and shining, as if he felt that his own confidences should be repaid in kind.

"Sure you haven't any bad news yourself?" he asked. ". . . Or good news?"

Gulian shook his head.

"None whatsoever."

Mr. Eyre sighed.

"Well, run along. . . ." He stretched out a detaining hand and grasped Gulian's arm. "See here, Gulian," he said. He was determined once more to break the rule of a lifetime and interfere in someone else's life; to repeat what he had heard. Such so-called sincerities had never appealed to him as any but the shortest ways of producing undesired results, but somehow this occasion was different. If, on top of Gulian's knowing what Ellis had said, he should also know that his father was troubled by his intimacy with Vida! . . .

"Gilly, you're not going to make an ass of yourself about anyone, are you?"

Gulian's face, smiling down at his father, hardened. "What do you mean?" he asked.

"Nothing. I've never done this before, but . . . I think Vida Prendegast is a good girl who's had a hard time. You don't want to get her talked about do you?"

"Who's been telling you that I'm getting her talked about?"

"A good many people I'm afraid. It isn't a secret."

"Yes it is—or rather—I mean I've been extraordinarily careful. . . . Good God! Why can't people leave decent friendships alone?"

"I'll take your word for it," said Mr. Eyre quietly, ashamed of himself.

Gulian suddenly leaned forward and laid his hand on his father's shoulder. "I know who told you," he said smilingly; "it was either Aunt Virginia or Margaret. In fact, I saw a letter to you from Aunt Virginia yesterday morning when I was looking over the mail; but don't you pay a bit of attention to it—not a bit. There's not a word of truth in it." His fingers tightened on the slender shoulder and his eyes grew dark. He stooped down and touched the grey head beneath him with his lips. "Goodbye, my very dear. . . ." he said softly. "Don't you worry. It's all right."

Mr. Eyre watched the retreating figure and then looked out at the moon again. The candle on the table, under its shade of filigree silver, wavered in the soft breeze. Little fingers of coolness touched Mr. Eyre's cheeks. The sky between the houses was like a thin green shawl of silk hung before the distant and diffused light of lanterns.

The moon was a very immature moon; thin as a girl. It had most of its youth to go through, and its fullness, and its wane.

Mr. Eyre wished that Gulian would tell him things more freely. This odd, disturbing mystery of father and son! Bone of the same bone, flesh of the same flesh; closer than wife or friend; the identical texture; a recasting of the same material; but between, a wall of personality impossible to see through!

Mr. Eyre thought again about this question of personality! . . . Death was especially queer when you thought about personality. Life was a matter of dual inhabitation; as everything almost in the world was. Spirit and body living together, almost indistinguishable, like an old man living in an old house until the characteristics of one were the characteristics of the other. And death was a separation of these and therefore a much more lucid, single thing than life. Too single, too lucid for the distracted mind of man to comprehend. It was in the separation that most of the dread that people felt resided. It wasn't that you feared the actual event; few people feared that; it was the homesickness you felt at the thought of leaving an accustomed residence; the good home of your body in which you had lived. It was your spirit that felt sorry for your house, not the house that felt sorry for the spirit. Your spirit could take care of itself . . . or, if obliteration was to be its fate, then it didn't matter. But who would take care of the house? It would fall to rack and ruin. Kindly muscles that obeyed your will; sensitive nerves; mouth that tasted sweetness; nose that breathed in a summer day or the sharpness of winter; eyes that knew silver and orange and all lovely colors, knew faces, and knew the velvet of grass. That was it. Death was nothing; at its best, a blessed simplification and clarifying, at its worst a forgetfulness. But the poor body, the poor kindly smiling body!

Mr. Eyre wished that it were possible for him to order a little champagne. He would have liked to drink a glass of champagne to his body. Even the most abstemious couldn't seriously object to that, could they?

CHAPTER XIII

MAY NIGHT

GULIAN and Vida, leaving the theatre and stepping into the prismatic dusk, stood for a moment motionless, caught in an eddy of the pressing crowd. The street glowed with electric lights and rustled with the sound of voices and the shuffling of feet; stammered with sharp cries for cabs and the closing to of doors and the starting of engines. Yet over all hung the relaxing spaciousness of the season. The noise seemed temporary and local.

Gulian held his companion close to him and peered above the heads of the people nearest.

He would not have chosen 'Liliom' on this particular night had he known just what 'Liliom' was to be . . . in view of what his father had just told him; in view of the problems in his own life he was trying to solve. He had sat through the first act, irritated by actors who insisted upon being symbolic, even when symbolism was not intended, convinced that here was another example of the credulity of over-sophistication which welcomes as great anything that is different, but with the sound of Liliom's gasp as he drove the knife into himself, his point of view had changed, and the tenderness and directness and tender bitterness of the play had gripped him. Only it was a little too tender and direct and astringent for his present mood.

Something of this spirit must have touched Vida

168

too, but with different results, for she looked up and
gave a little shiver and laughed. "Brr! Come on!"
she said. "Let's walk. I need exercise and air. Tell
the taxi-man to go home. I'm depressed. . . . I
hate thieves who kill themselves, don't you?"

Gulian looked down at her in astonished silence.
This question of simulated happiness was not a new
one between him and Vida; it was one of the subjects
—there were several of them—they had agreed not to
discuss. Like most of her countrywomen—and men—
Vida was irritatingly unaware of the functions of
tragedy; had no realization of its cleansing and re-
juvenating qualities; no appreciation of the truth
that there is nothing so heartbreaking as a presentation
of impossible happiness. She thought by refusing to
recognize tragedy you could prevent it. She did not
know that the doleful paradox of a comic opera is that
one cannot live continually to a waltz tune. Part of
the national sadness and dryness of the American, it
seemed to Gulian, came from this refusal to accept the
sweet acridity—the only real basis of gayety—of
reality. Tonight, Vida's remarks struck him as
peculiarly inapposite.

As an apology for his feelings, he gave her arm a
little squeeze, and made his way to the curb to dis-
miss the cab. When he came back, the street was not
so crowded and they walked comfortably and slowly
in the direction of Vida's apartment; through the
tangled dangers of Broadway and through the comparative silence and darkness of the streets beyond.
For a while they walked in silence. Then Vida spoke
suddenly in the blurred contralto notes that he knew
showed a stumbling passionate confusion of mind: "I
hate death," she said. "I hate even to think about it
or see it imitated. It's the one thing I feel incapable

before. I suppose it's because I'm naturally of a thrusting and ambitious nature. I only tried to fight it once. . . . I sat up two nights with my only brother. Years ago. It leaves you very bewildered and weak. I'd like to strangle it with my hands."

He thought he understood her better after this explanation although he didn't agree with her any the more, and he was frightened, as he had so often been in the past two weeks, by the prospect of a future of friendship with her filled with just such breaks in sympathy—breaks words could not weld together again.

She was so afraid of anything that smacked of coming to grips with reality that as result very often in her presence you were haunted by a sense of disaster; disaster she would not let you protect her from because she herself kept you from any attempts to see its face. Happiness is so much only for those not afraid to walk through unhappiness as a barefoot devotee walks through flame. . . . For some odd reason Gulian remembered a little German clerk years ago in East Africa who had annoyed him by much the same attitude towards actuality, save that the German's attitude had been that of the superman to whom actuality is what he wishes it to be. The German had eventually killed himself because of a spell of exceptionally hot weather and some garbled accounts. He had tried to blow his head off with a revolver almost as big as himself but hadn't quite succeeded. Gulian had helped take care of him for the week he lingered. On an especially warm night he had died. At the end he had raved and shrieked and fought against the conclusion. Gulian recollected this as one of the most disheartening episodes of his life. He had seen so many other men rise to a final dignity. The spirit of man could be so extraordinarily dignified, yet this little German

had been so extraordinarily shabby. His shabbiness
for awhile had discounted, since it showed so clearly
to what abasement the human soul could come, all
dignity. On the one side of life was his father, on the
other side was the German. And in between both of
them, between the vistas of the past and the prospects
of the future, walked this thing at his elbow, warm
and soft and alive, brave as his father where people
were concerned, cowardly as the German when stark
crises and exploration of the mind were to be met with.

But he supposed he shouldn't question Vida's attitude so much. She represented the present and love,
and neither the present nor love can in reality be either
dignified or debased. They merely are; they are
points in time. Only in retrospect or prospect do
moments take on philosophical or moral attributes.
The question before him was how he was to handle the
present so that there would be neither regret nor the
expectation of unhappiness.

"I hate death myself," he observed, "and I'm just
as thrusting and ambitious as you are."

She took his arm and pressed close to his side.

"I love life," she said with a little shudder and a
little laugh, "and I can't have too much of it. I've
never had enough. Somehow it always seems at the
last moment to elude me."

They had come once more to the many-paned front
door. Behind the heavy curtain of silk the light from
the hall glowed rosily, and Gulian opened the door and
followed Vida in. The gesture seemed for the first
time to express something definite. He had not been
asked to come in; it had been taken for granted that
he would.

He followed his companion up the stairs and stood
behind her as she slipped her key in the lock. She

turned around to him and smiled as the door opened.
Beyond he saw the soft lights of the cool gray room.

"I'm tired," she said, "and hot. I'm going to change
into something more comfortable. Go on in and wait
for me."

Gulian obeyed her, and seeking the lounge, pulled
a book towards him and opened its pages, but he did
not read.

The silence in the gray room deepened. The two
long French windows, open on to the little grilled
balcony, ushered in the soft thunder of the avenue
beyond, which served only to emphasize the quiet and
remoteness. Some crimson roses in a fawn colored vase
filled the air with their intermittent perfume. Gulian
reached over his shoulder and found a box of matches
and lit a cigarette. He put the book down and clasped
his hands behind his head and stared thoughtfully up
at the ceiling.

Presently Vida was back, wearing a clinging robe
of blue, of some lustrous almost sheer material girdled
with a loose belt of silver. "I am going to mix you a
drink," she said; "and take one myself. I'm going to
make you very happy, so that you won't go for hours
and hours. This is the first time in years I've felt
completely happy and I'm not going to lose it."

She busied herself for a few moments with bottles
and ice, and finally handed Gulian a long glass and,
standing at the corner of the lounge, lit a cigarette and
smiled down at him.

"Contented?" she said softly, and touched his hair.

He looked up and returned her smile.

"Very."

"Not altogether. Still thinking, aren't you? What
do you think about all the time? Poor Gilly, if I
could only teach you not to think! It makes you so

grim. Men aren't like women, are they? They've no ability for the moment. Are you thinking that you and I are very bad people, Gilly?—we're not."

He shook his head.

"What were you thinking about, then?"

"I was thinking of you and myself, and how it is that no one person, nor any two people, can act independently of the scores of complications that hem them in."

She put her hand suddenly over his mouth. "Hush!" she said. "For Heaven's sake stop philosophizing for once. Gilly! Look at me!" She sank down on the arm of the lounge and leaned over him.

He drew away. "We can't talk things over if we do that," he said harshly, "and I have to talk to you. We must make some sort of plan. For one thing, I've just seen my father and he's a very sick man. I can't do anything that would hurt him, can I? That's the first problem."

She laughed and slipped into the space he had left between himself and the end of the sofa. "What's your father got to do with it?" she asked. "Why should he ever know?"

Gulian raised his head and stared at her. She had said nothing that exceeded his own knowledge of what their meeting of the afternoon had meant, but the frank declaration of her intentions amazed him. Despite his experience he had never before met with the basic simplicity of women, possibly because he had had to do either with very good women or else women so little good that explanatory words were unnecessary. Now he was shocked. He did not know that women hesitate a long while before cutting a tangled knot, but that once they begin to cut they hesitate no longer.

"He does know," he faltered.

"That's our own fault—he shall know nothing further. Gilly ——" Her patience seemed abruptly to break and she stretched out her arms and drew his head fiercely down on her breast. "—— be still! Be quiet! Don't spoil this loveliness by talk. Listen! . . . No, I have you close now. You can't get away. . . . You've come all the way from the ends of the world for me, I knew that when I first saw you. Do you suppose we can let each other go now? All through that stupid play I was thinking of this. Do you hear me, Gilly? Don't make me ashamed of myself. If you only knew what I'd been through. But now I don't care; I don't care a bit." She laughed softly. "In all the world I don't care a bit for anything else but you."

Gulian felt that the waters shot with flashes of light were closing over him again. The thin texture of Vida's robe was as nothing between his hands and the body it enclosed; he felt the beating of her heart; the lovely, still immature curves of her flesh. The hurried pulse of her blood seemed to beat in his own veins; her scarlet, half opened lips pressed down on his. . . . And then he released himself and got to his feet. It was as if he had pulled apart the edges of a wound.

"No," he said dryly, "I can't. I shouldn't have come here."

She rested her head against the back of the sofa and stared up at him.

"Then you don't love me," she murmured in a small, awe-stricken voice, and as if speaking to herself, "after all, do you?" She laughed bitterly. "When shy, repressed people give themselves away they always make fools of themselves, don't they? I've made a fool of myself; I'm sorry."

Gulian looked down at her with a haggard face. This process of growing up was a painful one. His heart was torn between shame at himself and pity for the destruction he had wrought. He felt himself helpless before a dilemma. There was his father to be considered, and yet on the other hand here was this woman to whom he was now bound in a dozen different ways. No matter how innocent of intention he had been in the beginning—and no man of thirty-five can ever be wholly innocent—he had raised a genie. And you can't raise genii and then just go about your business. . . . Moreover, he was more involved spiritually than even he was aware. His suspicion that his Aunt Virginia was talking about him, that she had written his father a letter had put the final rivet in his edifice of obstinacy. Under no circumstances would he desert Vida. But yet, what was he to do?

He sat down on the sofa beside her. "Vida, my dear," he said, taking her hand in his. "No . . . Look at me. Don't turn your head away. . . . It isn't so very complicated. You don't love Sydney, so there isn't any loyalty involved and that is the only important thing. Divorce him. Nowadays even my father couldn't be very much shocked by that, could he?"

She turned towards him absent-minded eyes, as if she were coming back from a distant place of meditation.

"Divorce Sydney?"

"Why not?" He lifted her hand questioningly and brought it down upon her knee. In the midst of his stubbornly won reasonableness, the touch of her litheness set his blood racing again. "Otherwise . . ." he said lamely.

"And marry you?"

"Well, why not?"

He was beginning to feel uncomfortable. He disliked being put in the position of a prig even when he was right. It was a rather sardonic reversal of the usual formula that he should be the one pleading for convention and so-called virtue?

Vida's hand stirred in his. "I don't want to," she said slowly. She stared at the empty fireplace. "I don't want to marry you. I hate marriage. I wanted something lovely and free and just my own."

"And you think this is the way to set about getting it?"

She withdrew her hand.

"I don't know . . . why not?" Her lips twisted. "I know all about marriage—it's hideous. It means that somebody else owns you and your time and your comings and goings. It means you watch the love you once had die day by day. It has taken me years to fight my way to any sort of freedom, and now I have it, you want me to give it up again."

"You wouldn't even give up a little bit of freedom for me? I wouldn't ask you to give up very much. Remember, I'm giving up a lot myself."

Her hands, lying in her lap, twisted themselves together. "No," she said finally, "not even for you."

Gulian gazed at her half averted face for a moment and then he got to his feet and stood over her, his fists in his pockets.

"Look at me, Vida," he commanded. She did so.

"Do you know what you're talking about?"

"I ought to." Her stubborn eyes fell.

He laughed shortly. "I don't think you do, and I don't think you love me quite as much as you think. Hampering as marriage may be, and disastrous as it often is, and dangerous as it can't help from being, it is never as hampering and disastrous and dangerous as the other thing. Never. It couldn't be. I know; I've tried the other thing. There is no burden so strangling as the burden of a secret; no rule so strict as a lack of all rules. Nothing so irksome as the cruel disordered tyranny of license."

He hurried on: "I've tried intrigue and, to be brutal, it's boring. That's the long and short of it . . . it's tiresome and demeaning and subtracting. You've never tried it, have you? No, you haven't. Or not the real thing. Merely the silly little games that most women seem nowadays to be playing. Intrigue is stupid. Besides, there's my father. There's just one way and that's the way I've described. Even that isn't going to be as pleasant as it might be."

Vida shook her head wearily. "You use such ugly words," she protested.

"I use the words that express my meaning."

"You make everything seem so little worth while."

Gulian spread out his arms in a gesture of desperation.

"I've just asked you to marry me," he said. "Isn't that worth while?"

Vida stirred impatiently. "You don't understand, and I suppose you never will. I have asked you to love me—and that is going very far for a woman; I have offered you everything; and yet you stand about and argue like a schoolmaster . . . A damned schoolmaster!" she added with a sudden flare of passion. "I don't want a husband. I can't make you out."

She stood up with a swift movement and came close to him, touching him.

"Don't you love me, Gulian?"

"Yes."

"What more do you want, then? Why do you talk and talk?"

Her hands crept up to his shoulders.

"The whole place is ours. It will always be when I want it. We are hurting no one. I don't love my husband, as you said, and he doesn't love me. He only holds on to me because he can't divorce me and because I run his home for him. I don't think he would really care, so long as he actually didn't know. And he need never know. And your father need never know, either. Divorce would be much more public. Your family would hate it if you married me. You've never been married; you don't realize what it is . . . the staleness and the irritation and the weariness. I don't want you to grow stale to me, beloved. Can't you see?"

Gulian looked down at her. Odd that she should be using the very arguments against marriage he was using for it! Confusing. Perhaps, moreover, she was right; perhaps only moments counted, after all. Everything grew stale. . . . No, it didn't. It depended upon your heart and brain whether it grew stale. Trickery alone inevitably grew stale.

"It isn't your husband," he said quietly. "I don't care whether he knows or doesn't. It's you and I. Will you marry me, or won't you?"

She withdrew her hands slowly and stepped back, her eyes still holding his.

"Even if I wanted to, you know I couldn't," she said soberly.

"Couldn't? Why not?"

"You've known it all along. It's part of your cruelty. How could I get a divorce and remarry?"

"You mean . . . because you're a Catholic?"

She nodded.

It seemed to Gulian as if the quiet room had suddenly reechoed to a gigantic peal of laughter. The
extraordinary, distorted motives of humanity! And
yet he had never loved this woman so much as at that
moment when his heart was touched by her irrational-
ity and his mind and body separated from her by a
complete misunderstanding.

"Vida, my dearest," he said, in a final effort to convince her, "listen to me. It isn't necessary, you know,
for a man to love a woman for him to accept what you
offer; but it is necessary for him to love her to propose
what I am proposing. It will all be very simple and
easy. You won't find me the sort of husband you
dread. Such things as remarriages have been got
around in your church. Will you leave it to me?" He
spread out his hands passionately. "Good God," he
said hoarsely, "I'm begging for my life. Don't you
realize what you are doing? I'm trying to find some
coherence and clarity; trying to put my feet on solid
ground; trying to grow up; and you push me back."
He stood with his hands still stretched out towards
her.

She looked at them for a moment, then shrugged her
shoulders and walked over to the fireplace.

"I thought," she said wearily, "I had found something real at last; instead, I find only a lecture. You
have done, my dear Gulian, the most foolish thing you
can do to a woman. It would have been better if you
had left me completely alone. From now on, I want
you to leave me completely alone . . . please."

She stood by the mantelpiece, an arm stretched
along it, staring down moodily at the toe of her slipper.

The unfairness of her words stung Gulian, but he
controlled himself and went over to her. "Surely you
wouldn't be so foolish as that, Vida, would you?" he

asked. "We're the best of friends. I want to help you more than anything in the world."

She shrugged her shoulders.

"You're absurd. I don't want your help. I'm quite competent to look after myself, thank you. My two weeks of gayety have started auspiciously, haven't they?" She lifted her head with a little laugh.

"You're going to throw away our friendship?"

"Friendship?" She faced about on him and stared at him blankly. "You become more and more absurd. You're the most childish person I've ever met. Do you think a woman can be very friendly with a man who has refused her?"

Gulian flushed darkly.

"That's a lie!" he said fiercely, stepping forward, "and you know it. A lie your own oblique mind has made up. I refused you nothing. I asked you to marry me, and that's the best thing—poor as it may be—a man knows how to do. . . . I'm going now. Goodbye."

He turned away from her and started across the room, hopelessness and a despairing contempt filling his mind, but again, as a few hours earlier, he heard swift footsteps behind him and looked back. She had caught up to him.

"I didn't mean it," she said with a trembling quietness. "I didn't mean it, Gilly. I don't care what you do, if . . . you'll only love me. I can't let you go this way."

"You mean you'll marry me?"

She raised her eyes falteringly.

"Afterwards. . . . Can't we talk about that afterwards? There's been so much talk."

For a moment he hesitated, all his resolutions swept away. What did it matter after all? He was free to do what he wanted; so to all intents and purposes was she. What did this cold stupidity amount to that was holding him back? What did it profit him? Life was sunny and warm and episodical if only you could train yourself to forget. Exactly—just that! But forgetting was a difficult business. Why, he couldn't forget even now! There were other faces and lips even now coming between him and Vida. There was only one way to avoid interfering memories and that was to make no more than you could help.

He felt the coolness of the deepening night coming through the windows as he stood there; he felt himself trembling. In the street outside, a cab door slammed and a voice laughed.

He raised his head.

"I'm sorry," he said inadequately. "No, it wouldn't be fair. I'm sorry, my dear. Let me go, Vida."

She drew away from him, her hands hanging limply at her sides as if they had been hurt. Her fingers twisted themselves in the folds of her lustrous blue robe. Then she clasped them behind her and stepping back looked at him squarely.

"Yes," she said quietly. "I'll let you go. Poor, stupid, divided Gilly! And don't worry about me . . . it isn't me you've been thinking about, anyhow; it's yourself. In all your life you have never thought of anything else. No, not one single thing. . . . Don't forget your cigarette case."

It was just as if before his eyes there had occurred a transfiguration actual and startling; as if the texture and expression and even the coloring he had come to know so well had dropped slowly to her feet like a discarded garment and she stood clothed once more in the indifference and coldness of the first few minutes of their first meeting.

He went over to the table and picked up his case. "Goodnight," he said softly.

He dared not look back. Wings seemed to be beating about him as he went down the stairs and out of the door and into the street. Nor did he feel heroic. He felt more ashamed and confused and unheroic than he had ever before felt in his life; far less heroic than he had felt in similar episodes that had ended quite differently.

He reached St. Marks' Place long after midnight. A wind from the sea was rustling the leaves. He let himself into the cool spaciousness of his father's house and switched off the single electric light still burning. The little Artemis in her niche on the first landing—slim, poised, untrammeled—gleamed in her bronze nakedness an instant before darkness overtook her.

Gulian climbed slowly up to his room. He turned on the lights by the mirror and for a moment or two wandered aimlessly about, laying his cigarette case on one table, his watch on another. He picked up a book and put it down again. When he had taken off his coat he went over to the mirror and leaning both elbows on the bureau top, stared into the glass with an intentness that was youthful and unlike any in which he had indulged for many years.

Finally he spoke below his breath, "You damn fool!" he said witheringly. "You ass! She was right. You don't know what love is. You've never been in love with a woman since you were born. You've never done a direct and simple action since you were five. You were told a fact a little while ago. . . . You're in love with yourself and your own thoughts and your own emotions."

He continued to stare at his reflection for a while longer before he stepped back.

"That's true!" he said softly but out loud.

He began quietly to undress. He became more aware of the night. Sitting upon the edge of his bed, he thought, "I'll go to 'Hibernia' tomorrow. I'll go the first thing in the morning. I need space to size myself up in."

BOOK II

"*I saw moreover in my dream, that the interpreter took him by the hand, and led him into a little room, where sat two children, each one in a chair. And the name of the eldest was Passion, and the name of the other was Patience.*"

PILGRIM'S PROGRESS, BOOK I.

CHAPTER I

WISTERIA

Gulian had written Vida:

Hibernia,
Slaton-on-Hudson,
Sunday, May 22nd, 1921.

Dearest: I have been here five days and all that time I have done nothing but think of you. Try as I may, I can find but one obstacle that might stand in the way of our happiness, and that is your religious belief. But certainly such an obstacle can be got around, and certainly no just God or just church meant any such measure to increase the already too large total of human misery. Where is the logic to unnecessary suffering? That isn't religion; that's devil-worship.

Nor will there be any social penalty attached—if you dread that; but I know you don't—nor, and we are no longer children and can speak of such matters frankly, any material penalty. You will be better off than you are now. My family, especially my father, will not stand in my way when I explain matters.

Don't let's haggle. Time slips from us. When I hear from you I will come back to New York immediately. Meanwhile, I shall wait breathlessly for your letter.

I wish you could see this old red brick house as I see it at this moment from the arbor in which I am sitting. I spend my time imagining you in it, and I know you would love it as I do—I have not seen it in Spring now for ten years.

I am facing the back of the house where, upon trellises, above a terrace which leads down to a sort of formal garden, there is a mass of purple wisteria in bloom, and below the wisteria—yellow as buttercups in the sun—what they call, I think, golden-basket. At all events, a most gay, cordial, nine o'clock of a morning flower. And in the formal garden at the foot of the terrace and the stone balustrade—that's the right word, isn't it—I mean a low wall with a coping and short, portly balusters—are tulips and irises and forget-me-nots and lilac bushes, white and grape-blue; and even some snowballs, out earlier, I understand, than they should be because of the advanced season. But my botany is bad. However, the occasion is very moving and many colored and sweet smelling. I am eager for you to share the loveliness and the quiet.

To one side of the house, between the fold in the hills where it is tucked away, I can see, far below me, the river, and across the river the blue haze of opposite mountains. And everywhere are apple-orchards in bloom, and that astonished sort of greenness which overtakes the trees in spring when they have accomplished the fact of leafage. . . .

Somehow, between you and this place, I am recapturing a large part of the elations I thought I had left behind me.

Goodbye, my darling. I could not sleep last night because of you.

GULIAN.

Gulian read the letter over several times before he sealed it. He realized that he had slipped rather eagerly from personalities into a description of 'Hibernia,' but then he explained this to his own satisfaction by the fact that when he loved things—and he still insisted to himself that despite the clarity of vision with which he now saw Vida he still loved her—he mixed them all up together. He was rather proud, anyway, that he had avoided any semblance of the philosophical moralizing she so despised.

The letter had been a difficult one to compose, for he hadn't the slightest idea of just how he stood with Vida, and although his inclination and his sense of honor bade him be sufficiently lover-like, his knowledge of Vida and his pride warned him not to be too ardent.

However, stirred as all men of imagination are by

the tom-tom quality of words, he had gone further than he had intended and had composed a poetic letter as well, a letter as definite as a letter could be. The darling of the conclusion had been considerably easier than the superlative of the beginning. And when he was through, so exhilarated was he by rhythm, he wasn't sure but that he had meant everything he had written.

Also it was quite true that he had lain awake most of the previous night—and the three preceding nights as well—in the small four-poster bed of his room, with the moonlight—the little moon had become by now a portly more than half-grown moon—pouring in through the windows and the wisteria making the hours fragrant, but he had been thinking as much of what to write Vida, a thought that had been troubling his mind ever since he had left New York and which had caused him many fluctuations of feeling and decision, as he had been thinking of her lips and eyes, demanding as these latter were. And more even than letters or lips or eyes, his mind had been filled, as he had indicated, with the rare and recaptured ecstasy of being once more at 'Hibernia.'

The moonlight, hesitating at first, had filled the room to overflowing, turning the fluted columns of the bed to spear shafts washed with gold, regilding the severe narrow frame of a portrait, making the flowers in the pattern of the wall-paper expand like water-lilies in a mysterious pool. The perfume of the wisteria seemed to increase. Every once and awhile in the elm trees just beyond the window, there had broken in upon Gulian's thoughts the sleepy chattering of birds.

And every night for a long while Gulian had leaned upon the sill and smoked a pipe, brooding upon the silver and tawny landscape—an inlaid Oriental plaque

of silver convex work and lacquered gilt . . . round
dark masses of trees; sloping immaterial lawns; a
thread of scintillation where the river ran; the mysterious faunal shape of the distant hills. Above it all,
the high tossed, split coin of the moon.

> Ah, God! to see the branches stir
> Across the moon at Granchester!
> To smell the thrilling-sweet and rotten
> Unforgotten, unforgotten
> River-smell, and hear the breeze
> Sobbing in the little trees.

And then:

> Say, is there Beauty yet to find?
> And Certainty? and Quiet kind?
> Deep meadows yet, for to forget
> The lies, and truths, and pain? . . .

Ah, splendid! Never growing old! A great poet
suddenly and adventitiously made famous and as suddenly and adventitiously repudiated by those who
cannot bear too long to hear others praised! A metrical Aristides the Just! The damn fool world! And
all the while there was such a simple test for poetry
or anything else—merely a question of whether, within
the sphere designated, there was an authentic thrill.
If they—the damn fool world; that part of it that read
with any discrimination at all; would only overlook
for a while critics and fashions and on the whole trust
to its own instincts! A single conclusion arrived at
by the processes of thought being worth a hundred
conclusions handed down. Even a wrong opinion that
set the mind working being better than a right opinion
that left the mind idle.

A rage at everything arrogant and self-assured had

seized Gulian in the face of the calm implicitness of
nature. These butcher-boys from London and Paris
and Chicago and the New York Pale! Noisy, stuffy
men smelling of tobacco smoke, their minds obstipated
by clogged presumptions! Disappointed mothers. Unpleasant chambermaids dashing in unasked upon the
half-nakedness of strangers. In one night the moon
made more poetry and conveyed more criticism than
all the vocal crew that halloed up and down the world.

"And Certainty! And Quiet kind!" What about
these? . . .

Well, he had made for himself, as men will make
and keep on making until they die, a dilemma the ugly
horns of which had already several times thrust themselves above the surface of his perceptions. Pretty
soon he would have to decide definitely upon which
uncomfortable horn he was going to settle down. The
left horn of flight and a seriously damaged self-respect;
or the right horn of a very uncertain future. And he
supposed, considering his instincts and training, he
would have to accept the sharp point of the right horn.
There was nothing else to it; he would have to continue in his attempts to persuade Vida to marry him.
At the moment this seemed the only horn possible for
personal salvation. Willy-nilly he would have to see
the thing through as doggedly as he knew how. He
was aware that the cruelest sort of kindness is to pretend a whole-hearted love that is not whole-hearted,
for the single reason, if no other, that eventually the
pretense is seen through; but if he ran away just now,
if he even sophistically took advantage of the opportunities for running away that Vida's own attitude
presented, he would only be adding another scar to
that pride of his that had already been too often

scarred. And he wasn't so sure that he wanted to run away, anyhow.

Convalescence, physical or spiritual, is troubled by relapses. In the latter case there are too many memories of perfect interludes, of moments when incompatibility seemed unreal; bothersome visions as well—of eyes, of hands, of the turn of a head, of notes in a voice, of a quick way of moving, of brooding languors when a deep thoughtfulness, touching, provocative of hope, is suspected. A score of remembrances, especially when, as in Gulian's case, there has been given an opportunity hard to refuse. These things lie in wait for the heart and take it unawares. . . . There were moments when Gulian felt that he could not abide an existence without Vida, and there were other moments when he thought with shamefaced sardonicism of the use, in his reflections, of the word 'dogged.' But he need not have been surprised by the word. There is no clearsightedness so cruel as the clearsightedness of a man who sees suddenly the real woman with whom he has been in love.

Gulian tossed about in his four-posted bed while the moonlight grew more dithyrambic. It seemed to be adding its impalpable but oppressive weight to the breaking down of his resolutions. Morning after morning he heard the birds in the elms begin their querulous sunrise gossip. And then, the fifth morning, he wrote his letter.

He would no longer look forward or back. He would divide his mind in half and forget what one half of it contained. He would burn his bridges. A certain sort of peace overtook him.

The afternoon of two days later, a Tuesday, was the earliest hour at which he might expect an answer from Vida and so, about four o'clock, he comman-

deered the respectable but well-worn family station-
car and went down to the village four miles away for
the late mail, as that was the quickest method of
obtaining it. Abraham, who with his wife Hannah,
looked after 'Hibernia' when no one else was there
and had been doing so for twenty years, noticing the
underlying restlessness and the sharpness of the refusal to allow anyone else to perform the task, knew,
with rural intuition in such matters, that somehow or
other a woman was involved. Abraham possessed, furthermore, a universal bucolic truth, and that was that
without a permanent woman, no matter how often that
woman may be seized by the curious devil that seizes
women, a man is about as unfulfilled as an orchard
without bees. Better an unhappy marriage than none
at all. Except in moments when the devil was uppermost, he was so close, in the way of countrymen, to
Hannah in both flesh and spirit that half the time he
forgot which was Hannah and which was himself.
Silence and loneliness and a man and a woman busy
about their tasks produce as a rule satisfactory results.
Abraham had no idea of the centrifugal force of cities.

The mail had not arrived when Gulian stopped
before the white frame post-office behind its two huge
elms, and so he sat in the car, rendered temporarily
harmless, and stared down the macadam road under
its canopy of maple trees. The road and the village
pleased him. On either side were the butcher shops
and the baker shops, and the jeweler, and the stationer,
and the motion-picture 'palace,' and the millinery shop
—Miss Julie's—of the little town. The scene was
peaceful and self-contained. Fresher now than it
would be a month or so later, but never very far away
from a possibility of shade and the gayety of flowers.

It seemed to him at the moment that villages were

by all odds the most intelligent units of population yet devised for the average man. One knew, of course, what small town life was like in certain respects and how hard it frequently was on the younger generation, but that could be righted, was being righted, and there wasn't, as a matter of fact, much difference in the ways in question between the small town and the big one. The last citadel of a soul starved for excitement is always sex, anyhow. Until the moralists realized that, realized the necessity for beauty and adventure and excitement, illegitimate children would continue to be born. The point was that sparse settlement dignified the individual—the one essential, outside of food and clothing and shelter, that man required; the prime necessity of life; its innermost pursuit. Butchers and bakers and stationers and milliners and saints, even harlots, were people whom everybody knew and talked about and hated or liked. The terrible anonymity of cities was absent.

A man appeared with a number of striped canvas sacks, and Gulian awoke from his somnolent reflections and left the Ford and mingled with the small heterogenous crowd collecting before the postoffice window. His heart was beating fast as he returned to the Ford with the square, delicately colored letter which had been handed him and climbed into the front seat.

The letter was brief.

My Dear Gulian:

I cannot make you understand. Why, after all, should I try? It is only too obvious from what you have done and the way you write that you don't love me. If you did, you would understand me better and, possibly (this made him angrier than anything else) you would not describe at such length the scenery of the Hudson valley, which, incidentally, I know

very well. Why should I sacrifice a secure present, and one
I have arranged with some care, for a future that—since you
do not love me—would be anything but secure? Even if it
could be done? But it can't. There is no use of further
discussion. Arguments do not destroy my beliefs.

You need not come to see me. It would only make us
unhappy.

I am sorry I did what I did—I should have known better,
but there is no use crying over spilt milk.

Goodbye. I wish you all the happiness in the world,

VIDA.

P. S. It is strange. I do not think I demand very much of
life. I don't seem able even to get that.

Self-pity; self-righteousness! Damn self-pity and
self-righteousness! . . . Gulian set his foot to the
Ford and that extraordinary product of the human
mind leaped like a horse and swirled through the village in a cloud of dust and up the winding road towards
'Hibernia,' and past that place, lost in its elms, into
the shaded lane that led to the sloping heights beyond.

The lane twisted like a cool damp russet vine between the trunks of pine and white oak and ash, and
finally topped a ridge and came out upon a fine bland
rolling farm country that stretched away eastward
towards a blue horizon. The small square fields were
still charmingly immature and viridescent, and the
trees seemed to have distilled and re-chromatized
the sunlight into the shining dark clumps of the evergreens and the translucent yellow-green of the hard-
woods. Here and there a white farm house showed
itself or the darker buildings of an estate.

Gulian stopped the Ford and lit a cigarette and
for awhile regarded the landscape inimically, until
under the soothing influence of the peaceful countryside his set face relaxed.

He drew Vida's crumpled letter from his pocket and

read over once more the brief sentences. Evidently
Vida was quite through. She was putting him definitely out of her life. Pulling him up by the root.
. . . Well, she couldn't do just that. It wasn't decent.
Unsatisfactory as he knew it probably would be, he
would have to see her again when he returned to New
York, if only for a moment. As a man, with a man's
desire for spiritual order, he disliked this brutal lop-
ping off of a spiritual limb. He wanted the jagged
edges to be drawn together; the surface at least to be
smooth. He had none of a woman's hardy common
sense where such matters are concerned. He was
not so used to operations either mental or physical.
Above all, he did not want to carry with him a sense
of stupidity, or a sense of guilt, or a sense of vacancy.
He wanted some sort of healing episode, if it was
nothing more than he and Vida assuring each other
that no one had been to blame and that both had
been the victims of forces too great for them. He
wanted to be assured that life would go on much as
usual. Of course, life never does, but all men like
to be told that it will.

Very slowly he tore the crumpled sheets and envelope
into tiny bits and placed the pieces in his pocket. Some
crows flying across the near foreground loosed their
sardonic laughter at him, and from the well of placidity
below there drifted up the tinkling of cowbells. A
white cloud dragged its shadow bumpingly over the
sleeping land, and then, behind him, he heard the soft
clop-clop of a walking horse and, turning about, saw
a girl in a gray coat and gray riding breeches approaching him on a sorrel mare, her eyes fixed on the distant
view.

Gulian abruptly resumed his former position and
lit another cigarette. He felt vaguely annoyed. At

the moment he resented any form of feminine intrusion, especially if the intruder was young and good looking as this girl apparently was, and, moreover, a shyness under such isolating circumstances which pursued him even into maturity, made him suddenly uncomfortable.

The tread of the horse drew nearer and came abreast and altered to the stretching of chains and munching of bits that indicated that the rider had paused, and after a moment a fresh, crisp, unembarrassed young voice said, "You're Gulian Eyre, aren't you?"

Gulian raised a pair of deliberately uninterested eyes. Looking down at him was . . . he felt his interest revive slightly—the girl—what was her name? Lael something. . . . Lael Satori, that was it! . . . he had met weeks ago at that dancing place! The rude girl! What a splendid opportunity, he reflected grimly, to pay her back and incidentally, in the paying, achieve some sort of disconnected revenge upon the sex in general!

"Yes," he admitted dryly. "I'm Gulian Eyre. What can I do for you?"

The girl continued to peer down at him from under the little urchin-like brown felt hat she was wearing, the smile in her long smoky gray eyes beginning to cloud with the blank expressionless look of affronted youth. She had left most of her paint behind her, Gulian noticed; her half parted lips and soft cheeks were a faint azalea color.

"Are you trying to be unpleasant?" she inquired, at length. "If you are, I shan't bother you." Despite the brave sophistication of her words, her mouth trembled.

Gulian was abruptly alarmed lest revenge had gone too far; besides, he hadn't been prepared for this entirely candid and disarming method of approach. Moreover, he had never been able calmly to see a woman's mouth tremble.

"No," he protested hastily, "I'm not trying to be rude. I had no intention whatever of being rude. Really! I'm sorry, anyway. . . . You're Miss Satori, aren't you? I met you at . . ."

"Paul's."

"Yes, that's it—Paul's. And I really wanted to know if I could help you in any way. Really I did Can I?" He looked up ingenuously. His eyes were troubled under their half lowered lashes. He was unaware how small-boyish and engaging his appearance at such moments was.

The girl's expression warmed immediately and she laughed. "I know you're lying to me," she said, "for I know that you did recognize me and for some reason or other hated me. I think you're inclined to lie, anyway. However, I'll forgive you. Your sister, Drusilla, told me you were here. I had a letter from her this morning—I'm a great friend of hers, you know." She threw a leg over the pommel of her saddle.

"Yes, I know."

"She told me you were over at your old place and that I was to be nice to you, but—maybe you're hard to be nice to. Are you? What I really spoke to you for was a cigarette. Have you a cigarette? I'm not trying to pick you up."

She slipped from her horse and came over to the side of the car.

Gulian searched his pockets. "Lots! I hope you like the kind I smoke. Why don't you come up and sit here with me and smoke peaceably? We'll admire the view. Wait a moment; I'll help you." He made a motion towards her.

"Oh, thanks awfully!" she retorted ironically. "I'm very feeble and need help." She climbed nimbly to the seat beside him and stretched her slim, booted legs out in front of her. "I left my cigarette-case at home," she explained. "It is a nice view, isn't it?"

She stooped her head to his match, "I come here often. I'm staying with the Gates—just beyond you. Marian is a great crony of mine. But she doesn't ride, and I do, and so I steal off almost every day by myself, —afternoon or morning. See that house 'way off there to the left, the one with a green roof? The most unpleasant fat boy lives there, he's very rich and wants to marry Marian. He comes over almost every night, and I go out and sit on the terrace."

"There're no Gates young men, then?" concluded Gulian.

"No, there're no Gates young men. There's just Marian and her father and mother. Sometimes it is rather trying. Mrs. Gates doesn't like me because she thinks I'm wild; and Mr. Gates doesn't dare like me because he thinks his wife might think him wild if he did, so I've only Marian, and that's only in the intervals between the fat boy. Marian's my age—we're twenty-three." She hesitated for a moment and looked across the valley. "But then I've stopped liking men, except collectively," she added soberly. "I stopped two years ago."

"Good God!" exclaimed Gulian. "How young to be wild! And how young to stop liking men—except—collectively."

She studied him attentively. "Do you think twenty-three young? You're inexperienced."

Gulian hastened to defend himself.

"It's a piebald age," he said, "young in spots. That is, the women are; the men are altogether young. But possibly I'm all mixed up. I don't know. You see, I've been running around with women over thirty, and of course they're so young I'm confused. . . . Are you very wild?"

She turned her long gray eyes upon him.

"Some people think I am. You, I suppose, are extremely Tennysonian?"

Gulian assented mockingly.

"Frightfully! Women ought to be kept in their place, only the trouble is no one has ever found just what that place is. Now they know less than ever. Of course I'm Tennysonian. What nice American man isn't? Even our wild young poets are pleased by their own audacities—and that's Tennysonian. The thoroughly released person has no feeling about audacity at all. However, my present object in life is to study the younger generation, to which, I understand, you belong, and so I'm ready for instruction. . . . I remember a small Marian Gates years ago—a solid little girl."

"She's still solid, but she's very pretty. I should hate the fat boy to marry her. For one thing, their combined wealth would be appalling."

"The Gates are as plutocratic as ever?"

"More so." The girl sighed, and crossing one slim knee over the other, leaned back and inhaled her cigarette. Her throat, rising from the open collar of her white shirt, was the color of tinted ivory. There stirred from her the sweet faint warmth of young blood and exercise.

"Does this seem very peaceful to you?" she asked at length.

"Very."

"Often in the city you don't think there is such

peace, do you? And four years ago you didn't think
such peace would ever be possible again."

"Are you talking about the war?"

"I am. Do you mind? I haven't quite got over it
yet."

"No one has in reality. I think the present attitude
silly. Were you in France?"

"No, I was one of the home-guard, principally occupied in breaking up homes, I suppose. I was only
nineteen. I wore a foolish uniform and ran a motor-
car and thought if I didn't step on a Ford the war
would be lost. Like everyone else, about six times a
month, I nearly made a fool of myself. At one time
I rather think I wanted to marry a sergeant of marines,
but he wouldn't let me because he was thirty-two and
had a wife of his own and four children. That was
nice of him, wasn't it? But I didn't altogether make
a fool of myself—I was luckier than some of my
friends." She paused abruptly and looked at Gulian
with rounded eyes. "I am certainly talking very intimately to you, aren't I?" she decided. "Drusilla would
like this."

"I happened to be in France myself," observed
Gulian, "so I didn't have quite so much time, as you
did, to be altruistically patriotic."

The girl threw away her cigarette and locked her
hands over her knees and stared thoughtfully down at
the valley. "Women haven't so many ways to be
patriotic as men have," she remarked soberly. "They
usually think the only thing they have to give is some
sort of self-mutilation. It's difficult to reconstruct
now the way you felt, isn't it? But we're slowly
emerging, I think—except those who were ruined for
good. For a while I didn't think we were emerging;
recently, however, I've seen signs. People aren't half

as crazy about noise as they were a year ago, for one thing. Jazz is dying. And then one is beginning to remember that there're things like this, after all? But then, there always were things like this, weren't there?"

"Always."

She tightened the grip of her interlocked fingers around her knees.

"The trouble is coming out of it all—getting rid of the habit and mania of excitement—just when you're beginning to grow up, and especially if you're a woman and haven't anything to do. When you're young everything is equally exciting so you don't much care what the excitement is."

"Do you mind if I tell you something?" asked Gulian.

"No. What is it?"

"Well, I'm thirty-five," Gulian leaned forward earnestly—"and a man, and I find things just as difficult as you do. If I live to be eighty I expect to find them equally difficult."

"You're making fun of me."

"I most certainly am not. I'm merely telling you that bewilderment is the natural state of man." His mind reverted to the torn bits of paper in his pocket.

The girl was petulant. "I'm not going to be bewildered all my life," she announced, "I'm tired of it. I'm a definite person. I've reached out pretty definitely in some directions, and found out what I don't like; now I'm going to reach out pretty definitely in other directions and find out what I do like."

Gulian's tone was congratulatory. "I'm glad you're definite," he said. "It's a lucky thing to be, only I'm afraid your sex, having recently achieved freedom, hasn't yet thrown overboard its ancient idea that it can make definite certain things that aren't definite at all. I'm speaking of personal relationships. They're adventitious and haphazard. Men learned that long ago and so do their best to take them as they come; take them and go about their business."

He hesitated, suddenly realizing that he was, as was so often the case, expressing a general truth that did not, by any means, always join up with his own actions. He had very definitely in the case of Vida tried to bend a personal relationship to his own ideal of what it should be. He sat back and stared at the valley.

"I must be getting home," said the girl. "It's almost half-past five. Pity you haven't got a horse. We could ride back together. Do you ever ride?"

"Yes, there're a couple of ancient creatures in the stable. I had one out yesterday afternoon."

"Would you like to ride some morning before breakfast? I can't get anyone to go with me."

Gulian was startled by the eagerness with which he welcomed this chance for early exercise.

"How about tomorrow . . . about seven?" he asked.

"Splendid! I'll expect you. You'll have to come over to see the Gates sometimes, anyhow. They've been talking about you. They think you're rude. Now I must really go. I'll write Drusilla you're behaving yourself. Are you?"

"Not notably so." Gulian suddenly became gloomy.

The girl climbed down from the seat of the car and mounted her horse and turned the glistening sorrel head back along the woodland road. Gulian watched the two slim figures as they threaded their way through the green shadows and the pools of sunlight to where they reached the crest of the obliterating slope. At the edge of it the girl looked around and waved her hand.

Gulian resumed his contemplation of the valley. A new transparency was appearing with the lengthening light. The masses of trees, the scattered houses, became more distinct, but the general outline of hill and level grew softer, showed a tinge of violet. Behind Gulian in the woods a thrush broke into a dripping loveliness of song.

And so another woman was taking possession of him, was she? He supposed it was a weakness in himself. Women spied out a weakness uncannily and seized upon every advantage it gave them. But they didn't really like a man who exhibited such weaknesses. Gulian experienced a passionate longing to be cold and hard and determined. Something like Philip, only more so. Yes, that was it; to be possessed by no one. . . . However, he needn't worry much about this girl. She would amuse herself with him only in the absence of anyone else. He was a little ashamed of the ease with which, it seemed, he was able to forget Vida; still more ashamed at the relief he felt that such ease was possible.

He turned the Ford homeward. Dinner was served to him in the white-panelled dining-room, with two unshaded candles reflecting themselves in the brasses of the wide hearth and in the sober depths of the portrait of Philip Eyre, the founder of the race.

A moon flooded the terrace, and after dinner Gulian went out there and had his coffee brought to him. He lay back in a wicker chair and stared at the bulk of the old house, solid and friendly. The vines clung to its sides like a delicate carving. Extraordinarily wistful the whole thing—wistful and sweet smelling!

O God, the world was beautiful—damnably, hurtingly beautiful! You couldn't hate life even if it continually harassed you.

CHAPTER II

"THE DEEP, DEEP COUNTRY"

Six days later, Monday the 30th of May, Gulian returned to town. He had received a letter from Philip saying that there was a place open for him in Perry's office, and it seemed only sensible to accept the offer. His train landed him at Forty-second Street at ten o'clock of the morning, and as it was a Monday morning and spring, the streets showed an exceptionally young and fresh and new-washed appearance as he drove through them, rather like thin women in sheer dresses soon to be soiled.

The two weeks he had spent at 'Hibernia' had been a valuable experience to Gulian; a reconstruction and a discovery. A vernal clarifying interlude with a background of pastel blue and green, coming just when such an interlude was needed, not only for his own more personal return to mental health but for a general shaking-down of his wider view points.

In the long periods of reflection (rare enough nowadays) for which he had found time, he had begun to rid his mind of much accumulation; dissect out and throw away what he was beginning at last to realize were remnants of sentimentality, although at one time they had seemed to him the very latest hard-bitten panaceal thought. Like most young men of a radical turn he had mistaken sentimentality for science. Principally he had repossessed himself of the conviction that his father was right in thinking that, whatever

205

might be the faults of such a system, some system that
fostered tradition and an honorable ancestry and an
honorable root in the soil was necessary for the health
of a nation, and that if such a system no longer existed,
then there should be an immediate setting about to re-
produce an improved copy of it. Whether the ancestry
was ornate or simple made no difference so long as it
was coherent and clean-tempered. How, at the one
extreme of this theory, you could reconcile with the
common welfare the great holdings and great privileges that seemed necessary for beauty, he did not
know, but he did know that all previous attempts to
solve the problem had taken the wrong paths. His
reflections up to the moment, anyhow, had been more
eliminating than constructive. But then, his generation had been suffering from too much so-called 'constructive thought'; what it needed was an admixture
of simplification and common sense.

He remembered that in his 'The Confessions of a
Young Man' George Moore had disgustedly predicted
forty years or so of loose-lipped altruistic thought.
Altruism was necessary, but not the loose-lipped
variety. Unsafe as the world was for democracy, it
was even more unsafe for beauty.

There had been a Sunday when Gulian had gone to
the little church near 'Hibernia' and throughout a
droning sermon had studied on the sun-washed walls
the square white tablets that memorialized his family.
They read something like this:

"Philip Eyre, Esq. Gentleman. Born in Londonderry Co.,
Ireland, June 8, 1735. Emigrated to this country at the age
of 24. Died Mar. 15, 1819, in the 84th year of his life. Was
the founder of this church, a colonel upon the staff of Gen.
Washington, and for fifteen years a member of the New York
Assembly. A kind father, a loving husband, and a generous
friend.

"John Philip Eyre, Esq. Born April 10, 1765. Died Feb. 12, 1840, in the 75th year of his life. For forty years a warden of this parish; a major of militia; a member of the State Assembly, and for two terms a member of the National Legislature. A distinguished citizen."

And so on down to Gulian's own grandfather, whom he remembered well. A tall, thin, silvery, smiling old gentleman, like an upstanding birch tree.

None of these men had been great men, but they had all been useful men, and close to the soil, and men who had warmed their hands at the lamp of knowledge. Independent men, proud to be Americans yet well aware that America should be proud to have them as its citizens; their immovable yet expanding quality something like the spaciousness of their own American forests. After all, this quiet handing down of life and its obligations to sons and the sons of sons was the one concrete example of immortality men possessed; the one thing that made life actually understandable. Those born to the Araemic contempt for land and race, or those who had adopted this contempt as a possible salvation for the world, could not understand, failed utterly to take into account, the northern—nordic . . . call it what you will . . . passion for the homestead. The beautiful, black as blood, clear as black crystal, passion. They laughed at it, but their theories failed every time they challenged it.

And so, finding once more an interest and a virtue in the dead people of his own blood, and in the beauty they had created, Gulian had overtaken a something else; an amplification of the former passion; a something subtle and intangible that for ten years or so had been increasingly eluding him. A quintessence of his feelings towards his own country. Not the burly intolerancies of war; not the maudlincies of politicians; not the infatuation of this sect or that section; assuredly nothing to do with greed or ignorance or narrowness or provincialism; not patriotism at all as it is usually misunderstood; but a passion young and intrinsic. An inner flame of passion for the land itself. The poor scarred land! He had seen many Englishmen with this passion; many Frenchmen; only a few Germans and Japanese, caught up as they were in their bulbous clouds of imperialism. And practically no modern Americans. And yet it was necessary that a man should love his country as, after many years, a fortunate husband learns to love his wife; each line of her and secret loveliness. Nor did a love like this make a man nationally over-monogamous; to love one woman completely means to understand more or less all women. A man who cannot love nationally cannot love internationally. Passion, wisely controlled, is the secret of all greatness. The lover of the Pennsylvania hills is a lover of the Devon cliffs and the little blue valleys of the Seine.

Gulian thought he had lost this passion. It had been almost suffocated by the immense grotesquerie of the war; nor had the antics of a mean-minded government as related by newspapers read in Tokyo tended to revive it, but, very simply and easily, the mystery had been unveiled to him once more at 'Hibernia.' In the sloping fields, in the silent roads between the trees, in the old ruddy houses. This was America; the heart of it.

He was almost able to forget the sign-board he had seen on his way up the river; a huge hoarding where these touched elbows: 'The Forbidden Woman' (a motion-picture): 'Fifty-Fifty'; a girl show: The Inter-

Allied Church Movement: and "Buy Government Bonds."

In the lapis-lazuli mornings, filled with the songs of birds and light cool breezes, he had ridden with Lael Satori, and most of the nights of full and waning moon he had driven his car over to the huge Gates manorhouse, half a mile away, and had sat out on the terrace with Lael, or made one of a party of four in which Marian Gates and her plump cavalier were the other two.

His relief had been great when he found, once the formal greetings were over, and the health of his father and his Aunt Virginia discussed in detail, he was not expected to see much of Mr. and Mrs. Gates. Like their house, the elder Gates were large and unresponsive and did not welcome casual intrusion, and in their early fifties had settled down to the simple pleasures of the very rich; the hiring and dismissing of expensive servants; a continual worry about motorcars; and the attempt, usually successful, to disregard the petitions of numerous indigent relatives. Occasionally, in rare moments of passion, Mr. Gates invested in worthless bonds, or went out and glutted himself on golf. Both he and his wife belonged to that sizeable class of New Yorkers which possesses neither the gay clarity of tradition nor the shrewd imagination of the newly constructed. His father had appeared somewhere around 1860 and avoiding, like most successful men of that period, the Civil War, had made a fortune in a department store, a fact which his children had ever since been trying to live down by a rigorous disregard of anything which had any texture in it, mental or physical.

Marian was an improvement upon her parents. She was square and heavy boned and her imagination showed a tendency to become easily alarmed, but she owned a lovely skin and blue eyes and masses of fair hair and a directness and, if not a sense of humor, at least a present-day appreciation of its necessity. Almost always she managed to laugh at the right time.

Gulian agreed with Lael that Marian was much too good for her amorphous suitor. He had built up in his mind a sharp contempt for this suitor; possibly too sharp, since the suitor, at least in any spectacular way, was not harmful. A tall, pursy young man of twenty-eight or thereabouts, who walked with his feet stuck out and a curious motion of his hips, and who stole about the country timorously in a magnificent foreign car. His name was Elliott Hammond, and he was the especial worry, unnecessarily, of an invalid mother. This, combined with his figure, of which for some odd reason he was inordinately proud, had made him noticeably self-satisfied. Obviously he was biding his own time before honoring Marian with a proposal. Towards Lael he exhibited the kindly patronization of the carefully brought up rich young man who could not, of course, think seriously of marrying a poor girl. There was about him in such matters the gravity of an heir-apparent. To the frivolous-minded the gravity of any sort of mating was somewhat impaired at this season of the year by the vast amount of mating that was going on in every neighboring tree. On the whole it seemed a natural and sweet, and not too ponderous occupation.

Lael, in return, treated Elliot with a delicate and delighted cruelty. She wounded him with little darts and then ran away before he could turn his slow head.

"She's a nice little thing," Elliot confided to Gulian, one afternoon when he was taking Gulian home, "but— not much weight. I wonder what will become of her?"

Gulian turned a cold eye upon him.

"Does that bother you very much?" he inquired.

The ghost of a reminiscent smile flitted across Elliot's broad face. Gulian wanted to slap Elliot, for he knew the reminiscent smile was a lie. "She's pretty enough, you know," he added, "to marry anyone she chooses."

"You think so?" Elliot looked down at the wheel of his car. "There're disadvantages. There's her father, for instance."

"Charles Satori?"

"Old Charlie. The most useless man of his age in America. Spends every cent of his money. When he isn't playing bucket-shops in town, he's playing with a bucket and shovel down at some beach with a chorus-girl."

The description possessed the merit of a grim quaintness unlike Elliot's usual style.

"Lael ought to get a job," he continued judicially. "There's no sense in her trying to play about with people she can't keep up with. She's too handicapped, anyway, by her family. Roddie, her brother, isn't much better than her father; and her mother's an idiot."

"I'm glad I haven't met them," said Gulian earnestly. "I only know Lael."

All this might be true, in fact, more trustworthy witnesses than Elliot had said so, but Gulian none the less experienced a further desire to slap Elliot upon his overly-pink cheeks just where they bulged up to make two demure lady-apples under his round shyly insolent eyes.

Poor little Lael! Or rather, poor tall Lael! Slim and luminous as a branch of cherry blossom! Young people were infinitely more lonely and entrapped than mature people. Especially young people whose family, as was usually the case, was a stupid family. What could be done when excellent people were still permitted to disgust their children with excellence, and wretched people were still permitted to overwhelm them with wretchedness?

But it was curious, when you came to think of it, how apparently every woman he—Gulian—happened to run across nowadays seemed to have some sort of unfortunate history. Perhaps it was because at present most likable women were unfortunate. Certainly the more intelligent were unsettled and unsettling. The tide of restlessness was rising, and whereas the more stupid, like Marian Gates and his sister-in-law Margaret, became spiritual socialists and were driven to charity and reform, urging more laws for a land already legalized to death, the more imaginative became spiritual anarchists and marooned themselves on the rocks of personal unhappiness . . . ran away from their husbands; or wanted to run away from their husbands; or had already before marriage decided to run away from their husbands, should those bewildered animals falter once upon a road to perfection such as never before had husbands been called upon to travel.

With all his dullness, Elliot was right, only he hadn't gone far enough. Not only Lael but all her sisters ought to go to work. In the impersonal fever of the professional attitude lay their one hope of happiness. There wasn't any danger of their forgetting their main business, which was marriage. But of course they wouldn't go to work until they were forced to do so. No one did. Inertia was the favorite vice of the human race.

Gulian removed his gaze from the countryside drifting past and resumed the conversation.

"I should say," he remarked coldly, "that a girl like Lael had a better chance than most. . . ." He didn't want to talk about her to Elliot; there was something unpleasant in talking about her to Elliot; and yet he was forced to go on by a devil of curiosity and stubbornness. "She's lovely to look at; she has brains; she has a good deal of character. What more do you want? Of course, like all girls of twenty-three, if she marries very soon, what she turns into will depend to some extent upon whom she marries; however, I don't think she'll marry a fool. She's got one great gift, you know."

"What's that?" Elliot avoided a dog.

Gulian's eyes, suddenly turned upon Elliot, were penetrating.

"A sense of humor."

"She has?" Elliot was doubtful. "Well, her humor isn't going to help her much. A girl without money or real position is up against it nowadays. I'm not a bit keen about her hanging around Marian all the time. I told Marian so this afternoon."

Elliot became a mere dwindling speck in the center of Gulian's eyes.

"You did?" he said shortly, and turned away.

"What?"

"I said, oh hell."

"What did you say it for?"

Gulian stretched out a detaining hand. "Because, Elliot, you're an ass, and I've wanted to tell you so for a long time. . . . Here's my gate. Let me out and I'll walk the rest of the way home."

The car stopped, and Gulian descended to the road and studied the driver smilingly.

"Elliot, my son," he said, "when you get to my age you'll find that beauty, properly used, is a much more potent weapon even than wealth. If you're wise you'll try to bribe beauty to hang around. As for the rest of it, avoid gossip."

The lady-apples in Elliot's cheeks flamed to a deeper color.

"It's all very well for you to talk," he spluttered, "— and I consider your manner damned rude—but evidently you don't know anything about Lael. She's made a fool of herself ever since she came out three years ago. She's old enough to know better."

Gulian sighed. "Well, she never will know better," he said, "Put your clutch in, Elliot; I might get angry."

He turned on his heel. Behind him he heard the grinding sound of Elliot nervously shifting gears.

He longed to kick Elliot. Elliot had a kickable figure.

And yet he was annoyed with himself for having shown so much emotion. He had been given the choice of two evils; either to keep quiet and be ashamed of himself, or else to speak his mind as he had and convey an impression of greater fervor than he felt. He had no especial right to worry about this girl, Lael Satori, and certainly no especial reason to defend her, and yet here he was doing both. He imagined uncomfortably Elliot's haste to return to Marian and confide, with the slight lisp that conquered him in moments of excitement, his opinion that Gulian was more than casually interested. Elliot would heighten the details; that would be his idea of revenge.

And recently Gulian had been too badly hurt to have details of this kind heightened in any manner whatsoever. He did not want to be hurt in the same way again. He had suffered more than he himself realized except in moments like this when his feelings were aroused. He had really cared for Vida, he told him-

self; if she had been a little wiser he would have loved her deeply. He had been upon the edge of loving her deeply. At least, he had loved her far better than any other member of the rather formidable and international list he had thought he had loved in the past. . . . There is no memory so short as that of passion.

What a list! The mere thought of it sickened him! What a waste of time! What a weariness—and, sometimes, shame of recollection! It took a man until he was thirty-five even to learn to be a dignified fool.

He might have added that as a rule it took him until he was past sixty even to learn to be a lover—at least, retrospectively. The young man is too busy to remember his lost love-affairs; the mature man too stern to forgive them; and it is only the aging man who can cover them all with a cloak of understanding and humor and tenderness. Most old men have a portrait gallery in which the portraits are beginning again to smile.

Particularly Gulian wished that in intervals of reflection like the present one the memory of Vida would not possess him so utterly. He would like to forget her eyes, and their long lashes; the turn of her white throat; the fragrance of her lips. He had found that the only way to drive these things out completely was to think about Lael, but now even Lael did not seem able to come to his rescue.

Strange how mistaken he had been about Vida, how deceived he had been in thinking that with her he had stumbled upon an extraordinarily intelligent and contented friendship, when all the while the major part of this friendship had been no more than the avoidance of mutual disagreements; an avoidance that each day of increasing intimacy had made less possible. In the same way he was sure that with Lael he had at last

found a genuine friendship and a genuine placidity—
but who could tell? He was becoming cynical. At all
events, he regretted that disparity of ages and a difference of interests would in the future prevent him
from seeing very much of Lael. . . . He recalled
the dewy mornings when he had ridden with her
between the green shadows of maple and pine
and oak. Perhaps it was because he was not in
the least in love with her, and so avoided the irrita-
bility of love, or perhaps because she was so much
younger and so not too critical of his opinions, but
these rides had been increasingly satisfactory, and he
did not think the reasons mentioned explained everything. He believed the satisfaction and radiant quality was due largely to something in the girl herself; a
fairness of outlook; a candor of statement and intent;
an avoidance of mental reservation; a willingness to
stand punishment or blame; attributes he was beginning to think were a part of the rising generation.

This girl was a Rosalind; even Marian and the
despised Elliot had some admirable Shakesperian
qualities; frankness, moral courage, a sense of adventure; a fine un-shockableness that made for a real
understanding of life and its hidden beauty. They
were—well, one couldn't say quite so much for Elliot;
but leaving him out of consideration—the other two
were strong-fibered and fresh and sweetly blended and
delicately fragrant. Possibly there was a new power
abroad in the world, especially in womanhood.

Several times during these rides, Lael and Gulian
had stopped at the brow of the hill above the bland
valley where they had first come across each other,
and had got off their horses, and had lain at full
length upon the warm grass and smoked. At such
times it had seemed as if Lael had been upon the edge

of articulateness, but frank as she was, she was still too young for frankness about herself and, in the manner of the young, too proud. Gulian, however, had been able fairly well to construct the limitations of her life and perceive the passionate efforts she was making to rid herself of these limitations. He thought he understood her occasional tendency towards desperation, her occasional harshness, her occasional ferocity; her almost savage independence; although these, all save the first, and perhaps even that too, were the results to some extent as well of the unconscious philosophy of her age.

Her sense of independence delighted and amused him especially. She had a horror of being helped physically. She would have preferred to break an arm rather than allow Gulian to assist her. She spoke scornfully of his 'protective instinct,' called his more obvious gentlenesses 'Victorian.' Gulian over-emphasized the latter in order to provoke this charming juvenile rage.

In short, he felt that he was accumulating wisdom concerning these mysterious, much talked about, much libeled younger people, and he was anxious to confide the results of his investigation to Drusilla.

Succinctly they—these younger people—fell into the simple old divisions, usually forgot. Most of them were vulgar and loud and ugly, but then most of the rest of the world was vulgar and loud and ugly. Whenever the gentle and low-voiced and unselfish began to outnumber the loud and vulgar, the majority of problems now so vexatious would automatically be solved.

Even the mystery about them had been greatly exaggerated, as mysteries usually are. There was mystery, but it was merely the inevitable mystery of youth; of anything simple and inexpressive. As to the rest of it, just as he had always thought, these young people were what young people had always been; a little irresponsible, a little confused, a little self-seeking, a little cruel, completely sure that they had been granted a new dispensation and were going to change the world; but in the main, quick and fine, and hot-blooded, and chivalrous, and argumentative, and dreamers of dreams, and lovers of beauty. What differences there were, were differences of coloring and not of fabric; and what differences there were, marked an advance; an advance of courage, and sophistication, and clear-sightedness, and—most saving of graces!—intelligent skepticism.

Driven back upon themselves by the fact of the war, unable to explain its horror or reconcile it to common sense, these young people were angrily opposed to the romanticism which they thought had been its cause; and born into an age of increased illumination, both physical and mental, they were not to be frightened by the bogies of superstition nor the ordinary taboos. They were not, for instance, impressed by the unqualified command to honor their fathers and mothers, and very properly failed to do so unless the fathers and mothers deserved honoring. Some day this would result in parents ceasing to settle down to complacent physical and mental deterioration at the age of forty. Sentimentality, the greatest burden life has had to bear, was being thrown overboard. The evil magic of the spoken word behind which all bad men have sheltered since time began, was losing its validity. The fact that a man beat his chest and proclaimed himself a Christian or a patriot no longer was allowed to pass without investigation. Heaven help the hypocrite when these young people began to get things into their own hands! . . .

But Gulian at the moment was not thinking of these things, he was thinking of Vida and Lael and his own inevitable lack of intelligence where women were concerned, and he had reached the very lowest point of self-esteem by the time he had come to the terrace at the back of 'Hibernia' and, passing through the formal garden, had taken the path that led down through lilac-bushes and bridal-wreath to the little forget-me-not choked stream.

For a few hundred yards the stream twisted its way across a meadow and then plunged into the wood that separated 'Hibernia' from the hedges and fences of 'Hill House,' the name the Gates had given to their place. Where the stream entered the wood there was a path that led to a stile. Gulian had often taken this short-cut when he was in a hurry to reach 'Hill House,' and once or twice had brought Lael and Marian back by the same route to see his gardens.

Now he crossed the meadow and with no particular destination in view, turned into the amber gloom of the trees. A scarlet tanager uttered its chip-chúrr, chip-chúrr and shot past him like an arrow tipped with flame. Underfoot the ground was starry with myrtle, scattered years before by some hand that loved the spring. He was studying the myrtle with a mind not very intent upon horticulture, when he saw, walking towards him through the perpendicular maze of tawny trunks, a girl in white, and looked again, and recognized Lael. He had left her only an hour before drinking tea with Marian.

He stepped into her path smiling, and she raised her head and stared at him for a moment without speaking.

His smiling eyes became grave. He realized that she
was for some reason very close to tears. Two spots
of color burned in her cheeks and her mouth was
drawn into a straight line.

"You wanted to see me?" he asked gently, his
facetious greeting silent on his lips.

She nodded her head.

"Well, come along. We'll walk for awhile, and
then you can tell me what you want."

He turned about and fell in beside her and for a
step or two she maintained her silence. His laughing
Rosalind had been transformed suddenly into a tragic
woman; a woman of no age, for tragedy makes all
men and women contemporaries.

"Something has hurt you very much?"

She nodded her head again.

"Can I help you?"

She paused—they had come to the edge of the
meadow—and put out a fluttering hand that touched
his arm and was instantly withdrawn.

"Go on."

"I . . . I don't know why I bother you, but
you've been very good to me."

"Oh, yes—wonderful! . . . But go on."

"I . . . I'm not kicking; I deserve all I get, but
. . . Oh, damn!"

"Go on," said Gulian.

"I'm no good!" There was an edge of a wail in her
voice.

Gulian faced her and seized the slender shoulders between his hands and shook them with a fierce
gentleness. "Stop it!" he commanded, "and tell me
what you were going to tell me. . . . I thought you
were a good sport."

She raised her eyes to his as if she were an obedient child.

"There isn't much to tell. I'm going away. . . . I'd go tonight if it wouldn't look too silly. I've come to say goodbye."

"Marian's done something to you?"

"Well——"

"Marian's done something to you?"

"Yes."

"I knew she would sooner or later. You're silk to her buckram. What was it?"

The girl twisted herself out of his grasp and looked down. When she spoke it was rapidly and in a fairly even voice.

"I told you I was no good," she said, "and I'm not. I've been fooling you—all these fine things I've been saying. They're what I'd like to be, not what I am. I'm a darned idiot . . . only good luck has kept me from being worse. But I'm not kicking—I try to be a good sport; only these old things keep coming up when you think they're all done with. . . . And—I thought Marian was my friend."

She was studying the point of her white sandal as it dug a little trench in the damp earth of the path.

Gulian nodded his head with a grave sarcasm. "Yes," he agreed, "you've fooled me horribly. I'm very ingenuous—I've led a cloistered life. What have you done, robbed a bank?"

She looked up quickly, half indignant at his levity; then changed her mind.

"Two years ago," she said, "I had a worse fight than usual with my family."

"That was natural."

"They said I was staying out too late—they didn't like the people I was running about with. . . ."

"Well?"

"They said if I kept it up, some night they would lock me out."

Gulian drew a deep breath and spoke softly to the trees. "The damn fools!" he said. In his ordinary voice he asked: "And they did?"

"Yes."

"Left you in the street?"

"Yes."

"What did you do?"

"Why, I went home with the man I was with. . . . He was an old friend."

Gulian thought that the silence that followed was unnaturally prolonged. He heard again the chip-chúrr, chip-chúrr of the tanager.

"You mean. . . ?" he asked.

"I sat up all night in his library. He was very kind."

"You idiot!" said Gulian softly. "You blamed little idiot! You ought to have been spanked! I would have understood you better if you hadn't sat up all night in his library. . . . And you did this solely to make a point? Well, it was a silly one." He interrupted himself abruptly. ". . . What sort of a man was this friend?" he asked sharply.

"What difference does that make?"

"A great deal."

"He was a very nice man."

"Oh, yes, I know that, but what age was he . . . a mature man?"

"About your age."

"Then he wasn't a very nice man. . . . No, wait a minute! . . . or a very wise one. He was a blundering bad man. If he'd been a nice man he'd have gotten you into your house if he'd had to get a policeman to break down the door."

The color swept back into Lael's face. "I won't . . ." she began angrily.

"Yes, you will!" said Gulian, "you'll listen to me until I'm done. Now mark what I say. This 'friend' of yours afterwards did a lot of little things you didn't like, didn't he? Yes, he would. Ever since you've been just a trifle on your guard against him? Exactly! Well, that's because he's a coward, but he thinks if he's patient enough some day something will happen. I know his kind."

Gulian raised his hand. "Wait a minute, I haven't finished.

"Now to go a step further. How do you suppose this story ever got out? Your family certainly wouldn't tell. Marian has just accused you of it, hasn't she? Elliot, of course, was her immediate source of information—some day I'll try to get even with Elliot—but how do you suppose Elliot heard about it in the first place? Just remember, only you and the man and your family knew anything about it. Lael, think these things over. Think about them, and . . ." He made an impatient gesture. ". . . forget them. They aren't worth bothering about. They aren't important in the least. Nobody can really hurt you but yourself, you know. The same impulses that made you do this absurdity . . . and other absurdities, possibly . . . are the same impulses that can make you a great woman. I don't give tuppence-ha'-penny for a person, man or woman, who never committed a folly, anyway. Life doesn't consist in not doing foolish things, it consists in picking yourself up afterwards. It's only the fool who can ever learn to be truly wise, for he's the only one who can possibly know how un-

profitable folly is. It isn't morality that makes the
mature person weatherproof, it's boredom; a knowledge of the infinite weariness of sin. Don't worry,
Lael, my dear. You're getting over the things now that
ten years ago women used to save up for the purpose
of ruining the middle-age of their husbands. And
don't you, especially, worry. I know what you are.
I'm not a fool about women. . . ." He hesitated.
"That is," he continued hurriedly, "unless I happen to
be in love with one."

"And now," he said, stepping back, "I'll tell you
something else. I heard a much garbled account of
this escapade of yours long ago—shortly after I met
you."

"You heard?" A hand fluttered up to Lael's throat.
"Who told you?"

"My Aunt Virginia; she tells me most things. I
was expatiating on your good looks and I suppose she
was afraid I might fall in love with you. It was the
thing that made me especially want to know you.
Possibly it accounts for our present intimacy."

"But how did she know?"

"I've already tried to account for it."

For a moment Lael dug the toe of her shoe into the
ground again; when she looked up it was with a kin-
dling anger in her eyes. "If you knew so much, why
did you cross-examine me?" she asked. "It wasn't
very nice of you."

"I knew very little. Now I do know."

"You mean . . . ? I don't like you."

"No," said Gulian gravely, "I don't like myself
either. But then in this confused age one doesn't take
things for granted. I told you I was investigating.
Don't be cross. Come on. I'll take you back to the
stile."

She gave a little gasp but obeyed him and they walked in silence back to where the four-rail fence came down across the hill and through the woods. "I'll be back in town in a day or so myself," he said. "May I come to see you?"

She turned towards him and put out a hand impulsively.

"You're a good man, Gilly," she said shiningly, her gray eyes a trifle misty. "I'm sorry I was angry. You're the best man I've ever met."

"Good Lord!" exclaimed Gulian incredulously.

She crossed the stile and was gone.

Gulian walked slowly home, across the meadow and up the path through the lilac-bushes and the bridal-wreath. On his desk he found a letter from Doctor Ellis, couched in the warmly sympathetic manner of the modern specialist.

DEAR MR. EYRE: (it ran)

In answer to your inquiry of 17/5/21, I would say that your father is in a very dangerous condition. He may die at any moment; on the other hand, if he takes proper care of himself and experiences no worry or shock, he may live a long while.

If this is not satisfactory, I should be very glad to have you consult someone else.

Yours truly,

M. T. ELLIS.

Underneath in brackets was written "Dictated by Dr. Ellis, but signed in his absence."

Gulian twisted the letter between his fingers. He had wanted so much to be at 'Hibernia' with his father! . . . He raised his head. Well, by thunder, he would be! Doctors weren't infallible. They were no more readers of the future than anyone else. His father's bravery would be a factor in any illness. He had the gentle inflexible pride that makes even death respectful. Furthermore, there wasn't the slightest reason why he should experience any shock; or why he shouldn't take care of himself. Medicine as at present practiced was too material; it left too much out of account that inscrutable thing the human soul.

CHAPTER III

VANNYA BECOMES ARTICULATE

FROM a comparatively clear horizon, certainly with a celerity and an unexpectedness possible only to those who speak a language no one else will learn to speak, Vannya had burst into fluent, incorrect, and highly-colored English. It was a composite language, taken partially from the tradesmen around Washington Square, embellished with the solecisms of models, inflated with the absurdities of Greenwich Village, and only in places clarified by intercourse with Mr. Eyre and people of Mr. Eyre's kind.

Gulian had to some extent been prepared for this by the letters his father had written him while he had been at 'Hibernia,' Vannya, apparently, having been very attentive to Mr. Eyre during Gulian's absence.

"I am becoming exceedingly fond of this young captive Russian of yours," Mr. Eyre had written, "he is a charming, casual, earnest young man—that is to say, beneath an exterior of carelessness he conceals a highly-tempered singleness of purpose. However, he is too civilized to be ever anything but gay. Unlike most of us Americans, he doesn't worry about anything save what absolutely demands worry. Sometimes he doesn't even worry about that. He keeps his eye on what he is doing and accepts smilingly the rest of life. I think he will go far. Besides, one must remember that he is an aristocrat and so is accustomed to taking a large slice of life—and all its gifts—for granted.

"Drusilla has been asking him out to dinner, and so have some others, and he has bought evening-clothes. The first night he could not tie his white tie as he has been in uniform ever since he was a child. 'Eet wass ter-rii-ble!' he told me. 'I haf twenty meenutes! I cannodt do eet! Oh damn! I am punk! I run down to th' streedt. I see a vera kind man. I stop heem. 'Sare,' I say, 'can you tie my tie? I am what you call a dumb-bell.' 'Cartainly,' he say, 'coom to my house.' . . . Oh, a vera nice man! A doctor. He lif jus' aroun' th' corner. I haf coom to know heem vera well.' I consider this a typical Slav story."

Gulian called Vannya up the morning after his return and that afternoon at about four o'clock went down to Washington Place to see him. He found Vannya sitting in an exotic circle of nine or ten male and female compatriots dispensing raisin cake and very strong tea in glasses. "Hot Dog!" he said delightedly at Gulian's entrance.

Everyone was smoking with alternate intensity and languor and the conversation being mostly in Russian, Gulian understood very little of it, but he imagined the gestures of the conversationalists were typical. There would be moments of silence into which someone would cast a remark, and then a babel of ejaculation, comment, and dissent would break forth, during which those forced by sheer weight of numbers to go unheard would bounce gently up and down on their chairs with baffled eagerness.

A beautiful young creature with burning eyes, evidently mistaking Gulian for someone connected with the stage, insisted upon telling him of her troubles while trying unsuccessfully to get a position as an actress. She had had no experience as an actress, and Gulian could not understand why she thought she could be one, but no doubt her life had been always a matter of gusty Slavic idealism and carelessness of details.

"A Roussian!" she said, imitating a discourteous manager. "Th' place iss feel-thee weeth Roussians! And now . . . what do you theenk of that? He wass a bear, that man!"

Gulian was amazed once more at the incredible bravery of these people. He wondered what he would have done under similar circumstances. . . . Well, probably just what they were doing. Heroism, after all, is usually a matter of circumstance. It is extraordinarily difficult to kill the human race off. It has been tried unsuccessfully.

One by one the guests departed, leaving the studio to Gulian and its owner. The light, falling through the great sky-window and through the windows opening upon the street, lengthened. A hurdy-gurdy broke into wailing jazz. The unseen street became more vocal, as streets do in the expansive pellucid half hour that comes between summer afternoon and summer evening. A wagon rattled by, a truck droned; various people thought they were lowering their voices.

"Tomorrow," said Vannya, "weel be June."

Gulian had been looking about the studio. Its original bareness had been but little changed; a piano had been moved in, several chairs, a couple of tables; an old gilt-framed mirror and a couch. On the walls some prints had been tacked up. But that was all except the debris of Vannya's work; easels, canvases, stretchers, a palette, and scattered tubes of paint. Not quite all, the disorder was not completely masculine. On one table there was a cheap vase filled with flowers and on another a diminutive feminine hat and gloves, and in one corner reclined an unmistakably feminine umbrella. Gulian tried not to look at these things.

"You look at th' hat and glofes?" Vannya asked softly. "They are those of th' young woman who lifs in thees apartment. . . . But I hadt forgot. I am een America. I should not leef them aboudt."

He got up and collecting the offending articles, went into the bedroom and came back immediately, standing opposite Gulian, his hands in his pockets, a quizzical smile on his lips.

"My friendt," he said, "I could nodt egsplain to you or to my other vera kind American friendts. To them sooch a theeng means either lofe or a brutality. But weeth me eet iss not so. Thees young woman she iss a Belgian and vera lonely . . . she iss here for a year een a modiste's. I am vera lonely, too. We both speeg French. We laugh together at—I cannodt egsplain eet—th' way Americans do nodt laugh. We are vera happy. Eet iss—what you call—childish. We do nodt lofe each other, no; but we are vera goot friendts. Eef we lofed each other eet would nodt be so goot; we might be unhappy."

He was silent for a moment.

"She iss going away een two days," he continued thoughtfully.

"For good?"

"She iss going home—to Belgium. There iss a young man she iss to marry."

"Good God!" said Gulian. "You mean she is going to marry immediately after this?"

Vannya looked sorrowfully puzzled. "Why nodt?" he exclaimed. "I haf nodt hurt her. I haf only helped her nodt to be lonely, and laughed with her, and— what you say—petted her. That iss goot for any girl. Besides, thees young man, he iss a small trader; he will nodt care greatly even eef he knows—Oh yes, maybe talk, but een his heart he will be proudt. . . . I am a preence."

"I have always understood," said Gulian dryly, "that recently the Belgians have become shamefully democratic."

Vannya remained mournful. "You are ashamed for me, my friendt, are you nodt? Eet iss a pidy you ever saw th' leetle hat."

Gulian shook his head wearily. "Oh no, I'm not," he said. "It's none of my business, anyhow. Besides, I've lived too much out of this country to bother a great lot about things like that. I'm only wondering why Anglo-Saxons—Americans and English—make such a fuss about what conquers most of them anyhow. If we'd only cultivate an undivided mind and shut up about it; let those who want to go wrong, go wrong and be damned to them, and those who want to go straight, go straight and be equally damned."

He got up from his chair restlessly and walked over to the window and stared moodily down into the street, his hands in his pockets. In a moment or so, he faced around and came back. In the light of Vannya's insouciance his own recent experience troubled him more than ever.

"The bother is," he continued, "that the Anglo-Saxon can't do this sort of thing without involving his soul. He never gets off scot-free; neither does the woman. They fall in love with each other. We're sentimentalists; mystics. I don't think it's adventitious, or the result of training, I think it's ingrained, and so I suppose we'll go on to the end of time harried and devil-ridden and unhappy. But I imagine also it's what has made us do most of the fine things we've done. Loveliness is only the distillation of misery;

the essence of some soul's attempt to escape. That is why we write the finest love songs in the world, and you indulge in lyric politics. You're free personally but bound politically; and we're free politically but bound personally."

"You're upsedt," said Vannya soothingly. "I will play you sometheengs."

He crossed over to the piano and pulled out several sheets of dog-eared music from the pile on the scarred top.

"Thees iss Sibelus," he explained. "Eet iss a pippin."

Gulian left his chair and strolled over to the couch and sank down on it. He wished that music would either not come so near to explaining life, or else would go just a fraction further and explain it utterly. It led you up to the edge of mystery and then abruptly stopped. However, there was nothing else that went even half so far, except, perhaps, every now and then the glimmer of an experiment in the quiet of a laboratory.

"Would you lak' some more?" asked Vannya.

"No," said Gulian. ". . . That is, I would like some more, but I have to go." He arose to his feet. "Tomorrow, my father leaves for 'Hibernia'—you know—our place up on the Hudson. Wouldn't you like to go up with him, or join him later? He's very fond of you. I can't be there much myself, for I'm going into business, yet I don't want to leave him alone. It would be a great favor if you would. Besides, I would like you to see the American countryside just now. It's lovely. You could paint."

Vannya's face brightened.

"Goot," he said; "maybe I weel. Th' school iss closed. I am seek of cities. Also, I weel be vera lonely."

Gulian gathered together his hat and stick and opened the door that gave upon the steep flight of enclosed steps that led to the lower stories of the house. He looked over his shoulder, his hand on the knob. Vannya was again at the piano. The studio was bathed in the quiet light of the approaching evening. It was about half-past five o'clock. He went on down the stairs with the strains of a Slavic waltz accompanying him. In a dark corner of the second floor, a corner that smelled faintly of dust and cooking cabbage, he passed the shadowy figure of a woman ascending, and he had almost gone by unrecognising when something in her carriage made him look back and he saw that it was Drusilla.

He stopped astonished.

"Dru!" he called.

She paused on the step above him and turned her head, one hand grasping the rail of the balusters.

"Gilly! As I live! I thought you were still at 'Hibernia.' "

"I came back yesterday."

She faced about as he went up closer to her and smiled with a crinkling of her eyelids. She was dressed in a little suit of gray, a gray hat with a touch of rose on her head, and he thought he had never seen her look younger or more entrancing. But there was something in her manner, a sharp note of rather exaggerated cordiality, that made him uncomfortable. If it had been any other woman but Drusilla he would have suspected that she had known him from the first and had deliberately tried to avoid him.

"Is Vannya in?" she asked.

"I've just left him."

"He's painting my portrait," she explained, with a little laugh.

"At this hour?"

"No, of course not. He hasn't started, but I'm arranging for it. I don't know how good he'll be, but I want to give him a start. When are you coming to see me, Gilly?"

"When do you go to Stockbridge?"

"On the second. It's frightfully late and hot. In three weeks or so I'm going to have some people over Sunday. Will you come?"

"Most assuredly."

"Anyone you especially want?"

Gulian was thoughtful. "Yes, there is," he admitted. "I'd like Lael Satori. She interests me."

Drusilla tinkled into laughter. "So you did get on, didn't you? I judged so from Lael's letter. Well, she's a lamb. But people don't understand her altogether."

Gulian became resentful. "I like her very much," he retorted stiffly; "but I like her, and that's all. And for God's sake, Dru, don't get intuitive. I'm twice her age and I wouldn't marry the Queen of Sheba."

Drusilla's laughter was renewed. "Gilly," she said, "it's all I can do at times not to kiss you. Come for lunch tomorrow."

He watched her as she walked slowly up the stairs and disappeared around their curve. A vague uneasiness like the heat mist of a humid day surrounded him. Why had she—he was sure now that she had—wanted so much to pass him unseen? That wasn't like Drusilla.

He traversed the musty length of the front hall and came out into the pungent warmth of the street, and turned towards Washington Square. A stray taxi passed him and he hailed it.

"East Forty-fifth Street!" he said, giving Vida's address.

Something about the heat, the languid hour, his talk with Vannya was sending him on his journey. If Vannya took life so easily, why couldn't he? What difference did it make, anyhow? If he could only throw his cap over the mill with some degree of abandon! Lean back and relax! But even as he wished for this he knew that underneath his half-conscious desire was still a third layer of reaction, a thin stratum of resistance that probably at any crucial moment would render him comparatively safe.

That interview with Vida remained as an etching on Gulian's memory. There was an acid quality about it; a curious separate clear-cut distinctness that cut it off from any events that preceded or followed it; an arranged sequence of effect unlike casual modern intercourse. And yet, despite this clarity of line, the intention in its fullness remained mysteriously elusive, the inner point not completely explained. Gulian felt as if he had taken part in some odd irritating Oriental clash of purposes in which symbols and gestures stood for the franker methods of the West. And he was mortified, not only for his own lack of adroitness, but for Vida. Somehow the thing was too contrived not to be vulgar.

He had, indeed, taken into account the possibility of Vida's refusing to see him at all, and he would have understood such an abrupt dismissal, although it would have disappointed him and he would have thought it silly, but the normal haste with which the maid returned and informed him that Mrs. Prendegast asked him to step into the library, prepared him for at least conventional cordiality.

As he crossed the threshold of the delicately gray room he knew that this was not to be. He had the feeling of coming unexpectedly upon a tableau composed for his benefit. His heart, already beating uncertainly, faltered still more.

The three long windows were as usual open but not a breath of air stirred the warm coolness. The blue smoke of cigarettes hung in vanishing coils half way up to the ceiling; and in chairs near one of the windows, a wicker table between them, a silver tray and pitcher and glasses upon it, were Vida and a man. Vida was sitting erect with a languid straightness, her arms, half bare in their flowing sleeves, stretched out along the arms of her chair, her small shapely head, under a violet hat with a broad brim, turned in the direction of Gulian's entrance. She was wearing an evening dress of softly draped violet and the severe line of its neck made her face look especially cameo-like and immature. Back of her an evening wrap was spread out.

She surveyed Gulian thoughtfully with no expression in her dark eyes save perhaps a barely perceptible gleam of amusement. Then she smiled and spoke in a casually welcoming voice.

"It's nice to see you," she said. "I didn't know you were in town. I'm sorry I have to run away so soon —I wish you'd telephoned me—but I'm dining out with Mr. . . . Oh yes, of course! Mr. Eyre, this is Mr. Sedgewick."

Her companion had risen to his feet and was staring at Gulian with the same deliberate slowness of inspection with which Vida had greeted him, as if he too were in possession of a secret that interested and amused him.

"I know your brother Philip," he said briefly.

"Will you have a drink?" asked Vida. "It's some sort of stuff with gin in it. It's really a cocktail. It isn't bad."

"Thanks," said Gulian and accepted a glass.

Gulian sipped his drink and regarded Sedgewick's half-averted face broodingly. In some ways it was an uncommunicative face, excessively well-cared for, round, white, compact, self-assured, a short moustache rising above the full lips; what was left of the reddish hair brushed with infinite care into two smart little horns above the ears. But in other ways it was fairly easy to tell what the face had looked at for the most part during the fifty years or so of its existence . . . women, food, drink; occasionally some implement of sport so that its owner might be returned all the more vigorous to the main business of life . . . women, food, drink. The short powerful body was clothed in a beautifully cut suit and the short feet were incased in shining brown shoes and white spats. On the little finger of the thick short right hand a ring of two intertwined serpents, their eyes precious stones, twinkled.

"Did you amuse yourself in the country?" asked Vida languidly.

"I was very busy," Gulian stammered. "There was a great deal to be seen about—we really farm, you know—and then I had to get the house ready for my father. He's going up tomorrow."

Vida laughed softly. "You do love the country, don't you? I'm afraid I hate it. I'm too much of a cockney to enjoy it except when it's condensed into a neighborhood of pleasant people."

Gulian once more regretted his letter. "There are any amount of pleasant people where I was. . . ."

he began stiffly, and then he interrupted himself with a smile. He had an idea that nothing would please Vida quite so much as to entrap him into some show of childish irritation.

The atmosphere was oppressive. He would have liked to have taken his departure immediately had it not been necessary to say a few more sentences in order to avoid showing pique. He suspected that pique was what Vida especially wished to arouse in him—that, together with other uncomfortable emotions.

Vida was anxious to create—for her own satisfaction, he supposed; possibly to hold him up to the ridicule of Sedgewick; perhaps to corroborate something she had told Sedgewick—the impression that he—Gulian —was a tongue-tied and awkward creature. He imagined her describing him to Sedgewick as a gentle and gauche nuisance who had recently been trying to complicate her life. If this suspicion were true, he wondered if she had invented such a fabrication to soothe her own sense of loss, or to keep hidden from Sedgewick something she did not want Sedgewick to know? Possibly both?

At all events, the present experience was new in Gulian's fluent life; and enraging and terrifying. It was like suddenly losing your powers of coordination; like running against spider webs in the dark.

Either Sedgewick had been instructed in his part (had been told, that is, that Gulian was a very stupid man and a bore—and, worst of all an amorous bore) or else he had caught the coloring of the moment, for he promptly subsided into a silent lack of interest. He crossed his plump hands over his stomach and stared at Vida absorbedly. Gulian, looking at him, found this contemplation so naive, so pensive, so possessive and revealing that he was startled. The color rushed back into his cheeks. Who was this man? Vida had never even mentioned his name. And yet they knew each other excessively well—there was no doubt about that.

Abruptly his smouldering inclination to get away became a fire of baffled hate and nausea. Flames of disgust swept over him. He wanted to be clear of this white fat man and this shadowy secret woman; to forget forever this cool gray room with its undercurrent of intrigue. There was no longer any solace of humor in the situation, even humor of the most bitter kind.

"I've been telling Randall here," Vida was saying, "what a frighteningly learned man you are, and how much good the few times I saw you did me. I suppose you naturally would like the country. It would give you an opportunity to think. Did you do any writing? . . . You're writing a book, aren't you?"

"Yes."

"Or is it verse?"

"Both."

Gulian got to his feet. Strange how women walked so confidently upon the thin ice of a man's code of restraint. In two sentences he could smash the surface beneath Vida's feet and leave her to drown in the depths of her own duplicity. He wanted to say, 'You ought to know. I've read you everything I've ever written'; but instead he smiled down at her and took her hand.

For a moment his anger wavered. Her hand was very small and, it seemed to him, unnaturally cold. He did not think he was mistaken in imagining that it returned his grip with a convulsive, involuntary pressure. Then, too, his shadow had fallen across her shutting out Sedgewick, obliterating the rest of the

room, and this brought her for that instant close to him
him again.

"I think we'd better be going, as well," suggested
Sedgewick. "We've got a long drive ahead of us."

Vida glanced hurriedly up at Gulian. "Wait!" she
murmured. "Walk down to the street with us."

He wondered if he was absurd in believing that,
rather desperately, she was trying to prolong what she
knew, save for some accidental meeting, would be their
last sight of each other.

She arose from her chair and Sedgewick stepped
forward, almost brushing Gulian aside in his eagerness
to help her on with her cloak. But there his haste
ended. His short brutal hands, over-manicured, red,
hovered lingeringly above the white beautiful neck.
He twisted the owner of the neck about gently and
fastened the cloak under her chin. And, as if she had
remembered her role again, or regretted her temporary
weakness, Vida smiled up into his eyes; a little secret
knowing smile that once more shut Gulian out completely from whatever it was these two people understood so well between them.

"It's so hot," she protested.

Sedgewick shook his head. "I'm driving myself
. . . its my open car."

Gulian followed them out of the room and through
the tapestry-hung hall to the door of the elevator.

In the short flight from the second story to the first,
he thought Vida stood unnecessarily close to him. He
could feel her soft warmth touching him, smell the
perfume of her hair as he looked down at her. Perhaps she wanted him to feel a final pang at what he
was losing. Women do such things instinctively; even
very careful women do them without knowing what
they imply.

"You are going to be in town long?" she asked.

"All summer. I'm going into business."

"Into business?" They had left the elevator and were walking across the discreet lobby towards the many-paned entrance. "Then the butterfly—" she laughed "—the very serious-minded butterfly has been broken upon the wheel at last? Well, we all are, sooner or later, aren't we? Women—" there was an almost imperceptible but unmistakable pause "—especially, only in a different way. In the end they always become what events and people make them, don't they, . . . particularly what people make them?" She stressed the silence again. "I'm made." Gulian supposed she had been waiting for this opportunity.

The blood surged into his head. This was the final untruth. It was her own character; her own inability to face life squarely; her readiness for self-deception that had made her whatever she was. He heard himself speaking as if from a distance in an odd, thin voice.

"That's a lie!" he said wearily.

The fear in her face arrested him. Oh, of course! . . . She wouldn't want this fat man to know what they were really talking about, would she? Well, he wouldn't give her away. She could keep her shoddy little secret so far as he was concerned.

"I'm awfully sorry!" he apologized, laughing shamefacedly. He hoped that his voice was natural. "I say rude things without meaning them. Only, I feel very strongly on that particular subject. I don't think anyone worth his or her salt is ever made—once maturity is reached—to any great extent by circumstances or people. It lies deeper than that. . . . And—I'm not a serious-minded butterfly. . . . I'm neither a butterfly, nor serious."

Beside the curb a long-bodied runabout in brewster-green slumbered, the instruments on its dashboard glittering in the rays of the sinking sun.

Gulian helped Vida into the low-swung seat.

"I don't believe I'm supposed to park here," said Sedgewick, "but I took a chance."

"Goodbye," said Gulian.

For a moment he held Vida's eyes squarely. It seemed to him that the light went out of them, leaving them bruised and dull; dark with some vague terror.

"Goodbye," he said again, and lifted his hat and turned on his heel.

How strange and useless and baffling! Here was a woman who had come very close to him, almost as close as a woman can come. Across the narrow but abysmal chasm that separates personality from personality he and she had almost built a bridge, almost touched hands; and in the end all their pains had gone for nothing. The slow adjustments, the delighted discoveries, the delicate mortising of weeks had been ripped apart in as many hours. The tragedy of defeated understanding—the most common tragedy there is—appeared to him as the most hopeless, most pitiful tragedy of all. The universe was so big, men and women so small and temporary; for such a brief fraction of time were they given leave to occupy this miniature planet, thick with the dust of the dead, already crowded with the ruthless still unborn intentions of the multitudes to come! They were isolated and adrift. They came and they went. None save a tiny handful knew of them. Twenty years after the most beloved of men was dead all his capacity for loving had become at best but a thin mist of memory. And yet these little lonely men and women walked up and down the world cherishing their lonelinesses—

though it broke their hearts; strutting in their antag-
onisms, jostling their contemporaries, the only people
who would ever really care what happened to them,
destroying the only two things they knew anything
about, love and life; the two things that, once destroyed, could never be put together again.

The occupants of the same era should band themselves into a single great fraternity, if for no other
purpose than to fling a defiance into the faces of their
common enemies, time and death.

If Vida had wished to destroy Gulian's own immediate emotional life she could not have succeeded better.
Never before had he so wished to withdraw into himself; to avoid throwing out any possible future tendrils
of affection for any possible future wounding. The
more a man expanded the greater were his chances for
sorrow and rout. Nor, despite his re-assembled con-
victions that in Vida's case he had done the best he
knew how, was he free, any more than on the afternoon of her letter, from a sense of guilt. No matter
what he had proposed, or withheld himself from doing,
the mere fact that he had crossed her path and so had
perhaps confused it, was enough to haunt him.

Gulian did not telephone Lael as he had intended,
nor go to see her. His call upon Vida had put him in
no mood for such things. He was old, anyway, and Lael
was young. No good could come from their friendship
—probably it wouldn't even remain a friendship but
like all other male and female companionships would
turn into some sort of undesired agitation or recrimination. Undoubtedly both; the former preceding the
latter. He wanted neither.

CHAPTER IV

HEAT AND COOLNESS

THE weeks that followed were particularly hot. Gulian wondered if they had been designed to further test his determination to be a business man. The city lay down to sleepless nights and arose to glaring days. In Madison Place the leaves wilted around their edges and turned a faint dust gray above their green. All the houses in the discreet close were boarded up save for a couple which were clubs, and in and out of the latter, tired men came and went in the lightest of suits, their eyes absent-minded with the look of those temporarily bereft of their usual orientations—wives, families, homes.

Margaret had departed for Westbury, and Drusilla had gone north to Stockbridge, and Aunt Virginia, accompanied by Octavia Hiatt, whom she had kept in a humid state of suspense by refusing to disclose her plans until the last moment, and by Ella, and by the young chauffeur who still gloomily retained his position, had motored to her accustomed hotel in the Catskills, where she was received as always with mixed feelings of pleasure and dread.

"I honor you," she told the proprietor, Mr. Hacknall, "by coming to your place. I do it because I am old and it is a habit. No one comes to the Catskills any more. Tell that girl in your office to take the powder off her nose. She will give you a reputation you don't deserve."

Mr. Eyre the first of June had as usual betaken himself to 'Hibernia,' leaving behind him closed shutters and rooms filled with ghostly baize-covered furniture and an alpaca-coated Prescott to look after Gulian. Prescott had been glad to stay. He didn't like the country and recently, together with all his friends, he had become so engrossed in the making of homemade beer that he hated to leave his own kitchen even for a night. He attended to Gulian's rooms, from which the carpets had been taken up and matting laid down, and got his breakfast for him and his dinner, whenever the latter was desired, although most of the time Gulian preferred to go to a restaurant. The shrouded house was a trifle solitary after sunset, and Prescott's discreetly conversational presence was at times depressing. It was like having an uncle about who wouldn't really tell you things. For twenty years Gulian had known Prescott better than anyone else in the world except his father, and yet, he didn't know him at all. In his boyhood he had often borrowed money from Prescott and in his exultant, despairing youth, when life seemed almost too glamorous and close pressing to be borne, certainly too much so to keep away from in any or the least particular, Prescott had at times put him to bed and not infrequently protected him from the consequences of not having been able to find just the right step at the right moment in the dimness of early morning.

Afterwards Prescott had brought him his breakfast and Gulian had wanted to weep on the black-coated breast, had wanted to explain that it wasn't because he had any sinister or uncontrollable taste for evil but simply because there were moments when existence reached a brilliant agonizing climax from which it was necessary to try to go on. . . .

The secret of most of youth's misdemeanors . . .; not sordidness, but an attempt to pluck unpluckable stars. . . . Yet, for all this, Gulian knew Prescott no better than in the beginning. An absurd relationship!

A week after Mr. Eyre's departure, Vannya joined him at 'Hibernia' and to judge from letters was enjoying himself hugely; sitting up very late, and reading, and studying, and getting up very late in the morning, and painting persistently even in the middle of the day when all sensible people were avoiding the heat. "He is proving a source of shocked amazement to the Gates family," Mr. Eyre wrote. "He goes in bathing with Marian in the most abbreviated of costumes. But then a prince, even a Russian prince, is something."

As for Gulian, he felt that he was living in a strange vacuum of loneliness and concentration. This didn't displease him; he rather liked it. It was a new experience and restful. Only at times—particularly late at night when he was alone in the house —he felt a sudden new fierce desire to see Lael. He and she seemed to be the only people left in this great populated wilderness. Between him and her the multitude of intervening rooftrees seemed to melt away. He wondered what she was doing.

His days were regular, isolated, and unmarked. The city in its present state interested him. During the mornings and the afternoons it was busy enough and sufficiently crowded with familiar faces, but at night it took on a novel spaciousness. Not that it was any the less over-crowded, but the scarcity of familiar human contact made suddenly near and more distinct the presence of unfamiliar contact. You saw people you didn't know more clearly; the strange, pretty, over-dressed women who frequented roof-gardens; the burly business man from out of town; the listless,

variegated occupants of the streets; the frayed edges
of the metropolis that showed themselves in the late
hours of the darkness. Your senses became keener; the
sense of smell; the sense of hearing; the sense of sight.
Windows were perpetually open and that, if nothing
else, brought closer the seven or eight million other
inhabitants.

Two or three times a week Gulian broke this
monotony by getting hold of Cyprian Bland and carrying him off to a theatre or to dine on top of a hotel.
By this means they increased their stock of observation.
The women they saw fascinated them especially. They
were infinitely more emotional than the men but their
emotions, like their movements, were rigidly subser-
vient to the latest fashion in emotion. When they were
dancing they pressed themselves against the grotesque
fat waistcoats embracing them with a look of dreamy
rapture that in reality could have been caused only by
the rarest moments of life. The men were remote,
slightly embarrassed, methodical.

"An unconscious preparation for marriage," observed Gulian.

"More like a preparation for divorce," suggested
Bland.

Gulian liked Bland increasingly. A physical syba-
rite, but a very hardy man intellectually, and like most
good conversationalists, a rather silent man most of
the time.

Concerning the brokerage business, Gulian's original ideas suffered no startling change. He was eager
to learn all he could, and set himself earnestly to the
task, but he found about the task nothing essentially
epic, or lyric, or even dramatic. It seemed a dull enough
affair, this selling bits of paper; the very lowest form
of Adam's curse. These blithe young knights, after

twenty-one or -two years of preparation, plunging into the whirlpool of near-finance, struck him as pathetic. They cut short their mental growth and skirted, when they didn't bog-down, the morass of neurasthenia. And they were all so certain that the country depended upon them and that they were doing something important. Banking, of course, was different—that is, banking of the higher type.

Somewhere the race had made a mistake in its values. If all this eager youth could be put to productive purposes, or if the lowly, unproductive position of the middle-man could be generally explained and realized, coin-clipping might cease to engage the best talent of the country.

However, there was no use quarrelling with the instrument with which rather blindly you were trying to work out your salvation, poor as the instrument might be, and when business became intolerable it was always possible to refresh yourself with the thought that 'Hibernia' was waiting for you on Saturdays and that before very long you would be off for two days of coolness and leisure at Drusilla's. Furthermore, there was not the slightest doubt in Gulian's mind that if business continued to be as intolerable as it now seemed to him, the law of perversity, mentioned before, would begin to have its much hoped for effect and he would be able to write poetry again. He only wished, however—thinking of Drusilla's invitation—that he had not been so hasty in asking Drusilla to invite Lael. It would be embarrassing to see Lael.

Drusilla, as was her custom, and as was in keeping with her character, had planned a large and overflowing and expansive week-end party. Most of the summer she spent quietly and dreamily with flowers and

books and her children, but ever so often, as if abruptly
recollecting numerous obligations, she issued hurriedly
a number of invitations, and late in August, rather
against her will, she was in the habit of drifting like
a warm full-blown poppy broken loose from its stem
down the thorny road of various visits. She was
immensely popular but imagined herself not very well
liked and by no means conspicuous.

This time she had asked Cyprian Bland, and
Vannya, and the Pembertons—DeWitt and his covet-
ous wife—and the Hurds, and Lael, and another
young woman to keep Lael company, and a rich exquisite young man to perform the same task for the
girl as the girl was supposed to perform for Lael.

Perry had made known at an early date his unshakable determination not to be present. He loathed
Stockbridge and despised most of Drusilla's more
intimate friends and, besides, had never been able to
see the exhilaration of having a number of—on the
whole—middle-aged persons share the same house
with you for a couple of nights. Momentarily he may
have experienced some regret when he learned that
'that little Gertrude Pemberton' was to be on hand.
For some strange reason, in the same way that Philip
regarded artists, any woman of light-hearted tendencies
weighing less than a hundred and fifty pounds was
'little' to Perry: size being apparently a question of
levity and not physique. But no doubt he consoled
himself by the reflection that Mrs. Pemberton was
only a 'quarter-miler,' anyhow. A 'good starter,' but
a 'poor finisher.' He sent, none the less, a tender message to Drusilla and, as a mark of especial favor, gave
Gulian an extra day's holiday.

"Tell her," he said—that meant Drusilla—"to keep

those damned bugs out of the tea-roses and to dis-
charge Hutchinson if he's still drinking. . . . Rum
must be preserved for the upper classes."

Gulian took a late morning train on a very warm
Friday. He found Cyprian already installed and in
animated conversation with DeWitt Pemberton and
his wife, Mrs. Pemberton looking fragile and lovely in
her light summer-frock. Her corn-flower eyes beneath their bronze, plucked eyebrows were preoccupied and sad. One was at a loss to know whether it was
a new attitude on her part or merely the tranquillity
of an interregnum between flirtations. She turned a
mournful gaze upon Gulian and smiled sweetly, and
seemed to have entirely forgotten his lack of promise
at their previous meeting. The slave-buyer had turned
maternal. Life, because of some esoteric hurt, was
temporarily over save for a kindly, level-voiced, rather
distant interest in such important matters as Gulian's
business and Drusilla's children and Cyprian's writing.

Gulian, if anything, found this latter mood more
irritating than the former and disappeared into the
smoking compartment followed by Bland.

"Morgan le Fay lying fallow," commented Cyprian,
"The orchid lying in wait in the jungle for the next
fly. . . . This is the most deadly period, for every
faculty is alert. We were talking spiritism when you
came in—that is always a dangerous sign. A mental
thermometer would register a hundred and four. When
a woman like Gertrude begins to exhibit an interest
in disembodied souls it's a sign that she's become so
weary of embodied souls that she is almost ready to
take them up again."

In the early dusk of the brilliant afternoon the train
stopped at the little village and Drusilla's station-car

whirled her four guests through the elm-shaded streets and out into the country of small round hills and dark plantations of trees. Drusilla's house lay upon the edge of a long rolling valley; standing up so that you could see its firs and Lombardy poplars and catch a glimpse of white enclosing walls and white inner walls, a mile or so before you came to them. In the quiet gold-powdered light New England's resemblance to the Italy of the Primitive Painters was never more in evidence. One expected to see prelates with gilded crooks and women in flowing purple robes.

Mrs. Pemberton asked level-voiced questions of absurd simplicity about birds and trees and flowers. Early in life she had been told that the way to a man's heart was through his stomach and, secondarily, through his vanity, and the lack of observation which distinguished her, in common with her kind, had so far prevented her from realizing that this excellent rule had been superseded in a world that had grown more cynical.

"That bird?" exclaimed Gulian with raised eyebrows. "That's a robin-redbreast. It is common in the more savage parts of the Eastern States." He would have added a sardonic "——, sweetheart!" had he known Mrs. Pemberton better.

She did not understand him; she smiled like a gentle, happily instructed child.

Ten minutes later Gulian found Drusilla's warm arms around him. He liked Drusilla's house—it resembled Drusilla—welcoming and fragrant. He would be glad to be with Drusilla for a few days. In company with a good many other brothers, he forgot how fond he was of his sister until her presence reminded him.

In the background, in a group of people, he saw

Lael hovering. She smiled at him and nodded and shook hands. "I haven't seen you for ages," she said casually, and turned to Drusilla. " 'Bunny' and 'Chick'—" that was Yarnall—"and myself have a burning desire to go into the movies tonight—may we?"

CHAPTER V

DRUSILLA ENTERTAINS

GULIAN sat on the edge of Drusilla's swimming-pool in the pellucid calm of the June hour and dabbled his toes in the tranquil water. It was the second morning after his arrival. He was dressed in a pair of gray flannel trunks and a white jersey that showed to advantage his sinewy sunburned figure. It was Sunday and seven o'clock, and the sun had been up a couple of hours.

On three sides Drusilla's pool was surrounded by a thick wall of evergreens, ten or twelve feet high, but in the center of this wall, opposite Gulian, an opening had been cut so that you could look down across the shining valley and up and over to the hills beyond; and beyond these, to other hills that lost themselves in a blue haze. There were a hundred birds singing; cardinals and robins and song-sparrows and indigo-buntings, the last dropping from their hidden balconies like bits of a blue and burning sky their sharp-cut notes— "July, July, summer . . . summer's here! Morning, noontide, evening list to me!" A woodpecker tapped a tree and a solitary thrush matched his notes against the gurgle of the water as it left the pool.

Gulian drew his feet back and forth through the delicious coolness and reflected that this would be a perfect spot if it wasn't for Lael and, incidentally, Drusilla and Vannya.

Drusilla was too tenderly maternal towards Vannya,

253

and Lael . . . well, as for Lael, he couldn't make her out at all but the resultant figure of mystery made him angry. She was puzzlingly indifferent to the memory of only three weeks before; indifferent to the very reasonable apologies he had attempted to offer as an explanation for his not calling upon her. Not that there was any sentimentality involved, but he did think it would be pleasanter to be at least friendly during the few days they were thrown together. He recalled sardonically his insistence upon her being asked over the week-end.

He wasn't in reality seriously worried by the gentle intimacy which he had discovered existed between Drusilla and Vannya, and the more he thought about it the less worried he became. Indeed, he doubted—to be quite just—if he would have worried at all had it not been for the evil temper in which Lael had put him. There was no harm, after all, in gentle intimacies, and they were to be expected between two people placed as Vannya and Drusilla were. What, indeed, was there to go on? The recollection of his talk with Drusilla the night of his return home; the chance meeting on Vannya's steps—the little gray ghost of a doubt it had left—and, especially perhaps, the fact that Drusilla had told him the evening before that the object of her present solicitude was the conversion of Vannya's Oriental point of view to Occidental standards. The last was disturbing, for a woman is never in so much danger as when she is converting an Oriental point of view to Occidental standards. But where Lael was concerned Gulian's indignation was clean-cut. Drusilla would probably never make a fool of herself, she had the gracious pliability that does not break; but making a fool of herself he had definitely decided was one of Lael's pet accomplishments. She was childish and he despised her. He was so sure he despised her that his feet forgot their gentle rhythm and kicked the water angrily. He was doubly angry because having to reverse his opinion once he had had to reverse it again. He had been completely mistaken in Lael—she was no more or less than exactly what he had first thought her. It served him right for being even for a minute interested in anything so shallow and unformed.

Naturally he had expected Lael not to be too cordial over his lack of attention to her, and he had intended to explain fully what the trouble had been. To explain quite simply that there was no one in the world he liked better and that he hoped all their lives he and she would be the best of friends, but that as a man twelve years older he did not think it fair for him to take up too much of her time or complicate her life, and that for awhile anyway he had deliberately avoided seeing her lest his desire for her companionship get the better of his intelligence. That was fair enough, wasn't it? And decently candid? He knew, of course, that such an explanation would not be received gratefully by any but the exceptional woman near his own age, but Lael belonged to a new dispensation; you could talk to her as you could to a man; you could even swear at her if necessary and she would swear back. These modern Rosalinds were distinguished by a humorous clearsightedness.

He wished that he could go even further and disclose the fundamental reason, back of all the other reasons, for his dereliction, the sense of ineptitude that Vida had implanted in him; but that, naturally enough, was impossible.

Lael, however, had given him no opportunity for detailed explanation. She seemed quite content to leave things as they were. She had been at Drusilla's several days, and so had 'Bunny' Rogers, the other girl, and so had Yarnall, the rich, exquisite young man; and the three seemed to know each other well and to be happy in a lounging, exclamatory, uncommunicative way. The only possible method of intruding upon their intimacy was to make a fourth at golf or tennis should they be inclined towards exercise.

Dancing was ineffective. Both Lael and Miss Rogers had such a modern temper of abstraction where that sport was concerned that to dance with them barely assured recognition at the next meeting, let alone anything resembling conversation at the time.

Gulian refused to humiliate himself by athletic compromises, and so played golf in a tiresome foursome composed of Hurd and Pemberton and Cyprian Bland. Lael, going her scintillating way, flashing her smile upon Yarnall, emphasizing unconsciously by gesture and speech her complete understanding with him, abandoning, apparently, her theories about 'Victorian helplessness' by asking constantly that things be fetched to her or explained to her, became to Gulian an increasingly cool and debonair enigma. She had taken to painting again as if to indicate a return to a worldly hardness. Her mouth was once more an absurd button and her over-emphasized eyes held in their depths a look of aloof childish sophistication that enraged Gulian every time he saw it.

Part of his irritation arose from the fact that although he wanted a reconciliation with Lael, to make now any very open attempts in that direction would be to imply a jealousy and eagerness on his part he did not wish to imply. Dignity had entered into the question. . . .

A shadow fell across the end of the pool and he

looked up to see a slim shape in a crimson bathing suit of tight fitting jersey and trunks slipping into the opening between the cedars and regarding him steadfastly across the sun-flecked water.

"Hello!" he said. It was impossible to say less.

"Hello!" answered the shape gloomily, "I'm disappointed. I've always had this pool to myself. I hate crowds."

"So do I," replied Gulian, and looked away.

The shape left its position, outlined against the blue distance of the hills, and walked slowly around the circle of the cedars and sat down casually beside Gulian on the stone coping.

Gulian realized the futility and absurdity of trying to maintain haughtiness when two people were engaged in such a fraternal occupation as swimming and especially when they were clad in the costumes nowadays permitted. The evils of arrogance are largely a matter of dress, anyway. Even the savage when he wishes to be particularly disagreeable in a stately way paints himself. Two minutes of undressing make the wisest man look startlingly like the most foolish.

Gulian, moodily thoughtful, discovered, moreover, a further quarrel with the indecency of the reformer. This modern tendency towards an Attic disregard of clothes was something, he reflected, to be recommended, both physically and morally. People took more care of their bodies and therefore incidentally aired their souls. And although, to the middle-aged, the first glance might be somewhat startling, accustomedness cured all that and made comparative disclosure, like all disclosure, innocuous and spiritual. The custom had its practical advantages as well; one knew people better since the physical is so closely allied to the mental. One might say that with the exception of a few minor details one knew them completely.

Lael, for instance, had beautiful legs; slim, high-bred, pure of outline. Seeing them you realized that whatever she might do, it would never be anything vulgar or mean. There are no features more distinctive than legs, male or female. Hands are mental; but legs and feet are unconscious and express not mentality but fundamental character. Gulian was glad he had seen Lael's legs.

"It's lovely out here, isn't it?" he said amicably—declaring a temporary truce.

"Lovely!"

Lael continued to study her feet which, close to Gulian's, were also dabbling in the water.

"What makes you so queer?" she asked suddenly, rather as if Gulian were more a specimen for psychological research than anything else.

"Me? Queer? I'm not queer!" Gulian's indignation, held in abeyance, rose to the surface. The truce would be short-lived if Lael continued to use such a tone and indulge in such unjust accusations.

Lael sighed. "Then it must be," she decided, "that you don't know what being queer is."

Gulian turned a wrathful face in her direction.

"Hush!" said Lael, increasingly irritating, "here comes someone. Do be quiet!"

Gulian's face and neck showed a sullen red under his sunburn. "I haven't said a word—" he began furiously, and then, as the quickest insult he could think of, "I wish to God you'd take about half that paint off your lips. It's disgusting."

"Is it?" inquired Lael pleasantly.

The figure of Charles Hurd, rhomboidal in a bathing suit, but splendidly vigorous, the sun shining into his high-colored face and intelligent eyes, came around the corner of the cedars.

He paused when he saw Gulian and Lael. "I consider ourselves," he said, "by far the finest people of this household. Only fine people go in swimming at this hour of the morning."

"Listen!" breathed Lael quickly in Gulian's ear. "Will you play tennis this afternoon? And tonight I want to see you. . . . We can walk in the garden. I want to see you. Will you? . . . Come and sit down, Mr. Hurd."

Gulian nodded his head. His heart beat more quickly, and that gave him a new cause for annoyance —this time with himself.

He greeted Hurd, plunged into the water, and swimming around the pool once or twice, climbed out and hurried up to the house. He did not see Lael at breakfast, nor afterwards at church, and at lunch she was a shadowy figure that sat far away from him, engrossed in the lazy conversation of Yarnall. After lunch, Gulian purposely avoided her. He did not want to seem too willing and he even decided once or twice that at the last moment he would offer some excuse not to join the tennis game. But when three o'clock came, he went upstairs and changed into his flannels and made his way to the court.

Lael and 'Bunny' Rogers and Yarnall joined him on the terrace.

'Bunny' Rogers—an excessively inappropriate nickname for a strong green eyed girl of twenty—decided without any pre-knowledge of Gulian's playing that he and she should play against Yarnall and Lael. "I think that would make it about even," she said in her absent-minded young voice. " 'Chick' is good, but lazy, and Lael is wild."

"All right," agreed Gulian, and helped her stretch the net.

The game began, and it was with a ferocious enjoyment that Gulian in the first few minutes found himself and 'Bunny' defeating Lael and her partner rather easily and found himself serving to Lael with an accuracy and speed that astonished even himself. It delighted him to hear her occasional gasp. He wanted her to be afraid of him. He was additionally light-hearted when, before long, he realized that she had guessed his intention and was becoming silently angry.

"Too hard?" he asked insultingly.

She did not answer him, but the next time returned the ball with a calculated viciousness. He understood that the match was becoming a duel of hidden intentions.

Once, early in the second set, while he was up at the net, he missed his stroke completely and the ball sung between his racket and his head and skimmed past the latter by a fraction of an inch. Lael, coming up to return some balls to 'Bunny,' did not look at him. "I wish to thunder it had hit you!" she murmured vindictively.

"Thank you!" said Gulian; and a moment or so later was sorry he had not made the retort more caustic, for Lael, out of position, and not ten feet away from him, caught a weak return from 'Bunny,' and smashed it with all her considerable might in Gulian's direction.

The ball had no drop to it and Gulian had no time to get out of its way. He put up his racket automatically, and the next moment found himself whirling around in little stooped-over ridiculous circles of agony.

The world danced and spun and sung incoherently. He felt hands touching him and voices speaking; particularly Lael's voice, high and scared. "Oh, I'm so sorry!" she kept saying. "I didn't mean it! . . . Oh, I'm so sorry! I didn't . . . Yes, I did! I'm a liar! I did mean it! I meant to hit you! . . . Oh, Gilly, if I have hurt your eye!"

Someone brought water and Gulian pressed the wet handkerchief against his eyelid, and presently the pain subsided, leaving no more than a slight throbbing. "I'm quite all right, thank you," he said, straightening up and feeling embarrassed and clumsy. "I don't think anything's wrong at all."

"Let's look at it," said Yarnall. He pulled the lashes apart and Gulian made a grimace of anguish. "You ought to see a doctor at once," Yarnall concluded.

"I'll take you," volunteered Lael eagerly.

The world had suddenly changed into a small and friendly community, solicitous and earnest, and, on Lael's part, remorseful.

"But I'm sure it's all right," persisted Gulian.

Lael stamped her foot. "Will you please stop being an idiot?"

Gulian shrugged his shoulders and grinned in acquiescence. "If it gives you any pleasure," he capitulated.

She walked up to the garage with him, avoiding the terrace upon which the others were having tea, and commandeered a small car and placed Gulian in it as if he had been a wounded child. Then she thrust a cigarette into his mouth and held a match to it.

"The only thing I learned in the war," she commented.

"But I'm all right," said Gulian. "Absolutely."

"Keep your eye shut!" commanded Lael. She paused with one foot on the step, her face, white and strained, turned up to his. "Gilly, when we get home you can beat me if you want to. . . . Trunk strap if you like. I nearly killed someone else once when I was very small."

"Get in," ordered Gulian, "and stop talking nonsense. I deserved everything I got and more. You're a better sport than I am."

The countryside flew past. Gulian decided that Lael was an infinitely more skillful driver than he was himself; he also decided that on the whole women were more courageous and reckless than men.

The doctor, whom they found watering his nasturtiums after the heat of the day, corroborated Gulian's diagnosis that no permanent damage had been done, although it would be necessary to wear an eyeshade for a few days. "However," he added, "it was a narrow enough squeak. That's an easy way to lose an eye." And then, happening to look in Lael's direction, "Hello!" he said, with a professional cheeriness now confined to country practice, "what's this? . . . Someone going to faint? Wait a moment."

Lael struggled to her feet with a dogged slowness, her mouth drawn tight, her eyes staring. "Certainly not!" she said indignantly. "I never fainted in my life. I'm tired."

But as they were getting back into the car she confided indifferently, "I'm glad I'm not a criminal." Gulian realized that if she had been born fifteen years earlier she would have been crying.

"Get away from that wheel," he retorted. "I'm going to drive."

"No, you're not."

"I am." He was unexpectedly truculent, forcing her down into the other seat. "I am, and be damned to you. Hereafter, on the few occasions when you're with me, you mind what I tell you."

Above the roar of the engine her words reached him. "You're a bully," she was saying, but in a small, delighted voice. "You take advantage of a situation. You're hopelessly Victorian."

Gulian grinned at her.

By and large, he considered his injury a beneficent one. It would save endless explanations where Lael was concerned, and the shade over his eye made him feel romantic and piratical; so much so that he did not mind in the least the jokes at dinner referring to Lael's unduly rough ardor for him, and so much so that he was able to entertain Mrs. Pemberton who sat next to him in a manner that left that for the moment unoccupied lady wondering why she had neglected her opportunities so aimlessly.

And yet all the while an inner voice kept warning him that after the episode of the afternoon he would have to be more careful than ever. The reaction from the last two days of irritation and wounded feelings to the present state of fortified friendship in which he and Lael found themselves was dangerous. He had no idea what Lael wanted to tell him that night, but the fact that she wanted to tell him anything was a sign of interest on her part that was provocative. Nor would the setting be un-perilous. Gulian knew the effect of moonlight and roses and gardens upon even the most stable minds. And he wasn't in love with Lael, fond as he was of her; he was even inclined to go to the other extreme in not being in love with her, for he was held back by a pitying conviction of her mental confusion; determined that he would not permit himself even the harmless philandering in which he would probably have indulged with any other woman he liked as well as he did her. Lael's present deep-rooted lack of self-esteem and the real strength and sweetness of her were so delicately balanced that the slightest pressure one way or another might be final.

If he could only show her how exquisitely she did matter, without in any way forcing his own personality into the argument. If he could only convince her what, upon a stupid earth, rareness of personality meant. Life hadn't so many gifts that any of them could be squandered.

And yet if he attempted to show Lael what a fine person she was—rather, what a fine person she could be—he would be far too likely to become himself too interested in the telling and in the recipient of the tale.

And so it was with some trepidation that he left the library after dinner and found Lael in the hall and stepped with her into Drusilla's garden.

CHAPTER VI

"A LITTLE LOVELY MOONY NIGHT"

DRUSILLA'S garden was outlined in perfume and moonlight. The roses eddied up to the retaining shores of the hedges like a quiet sea white with spume, and the walks and arbors with their walls of privet and box were a dark arabesque upon the gold of the open spaces. Below the garden the valley slept in an opal haze, at the heart of which here and there the lights of a house glowed with the soft warmth of the inner fire of the jewel.

From where Lael and Gulian sat, on a stone bench beneath a canopy of crimson ramblers, they could look down a path to the eastern wing of the house, beyond an open window of which, outlined with the sharpness of the wrong end of a telescope, was the sturdy back of Cyprian Bland as he played bridge with Mrs. Pemberton and Mrs. Hurd and the latter's husband. In another room an invisible Vannya was playing the piano.

Bland had been particularly amusing at dinner and he had directed most of his conversation towards Mrs. Pemberton as if he wished to see if he could shock by frank brutality that subtly indecorous woman.

"Of course," she had commented to Gulian with her usual originality, "it makes such a difference how things are said." As a matter of fact, it doesn't. The most indecent people are those most careful to clothe their indecencies delicately.

Cyprian had discoursed on the cultural significance of advertisements. He claimed he was writing a his-

265

tory of them. "They are barometers," he exclaimed.
"They march hand in hand with what I shall call the
younger, or B. V. D. school of literature. Give me the
advertisements of a nation and I will tell you what the
nation is. For instance, we are, and always have been,
as a race, flooded with a pseudo hearty frankness and,
also as a race, we number countless worthy women
who desire a speedy culture that won't hurt. Hence
such advertisements as, 'We keep faith with the
chewer'—Magnificent!—and the one about French
house decorations addressed to Mesdames of America,
and made up of a jargon of English and Gallic, the
latter so scattered through the context that its meaning cannot be mistaken—charming! Imagine how
that flatters the aspiring but ignorant reader. She
thinks she speaks pretty good French after all. Well,
there you are. And my friend the woman of the lin-
gerie—I have been watching her breathlessly now for
three years and the artist has been steadily taking
things off until one began to wonder what he'd take
off next. Now he's beginning to put them back. Why?
Because the burning interest in the female form supine
which has obsessed us since the war is beginning to
wane. . . . Incidentally, I would like to know why
it is that the more pornographic a magazine is—I refer
you to one especial charming little string of them—
the more it cheers for all kinds of reform save one.
It is an interesting psychological investigation. I
intend to devote a couple of chapters to it." He glared
at Mrs. Pemberton from behind his convex spectacles.
. . . "Why, why should we refuse liquor advertisements and yet advertise albums of nude young women
in every conceivable form of setting up exercise? There
is some fundamental psychological, sociological reason
for this. Can you tell me, Gertrude?"

Mrs. Pemberton couldn't. "He puts things in such an unnecessarily coarse way," she murmured to Gulian —"I find almost everything beautiful if looked at correctly. . . ."

Gulian smiled now as he watched the distant, self-reliant back.

Lael, a silvery figure in a cream-colored dress, drew herself together as if aroused from reflections in which Gulian had no share. "That's 'Louise,' Polienoff is playing, isn't it?" she said. "The Louises of the world are pretty much scattered about everywhere, aren't they?"

Gulian turned his head and looked at her. "You become older," he observed. "You have become older ever since you put my eye out. I hope it hasn't unduly depressed you?"

"Don't be silly," she replied; "and give me a cigarette. I'm twenty-three, and when you're twenty-three you stop and wonder sometimes what is going to happen to you."

"You are very late about starting it. When I was eighteen and a freshman at college I frequently couldn't sleep for thinking how old I was and how little I had accomplished." He sighed. "Now, it's such a worn-out thing it no longer keeps me awake."

"Aren't you happy, Gilly?"

"Oh . . . sufficiently."

"Aren't you satisfied, now you're in business?"

Gulian laughed and threw back his head. "Underneath the exquisite exterior of the much-travelled young woman the fine typical American girl speaks, doesn't it?" he exclaimed. "No, why the devil should I be satisfied just because I am in business."

"What would satisfy you?"

"Do you really want to know?"

"Yes."

"Well, I'll tell you then." He shifted his position and half-faced her, his arm along the back of the bench, his one good eye thoughtful, the other concealed by the piratical eyeshade. "Three very simple things, but the hardest things in the world under modern conditions to get . . . at least, hardly anyone ever gets them. Most modern men don't even know that they want them, although they do. I'm not sure, but I think Anatole France mentions them."

"What are they?"

"Work—work that fills every crevice of your passion for work; love, as much a part of you as your breath; and a background of quiet beauty. . . ." He interrupted himself with a laugh. "There! I'm sorry. By nature I'm a poet and that's fatal to a proper cynicism, or a pleasant conversation."

Lael opened her eyes scornfully at him. "You make me angry," she said slowly. "You're self-conscious and disgusting. You constantly insult my intelligence. . . . And can't you find any of these things, Gilly?"

"Yes, to some extent. I think I've just regained the last in my father's house—up there on the Hudson; as to the other two, I believe some day I am going to write something really worth while; but the second, and most important—well, do you see much of it around?"

"You mean there's no girl—no woman, you've ever seen. . . ?"

"Not yet. It's all a matter of chance anyway."

Lael drew thoughtfully at her cigarette and then flung it suddenly from her, so that it described a little arc and fell on the path before her, where it glowed like a broken-winged firefly.

"I wonder?" she said. ". . . I think so often it's

a person's own attitude. Your heart is very open to
the world, Gilly, but I don't think it's altogether open
to other people. You're very kind and sympathetic
and all that, but beyond a certain point you're suspicious and elusive. I wonder if you haven't hurt a
good many people by laughing too soon—even by
laughing too soon at yourself? Have many people hurt
you?"

"Oh, yes," said Gulian dryly.

"They will do it, won't they?" She sat with her
hands crossed in her lap, gazing at the distant house.
"And half the time they don't even know they're doing
it. . . . That's the most pathetic part of it." She
straightened up abruptly and leaned towards him,
her voice losing its pensive quality. "What I wanted
to ask you, Gilly, was this."

"Oh, yes!"—he leaned forward too.

"You see, I haven't one single older person I can go
to—not one; and I thought maybe you'd help me."

"I'll try to. . . ." He stiffened. "I'm sufficiently
old, I suppose. I've reached the gigantic age of thirty-
five."

"Please!"

"All right—I'll be decent."

"There's a man, Gilly, who wants to marry me."

"Is there?" Gulian peered down at the averted
face. "But there're a lot, aren't there?"

"Oh, yes, but this one especially. And I don't know
what to do about it."

"Well, good gracious, can't you settle that for yourself?"

"No . . . I can't. You see, I'm not in love with
him."

"What's he like?"

"He's very attractive . . . not much older than I am; and he's horribly rich."

"It sounds perfect."

"It isn't."

"Can't you love him?"

"No; I've tried."

"Is it Yarnall?"

"It isn't Yarnall . . . but I wouldn't tell you his name even if it was. . . . What am I to do, Gilly?"

Gulian laughed shortly. "How can I tell?" he asked. He was surprised at the bitterness in his voice.

"But there're so many things to consider. You see, you've never been poor the way I have. You don't know what it is to be poor—especially for a girl. And there's my family, too; they're getting poorer all the while. And they're so helpless and silly and heart-rending. It would be such a blessed relief just to know that all the rest of your life you wouldn't have to bother about money."

"Why don't you go to work?" suggested Gulian harshly.

"Maybe I will. But men say that, and it isn't so easy. They're trained and women aren't. . . . What do you think?"

Gulian was silent for a moment.

"If you really want to know what I think," he said finally, "I think the whole secret of life is making it as much as possible a series of high-hearted adventures. and since, of all these, marriage is one of the greatest, if you squander the chance, you lose an oppor-tunity. In fact, with your blood you can't do it and get away with it. I've never yet known an American woman to marry for money and not regret it. In Europe it is different for they make other arrangements; but American women can't do that. It may be a pity, but it's true. And sooner or later all women fall in love, and if they are already married it only means a futility or an ugliness. I'm not a romanticist; money—some of it—is almost as necessary for a happy marriage as love. There ought to be a just proportion of both. But you have to start with love, or what you think is love." He hesitated. "And yet, it's all mixed up. Even an unfortunate marriage seems to me better than none. Not to marry simply means missing an ultimate experience. . . . How can I tell?" he ended irritably. "I don't want to interfere with your life, anyhow."

"You won't," said Lael quietly; "and I think I agree with you. Although lots of my friends look at it differently. They feel that a divorce is easy to get if they're not satisfied."

"So I've heard. But they must be very young and inexperienced. There's just one thing no man or woman can deliberately sell and get over it, and that's his or her body."

"No, that's true, isn't it? Queer, too, for so often you would be so happy to give it away . . . even if you got nothing in return."

"Women, not men. Men want to give other things." He stirred uneasily and put out his cigarette.

"Do you want to walk about a bit, Lael? This bench is getting hard."

"Yes. Let's go down to the pool. I'd like to see it by moonlight."

"Was that all you wanted to ask me?"

"Yes. It's enough, isn't it?" She touched his arm lightly. "Oh, Gilly, it means everything to me. I'm afraid for the first time in my life. I used to think life was only complicated by other people, and now I know most of the complications lie in yourself."

They turned at right angles and took a path that led through masses of phlox and iris and larkspur toward the little circle of cedars at the crest of the hill.

Lael was silent, her feet making hardly a sound on the damp earth. It seemed to Gulian as if he and she were moving side by side through some unknown medium of which the recognizable parts were this refulgence of golden light and this soft breathing of tree and plant; a medium that was shutting out more and more completely the house, and the sound of Vannya's playing, and all the ordinary experiences of the day and the night. And suddenly he felt very sorry for Lael, and very close to her, and anxious not to break the silence, and regretful that such moments as this were so short and so easily intruded upon. He did not like to think of Lael walking this way with anybody else—in this wordless intimacy. And yet, of course, some day she would.

They came to the edge of the pool. The cedars cast dark shadows into its depths, and between the sides of the opening opposite the blue of the sky had changed to an ultramarine.

Lael picked a sprig of cedar and twisted it between her fingers.

"Only this morning," she said, "we were swimming here. It was a long while ago, wasn't it?"

She tossed the sprig of cedar into the water.

"Gilly," she said, "I'm going to marry that man."

The motion she had made had loosened one of the straps of her dress, and her white shoulder and arm gleamed in the moonlight. Gulian could not take his eyes away from this unconscious revealment. The shoulder, the curve of the neck, were so young and yet so gracious and warm of outline; so pathetic in their loveliness, so living and appealing. His heart seemed to turn over in his breast.

"Lael!" he said almost inaudibly.

"Yes?"

She turned her head slowly in his direction and he saw that her lips were drawn down in some mysterious sadness or expectation.

He wanted to say, "You can't marry that man!" but somehow a final hindrance at the back of his brain held him silent. Yet he couldn't have this girl go away from him forever. He couldn't bear the thought of it. . . . She was very close to him; she must have stepped nearer. The garden was very quiet; the moonlight and shadows unsubstantial. "Lael!" he said again suddenly and caught her to him.

He felt her momentary tautness give way and relax into a little nestling movement, and he bent his head and found her lips and kissed them. . . . The silence of the garden seemed to increase; to become an emptiness in which there was nothing but the beating of his blood; the small shaken breathing of Lael; and . . . the presence of Vida! Yes, the presence of Vida! A vision of the last time he had held a woman in his arms rose up before him. Vida seemed to be looking over Lael's shoulder. And then, with an abruptness that frightened him, both women, the actual woman and the misty woman of his imagination, struggled free from him, pushing him away.

"That's enough!" said Lael sharply.

"You mean?"

She laughed. "You're no different from the rest, are you? You're a little worse, for I gave you my confidence and you abused it." Her voice grew harsh.

"You think I'm cheap, don't you, because I told you so? Well—I am cheap."

"Lael!" Gulian stretched out an arm.

She eluded him.

"Don't touch me! . . . I despise you!"

"Lael, you are mad!"

"I am not mad. . . . Let me go!"

She tried to pass him but he grasped her arm fiercely. "Listen to me!" he said, "you silly little idiot! Kisses are plentiful. I've had enough in my life. They don't amuse me any more even for a minute unless I love the woman who gives them to me. Do you suppose I kissed you for fun? . . . Lael, I love you. I'm asking you to marry me. I was only afraid because I was so much older than you. I didn't want my pride hurt again."

"Hurt again? Then you do this often?"

He did not answer her, and she looked down at his hand holding her arm and up again.

"You amuse me," she said coldly, all the humorous Rosalind gone and the white logic of feminine illogicality uppermost. "Ten minutes ago you told me there wasn't a woman in the world you cared for, and now you tell me this. You're not even a dashing lover; you're sentimental and absurd up to the end. Do you think I will marry you just because you think that now it's your duty to ask me? No, thanks! . . . Let go my arm, please; you're hurting me."

"I'll hurt you worse," said Gulian, his white face near to hers," "before I get through with you. I love you. Do you understand?"

"Let go, please."

"Will you answer me?"

"I have."

"Lael! I'll ask you once more, and then . . .

and then, by God, I'll never ask you again as long as I live."

"I've answered you."

"You mean you don't care for me? . . . Answer me that directly! Whatever you may think of what I've said or done, do you care for me or not?"

She met his eyes boldly.

"No," she said, "of course I don't care for you. Why should I?"

"Why did you kiss me then?"

She smiled patiently as if she were talking to a child. "How silly you are! Do I have to love every man I kiss? Maybe I do think I love him until I kiss him. . . . Afterwards. . . . well—I know."

Gulian released her and stepped back.

"Thanks," he said quietly, but with twisted lips. "And remember in the future, my friend—since I won't be there to tell you—that kissing is like quarrelling, it takes two to make it."

"You cad!"

He shook his head with a laugh. "It's you who are being old-fashioned, my dear," he said bitterly. "I'm no cad. I'm simply a man who discovered a few minutes ago that he was in love with you. Forgive me for my folly. . . . And you're quite right. I'm no good. I had no business even to dream of you. I'm old and—" he laughed again—"what's more, getting extraordinarily fed up." He turned his back and lit a cigarette and stared across the pool. He could almost imagine Vida standing there in the opening between the trees, a small amused smile on her lips.

When he looked around again, Lael was gone. He saw her, a silvery, translucent figure, walking slowly through the silent turbulence of blossom towards the house.

He had done exactly everything he hadn't meant to do, and, in doing it, he had realized too late that he was despairingly in love, and in a new and strange and dizzy way, with a girl who despised him. Ten years earlier, with the persistence and egotism of youth, he would have tried to alter this contempt, but now . . . not he!

He did not see Lael again that night. She had gone to bed when he got back to the house. The next morning he left on an early train before she was awake. When he arrived at Madison Place he found a note from Philip asking him if he could arrange a small dinner for the Reverend Doctor Hartley, of Holy Trinity, and Mr. Matthewson, of St. Jude's, the following Wednesday night. "I especially want you to know these men," wrote Philip. "The church is on the eve of a great departure, and somehow you can always get to know men better in your own house than anywhere else. I know also that Prescott is the best of cooks."

CHAPTER VII

THE NECESSITY FOR A USE OF INTRIGUE

On the afternoon of that particular Wednesday night, Sydney Prendegast, returning unexpectedly from another of his periodic motor trips, this time to a New England seaside resort but in the company of the same three red-faced friends with whom he had gone to Saratoga, let himself into his apartment shortly after five o'clock and found his wife, Vida, giving iced-tea to Randall Sedgewick.

In itself the act could not have been more innocent, but the coincidence was unfortunate. Sydney's trip had not been an altogether pleasant one and he was in a bad humor. For one thing, he had been drinking too much, and his libations, spread over six very hot days, had left him with a vague bellicose wounded feeling all the more trying because at first it had had no particular object upon which to fasten. He also had been losing money steadily at cards, and he was beginning not only to question the honesty of his three red-faced friends, but the stability and worth of friendship in general.

There is no man so exacting of loyalty as the inherently disloyal man, and no man so sentimental about friendship as the man whose friendships are based upon such cold-blooded affinities as a common taste in the minor and major vices.

Moreover, although in the press of other excitements they had slipped his mind, recently disturbing rumors had reached Sydney's ears concerning Vida. Vida apparently had not been behaving with her customary discretion, had not been living up to the illogical but—as far as he was concerned, at least—satisfactory unspoken agreement which had for so long existed between them. An odd, yet not uncommon agreement in a land that still chivalrously insists, even in the most elastic circles, that a woman is just exactly what she is not.

And the hero of these indiscretions—the principal figure in these rather foolish public appearances—was no other than this same self-satisfied, shortish, expensively dressed man whom Sydney had never liked and whom he now discovered lolling in a chair across a small table from the cool, gray-clad figure of his wife.

Ordinarily Sydney would have disregarded the rumors he had heard until they had reached a point where the evasion of them was no longer compatible with his curiously sensitive and uncertain pride, for underneath he was afraid of Vida and in order to overcome this fear had to lash himself into rages that left him exhausted; but the present opportunity seemed to offer a convergence and release of irritations too convenient to be overlooked. Vida was to suffer not only for her own folly, but because the weather was hot, and because whiskey is strong, and because cards are frequently unlucky. Wives are not as aware as they should be that the waves of temper which overtake their husbands frequently have little to do with the incident chosen. They should search—if they are sufficiently interested—for the underlying cause. A contemptuous glance from a comparatively strange woman on Monday may result in a matrimonial quarrel the following Thursday.

Sydney put his straw hat down softly upon the

table in the darkened hall and strode into the living-
room of his apartment. In his own mind he represented a picture of close-lipped, rather beautiful
masculine austerity.

"Hello!" he said coldly.

His wife looked up without interest.

"You're back a day or so earlier, aren't you?" she
asked.

Sedgewick had got to his feet.

"So I perceive," said Sydney, and went into his bed-
room beyond.

He had, he felt, scored the first point in the contest
that was about to begin. Vida would either have to
ask him what he meant or else remain unsatisfied and
silent. The position of the interrogator is always
weaker than that of the informant.

Sedgewick had sat down again and was staring
blankly at Vida. She held his eyes for a moment and
then shrugged her shoulders and, looking down, began
to play thoughtfully with the string of pearls around
her neck.

Sedgewick's thick mouth under its short moustache
became an O of surprise. "Do you suppose he knows?"
he asked softly.

"How could he know?" Vida shrugged her shoulders
again. "But he's probably heard enough so that I will
have to put him on another track. Long ago I gave
up trying to understand Sydney's moods, but I can
control them. I will bring him back to a proper frame
of mind. It may require brutality, or it may require
flattery." She sighed. "Life is complex, isn't it?"

Sedgewick frowned in the manner of a ruthless man
puzzled by nuances that offend his sense of reason.

"You make it a darn sight more complex than is
necessary," he complained. ". . . Why don't you

cut out this nonsense, Vida, and come away with me?"

Vida laughed.

"And marry you, you mean?"

Sedgewick looked startled. "Why, yes," he said hastily. "Yes of course."

"Good Lord! Don't you know enough about marriages not to want any more? I do. Where's your ex-wife, Randall?"

"In Baltimore."

"Doesn't she look a lot like me?"

"Well . . . yes. She does."

"I thought so. Men like you marry by types. Probably I'm very similar to her in character, too. You'd be jumping from the frying-pan into the fire, my friend. Be satisfied when you're well off, and thank your stars I'm not sentimental. I've hardly ever known a divorced man who didn't marry the exact duplicate of the woman he couldn't get on with in the first place. Now go . . . will you?"

Sedgewick stood up and moved towards her, but she got to her feet and avoided him.

"Not now," she said smilingly.

When he was gone, she went over to the table and pulling out of a vase one of the roses she was so fond of, placed it against her lips and inhaled its fragrance meditatively. Finally she pinned the rose in the bosom of her dress.

In the interview to come, she was not sure whether the rose would symbolize a necessary softness or the thorns of her anger. In either case she would have to behave circumspectly; choose the weapon that seemed apposite. . . . She was shortly going on a round of expensive visits; she had purchased numerous expensive clothes. She didn't want Sydney to make a fuss about money, and she still shrank from

asking too many material favors from Randall Sedgewick, even if they were of a kind that would go unnoticed by Sydney. She preferred to have Sedgewick
give her things of his own accord.

The soft parti-colored veils of the late afternoon
were being drawn one by one, imperceptible at first,
perceptible only when their numbers were endlessly
multiplied, across the heady azure of the June day. In
the corners of the room, violet tints began to appear;
grow deeper, spread out across the pile of the blue
rug; strange little ghosts of twilight; peaceful household ghosts. The big shining center table was a pool
of quiet in which gayly covered books lay like feluccas
at anchor.

Vida moved quietly across the room and knocked at
Sydney's door.

"Come in," he said.

She opened the door and stepped across the
threshold, on her face the demure half-amused expression she so often saved for her husband.

Sydney was in his shirt sleeves before the mirror,
tying a tie of bold and contrasting stripes. His thin
hair was brushed back smoothly from his equine face.
Evidently he had just bathed.

Vida went over to the window and peered down into
the narrow courtyard beyond. A stout woman, lightly
clad, fanned herself in the house opposite. Vida was
disgusted. She wondered why it was she couldn't
have a country place like other women and so avoid
the unpleasantnesses of heat. She turned about
abruptly.

"Would you mind telling me," she asked, but not in
the least in an unfriendly manner, "why you insult my
harmless guests?"

Sydney paused for an instant and opened his eyes at

his reflection in the mirror as if he had heard a distant sound; then he allowed himself to become absorbed once more.

Vida walked close to him, her demure veiled expression changing to a little hovering smile.

"Would you mind telling me?" she asked again. "No? . . . You won't?"

Sydney patted his tie into perfection.

"It's very hard," Vida reflected to herself. "I can't tell what is expected of me. Am I to go back to the sweet old Victorian custom of seeing no one except my family; or am I to behave like a civilized human being? The former would be rather hard on you, Sydney, wouldn't it? You'd have to be so attentive to me . . . Why do you object so suddenly to my seeing Randall Sedgewick?"

"Did I say I objected?"

Sydney picked up his brushes and examined critically his already faultless hair.

"No, you implied you objected."

"Did I?"

"Oh, for heaven's sake, don't be impossible. Either tell me what is on your mind, or else don't behave again as you did just now. I'm bored."

Sydney turned and crossing slowly the intervening space, stooped above his wife like a hovering bird of prey. She returned his stare unwaveringly, the little vague smile still on her lips, her eyes starry and wide.

"I don't give a damn whether you're bored or not," said Sydney between his teeth.

She shook her head mournfully.

"You don't?"

"No."

"Why? What have I done?"

"You know what you've done."

"I haven't the vaguest idea."

"You liar!"

For a moment Vida looked startled, and then her mouth hardened and the little smile disappeared. She stepped back. When she spoke her voice was matter-of-fact and no longer coaxing.

"I have tried, Sydney," she said, with a grave gentleness, "to be friendly and pleasant. I'll try a while longer; but I don't propose to be insulted. If you don't explain you'll be very sorry. You ought to know by now that you can't bully me, and that if I really lose my temper with you you'll regret it. . . . I've told you I haven't the faintest idea what you're talking about; and I haven't."

She sat down on the edge of the narrow rosewood bed and crossing her knees, took one of them between her hands. Her expression was patient. Over the bed, framed in a dark frame, was a print of Watt's Sir Galahad. Vida had revolted against this once too popular picture—in this case a wedding-present—and had relegated it to Sydney's sleeping quarters. Sir Galahad had gone out of fashion (there seems to be no doubt that he has, literally as well as artistically), and Sydney anyhow never knew what was on his walls. If he looked at the print at all, he probably imagined it to be a photograph of Maude Adams in 'Peter Pan.' Neither he nor Vida realized the sardonicism of the close proximity of this wistful knight to Sydney's bed-head. Over many bedsteads throughout the world are similar paradoxes.

"Are you going to tell me, Sydney?"

Sydney considered this challenge. "Yes," he said at length, "I will." Like Vida he also was in doubt whether a heroic display of temper or a thoughtful reasonableness would be the more effective and relieving. The latter gave more opportunity for soft, unforgetable insults. He thrust his hands in his pockets and looked down at his wife.

"Vida," he began, "I'm a pretty liberal husband, aren't I?"

"Of course you are. What else could you be? Besides, it's convenient—you can go your own way and yet know that I am being amused. Is that all you want to tell me?"

"No. I want to ask you if you don't think there're limits?"

"For me, or for you?"

"For both of us. I'm pretty darn careful not to make you a laughing-stock, and—" Sydney suddenly took his hands out of his pockets and brought the fist of one hand down into the palm of the other "—and, by God, you won't make a laughing-stock out of me." He narrowed his eyes. "There're certain things you can't do and get away with them. You know that as well as I. You can play about all you darn like, but you can't do it too recklessly, and you can't go to queer places. Whatever I may be, I've got a decent name and it's going to be kept decent. I've always remembered that at the worst; you will too."

"Have I ever forgotten it?"

"Recently people have been talking about you."

"Recently? I thought they always had. You can't prevent people from talking. It's invariably the innocent friendships that are talked about, anyhow. Guilty people keep quiet—like you, Sydney, dear. . . . What have they said?"

"You know what they've said."

"I? . . . You mean about me and Randall Sedgewick?"

"Exactly."

"A few little parties out in the country; a few motor trips. . . ." Vida stared thoughtfully at her interlocked fingers. "What's to be done?" She raised her eyes. "Suppose there was any truth in it, Sydney—which there isn't; suppose I did decide to claim for myself—oh, discreetly, I mean; discreetly, of course—all the privileges I've given you? Wouldn't it be fair? What would you do about it?"

Sydney's voice was purring. "I'd divorce you," he said softly. "I'd divorce you like a shot, and you could explain to your church and the world afterwards. . . . Look at me, Vida." She did so. "Do you believe me? Have all the parties you want, but don't make me a laughing-stock and don't go over a certain line. Women are different from men. And there's no use telling me I'm old-fashioned or illogical. I'll admit it. There's another man that's been around here, too, I don't like at all, and that's Eyre. . . . He's too damned foreign for me."

A sudden light flamed in Vida's eyes and went out. "Yes," she said wearily. "I do believe you. You'd divorce me like a shot. It's about the only thing I am sure of. . . . Weak men always do. They're too vain even to give up a woman they've no more any right to."

For a moment she sat lost in thought and then she got to her feet suddenly, as if she had arrived at a decision. She crossed over again to the window. "Sydney," she said over her shoulder in a level voice, as if the narrative was painful to her, "I've made up my mind to tell you a secret. I'm going to do it for your own good, so that you'll see how untrue and worthless gossip is and in the future leave me alone; and I'm going to do it so that you'll understand how much all men are in the power of their wives. Any woman if she really wants to can cheat a man." She hesitated. "And finally," she added breathlessly, "I'm going to tell you so that if you still have any desire to work off your bad temper and exercise your well-known powers of intuition and detection you can work them off in the right quarters." She faced about and leaned against the window-sill, her hands gripping the wood behind her, her face curiously white. "Randall Sedgewick and I," she said coldly, "are the oldest and most innocent of friends; the man you should have feared was Gulian Eyre. You were right not to like him."

Her husband stared at her and took a step forward. "Eyre? That damned pup?"

"Yes. Only he isn't a pup, he's the most fascinating man I know . . . that is, until you realize what he is."

"What is he?"

Vida twisted her hands together as if she was being tortured. "The cruelest, the most selfish, the most cold-blooded person in the world," she said in a low voice.

"What's his cold-bloodedness got to do with you?"

"I'm trying to tell you. And can't you stop asking me questions? It's all over now anyhow. I'm only trying to show you what talk amounts to."

Sydney looked at her with narrowed eyes. "I'd like to know just what you are trying to do?" he said sneeringly. "Get Eyre into trouble? What's the matter? Did he turn you down?"

Vida sprang at him with raised fists. "You beast!" she cried. "You little nasty minded beast! Gulian Eyre doesn't turn any woman down. He takes what he can get. That's my thanks for not becoming his mistress." She checked herself abruptly. "You're

not worth getting angry with," she said quietly.
"I'm through. Goodnight. Make of it what you can.
. . . Are you dining here tonight? If you are, I
won't."

Sydney barred her path to the door. "Wait a
minute!" he said. "I want to ask you some more
questions."

Vida lifted her head and looked at him and walked
past him. She paused with her hand on the knob.

"Sydney," she said, half facing about," "it's a
secret I told you. I know you loathe Gulian Eyre,
but—don't do anything foolish. Don't make a scandal." The wistful look in her eyes disappeared and
two little lights danced in their depths as if a new and
exciting idea had occurred to her. Her red lips seemed
to grow redder. "But don't forget," she said softly,
"that I hate Gulian Eyre even more than you do."

"Get out of here!" said her husband savagely.

For several minutes after his wife had closed the door
behind her, Sydney remained staring thoughtfully at
its unresponsive panels before he walked with equal
thoughtfulness over to a small cabinet of brown-oak
that stood in one corner of his room and unlocking
the little gates that barred its upper shelves, took out
a bottle of whiskey and a glass and sitting down at a
table, poured himself several drinks in rapid succession. His right eye, marvelously like that of a minor
bird of prey, focused itself upon the print of Sir
Galahad but failed to envisage that warrior. Before
the right eye and its, at the moment, somewhat un-
coordinated mate there was beginning to pass a series
of images that had nothing to do with Sir Galahad
whatsoever.

Sydney had an uncomfortable feeling that in some

way or other Vida had got the better of him as usual in the interview he had so carefully planned and that, as usual, where she was concerned, he had made a fool of himself. This destroyed temporarily the picture he cherished of himself as a hawk-like, direct man; a picture the existence of which at the back of his brain was necessary for his peace of mind. His discomfort increased with each glass of whiskey he took. He grew sentimental.

Vida didn't understand him. Perhaps if she had, things would have been different. There wasn't any real harm in him—other women didn't think so; all he wanted after all was a little sympathy and a good time. But Vida had never been willing to grant him the former or participate with him in the latter. Hard as nails, that's what she was! Hard as nails! Of course, he didn't really suspect her and Randall Sedgewick. She might have known that. If nothing else, she was too callous—he would have thought more of her if she hadn't been so callous. A little softness in the best of women was not out of place. But he had come very close to scaring her. . . . His thoughts reverted to Gulian Eyre! That's where he should have been watching all the time, but he hadn't been. Too easy—Well, you never could tell. But it made him damned angry. Tried to run off with another man's wife, had he? Well, Vida had turned him down. She was crooked—all women were crooked; half the fun of knowing them was to catch them out in their crookedness and then bully them—Vida was crooked, but she knew which side her bread was buttered on. You bet she did! . . . Besides—cold! Cold as ice!

As far as he was concerned she could be as crooked as she wanted so long as she didn't go too far. He didn't care, but he was old-fashioned—that's what he had told her he was, and he was. An old-fashioned American gentleman when it came to some things; and damned proud of it. None of this French stuff. . . . There was that wife of the French officer he had known overseas when he had been in the Quartermaster Corps, for instance. Disgusting, when you looked at it properly. Thank goodness he, Sydney, might be pretty wild but he never mixed up his moral values. Whenever he was wrong, he knew it. That was the difference anyway between Anglo-Saxons and these darned foreigners; never mixed up their moral values, Anglo-Saxons didn't; might be just as bad as anyone else to all practical intents and purposes, but never mixed up their moral values. . . . What had been the use of going to war, when you came to think of it? Nobody appreciated it any more. Nobody. . . . People laughed too much. That was the trouble. Always laughing—not serious enough. That damned sneering snob, Gulian Eyre, laughed too much. Probably laughed at him—Sydney. Damned sneering snob! . . .

Sydney arose with the earnest unsteadiness of a certain kind of drunkenness and frowned at Sir Galahad. Now that he came to think of it, 'the mutt in armor' looked something like that Eyre pup . . . same straight features; same curly hair; except that Eyre was older and sunburned and harder. Same sort of silly face, however. . . . Sydney walked over to the bureau and opening the top drawer took out a service-revolver and held it in his hand. He regarded the bland trumpeter of death with deep attention.

No, that wouldn't do. That would be silly. Couldn't shoot a man—not in New York. They hung you sometimes for shooting a man in New York no matter how good your excuse was. It wasn't like other parts of the country that were still American—couldn't defend your honor any more. Besides, he didn't want to kill Gulian, he wanted to frighten him. And you couldn't frighten a man after he was dead. He held Gulian Eyre in the hollow of his hand—could hold him there as long as he wanted. All he had to do was to hint to him that he would tell his brother, Philip, or his father; or his—Sydney's—own father. Could raise hell, that's what he could do! All that would be necessary was to let Eyre realize that his secret was known. That would be enough. He would like to see Eyre's face when it happened. No necessity for 'rough stuff.' None at all. Modern men didn't fight. Didn't have to. . . .

These reflections pleased Sydney immensely. He smiled thoughtfully and gently. Someday he would take this matter up with Eyre, show him where he belonged—meanwhile he would go to his club for dinner.

He dropped the revolver back into the drawer and reached for his coat and put it on. Then he turned out the light and left the apartment.

. . . In her own room, next door, Vida had laid aside her pretty, soft, clinging gray gown and had taken a bath before dressing for dinner. Now she stood before a long cheval-glass in the subdued light of two rose-shaded side-lamps and stared at her reflection; the hidden loveliness of her slender figure. This was an old habit in which she took infinite satisfaction. There was about it a Narcissan pleasure and a sense of freedom in secrecy; a sense of being one of the rare spectators of a beauty absolutely her own possession and her gift, if so she wanted.

Her dark hair above the white pool of her shoulders and arms was like the shadow of trees in the moon- light of a forest. Her waist was as slim as a boy's. But tonight she was not happy; she was overwhelm- ingly, acridly depressed. She sighed, turned away, and taking a gorgeous dressing gown of Chinese silk from a chair, put it on and rang a bell. To the maid who answered her ring, she gave instructions to have dinner brought to her where she was.

After the maid had left, she turned out the rose- shaded lamps and going to the window-seat, pulled aside the curtains and resting her elbow on the ledge, cupped her chin in her hand and stared up at the, by now, green, faintly star-illumined night. Presently she put her hand down, and although she did not cry, her throat ached as if a wire band were pressing upon it.

She had saved Randall Sedgewick and herself, she had switched Sydney's single-track mind in a direction that would occupy him for many months to come, she had even satisfied to some extent a vague desire to be revenged upon Gulian and, above all, upon Margaret— not that Sydney had the courage for any very overt act—but now that she had done all this, none of it seemed worth while.

CHAPTER VIII

But there it is, as we said, a man joins a sect and becomes one-eyed.

New Letters: STEVENSON.

IT WAS unfortunate, or perhaps fortunate, since on the whole it is better to have such things over and done with as speedily as possible, that Sydney, entering his club, should have found Gulian leaving it. Oddly enough, too, since it was a club Gulian seldom if ever used—an organization supposed to be devoted to sporting and drinking purposes but now that drinking had to be done fairly secretly, given over almost entirely to card playing. A painful place Gulian found it, where well-dressed, hard-faced, rich young men pretended to like each other. He had dropped in this evening merely to write a note to Drusilla, and he was pausing by the letter-box near the front door when Sydney passed him.

"Hello," he said casually.

Sydney nodded and stopped and came back.

"I want to see you, Eyre," he announced a trifle breathlessly.

"Me?"

"Yes, you."

Gulian's brow wrinkled and he looked at his watch. "Right now? I'm awfully sorry." He smiled. "I've just about time to get home and dress—there's some people coming to dinner. Call me up and make an appointment, that is—Is it really important?"

Sydney nodded in silence.

"I'll expect you tomorrow then, or some time," Gulian cheerily agreed and waved his hand and hurried along the hall.

"Now what the devil," he wondered, as he went down the outer steps, "does that poor fish want with me?"

Sydney was left standing aimlessly by the letter-box. He found that his heart was beating rapidly. He looked about him as if he feared someone would hear it, and then, after a further moment of indecision, squared his shoulders and marched off rather proudly in the direction of a small room at the rear of the club where there were a number of men sitting around tables against a background that resembled the dressing quarters of a gymnasium, except that the serried ranks of wooden lockers were too small to hold clothes.

Sydney peered through the tobacco smoke until he found a table inhabited by some particular cronies. He crossed over to this and sank into a chair.

"I'll take a bronx," he said.

He felt considerably elated. He had not been afraid to face Eyre; he had hesitated only a moment before he had stopped him. Funny, meeting him that way, just after the talk with Vida! Damn insolent snob!

After the third bronx, Sydney began to wonder why he had hesitated even for a fraction of a second —why he had ever hesitated about anything. There was nothing like taking the bull by the horns; nothing! In fact, he was amazed at himself because he hadn't had it out with Gulian then and there. He pictured himself rolling over and over—but most of the time on top—in the hallway of the club, Gulian's

piteous face staring semi-consciously up at him and
club-servants, possibly a member or two, trying to
pull him—Sydney—off. Of course such an exhibition
of rage and strength would result in his being expelled
from the club but then Gulian would be expelled too,
and as for his own expulsion, Sydney decided, he didn't
care very much, anyhow. He had never thought about
it before, but as a matter of fact he hadn't any real
friends in this club; these men he was sitting
with weren't real friends. They merely took your
drinks and pretended to be friends. There were very
few real friends anywhere in the world. It was a
matter of tooth and claw. . . . This last reflection saddened Sydney so greatly that he abruptly left
his pseudo-friends and went upstairs to the restaurant
where he ordered dinner and drank a pint of burgundy from his private stock. The mellow wine re-
stored his good-humor, and it suddenly came to him
with a pleasant glow that ran along his arms and
shoulders that he not only had a moral advantage over
Gulian but a physical one as well. Gulian was afraid
of him. He had seen it in Gulian's eyes. . . .

"Bring me another pint," he said to the waiter.

Like a great many men who, returning to their own
country after a long absence, are more than casually
interested in what has happened to it and where it is
going, Gulian had heretofore taken not the slightest
interest in what certainly is one of the most characteristic revelations of any nation. He had heard that
the churches were in a parlous state but this did not
excite him, and his calmness on the subject had been
fortified by Philip's clumsy attempts to worry him
into an open show of orthodoxy. After attending one
service at Holy Trinity he had flatly refused to go
to any more . . . spiritually certified millionaires

who regarded Heaven as an eleemosynary institution, privately endowed, but open to their inferiors upon certain conditions, failing to please him. And although he had also accompanied his father to St. Jude's two or three Sundays, he had been more depressed than sanctified by the sight of that dwindling congregation. Earnestness and simplicity and goodness in the pulpit seemed to be no more effective than modernity and carefully calculated mental antics. It was therefore with considerable amused mystification that he looked forward to Philip's ecclesiastical dinner. He supposed that it was Philip's last desperate assault upon his worldliness.

They—Gulian and Dr. Hartley and Mr. Matthewson and Philip—had come out after dinner into the garden of 15 Madison Place and were having their coffee under a trelliswork whose summer dusted vine Prescott had that afternoon carefully washed for the occasion. There were four wicker chairs in a semicircle and between the chairs was a wicker table. In the subdued radiance the garden looked as green and fruitful as it had done in the spring, and the bronze boy of the fountain added to this impression of verdure and restfulness with his conch shell. He did more than that; he overlaid the whole occasion with the curious implication of a secret existence of its own and of perpetuity that running water gives. . . . You go away; you come back. It is eternally there, engaged in its busy, aloof, absorbed, hurrying business. And while you are within hearing it furnishes, despite its haste, a continuous comment, ironic and good natured, to all your thoughts and conversations. No wonder men invented Naiads.

"You didn't exactly answer my question, did you?" repeated Gulian.

Dr. Hartley crossed his graceful Episcopalian legs.

"No," he admitted with an engaging frankness, "I didn't; and to tell you the truth, I didn't because I take very little stock in this assumed spiritual superiority—Christian or otherwise—of other ages to our own. I know them too well; I've studied them too deeply. We—I am convinced—are an improvement. We have grown in humanity and humor and clearsightedness." He straightened up in his chair. "In short—" he waved a conclusive cigar—"I think it marvelous, considering the multiplicity of interests, the myriad distractions, how the light of faith still burns so brightly in the modern man's breast; how it spreads; how it becomes warmer. I wish, for instance, you'd make a habit of dropping into my church, Mr. Eyre. . . . Not now, of course; most of my people are in the country—I am going myself shortly; but during the winter. You'd be astonished. The richest people in the city, the last people you would think would be interested in religion. Earnestness, generosity, good works. Does that mean nothing?"

"I've been there," said Gulian dryly.

"And you were unimpressed?"

"I saw no signs of a desire, or an ability, to dance before the Lord—or, for that matter, before Apollo either. And that—fundamentally—is what I am talking about."

"Dance before the Lord? Apollo?" Dr. Hartley's polite laughter held a trace of bewilderment.

"Yes." Gulian's voice was troubled and uncertain, as if, against his will, he was being forced to state views that were deep seated in his mind but by no means clearly formulated. "Exactly. Dance before the Lord." He leaned forward even further in his chair. "If the object of life is to find joy, and one of the ways of finding joy is to find God, then if there isn't any joy, God hasn't been found. You see, I'd like to know what has become of ecstasy. It doesn't seem to exist any more except in exercise or in a few love affairs. Whatever other ages may have felt, we at least have lost the trick of being joyous citizens. I don't expect, to be sure," he added hastily, "a mature banker or an elderly lawyer to do a *pas seul* in public, but I would like to see in their faces some reflection of a shining inner vision; and I didn't notice any the other Sunday, Mr. Hartley. In fact, I was greatly depressed by the fact that your bankers and brokers and lawyers who ought to be the leaders of the community had very obviously lost sight of the three or four primary pursuits of man. I should say that they don't believe in God, except in the same way that they believe in the Union Club; that they don't believe in beauty except as something some hired man can make for them; and that as for love, they regard it as a rather unpleasant form of poison ivy which they are managing to avoid as they grow older by no longer venturing into the woods on picnics. . . . That may be all right, but it isn't a very inspiring point of view, and it isn't even a very safe one. No man ever gained his soul except by losing it. And now to come to my point, the fault, I think, lies chiefly with the Protestant idea—or rather, the way the Protestant idea has been worked out. The other great division of the Christian church seems to get considerable comfort out of its faith and, by so doing, considerable comfort out of life in general."

Dr. Hartley sighed. "It's the fashion now," he said, "for earnest young men to blame all the troubles of the world on the churches."

Gulian laughed. "Thank you for the earnest,—

but as for the rest of it, I'm afraid you're behind the times . . . the church has begun to factor so very little in the minds of earnest young men that they have begun to look around for another scape-goat. It's only the frivolous who still subscribe to doctrines they are too lazy to question."

He was astonished and diverted to find himself in the heat of a religious discussion, and it bore out his theory that there were only two or three real questions at the center of the heart of man, and one of them was his search for God. Moreover, somehow or other he could not help feeling that something that had once been in the world had been lost and that the world was overwhelmingly poorer. Humanity could be forgiven for not realizing what it never had discovered, but it could hardly be forgiven for discarding what it had once possessed. The signs of this self-mutilation were everywhere visible. The present age physically was the most comfortable of any in history; mentally it was the most uncomfortable. The modern man spiritually was the loneliest man of all times; far lonelier even than his shaggy ancestor who had roamed an almost uninhabited sphere. It was difficult to tell whether this discomfort was the result of growing pains or a vacuum.

Meanwhile Dr. Hartley had at last found something he could set his teeth into. "That," he said, sitting upright in his chair, "is one of the most subversive statements I have ever heard. And why you blame the Protestant churches especially, Mr. Eyre, I do not know. Why do you blame the churches at all? Isn't most of the fault—if there is any fault—due to changing conditions? As I understand it, your line of reasoning is this: one of the essential pursuits of man is the search for God; basically this search is the same as the search for beauty; therefore, since modern man is still so far removed from God, and, as a consequence, so far removed from beauty, the church, which has had charge of this search—these combined searches—is in some way the principal culprit. But may I ask what the churches have ever done except to humbly preach the necessity for worshipping the Lord in the beauty of holiness; and may I ask when, in recent times, they have failed to be aware of their own imperfections and the imperfections of their congregations?"

He was a very adequate clergyman, Dr. Hartley; a youngish, florid, sanguine, very well-dressed, well assured clergyman. The tails of his coquettish coat flapped briskly about him as he walked; he seemed always to be in a hurry to keep an appointment with one of the more executive of the archangels. He presented a striking contrast to Mr. Matthewson; about Mr. Matthewson there was something human and uncertain and humbly courageous, rather like the weather-beaten façade of his own church, St. Jude's. But at the center of this, like the high-altar of St. Jude's, one suspected that there was an unconquerable unimpairment, shining and adequate. You could conceive of Mr. Matthewson in the privacy of his study doubting many things—man-made things—but you could not conceive of him doubting for a moment the ultimate triumph of love or character or humility.

His parish, as has been said, was a poor one; mostly elderly people of long descent, whose families had been saved for so many generations that salvation had become practically hereditary, and a scanty handful of the neighboring less well-to-do, who conducted themselves with the modest sinuosity that seems inseparable from being an humble adherent of the most fashionable of denominations. . . . Mr. Matthewson had outgrown religious discussions. He sat with his hands in his lap listening to the fountain.

Gulian gesticulated slowly in the moon-dusted twilight; the moon was just beginning to rise over the edge of the house. "The churches have never been humble," he said, "they have never preached that beauty and God were the same thing; they have taken a joyous and splendid desire and made it something stupid and hateful and oppressive. In every instance they have stood against advancement and light; in every crisis they have gone back on the doctrines to which they subscribe. But at one time man had little else to think of, so they could not kill his desire completely. At present man has a great deal to think about—so they have almost succeeded in killing it. The fact that the desire is not dead shows what a powerful desire it is. The reason, Mr. Hartley, I especially blame the Protestant churches is because they have had hold of a further truth and represented, as it were, the intellectual side—the more modern side— of the Christian belief, and yet they have deliberately contradicted intelligence and deliberately contradicted the very reason for their existence.

"You say the churches tell people to worship the Lord in the beauty of holiness; have you ever heard them tell people to worship beauty in the holiness of the Lord? Have you ever heard them tell people that joy was goodness and that honest merriment was the same thing as God? I never have. What I mostly hear is a bored repetition of the phrase 'be good and you'll be happy,' which, incidentally, is the greatest lie ever invented. No man was ever made happy merely by being good—as a rule he is only made re-

gretful. He is made happy solely by the feeling that
in some mysterious way what he calls God has caught
him up and is invisibly near. From the very beginning the churches have denied the intrinsic teachings of
their own Master: have denied, that is, the righteous-
ness of life itself, and assumed that it was a wearisome
preparation for an even more wearisome future. What
a vast corporation of taboo has been built up, when all
that was needed were loosely organized trading-posts
where a man could exchange his bundle of doubts for
the simple merchandise of 'try to love your God (whatever God you can find) with all your heart and all your
soul; and try to love your neighbor as yourself.'

"And the trouble is that the churches have been so
strong that their influence has permeated everything
else. Nowadays most men think that duty is a condition of life. They only think so because they've got
the cart before the horse; because their point of view
has been perverted. Fun is the natural condition of
life. There is hardly a duty which if looked at properly and undertaken by someone properly trained from
the beginning isn't fun. It's fun to hunt God because
it keeps you keen spiritually; it's fun to hunt learning
because your mind is a muscle and it gives you the
same glow to conquer a mental problem as it does to
conquer a physical one; it's fun to be decent because
you are outrunning yourself; it's fun to be faithful to
one woman because she laughs and you do too. Tears
aren't fun.

"If I had my way, Mr. Hartley, I would first cause
to be issued a brief of just what Protestantism is; and
then I would call a great convocation and force the
warring sects to pool all their material and spiritual
property. Thirdly, I would have a man to man search
made among the congregations and, an agreement hav-

ing been entered into with the other principal division of Christian thought for reciprocal action, by every use of argument and advice weed out of Protestantism the born conservatives and welcome into Protestantism the born radicals. Finally, using the vast funds and power collected, I would build wherever possible great houses —temples—for the worship of God; lovely as the thought of man could make them; dominating the countryside; brooding over towns like the shadows of warm great clouds; open night and day; into which any honest—or for that matter, dishonest—man could go, assured that he would be free from any catechism, actual or implied; from the prying or advice of any senile fanatic or ignorant boy, and I should have my guardians of the temples use their missionary efforts solely in trying to persuade men to enter the temples— that and that alone. The preaching of any doctrines would be a theological offense. An official priesthood where Protestantism is concerned is a contradiction in words. Once you got a man inside one of these temples I would let silence and music and beauty do the preaching. There would be services, of course, for those who liked them and who needed this additional stimulation and symbol—services in side-chapels. But these temples—these cathedrals—wouldn't be churches at all in the accepted sense of the word; they would be laboratories where any man could go to conduct undisturbed his own experiments. Perhaps there would be a small staff of especially qualified experts attacking historical and ethical and spiritual problems, but with no more validity attached to their solutions than is attached to the results of the researches of any ordinary scientist; perhaps there would be a few great itinerant preachers to be used in times of festival or doubt; but purely inspirational preachers, no dogma;

and carefully chosen, for oratory is a rare gift and usually of the devil. . . . I don't know. All organization is dangerous, especially to the Protestant idea."

Gulian paused and spread out his hand helplessly. "In brief," he concluded, "that's my idea of Protestantism. Probably it's absurd; obviously it will never be put into effect; but until something of the sort is done there will be no such thing as Protestantism. And remember this, Mr. Hartley, the agnostic isn't necessarily an unbeliever; he is more likely than not to be a super-Protestant—a Protestant who has been driven from church to church until in disgust he is driven out of the churches completely. Each Protestant sect has been founded by a man who was regarded as an agnostic by the sect he left. Even the atheist is merely an agnostic who has lost his nerve. As a rule they are the very men the Protestant churches most need. The most honest of Protestants; the quintessence of Protestantism—Protestants without a spiritual home. If you want to look for real unbelief, hunt the sleepy pews of your churches."

Gulian sat back in his chair, a little ashamed of his eloquence; astonished at the concreteness of his thoughts—once he set himself to codifying them— upon a subject to which he had given so little formal attention. But the thoughts—his passionate eagerness—must have been there all the while.

Philip stirred uneasily and reaching over to the table, took a cigarette from the box and began to tap its end on the arm of his chair. He continued to tap it vaguely, absent-mindedly.

"Succinctly what you mean," he said to Gulian, but without looking up, "is that never before have the outlines of God and beauty, and the necessity for combining them . . . their essential similarity . . .

been so clear in men's minds and never before have they been so distant from men's ordinary lives? You mean we don't seem to get these things actually into our fibre? We're objectivists; lip-worshippers . . . if we're anything at all. Is that it? . . . Yes, I think you're right."

In the silence that followed, Dr. Hartley spoke with amazement. "Philip!" he said. "You of all men!" He drew his breath in slowly. "It is difficult to argue with you, Mr. Eyre," he continued, his voice recapturing its bland good humor. "You touch such a huge subject so lightly. It would take me many hours to answer you. Where shall I begin? Give me a point of attack—where shall I begin?"

"Where most people like arguments to begin," suggested Gulian, leaning forward again, "with their own personalities and problems? Tell us why it is, for instance, that I, with the best intentions in the world and a predestined Protestant, for intellectually I could be nothing else, and Philip, who has certainly, unlike myself, striven hard enough, can find little but disgust and weariness in the church to which we wish to belong. . . . Incidentally, Philip astonishes me as much as he does you. But no matter. Answer me that question, Mr. Hartley. . . . I don't want to seem didactic. I realize I am an amateur talking to professionals. I am merely, like the present-day average man all over the world, asking for enlightenment. Perhaps Mr. Matthewson will collaborate with you."

Mr. Matthewson shook his head in the moonlight and smiled.

"I will try to do the best I can," began Dr. Hartley, taking his cigar from his mouth, but he got no further, for Prescott, treading softly on the brick pavement, had appeared from the house and was stooping over Gulian.

"Mr. Eyre, Mr. Sydney Prendegast is anxious to see you, sir, on important business," he said.

Gulian followed Prescott through the side door that led from the garden, and along the hall, and into the dimly lit drawing room, with its ghostly baize-covered furniture and its strange June smell of stored up heat and tropic dust. A figure ghostly almost as its surroundings moved from a corner and stepped towards him.

"Hello," said Gulian.

"Is that all, Mister Gulian?" asked Prescott.

"That's all, thank you."

Prescott vanished, his departure leaving a still greater emptiness.

Through a back window, staring, uncurtained, the moonlit garden was visible and the comfortable backs of Philip and Dr. Hartley, and the long shadow of Mr. Matthewson. Their cigars glowed like fireflies on a new, not yet thoroughly illumined planet.

Gulian felt grimly alert, sardonically amused, on the edge of irritation. He could have wished for no more pointed conclusion to his thoughts concerning the seemingly hopeless space between the arguments, the desires of thinking men, and actuality, than this unwelcome visit. Had Sydney Prendegast deliberately chosen it, he could not have picked a more dramatic moment than this, with its background of soft moon and quietly smoking clergymen and chuckling fountain; with its talk of mysticism and God and beauty and the church; its memories of good food and placid wines.

Sydney had not as yet spoken, but there was something in his manner, in the gravity of his long sallow face, in the aroma of whiskey—or brandy, or whatever it was—that surrounded him, which, in connection with the remembered portentousness of his manner a few hours before in the hallway of the club, warned Gulian that when he did speak what he had to say would not be pleasant.

"Is there anything," asked Gulian smilingly, "I can do for you?"

CHAPTER IX

THE LAYING OF A GHOST

SYDNEY, as he had stepped forward to meet his host from the dark corner of the Eyre drawing-room in which he had been waiting since Prescott had left him, had experienced a disagreeable twinge of doubt. Gulian was a more powerful man when you inspected him closely than Sydney's recollection had led him to suppose. One of the accompaniments of Gulian's lean face and slender build was the impression— while you were away from him—that he was a man of medium height and over-thin. You had to look at him carefully to realize the breadth of his shoulders and the easy grace with which he walked.

Sydney was looking at him carefully; he was looking at him with extreme care. He knew himself to be heavier, but the margin of difference was not as great as that required in any question where there was a possibility of final recourse to physical weapons. Sydney was no longer actively drunk, and he was beginning to think of himself more as a pleasant but not to be trifled with mature man, than as an adventurous youngster. The long ride down town in a taxicab had sobered him considerably; the discreet figure of Prescott, the shadowy, half-lighted room had about completed the process. There was left only a small nucleus of intoxication and desire for revenge. Had he been a less timid man and, therefore, less afraid of himself, he would have gone home at once. But self-consciousness kept him where he was. He decided, however, that the interview would be more polite than he had at first intended.

There would be not the slightest occasion for anything but diplomatic threats, anyhow. Both he and Gulian had passed the fighting age and both were restrained by the code of gentle-folk. And Sydney received a new wave of confidence in remembering once more the supposition that had sent him on his errand; the supposed fear of the Eyres where scandal was concerned; their old-fashioned horror of public nastiness. He saw himself in a quiet way bullying Gulian to his heart's content.

None the less, Gulian's good-natured, a trifle patient expression, as he stood in the middle of the room, annoyed Sydney considerably. He deliberately avoided his host's outstretched hand. Gulian looked down at the offending member, smiled, and pointed to a sofa.

"Sit down," he said. "Have a cigarette?"

"Thanks. . . ." Sydney brought out his own case. "I have a match."

"You wanted to see me at once, then?"

Sydney looked up from the table upon which he was depositing the burnt match and narrowed his eyes.

"Yes," he said, with a deliberateness which concealed his trepidation, "I do."

"Won't you come out into the garden? There're some men out there. It would be more comfortable."

"No. I can talk to you better in here."

Gulian, perceiving the nervousness and hesitancy in Sydney's manner, felt sorry for Sydney; he knew only too well that Sydney's domestic life was not a very happy one and he knew that Sydney not only drank too much ordinarily, but that he had been drinking too much on this particular occasion. But then,

Gulian felt sorry for undeveloped humanity generally. It was only for the full-armed rogue that he experienced no pity. In reality Sydney was only a drunken boy of fifteen who had been drunk from babyhood. The world was full of such drunken children. Life was pitiably beyond their grasp. He felt a desire to help his faltering visitor out.

"What is it you wanted to say to me?" he urged gently.

Sydney took a mental lurch, and spoke rapidly. As he spoke his confidence increased—to the timorous there is nothing so encouraging as the sound of their own voices.

"Eyre," he began. "Well, there's no use beating about the bush . . . I've come to tell you pretty clearly what I think of you, and I've come to warn you." Gulian looked astonished. "If it wasn't for the fact that your father and my father are old friends and that we belong to the same business family, I wouldn't have taken the trouble—I'd have let you get into the jam that sooner or later you'll get into. It isn't too pleasant for a man to drag his wife into a thing like this, but in this case I'm going to."

"Your wife?" asked Gulian softly.

"Yes, my wife."

Gulian had been watching the unpleasant equine face with a growing attention, his eyes looking up steadily from under eyelashes slightly lowered. Now he got to his feet. "Let's sit over here," he suggested casually, indicating two chairs near the empty fireplace. "We'll be nearer each other."

His eyes studied Sydney's tall, stooping figure as it crossed the intervening space. The coat of Sydney's gray light-textured suit was buttoned and to Gulian's relief there was no suspicious bulge to any of the pockets. It was just as well to be assured of such things. When neurasthenics like Sydney begin to talk of wives and loyalties it is best to make certain that they are not armed.

Gulian took the chair opposite Sydney and leaning back, regarded him with a kindly expression. "Now," he said, "go on. What has your wife got to do with it?"

His visitor was not prepared for such friendliness. For a moment he was disconcerted. Things were not going just as he had expected.

"Everything!" he blurted out hastily.

"Everything?"

"Look here, Eyre! ——" Sydney recaptured his fierceness. "I'm not here to pass compliments; and I'm not here to waste my time or yours. . . . I'll come to the point. You can put it over me when it's a question of talk—you've lived all over the world and I'm only more or less of a simple citizen; but by God, there are certain things which you can't put over on me, and that's what I'm here to tell you. You can't come back to this country and try to steal other men's wives and get away with it. If you want to make love to another man's wife, you at least have to do it decently—you have got to let her get a divorce and then marry her. There're a few people who do otherwise, but not many. I'm telling you this for two reasons; in the first place, as I said, I want to warn you; and in the second place, I don't mind, while I'm about it, letting you know what a dirty sneak I think you are."

"Thanks," said Gulian as if relieved.

Sydney breathed heavily through his nose. He had accomplished something. He was rather proud of his final sentence.

Gulian's expression had remained unchanged except

for a momentary look of bewilderment; now he leaned sideways towards his accuser. "I'm not sure," he commented, and anyone listening to him would have thought that in his voice there was a trace of a chuckle; as if, in some outlandish fashion, he was amused by this strange interview, "whether this is an academic discussion or whether you have some concrete point in view. At all events, it's very nice of you to drop in this way and inform me about the customs of the country—I mean the present national point of view about clandestine love affairs. I shall treasure your words. As I understand it, nowadays no husband minds if another man steals his wife, so long as he does it publicly and does it in the courts. Is that it?"

Sydney glared at him.

"Don't you try to be funny!" he said threateningly.

He had by this time come to the conclusion that Gulian's continued amiability was not the result of a lack of fear, as he had at first imagined, but the result of a rather desperate attempt to temporize and evade the issue. Then Gulian was the sleek coward he had always thought him.

"I'm not trying to be funny," said Gulian soberly. "I've never been sadder in my life."

Sydney abruptly got to his feet and stooped over his interlocutor, his long face a dusky red.

"Eyre," he said, "you tried to make a fool of my wife and she wouldn't let you—That's true, isn't it? She has too much sense. Besides, she saw through you and what a cad you are. And you sneered at me, too, didn't you? Well, I've come to tell you tonight that you can't sneer at me and, moreover, that you'd better not try to make a fool of anybody's wife." He stooped nearer to Gulian. "From now on you do one single thing I don't like—one single thing—and I'll fix you

for good. . . . I'll tell your brother what my wife told
me this afternoon—I'll tell your father, if necessary;
I'll tell my father; I'll tell the whole damned world.
I'll make a public goat and fool out of you. Does that
get through? That's what I've come to tell you."

Gulian continued to smile absent-mindedly at
the empty fireplace. "So your wife told you that I
had insulted her, did she?" he murmured. Vida having tested his sense of honor once and found it secure,
had evidently decided to rely on it continuously.
". . . Well, the whole thing is very noble of you. It
reflects credit on your intelligence and courage—even
if you are a little drunk. In telling your story you
couldn't very well have left out Vida's name, could
you?" Suddenly he looked up at the equine face bend-
ing over him. "What is this anyhow," he asked
sharply, his words cracking out like the lash of a
whip." "Blackmail?"

Sydney's stooping face grew darker. He clenched
his fist.

"Don't you get insulting ——"

"I don't intend to be. I want to know. I'm living
now on a small salary I earn at my brother-in-law's,
and I would like to know what other expenses I am
to expect——"

"You dog!" said Sydney. "I've explained my
reasons."

"Altruistic. Well, thank you." Gulian stood up,
brushing Sydney aside. "Now Prendegast," he said,
"let me do some talking. If I'm not mistaken, for
some reason you don't like me and, having got hold
of what you think is a disastrous story, you intend to
dangle it over my head as long as you see fit. The idea
being that if at any future time I do anything you
you don't care about you'll try to ruin me with my

family. Is that it? Well, you must have a queer family. I don't believe I could be ruined quite so easily with mine. Of course what you propose isn't actual blackmail, but it's mental blackmail. Did you ever hear the story about the Duke of Wellington and a certain lady? She wrote she was going to blackmail him and he wrote back: 'Dear H: Blackmail and be damned.'" Gulian moved slowly towards one of the windows that opened into the garden.

"What are you going to do?" asked Sydney in a startled voice.

"I'm going to open the window," replied Gulian evenly, "and call in my brother. I'll call in Dr. Hartley of Holy Trinity and Mr. Matthewson of St. Jude's too, if you want them."

"You idiot!" snarled Sydney. "Get away from that window."

Gulian wheeled suddenly about.

"If you move a step forward," he said, "I'll knock you down."

He flung open the window and leaned into the moonlight. "Philip," he called, "will you come in here a minute?"

* * * * *

Afterwards, thinking it over, Gulian remembered with a glow of surprised affection Philip's unlooked-for broad-mindedness. In a crisis Philip's formalism dropped away from him.

Puzzled, blinking from the darkness, he had stepped into the room and had taken a position before the empty fireplace, his hands locked behind his back, and Gulian, without waste of time, had told him the situation. Philip had listened in silence.

"I'm entirely guilty," Gulian had finished, "and I want you to understand it." (He did not know exactly what sort of a lie was expected from him, but he was aware that whatever story Vida had told, the broadest sort of lie was necessary.) "I did make love to Mrs. Prendegast and she's a damn fine woman, as I discovered when I made an ass of myself. That's all there is to that. But that isn't my point. I'll leave her out, even if her husband won't. What I object to is what Prendegast has tried to do to me. He has tried to frighten me. He has tried to hold a whip over my head. Well, here's his whip; I give it back to him. I'd have respected him a little bit more if he had tried to fight me, . . . but he wouldn't fight. The whole mix-up is grotesque and absurd. What do you think, Philip?"

Philip had swayed slightly backward and forward on the balls of his feet.

"Did Mrs. Prendegast send you here?" he asked Sydney gravely.

"No," said Sydney. "Of course not."

"Um! I thought so. Gulian," Philip turned to his brother, "this man, as you probably already know, is drunk. I doubt if even he would have made such a fool of himself if he hadn't been. If he bothers you again, thrash him, or let me know, and I'll speak to his father. . . . He lives on his father. As for you, it is none of my business what you do—you are a grown man. I may regret that we disagree on some things, and I may regret that you can find time or heart to do a thing like this—that is, if you did do it— but assuredly I have no intention of interfering with your life. . . . We ought to go back to our guests. Goodnight, Prendegast."

"I'll see him out," Gulian volunteered.

He led Sydney to the front door and flung it open.

St. Mark's Place lay bathed in moonlight. A cool breeze stirred the leaves of the trees.

"Goodnight," said Gulian cheerily.

"You damn ——" began Sydney.

"Oh, shut up!" Gulian interrupted with a passionate weariness. "Shut up! Shut up!"

He watched Sydney's retreating figure until it disappeared in the distance, and then he went back to his guests.

Philip was already there, and he and Dr. Hartley— Mr. Matthewson had very little to say—were engaged in a placid conversation about politics. The new administration was going to bring order out of chaos. The country was going to return to sanity and quiet and business-like methods. There was to be a millennium of normality; a sort of heavenly Wall Street; an apotheosis of fat, white-haired kindly men engaged in killing uncomfortable facts; not killing them, but sitting upon them; pretending they weren't there. . . . Gulian thought of the really great and sick man in his retreat in Washington. A brooding eagle; a real American, with all the American faults and virtues. Not the American of the ponderous decline; not the 'one hundred per cent American' of small towns and smaller meannesses, but the American with the falcon nose of the breed which had pushed forward frontiers of land and thought. Nothing left of this brooding eagle much but flame. Selfish, near-sighted where other men were concerned, inhuman, Jesuitical, but brave to folly, great-horizoned, a poet, an artist, a passionate lover of his nation, an emperor, a bugle call. The world rewarded well its rarer spirits. No man could attempt to tell the ultimate truth and not be slain. . . .

But Gulian didn't want to talk politics; he didn't

want to talk about anything; he was depressed. A familiar that had been his shadow for many weeks had departed; a wraith that had been near to him was gone; and, as is the case with all men who have been haunted, where the ghost had been there was now to be for awhile nothing but loneliness.

CHAPTER X

JUNE DUSK

THERE were only a few days left to June, but they proved to be momentous days, marked by two events that disturbed Gulian greatly and by a third which, although at the time it seemed of no importance, was to have not a little bearing upon his future. . . . To take the third, and apparently unimportant incident first, Margaret coming up to town on a Saturday and bringing her son, Philip Junior, to see the dentist and discovering with her usual efficiency that Gulian had no pressing engagement for that afternoon, and having herself a great deal to do, turned Philip Junior over to Gulian from lunch until half-past four.

Margaret, her voice a little shining disc of fool's-gold, a bit of metallic cheerfulness surpassing the cheerfulness of any person actually ingenuous, a voice she used whenever she wanted anything, called Gulian up at his office. Could he lunch with her and Philip Junior? He could (not being brilliant at thinking up excuses on the spur of the moment). . . . Where? . . . Well, would Delmonico's do? . . . At what time? . . . One o'clock?

At the appointed hour he found Margaret and Philip Junior in the narrow hall and took them to a table near a window.

Margaret was, for her, in exceptionally good spirits; full of health, vitality and scandal. All her neighbors on Long Island were behaving in their usual outrageous way and the only possible hope of the world was, as usual, for women to organize. What they were to do when they organized was not so clear. Drink was on the increase. Young girls carried flasks in their stockings, and were subsequently carried home. . . . Since they rolled their stockings, sometimes showing those vile things their knees, how they could make satisfactory ambulatory bars out of something that practically did not exist, was difficult to see . . . but no matter, they were bad. The one solution seemed to lie in a rumor that stockings were going to be abandoned entirely and replaced by paint.

During one of these somewhat distracted flights of conversation, Margaret hinted darkly at the growing intimacy between Vannya and Drusilla.

"It's very silly of Drusilla," she observed. "Criminally silly. But then, I've always said that women out of a job are constantly at the mercy of mischief. Take the mere matter of gossip. . . . You have no idea, Gulian, how idle women gossip."

"Oh, yes, I have," retorted Gulian sombrely. He turned to Philip Junior. "June," he asked, "what do you want to see? We've got the whole afternoon before us."

"Elephants!" murmured Philip Junior ecstatically.

"Elephants . . .! We share a passion. . . ."

It had been a long while since Gulian had seen anything of children and he had rather made up his mind that he didn't like them, but about Philip Junior there was something that touched him instantly and infinitely. They left Margaret at the door of Delmonico's and started for the Zoological Gardens and as the afternoon wore on, Gulian, to his surprise, found himself rather wishing that Philip Junior was his son. A straight-legged and very blond baby, Philip Junior was, with the most absurd and delicious big ears and a big sensitive nose. His eyes were as blue and crisp as periwinkles, and he was exceedingly silent, except when aroused—then he let loose a flood of questions. You could feel him tremble when he saw anything new or interesting. He trembled equally over a bird and over a steam-roller. But he was sturdily determined not to give himself away despite this weakness.

That was his one sense of himself; otherwise he was completely un-selfconscious, so keen that you could perceive, as through a shell of amber, the new born thing struggling to adjust itself to its environment; the child trying to evoke the shadow of the man beginning to enwrap it and shut it out from life.

Gulian and Philip took the subway to the Bronx and came to a nice warm pungent smell of animals and trees and grass. Just inside the gate several snowy-white goats within a large wire enclosure climbed up and down precipitous roofs and ledges, or slept in the shadows like snow-balls left over from the winter.

Gulian and Philip regarded these creatures for many ruminative moments and afterwards a bewildering multitude of others, and discussed their habits and previous condition of life—and their souls, but they saved the main treat for the end, and it was breathlessly and on tip-toe that they entered at length the house of the great grave pachyderms.

"How did you come to like elephants, June?" Gulian asked. "It's a most refined taste."

"What's refined?"

"Well . . . nice; wise; sensible—you know. What only a few people like."

June considered this statement.

"Then is it refined to like children," he concluded. "Are you refined?"

"Sometimes. . . . Why? Do I like children?"

June seemed stricken dumb.

"Don't most people like children?"

June attempted a diversion.

"They eat with their noses, don't they?" he observed speculatively.

Gulian realized that with true juvenile tact he preferred not to discuss what were obviously domestic disappointments.

"June," he said suddenly, "I want you to come to see me a lot, will you? I'm coming out to see you on Long Island, too."

June trembled. "Peanuts!" he continued with grave unconcern. "And straw—and matches! . . . Did God make elephants?"

"I suppose so."

"And goats?"

"Yes."

"And seals—and aw-striches—and all these things —and bugs?"

"Certainly."

"What a lot of old bones he must have had to start with." . . .

They headed for home at four o'clock, caught up for a while in the breathless, airless rush of the subway, and met Margaret waiting for them in her motor in front of her closed house.

"Has he been good?" she asked.

"Perfect."

"He isn't usually."

Gulian noticed that June regarded the sky thoughtfully.

"He's been a lamb!" he exclaimed vehemently and

angrily, "and as good as gold. If you don't like him, send him to me. I'd like to have him live with me."

He did not know how soon this wish was to be fulfilled.

June's big nearest ear twitched but he did not abandon his impersonal gaze.

"Goodbye."

Gulian watched the landaulet drive away, a corner of June's head visible around the side of the lowered top.

It was a serious problem, this question of childish grown-ups living with their grave and wise offspring. The giggling stolidity of those over ten years of age, increasing as they grew older, looked rather shabby beside the earnest exhilaration of human beings still in touch with the earth.

This was incident number one—or rather, three— on the surface, as has been said, of no particular significance, except that Gulian had discovered a nephew; but incidents one and two were obviously of moment, although the latter was a shadowy thing; a shadow-play; a matter of suspicion and intuition and innuendo; leaving the uninformed participant baffled as to its full meaning.

As for the former incident, somewhere in the dishabille West Forties Gulian and Cyprian had discovered a new parasitical gentleman who had opened a new parasitical dancing place. A parasitical gentleman, because there was no need for further cabarets . . . no need, in fact, for any . . . and a parasitical dancing place because the space reserved for dancing was too small for any but the half dozen professional performers hired at great expense to engage every night in the simple act of taking off their clothes; parasitical also because an indecency was hinted at that did not exist. To be sure, the space was so small that the aloofness of the professional broke down and a common adventure in vulgarity took its place, the performers beckoning the audience with their gestures and the audience beckoning the performers with their eyes, everyone, moreover, being so near to everyone else that the more unpleasant features of life in Brobdingnag were uppermost, but there was no actual indecorum. There seldom is in public exhibitions in Anglo-Saxon countries, those advertising such inducements living for a while on the hope that springs eternal in the human breast that somehow someone has at last managed to evade the explicit police laws on the subject. But most of the men who went to this new cabaret went for the extremely direct emotions they thought they were going to receive, and most of the women for the extremely indirect emotions they thought they were going to receive. As a result, they were disappointed and felt themselves cheated.

The only baldly immoral feature was the lighting, which came from a huge harvest moon and little out of place stars of a strange uncanny blue. The effect was to make you feel that all health had suddenly become unhealthy . . . incidentally, your mind was taken off the food, which was bad, and the bill, which was exorbitant. Nowhere could there have been found a better example of what happens if you suppress hearty and open enjoyment.

You went up in an elevator and were flung into this subversive illumination, and sought a dark table, and were immediately overcome with depression. At least, Gulian and Cyprian were. . . . They had dined together and gone to the theatre and had ended up here for no other reason except curiosity and a disinclination to go to bed.

"Another one of the strange meetings of Africa and the inner chambers of the Orient," observed Cyprian. "They've crossed half the world and two thousand years to meet. This savage sluggish tom-tom and this nasty subtle massage of tired nerves. At his best the negro is the sunniest and jolliest creature alive, and at his best the Oriental is a bearded saint and ascetic. But look what so-called civilization has done for both of them! The music of one, the shrewdness and love of texture of the other! If people want to run wild I wish they'd go back to the out-of-door faun stuff. . . . In a short while, when this place is more popular, they won't let us in without a woman, will they? They bank on the male's natural extravagance and bravado in the presence of the hoarding sex. There are getting to be so many places in New York that you can't get into without a woman, that a man will either have to get married, or go to the bad, or else stay at home."

The professional dancers retired to put on a few clothes, and the orchestra, huddled against a back-drop that was supposed to represent the Congo, thrummed their way softly into a dance. The management was kind enough to permit their patrons occasional intervals of normal pleasure. A few couples appeared in the dim radiance and began slowly to circle the floor.

Gulian raised his glass to his lips and abruptly set it down untasted.

"Not enough whiskey?" asked Bland, pushing the flask towards him.

"Oh plenty, thank you."

"What's wrong?"

"Nothing."

"There's nothing wrong with the whiskey, I know—it's mine."

"Let's get out of this damn hole," said Gulian passionately.

A girl in white, dancing with a man in a dinner coat, had almost touched Gulian and Bland as she passed the alcove where they sat. The man was a small compact man, very neat, very self-assured; his blond hair gone from the temples—giving him a pseudo-intellectual look—and his crisp moustache waxed and turned up. His prominent, not unhandsome eyes had the distant, insolent look of a man who has had a great deal to drink over a period lasting several hours.

"Do nice girls come to a place like this alone with a man and dance?" asked Gulian.

"I imagine that nowadays they go any place alone with a man. . . . Why? Do you think you've seen a nice girl? What makes you think that?"

"Because I know her," said Gulian, "and so do you. . . . Ready? Very well, here's my share of the bill."

He flung a note on the table and stood up. The orchestra had stopped playing and the dancers were seeking their tables; all but the girl in white and the man in the dinner-jacket. For some mysterious reason they lingered at the edge of the floor, engaged in earnest conversation. Gulian had to pass them on his way to the elevator. Bland, ahead, was walking in his usual manner of a reflective swaggering insect.

As Gulian came up to the laggard couple, the man spread out his hands in a gesture of disgust. "I'm through," he was saying. "If you want to go home, do so by all means. I won't stop you. This has happened every time I've gone anywhere with you recently. Just as I'm beginning to have a good time, you want to quit. I'll put you in a cab. . . . No, I'll go home with you and come back later."

"You needn't," said the girl in a small voice. "Just go away."

"By thunder, I will! You've said that once too often. I most certainly shall."

The girl did not answer and, after a final moment of hesitancy, the man turned away and walked across the empty space.

For a moment the girl watched him, twisting between her fingers a bit of paper, or the remains of a flower, before she herself started in the direction of the elevator.

Gulian had stopped in the shadow of an imitation palm; now he stepped forward.

"Well, Lael," he said.

She raised her head with a startled expression.

"Oh, it's you, is it?" she asked coldly.

"Yes, it's I. I'll take you home."

"You needn't bother, thanks."

Gulian fell in beside her without speaking. At the elevator they found Bland waiting.

"Cyprian," said Gulian, "I'm going to take Miss Satori home—she was with a party of men and women who bored her."

"I'm so glad," said Bland, "to find anyone as equally bored as myself. It is a tribute to the growing intelligence of youth. Was Miss Satori your nice girl?"

Lael smiled wanly. In the radiance of the elevator she looked pale under her paint and there were circles under her eyes.

When they reached the street they waved goodbye to Bland and Gulian hailed a cab and put Lael into it.

"I don't want you to come," she said breathlessly.

Gulian stepped in beside her and shut the door.

"You think you're very wonderful, don't you?" she remarked, as the motor started.

"I don't think anything," answered Gulian.

Suddenly he put his hand out and laid it on hers.

"Can't we be friends, Lael?" he asked. "This is silly."

She snatched her hand away.

"I hate you!" she said bitterly. "I loathe and despise you! I never come near you but you make me feel like a fool and cheap. Why should you, of all people, find me in that place with that man?"

"Because," said Gulian gently, "I think I'm going to find you in different places all my life. . . . I don't think it can be avoided. . . . Was that the man in whose library you spent the night?"

She did not answer.

"I thought so. . . . He's not even very pretty, is he?"

Presently they came to Lael's door and Gulian helped her out and followed her silently up the steps. She stooped to insert her latch key.

"Lael!"

"Well?"

"Won't you say goodnight to me?"

She shook her head without looking up.

"Won't you?"

"I've told you," she said, still fumbling with the key, "what I think of you—you're a prig and a hypocrite, and I wish you'd leave me alone."

Gulian took her by the arm and turned her about. "Then, by God," he said in a deliberate voice, "you will listen to me."

"Now you be still until I'm through   You are a fool and you are cheap, because, like most of your little friends, you're a poor steward of the real

talents you've got. You've got youth and brains
and beauty and a heart, if you want to use them . . .
but you don't. And you never will until you begin to
think of somebody else but yourself. You're a silly,
spoiled, headstrong little girl and you ought to be
whipped. You've no real knowledge or experience—
you're half-baked. All you know are the ugly little
innuendoes and thoughtless vulgarities of your equally
ignorant playmates. You don't even know what all
really worldly people know, and that is that kindliness
and decency are essential worldlinesses, and that an
honest friendship is never to be refused. I didn't kiss
you any more than you kissed me, and you know it.
I'm sick of the self-protective lies of women. . . .
Utterly sick. Goodnight. If you want to apologize
to me I'll try to erase everything that either of us have
said, not otherwise."

He turned on his heel and descended the steps. He
had an idea, as he walked along the deserted street,
that Lael was standing where he had left her, watching
him.

. . . . The shadow-play, the event of innuendo
and suspicion, the incident that seemed at the moment
to transcend in its gravity by far the other two had to
do with Vannya's coming down from 'Hibernia.'
Gulian had learned from a letter of his father's that
Vannya was in town and thought it odd that Vannya
had not let anyone know. He would have considered
it even stranger had he not realized Vannya's vagueness and complete absorption in whatever at the moment he was doing. After a day or so of silence, he
decided to call Vannya up and ask him to dine with
him that evening, but the difficulties of telephoning
Vannya were great—the telephone at the apartment
house being in the basement and a number of drawling

unknown females always to be got rid of first—so
finally he concluded to take a chance of finding Vannya at home and drop in at the studio about six
o'clock. If Vannya wasn't in, a message could be left
for him.

And it was a necessary telephone call, made at
Perry's request earlier in the afternoon, that brought
to life again certain uneasinesses concerning Vannya
and reminded Gulian what an uncanny, sometimes illu-
minating, frequently disconcerting and complicating
invention a telephone could be.

Perry had left some papers in his safe at home and
a couple of hours after lunch, he had asked Gulian to
call up his secretary-valet and have the papers sent
down to the office.

"Mudge is his name," he had added, "and he has a
lovely bass voice."

But the voice that came over the telephone in
answer to Gulian's ring was not Mudge's, it was a
soprano, and it was not the soprano of a housemaid
or even a housekeeper.

"Yes, this is Mr. Shipman's," it had said.

"Who is speaking?" asked Gulian.

There was a moment's hesitation. . . . "What do
you want?"

"Drusilla!" ventured Gulian. "Is that you, Dru?
. . . What are you doing in town? I thought you were
in Southampton. Why didn't you let me know?"

"This is not Drusilla," returned the voice coldly.
"Wait a moment. . . . I will call Mr. Shipman's man."
Presently Mudge came to the telephone.

Gulian gave the message and went back to Perry
at his desk in an inner office. "Have you got a maid
up at your house who talks like Drusilla?" he asked.

"Maid?" Perry's curly face and curly moustache were interrogatory.

"Yes."

"So help me bob," said Perry solemnly, "there isn't a woman in the house—just Mudge and me. We're living in a state of complete and lonely virtue. . . . Why do you ask?"

"Because there's a woman there who's either Drusilla or her double."

"Drusilla? Why, Drusilla isn't in town. . . . Not unless she's come up unexpectedly."

"She said she wasn't Drusilla. . . . " interjected Gulian hastily. He had decided abruptly that if it was Drusilla and she didn't want anyone to know her whereabouts, Perry would be the last person in the world to tell. "Has Mudge got a wife?"

"One, at least. She's around the house a lot."

"Oh, that's who it was then."

But he knew that it wasn't Mudge's wife; he knew that it was Drusilla, and the knowledge troubled him. Secrecy was so foreign to Drusilla and this present secret possessed curious features. If Drusilla didn't want anyone to know that she was in town, why then had she gone to her own house and why had she so carelessly answered the telephone? She would know that Mudge would inform Perry of her arrival upon Perry's return home that evening. Obviously, then, her secret, whatever it was, was one that at the end of the day would no longer be a secret.

But what kind of a secret could that be? Gulian was unable to decide. A woman might come up to town and not let her husband know merely because she disliked her husband; or she might come up to town and not let her husband know because she had an engagement with another man; but in either case she would act with extreme care. What would cause her to act with secrecy and yet, where certain details were concerned, with a cold recklessness? What would cause her to lie to her own brother? And why would she go to her house at all except to get certain articles that she needed—letters; clothes?

Anyway, Gulian decided, he would leave the office at once. He did not in the least care what Drusilla did to Perry, and in his secret heart he saw no great difference between taking Scotch leave of your husband and leaving him by legal processes, but since the world was what it was, he preferred—if his suspicions were correct—not to have Vannya and Drusilla ruin their future by any childish indiscretion.

And then—Why, yes, of course! He had forgotten that! The thing was impossible, anyhow. There was his father to be thought of . . . but then Drusilla of course knew nothing of her father's condition. . . .

Possibly it was all a chimera. He hoped so. A fantasy resulting from his own recent experiences and Margaret's gossip. However, he would go up to Perry's house and see if Drusilla was there.

He took the subway and arrived at Perry's partly shrouded doorway shortly after four o'clock. A dark wheedling man—evidently Mudge—answered his ring.

No, Mrs. Shipman had not been there. She was in the country.

"Are you sure, Mudge?" Gulian asked.

There was an evasiveness in the crossed eyes that made Gulian suspect Mudge's honesty.

"Mudge," said Gulian, "you've got a good job, haven't you?"

"Yes, sir. An excellent one, sir."

"You'd hate to lose it, wouldn't you?"

"Oh yes, sir."

"Well, maybe you will. You are in a delicate position. I am Mrs. Shipman's brother, as you know. Should anything happen to Mrs. Shipman and Mr. Shipman find out afterwards she gave you money, you'd get into trouble. . . . Did she give you money, Mudge?"

Mudge's crossed eyes became obstinate.

"You are a secretary as well," continued Gulian, "And that is a confidential position. Mr. Shipman's interests are yours—you can have no others while you are taking money from him." He suddenly thrust a fierce face close to Mudge's. "Give me that twenty-five dollars, Mudge, Mrs. Shipman gave you."

Mudge backed away.

"She gave me no money, sir."

Gulian followed him.

"You liar! . . . Then she was here, wasn't she? Mudge, give me that money and tell me what directions Mrs. Shipman gave the driver when you put her in the taxicab. Quick! Or I'll have Mr. Shipman here in half an hour."

Mudge drew some crumpled bills from his pocket.

"It was only twenty dollars, sir," he said. "It's hard; Mrs. Shipman's my mistress, too, you know. You won't tell Mr. Shipman, sir, will you?"

"Not if you tell me where Mrs. Shipman went."

"I can't remember the number exactly, but it was on Washington Place."

"How long ago?"

"Not over quarter of an hour."

Gulian turned and raced from the vestibule and out into the street. An empty cab was rolling slowly westward.

"Washington Place!" he ordered, as he flung open the door. "And drive as quickly as you can!"

He wasn't sure. Maybe it was all folly. Yet, from what he now knew, he was afraid that it was the most sober kind of actuality.

The drive down town seemed unbearably long. Traffic policemen, unconscious of what they were doing, caused heart-breaking delays. What a sinister joke on the part of fate if the uplifted arm of an unknown Irishman should alter the whole future of a man's only sister! But finally the cab came to Washington Place and Vannya's stoop.

Gulian paid the driver and hurried through the hall and up the long flights of uncarpeted stairs, dust-moted by the quiet sun of the late afternoon. He found that his heart was beating almost to suffocation as he paused in the darkness at the top of the final boxed-in ascent that led to the studio. Only a thin door separated him from final knowledge; possible success, or possible failure. And then he heard voices and was relieved.

He shook himself into a state of casualness and knocked. The voices ceased and there was a moment's hesitation before one of them—the man's voice—said "Come in."

Gulian entered smiling. About him there was not the slightest hint of his recent haste and anxiety.

The big disorderly room basked in a slanting light that touched with misty gold the edge of easel and sofa. On the sofa Drusilla and Vannya were sitting—or, rather, had been sitting, for Vannya was now on his feet, his lips half parted, staring uncertainly towards the door. The half-moon scar on his face shone white.

At the edge of the sofa were two bags marked with

Drusilla's initials. Their owner was leaning forward, little spots of red burning in her cheeks, her gray eyes wide and startled.

There was something about both these people very touching. Gulian loved them both—at the moment he loved Drusilla with a sharpness he had not felt for years. He could not find it in his heart to be angry with her. The small boy, the small girl are so inextricably mixed up with the wistful distracted maturity of people you love! Drusilla, for all her years, was only the long legged, long haired, starry eyed, tender, un-get-at-able creature of not so many years before. Gulian heard his father's outraged, delighted commands to her. People you loved never grew up. He wasn't even sure he was doing the right thing now. One moment of ecstasy might, after all, be worth a lifetime of regret. Who knows? He took in each detail of the situation with a glance.

Vannya broke the embarrassing silence.

"Fine andt dandy!" he said with a brave carelessness. "Where deed you coom from?"

The spell—the reminiscent, pellucid, beautiful and dangerous spell that had held Gulian for a moment, disintegrated like the outer rim of a thin cloud.

"Haf tea?" suggested Vannya. "Sidt down."

"Oh, no, thanks! It's too late. I came to take you out to dinner—now I'll take Drusilla too. . . . How in the world did you get here, Dru? Where did you come from? Why didn't you let me know? I thought you were in Southampton."

Drusilla raised her head and looked at her brother, and then turned her eyes away again.

"I was at Southampton," she said, "but I had to come up to town, and I dropped in to see Vannya about the portrait. . . . I want him to come up to Stockbridge and finish it."

"How long are you going to be here?"

"Just over night."

"You've just arrived?"

Drusilla waved at her suit cases.

"On my way from the station."

Gulian was aware that had this been an ordinary intrusion on his part he would have left immediately. The atmosphere was one—especially on Drusilla's part —of waiting. He could almost see her trying to invent some plausible excuse to be rid of him, and he felt that his best chance for success lay in wearing down by patience the original determination that had brought her here, by cooling it with boredom. Just the sight of him, sitting there apparently so innocent, might begin to dull slightly the edge of her first hot recklessness.

But it was uncomfortable. Gulian felt as the unwanted person always does feel; that he was sitting with inhuman heaviness upon his chair; that his hands and feet were unaccountably clumsy. He knew himself to be constantly on the edge of blushing without reason. The conversation was disjointed; heavy as separate pieces of lead.

Curiously enough, however, as it proceeded, he perceived that a subtle difference was taking place in Vannya. Vannya was momentarily becoming more light-hearted; more like his usual self. The balance of the mental attitude was turning slowly in Gulian's favor. It was almost as if Vannya was deserting Drusilla and throwing his support to Gulian. As if, after all—upon thinking it over—he was secretly relieved that Gulian had come.

Gulian smiled gravely in the gathering darkness.

He knew his Vannya. In all the world there was no
man who could commit evil more innocently. Vannya
had the heart of a child and nothing could touch it.
Later on, when he got Vannya alone, with a few words
he would put an end forever to this folly. All that
would be necessary would be to explain to Vannya
that one did not run off, no matter how one felt, with
the sister of a friend. Even at the moment Gulian
could not find it in his heart to blame Vannya greatly.
Vannya would run off with any woman he liked if he
thought that by so doing he would cause her a moment's happiness. And he would run away from her
with equal kind-heartedness. Nor would he afterwards
ever understand what all the fuss had been about.
. . . Gulian was by now quite sure that Vannya was
not really in love with Drusilla. He imagined that
Drusilla's will had been the stronger in this affair. He
wasn't even sure how much Drusilla was in love with
Vannya. In every discontented woman's life there
comes a breaking-point where the man upon whom
for a little while affection is bestowed may be no more
than a symbol.

No one lit a lamp, and the studio changed from a
place of misty gold to a place of purple shadow, and
finally to a place of haunted darkness. Vannya's
cigarette glowed in the dusk; his face and Drusilla's
were pallid oval masks. Gulian played his trump card.

"Dru," he said, "I think I ought to tell you and
Vannya something I've just learned. . . . It's about
father." He experienced the distaste that all honest
men experience when they betray a confidence and use
a secret weapon.

Drusilla stirred in the dusk. "What about him?"
she asked.

"The dear!" murmured Vannya.

"He's a very sick man."

Drusilla sat upright.

"Why haven't you told me this?" she asked harshly. "What's the matter with him?"

"Nothing perhaps, if things go right. He may live a long while if we can only keep bother and shock away from him. I don't know much about such things —it's his heart—but Ellis said a shock might kill him. Any kind of a shock."

"Doctor Ellis? . . ."

"Yes."

The white oval of Drusilla's face became motionless.

"Which way are you going, Gilly?" she asked at length.

"Back to Madison Place."

"Well, I must get up to the house. Is there any way of telephoning for a cab?"

Gulian stretched out a hand.

"Oh, please stay down town and have dinner with me!" he begged.

Drusilla arose and touched his shoulder gently.

"No," she said softly, "I must be getting back. . . . Telephone, will you, Vannya? . . . And Vannya can't dine with you either, Gilly. He has some work to do." It was as if she wished to protect Vannya from any further distraction; as if she wished to put things back where they were before; to dissolve this meeting into the mist from which it had arisen.

Vannya started for the door with an eagerness that was not altogether flattering. Drusilla and Gulian followed him more slowly.

"It is very dark, isn't it?" said Drusilla tremulously. "Will you write me in detail about father? . . . I—tonight—It's been so hot. I'm worn out."

"I don't blame you. But won't I see you tomorrow?"

"No, I am going back to Southampton."

Vannya reappeared from the basement and the three of them waited at the curb until the taxicab drew up.

"Goodbye, Dru," said Gulian. He leaned into the cab. "Nice girl!" he said, patting her hand. "Nice girl!"

He knew that as soon as the cab door was closed Drusilla would begin to cry.

It seemed to Gulian that the world was falling down around him—the secure world to which he had returned so short a while before. This world was no more secure, no more imperturbed than the world he had left. His shining family, seen close at hand, were like everyone else; hot, dusty, confused. Wealth was no protection; nothing was a protection. The common lot of humanity was perturbation, as he had so often told himself. Only the wrong end of the telescope made things appear anywhere perfect. Close at hand you realized the thickness of the apparently faultless nose; the dust behind the door; the weakness beneath strength. And then—if you were wise—you realized something else, and that was that nothing really mattered after all save courage. Nothing at all.

That all beauty had something to do with courage; that courage was the only near approach to perfection the human race had as yet made.

In actual truth, the knowledge of imperfection was the beginning of happiness. When you reached the point where you saw that everyone was more or less like yourself, you reached the point where your own vices seemed less contemptible and your own virtues less unimportant.

. . . Gulian perceived a new sort of contentment ahead—very far ahead as yet, perhaps, but none the less ahead. He knew now that he was by no means the worst of the Eyres, that, as a matter of fact, he was of exactly the same stuff as the rest. . . . Part of the teaching of history should be the teaching that all great men and women are pitifully small and yet out of their smallness make something unexpectedly large.

BOOK III

"So he had him around to the backside of the wall, where he saw a man with a vessel of oil in his hand, of the which he did also cast (but secretly) in the Fire, . . . by the means of which notwithstanding what the devil can do the souls of the people prove gracious still."

PILGRIM'S PROGRESS.　BOOK I.

CHAPTER I

AN INTERLUDE AND A MEETING

POSSIBLY the increasing heat and the loneliness accentuated Gulian's depression. June went out in a blaze of sunshine and brought a July that showed no prospect of relief. The city became increasingly deserted as far as Gulian's acquaintances were concerned. Even Cyprian Bland departed for Maine, protesting bitterly against a climate which refused to allow you to remain where you wanted to be and sent you where you didn't want to go; and Gulian settled down to unbroken hours of work and late afternoons in deserted club rooms and quiet evenings of reading, in which the only sound was the lisp of water from the garden, or the blurred passing of a stray mothmiller. Occasionally he varied this routine by motoring out to the house of some friend. But the carefully organized drinking and the completely disorganized thinking of northern New Jersey and Long Island seemed hardly worth the bother necessary to obtain them.

He had an impression that once people used to sit on porches in the insect-loud hush of summer nights and really talk, and smell the perfume of gardens, and get into their hearts some of the quiet of darkness; but now all that had been abandoned for bridge or the partially naked and unreal philandering of fatigued brokers' wives. He preferred books and his own secret, passionate experiments in verse.

341

He had been reading Wells' 'Outline of History' and was amused at the pompous academic critics who failed completely to understand what Wells was trying to do, mistaking a gigantic philosophic thought for the petty investigations of a pedant. Probably for Americans this was the most important book that had been published in three decades—this, and 'Main Street.' Americans needed more than anything else to acquire a faint conception of what is meant by 'the historic sense.' There was nothing they so much lacked as the knowledge that everything they thought or did had been thought and done a thousand—ten thousand—years before. And since they wouldn't read careful history it was good that they would read Wells. Perhaps a few of them might begin to cease thinking of themselves as 'the greatest experiment' of the ages. History was nothing but a series of great experiments.

Gulian remembered his own university career and the hopelessness that had sometimes overtaken him because he had not been able somehow or other to connect things up; to synthesize them. Had there been one great-visioned man such as Wells to tell him that the basis of chemistry and philosophy and mathematics and music and football and poetry and everything else in the world was the same, he would have found an infinite zest where there had been only dullness and shirking; would have leaped in an instant into some sort of full-fledged manhood. It wasn't so much that each new generation had to start at the beginning, as it was that each new generation had first to overcome the stupidity of the generation preceding it.

He also read a book of Galsworthy's and was glad to find that limpid gentle soul beginning to recover from the wounds of the war; and he discovered the

tender hardihood of Sheila Kaye-Smith; and he dipped
into several volumes of the more radical Englishmen
and despised their disguised cockney cleverness and
nickering vulgarity.   They rolled pseudo-smartness
about in their mouths like Germans drinking from
finger-bowls.

A native book or two gave him goose-flesh, distinguished as they were by ejaculatory protestations of
strength that could come only from undisciplined
weakness.   America had best be careful lest it end by
being not only the most feminized but most feminine
of nations.   Chunks of virility out of the Middle-West!
'Big strong stuff' from narrow-chested Orientals and
poor little men with round spectacles and demanding
wives!

He wished Hergesheimer would get to know people
as well as he knew colors; and he wished that Hergesheimer would forget Hergesheimer and become the
really great man he then could become.   Lacquer
wasn't life.   Here was an opportunity being wasted.
A splendid passion somehow truncated.

As to his own writing, he was finding something in
it that had never been there before; a direct impact of
word upon thought; an increasing ability to cut out of
vagueness the silhouettes of emotion.   O beautiful,
long, undisturbed nights!

The 4th of July he spent at 'Hibernia,' going up
there on a Saturday and returning on Tuesday, and
the following week-end he spent there as well, and
on both occasions, Vannya, much to his satisfaction,
was absent.   Greatly as he loved Vannya, an interval
of time would have to elapse before their former entirely candid relationship could be resumed.   And
Vannya, with his Slavic tact, seemed to realize this
painful truth, for he had disappeared into the heart

of Pennsylvania and was busy at a summer art school.

On two successive Saturdays, Mr. Eyre, driving the Ford station-car himself, had met Gulian upon his arrival with a fine, holiday, silvery sort of gayety. He had adopted his usual summer garb of well-to-do gentleman-farmer . . . a panama hat, a loose tie, a crisp suit of golden panama-cloth . . . and above his white moustaches, his cheeks were sunburned. There was not the slightest evidence that here was a man under sentence of death, save perhaps now and then an eagerness for life too tremulous and a distaste for littleness and hatred too intense.

"Why the devil do people talk so much," he exclaimed, "when they'll all be dead a hundred years from now? . . . I drive the Ford myself, in special honor of you. You don't come up half enough. But, except for occasions like this, I can conceive no duller occupation than driving a car, can you? You miss the sweet living ripple of a horse's flanks. . . . I like their ears, as well."

Luncheon was served in a dining-room with shutters partly closed to keep out the heat, and it was—all his luncheons at 'Hibernia' were—just the sort of luncheon and just the surroundings that Gulian remembered as a boy and which had troubled some of his waking dreams ever since.

There was a smell of matting; cool and Oriental and reminiscent of clipper-ships and the '40's, and sea-captains with a Puritan background but a vivid experience, but to this was added a touch of Middle-State urbanity; a smell of old painted woodwork and flowers and polished mahogany. In the hall beyond a tall clock ticked somnolently, and the sunshine entered between the partly closed shutters with the sleepy softness of a tortoise-shell cat. Nor was the smell of matting and woodwork and flowers and polished furniture and rugs all, for from the outside came a drowsy distillation of moss in sheltered corners, and mint beside a stream, and an aromatic warmth of gilliflowers and zinias and petunias and hollihocks. The humming and the flight of bees were like flakes of sunshine made audible.

On the table was cold ham and meat with aspic; and a lettuce salad; and cottage cheese, sweet as the gloom of a spring-house; and a light beer, the brewing of which Mr. Eyre, adapting himself to circumstances, superintended with the care exercised by his ancestors of a hundred and fifty years before.

Here was the perfection of a highly specialized and individual civilization; something essentially republican yet ruddy and gentle; aristocratic but sensitive; something far finer than any king could produce; something that if it had been left alone would have flowered into a sinewy beauty greater probably than any the world had known. Something that had gone down temporarily, but might some day raise its head again above the flood of Alsatian hotels and battalioned meals, and products put out by men who themselves never ate them. Products which, not satisfied with destroying the stomachs of the country, blithely destroyed its loveliness with their blaring catchwords. . . . Silver and mahogany and sunlight; sunlight upon silver and mahogany!

Into Gulian's mind as he sat in this dining-room there came certain misty, disconnected abstractions as well; abstractions that had to do with the association of men and women suggested by this old house and these prompting aromas. He could not tell why they were there, except that all emotions are links in the same chain. He had never known his mother, but in the figure of his father he had long ago recognized one-half of a perpetual love affair; a mutual decision unshakable by death or separation. The living half of what had been an intimate, untalkative union, continuous and satisfying. On an afternoon like this a wife and husband—if they were at leisure— would have been content with each other's company, reading, reflecting, sometimes talking together; afterwards, in the cool of the evening, walking between hedges of box. And at night they would have gone up to a room smelling of lavender and, in their still unshaken innocence, have continued to wonder about this mysterious soft-lipped thing, woman, and this mysterious hard-muscled creature, man.

They would not have felt that every hour of liberty not spent having tea with friends or flying through the country in a cloud of dust was wasted. They would not have endlessly discussed together—or with equally restless acquaintances—their more hidden relationships. Why a man was a man, and why a woman was a woman, and why it was they couldn't get on without each other and yet had no alternative save the obviously unpleasant one of marriage.

Honesty was to be encouraged—it marked an advance; eliminated the stuffy horrors and tragedies of repression; but the periods marked by newly acquired honesty were uneasy to live in mentally and socially. The world echoed with chattering discussion. Nothing was clear-cut and simple. There was no place where an honest man could be at peace. The solution lay possibly in an honesty that eventually would become so habitual and an eventual articulateness so perfect that they would result in a complete understanding and, at the same time, an almost complete silence; but until then there were ages of wearisome talk to be anticipated.

Gulian longed to possess some woman with the passionate silence and simplicity that must have marked the courtship of his father; to break down and hush with his lips and arms her impatience and her queries. To say, or imply, 'What do I care what you say and think, it is *you* I am in love with, *you* who are a something—an essence, an intrinsicality—having little to do with speech or present action.'

He was experiencing the old human desire for unity; for autogenesis; for entire absorption. And these drowsy days and this house whose many generations made it greater than the sum total of any one generation implied that some such sort of absorption was possible.

After lunch Mr. Eyre invariably took a nap and the weather being too hot for exercise, Gulian usually read —Don Quixote, or some equally replenishing book—in the brown, silent library, until it was time to take his father for a stroll or a ride in a motor, and at night he slept endlessly and dreamlessly, waking in the morning with the surprised delight of a man coming up from a plunge into cool waters. He avoided golf, a game which Mr. Eyre remarked with some truth, 'was not a game but a sorrow,' and he avoided tennis; he had no desire to see any of his neighbors. . . . The height of summer was beginning; gorgeous; blazing. There was a perpetual sound of someone cutting hay—a whirring like a gigantic cricket—and the darkness was heavy with the syllables of katydids and tree-frogs and night-jars. Contentment and sadness as well; a sense of finality and yet of evanescence.

It was on his second visit to 'Hibernia' that Gulian discovered that Lael was staying with the Gates'.

He made the discovery in this fashion. On a Sunday afternoon Mr. Eyre suggested a call of politeness. "You really ought to go over to see them, you know," he complained. "They were very nice to you when you were up here in the spring. . . . Yes, I realize how you feel about it—but you can't be rude to them."

"Do you go over to see them?" Gulian asked.

"I?—I'm an old man. I take advantage of the lee-way permitted old age. That is—" Mr. Eyre reflected "—that is, except where very pleasant things are concerned. . . . Give them my love."

"I've noticed," commented Gulian grimly, "that you do take advantage of the leeway permitted old age where visits are concerned."

But none the less, he procured his hat and stick and set off by the garden path that led through the woods.

The periwinkles were gone and the violets, and there was nothing left but the unbroken green of moss and rank grass, above which swam the transparent shapes of midges. The woods were silent as well. Shadow and open place lay steeped in the quiet of a hot afternoon, except that far-off, faint bells called a sleepy congregation to church.

Gulian crossed the stile and came out of the trees and ascended the series of steps that led through the overly-formal formal gardens of 'Hill House' to the eastern entrance of the house itself. Somewhere at the bottom of the steps, in what they thought of to themselves as 'coppices' and always spoke of as 'the park,' the Gates kept a herd of rather embarrassed looking deer. This gave them somehow a feeling of relationship to the English peerage more subtle than any mere acquaintanceship with its members could bring about.

At the top of the steps was a brick terrace furnished with a couple of green tables and green chairs and gay umbrellas and awnings of striped yellow and blue canvas. The terrace was entirely deserted when Gulian came to it save for a magazine that had been dropped from some listless hand and a woman's embroidery bag hanging from the edge of an ornamental flower pot.

Evidently the Gates' and their guests were all asleep or else away on some expedition, and a moment afterwards the footman who answered the bell assured Gulian that the latter was the fact.

They had gone on a picnic, but they would be back almost immediately for tea. And Mrs. Gates had given word should anyone call to inform them of this. Would Mr. Eyre wait?

"No, I won't wait, thank you," said Gulian. "Tell Mrs. Gates how sorry I was not to find her home."

He turned back to the view he had just left. Below him lay a blaze of gardens and the violet tinged emerald of a lawn whose scattered trees ended in the shining disc of a pond. Already garden and lawn were beginning to be touched by the soft light of the fading afternoon. Beyond there stretched to the horizon woods of a paling blue, only a scarf of smoke rising here and there in the thick tumult of branches indicating that this well-mannered forest was merely a summer screen above the elbow-touching population of soporific millionaires and the alert people who waited upon them.

Gulian hated to leave such a view—it was a Sunday afternoon view; on any other day of the week it would have been subtly different.

He took a cigarette out of a box on one of the tables and bent down to light it. As he did so, he heard the sound of motor-cars coming to a stop on the other side of the house. Either the Gates' were returning or other callers were arriving, and in the first instance there was now no chance for escape. The steps below were too long and it would be undignified to try flight through the neighboring walls of vegetation. He sighed and sank into a chair, only to arise immediately as Mrs. Gates, large, panting in her hot-weather fashion, appeared with a Danish guest who looked rather like a blond, muddy-complexioned cherub.

After them streamed out a variegated collection of young and old people who arranged themselves on chairs and benches and the retaining walls of the terrace, gracefully or negligently, according to individual characteristics, and who immediately began to make themselves quietly noisy.

The Dane was evidently absent-minded with the problem of whether he should or should not ask Marion to marry him. Being a Dane he was not wasting his time thoughtlessly. His eyes, partly desirous, partly financial, followed Marion. He lisped incoherencies to his hostess and Gulian.

Mr. Gates, accurately attired as sporting country-gentleman, patronized Gulian amiably. He called him 'Gulian,' for one thing; and he implied that, after a not too creditable life, Gulian had at last settled down to some degree of intelligent usefulness—'Every dog has its day.' . . . 'Youth must be served.' . . . and so on. 'Ah, well, we can forgive that sort of thing, if afterwards a young man shows his mettle. . . .'

"And so you really like it," he said; "business, I mean? I thought you would like it. All reasonable men do. Red-blooded men. There's nothing like work to keep a man happy and contented." He snuggled back into his chair, thus changing the plane of his undisciplined stomach.

"It depends on the work," lisped the Dane, exhibiting a roguishness one would not have suspected. "I haf no feeling for work in itself. I would not like to be even the busiest of undertakers, for instance."

He was not aware that the moment was a crisis in his life, and that he was being found wanting in the cold, blue, sentimental eyes of Mr. Gates. One should not joke about work—especially to a man who has given it up himself. Gulian realized the awkwardness and was sorry for the Dane, but his experience had taught him that Scandinavians invariably rush in where angels fear to tread. One can do nothing to help them.

"I spend all the time I possibly can myself," he announced with deliberate provocativeness, in order to divert Mr. Gates' mind, "writing poetry."

Mr. Gates stared and sucked in his upper lip.

"Oh—poetry!" he said doubtfully, as if it were something he had heard about but in a connection he could not remember, and then he turned his head to peer at Lael who was coming towards them, her arms full of flowers, deep blue against her white sweater and white skirt, two young men trailing behind her like insouciant clouds. Gulian and the Dane got to their feet and Gulian stooped over Mrs. Gates. "Goodbye," he began.

"You're sure you won't have another cup of tea . . . or a whiskey or soda, or whatever it was you had?" Mrs. Gates asked.

"No, thanks," said Gulian. "I really must be going." He straightened up and almost fell into Lael's occupied arms. She hesitated for a fraction of a moment before she held her flowers out to Mrs. Gates.

"We stopped to pick these," she explained. "Where shall I put them?"

Her shining beauty, her intention to ignore him, changed Gulian's vague indignation into an unexpected bitterness of scorn, cruel and dangerous. What was she doing with two men anyway; and late for tea?

"Hello!" he said with an edged slowness. "I didn't expect to see you here. How are you?" His tongue lingered meaningly on the final words of the first sentence.

Lael's wide eyes opened more widely.

"Didn't you?" she commented indifferently. "Where did you say to put these, Mrs. Gates?"

"Give them to Henry. He's just gone in. Goodbye, Mr. Eyre."

Somehow Gulian found Lael walking beside him towards the screened door that led into the house. He had not intended this awkward juxtaposition and it angered him still more and embarrassed him. Why did she walk beside him? He didn't want her to walk beside him. He wanted to be left alone.

"Are you seeing me off?" he asked dryly.

Lael closed her lips demurely as if she was determined not to quarrel. "I am taking these flowers to put them in water," she said at length and patiently.

"Oh! Why, however, do you pick me out for this especial attention if you dislike me so much?"

"Did I say I disliked you? . . . And am I picking you out for any especial attention?" And then; "I suppose," she continued hurriedly, still with half averted face, "you think I have no character at all being here, don't you? But Marion asked me, and the city was hot and horrid. Besides, I've grown older. Quarrels seem silly to me. Young people are like beetles; they tumble about and fight and make up and

fight, and none of it means anything. . . . Yes, I'm
here."

In this eagerness not to be misunderstood, in this
personal twist immediately given the conversation,
Gulian saw further proof of the girl's self-centered-
ness and selfishness. Why did she suppose he cared so
much what she did or where she was?

"It's pleasant to settle things so easily," he said
smilingly, "only it's a trifle annoying to the people
whose sympathy you ask for and receive. I thought
Marion had insulted you."

"You're the only person whose sympathy I have
ever asked for."

She opened the screen door and Gulian followed
her into the partial darkness of the Gates' living-
room; an inert lifeless room with a gray stone fireplace stolen from some French chateau and on the
heavy tables, in heavy silver cups and vases, masses
of ponderous blossoms arranged with the perspiring
listlessness of hired hands.

Gulian laughed shortly. "It's extraordinary," he
commented, "how all conversation comes down to what
you are doing or planning, isn't it? The world re-
volves about you. Why should I care whether you're
here or not? What business is it of mine? You have
shown me how silly it was to care. I've given up
wasting either advice or emotion."

"You child!" said Lael scornfully.

In the shadows, now becoming lighter to their accustomed eyes, she walked over to the table and
dropped her burden of flowers wearily upon it, and
then walked back to Gulian and stared up at him, her
hands hanging by her sides. "You can say," she retorted slowly, "the cruelest things of anyone I have
ever known. You must have had a great deal of prac-

tice." As if she had suddenly changed her mind, she smiled with her red lips and long gray eyes. "How silly we are," she said lightly. "We do nothing but spoil each other's good times, don't we? Let's stop. Shall we?"

Gulian looked down at her and her eyes wavered. In the whiteness of her throat, her head thrown back, a small pulse throbbed.

He wanted to hurt her—hurt her horribly, as he found she could hurt him.

"It is women like you," he said slowly and thoughtfully, "—no, you are not a woman; I doubt if you ever will be. . . . It is little fools like you who give men practice in saying things that hurt. I don't call it a good time seeing a person you once liked making an idiot of herself."

The beating pulse in Lael's throat seemed about to rise into an exclamation of anger and pain.

"A thousand times," Gulian concluded, in the same soft precise voice, "you've played with men as you're playing with me and a thousand times you've gotten away with it. You think you can wound them beyond expression and then make it all up with a smile or a word. Well, you can't. This is the thousandth and first time, and you lose. I'll make you hate me—I hope to God you will."

With an abrupt casual fierceness he leaned forward and caught Lael to him and bent her backwards, his mocking, agonized face close to hers.

"I love you," he said, "and you know it. I love you so that every minute of my day is bruised with it. But you've got to leave me alone . . . you . . . you . . . ! What are you anyhow but something to be kissed and forgotten? Why shouldn't I kiss you? What difference would it make to you?"

For a moment Lael struggled against him and then, as if a flame had scorched her, she shrank into herself and became smaller and lay quiet, her eyes closed, her only movement the beating of her heart beneath her little breast. Gulian heard it, the beating of her heart, fluttering like a bird against his own, and he raised his head and looked at the wall opposite. His mocking, stricken face became grave.

"No," he said to himself as if surprised, "not even that! It can't be done!" and he set her free. He searched the floor vaguely with his eyes. ". . . Where's my hat?" he stammered. "Oh, here it is."

He stooped and picked the hat up awkwardly and brushed it off, and Lael watched him without moving, her hands by her sides.

"I'm sorry," he mumbled helplessly. "I'm always sorry—sorry for every damn thing I do. And I've never finished anything in my life. Never. . . . anything. I'm sorry."

And then, realizing the absurdity of his position, he straightened up with a red face, bowed, and strode towards the hall without looking back; out through the house on to the level stretch of lawn, where fire-flies danced their masque of sparks beneath the great elm trees, and out through the gates beyond. He swung his stick as he walked. The world was a place of reckless disgust. He did not care what happened to it, and least of all did he care what happened to himself.

CHAPTER II

A man is never better than when he has the humblest sense of himself; he is never so unlike the spirit of Evil as when his pride is utterly vanished.

DONALD MITCHELL: DREAM LIFE.

THE slim white pitifulness of women's throats was something to be thought about. You could not get it out of your head once you got it in. No matter how you twisted and turned, there it was coming up to disconcert you in the midst of your most passionate attempts to think rationally.

The memory followed Gulian each moment that was left of that Sunday; through a monsyllabic dinner with his father, and through the drive down, cleaving the heavy night with peering lamps, to the station, where he caught a late train in order to be at the office early the following day; and on the way into town, the cars clicking a rhythm on the hot, damp rails; and in the taxicab to the deserted tree darkened vistas of Madison Place; and up to his room and into a restless bed.

And it wasn't fair. Very evil women had slim white throats as well as very good women; and selfish, ignorantly provocative girls had them too. Moreover, since happiness is a matter of self-discipline plus the ability to direct the disciplined self into channels where it is released by congenial activities, governed, of course, by a proper sense of relationship towards one's

fellow human beings, and since frequently a shock—
or a series of shocks—is required to begin the ad-
justment, Gulian assured himself that it had been only
noble on his part to be the necessary, if despised, instrument of Lael's possible salvation—especially as
he had already fallen so low in her estimation. Lael—
he winced every time he thought of the name; it
brought up too concrete a vision. He tried to think in
more abstract terms—Lael had 'fine stuff in her' but
she needed just such a shock.

In such a manner he tried to explain to himself his
entirely spontaneous action, the result of momentary
desperation. Most actions are explained in this fashion; after and not before they take place.

But this carefully evolved and thoroughly masculine
self-justification was by no means satisfactory. Masculine self-justification seldom is. It has none of the
fine, fierce, insensate quality of feminine subjective
absolution. Men have an extraordinary ability, greater
than women, to excuse themselves, but at the back of
their excuses sits always a leering imp of remonstrance;
a sense, however stifled, of fair-play.

Whatever a woman did, a man who took advantage
of his physical strength where she was concerned was
a coward. . . . Yes, that was the flat of it—a
coward! And he, Gulian, had been a coward. No
matter what his temptation had been or how much he
might try to defend himself on the score of higher
motives, the fact remained.

. . . Besides, there was that business of throats.
. . . They were damnably pathetic! There was no
getting away from it, they were.

He heard the sparrows begin to chatter in the hot
gray dawn, and the rattle of a passing truck, and the

broken noises of the city's awakening; and finally he
sighed and got up and gave himself a shower-bath and
went to a breakfast that despite its awning-shaded
remoteness seeming a glaring performance to his sleepless eyes.

There was not the usual interest to be found in
Prescott's personal affairs, related in a soft impersonal
voice; and there was not the slightest interest to be
found in the recurrent ineptitudes, political and private,
which graced the morning papers. Even an after-
breakfast cigarette, usually the one imperishable thrill
left to otherwise hopeless men, tasted dry and habitual.
The walk to the office brought no lightening of this
mood.

A Perry, disillusioned and bitter as himself, greeted
Gulian. Perry had returned from an esoteric week-
end at Atlantic City, and although the week-end had
been just what he had planned it to be, the remem-
brance of it was by no means as enlivening as the
anticipation. Under Perry's annoyingly amused eyes
there were dark circles, and he was gently uncommunicative with the white, saint-like patience of the
fatigued, which is not the same thing as real saintli-
ness or real patience. The market, furthermore, had
opened jumpily and Perry was worried. With the egocentric point of view of the very wicked or the very
good he could not help but feel that this erraticism had
something to do with his own derelictions.

At half-past ten he thrust a grave face into the office
where Gulian was at work and commented on securities in general.

"Some damn fools must have been drunk over Sunday," he remarked. "They're raising hell with 'the
oils.' We haven't much in personally, but we've got
enough, and I know some people who have more."

"It's just a question of margins, isn't it?" asked Gulian. "The value is there all right?"

"How do I know? I guess so. There're lots of rumors about, of course. There always are, no matter what steps are taken to prevent them. But I think it's merely a group trying to get control. We haven't smoked them out yet." Abruptly he became an old and world-weary man, the lines about his mouth deepening. "Stick to bonds, my son!" he advised. "Stick to bonds!" And disappeared into his own quarters with the solemn haste of a disturbed rabbit.

Gulian resumed his correspondence. It seemed appropriate that the day should be muggy and that stocks should be uncertain. The hatefulness of things in general was rising to a climax. His jaundiced eye rested for a moment upon the permanent-waved, calcimined intentness of the blonde-haired stenographer to whom he was dictating. He felt annoyed by the girl and her assumption, belied by her appearance, of business indifference. Some time masculine ingenuity, wearied by sex interruptions, would invent a machine whose secretarial functions would not be confused with those of a blind and unconscious desire for maternity.

Mr. James Smith,
  The New Rotterdam Trust Company,
    New York City.
Dear Mr. Smith:
  In answer to your inquiry of 8/7/21, I shall be most happy to call upon you at any time convenient to you and lay before you the proposition in question. . . .

Silly asses! Writing to each other in this silly pompous way! He wouldn't in the least be happy to

call upon Mr. Smith—why should he be? And probably Mr. Smith, under his outer pretense of dignity,
was a grotesque timid little man who wore union suits
that bagged at the knee, and snored in his sleep, and
had a fat intimate pouchy stomach!

. . . Well, to get on with it! . . .

At one o'clock he dismissed his stenographer and
went out to lunch.

He had never before seen a serious break in the
stock-market, or a near approach to it, and he was surprised at his own lack of curiosity. Undoubtedly a
great deal was happening; undoubtedly the hidden
forces and their regurgitations were dramatic; but it
was difficult to find them so without an intensive effort
of the imagination, and even then it was the edges of
the whirlpool that were fascinating, not the heart of it.

Certain men were 'driving down' certain stocks in
order to buy them for less than they were worth and
subsequently sell them for more than they had paid
for them. The profit would go into big useless houses,
towards the decoration of superfluous wives, to the
buying of golf balls and the eating of too much food.
To those at the center of this transaction there accrued
undoubtedly some of the excitement of a dishonest
horse race; but to the vast majority concerned, and
whose money for the most part was being used, there
would be no more than the dull bewilderment and
agonized feeling of loss that follows robbery by means
of chloroform. A night of roulette or baccarat would
have been infinitely more satisfactory; at least a man
would see where his money went.

As to the more obvious manifestations of this financial distemper, they consisted principally of ticker-
rooms crowded with anxious investors, in streets un-
usually congested, in the hurrying to and fro of mes-

sengers and gray-faced, tight-lipped men, and in a succession of conferences in Perry's office between Perry and his partners, and a series of visitors. Apparently decisions were being made and reversed and made again. Whatever might be true of Beadlestone, Shipman, Endicott & Co., evidently a number of their clients were heavily involved.

And the ripples of these stones being flung were far-reaching. Even at the moment dozens of unsuspecting wives—Nutley, the Oranges, Long Island; the pretentious reaches of Morristown and Southampton— were by word or action implying to other wives the glittering solvency of already ruined husbands. Whatever might be said of the unreality of the present, that night scores of gaunt realities would be let loose. They were already gathering like ravens. Small painted faces would become thoughtful for the first time in years; they would be unjustly accusing; a few men might disappear; for numerous people life would be stripped bare. But to visualize all this required a strain upon vicariousness, and Gulian was more engrossed with his own misfortunes.

He supposed that his impassiveness was due partially to the fact that he did not own a share of the affected stocks, nor, so far as he knew, did any of his family, and that his own branch of work had to do with permanent and conservative investment, but the real basis of his sardonic disgust, his amused contempt, was his present despair with himself.

He had never lost his earlier point of view that trade, commercial or fiscal, was not in itself a fundamentally important occupation, and that it was a dangerous and devastating and perverting one unless those engaged in it kept clearly and always in mind that it was merely a means to an end. The main business of life was the business of human contact, and the only professions that contained in themselves the slightest trace of inherent dignity were those professions connected with this main adventure. Men justified themselves not by what they did in order to live, but by what they did with the surplus of time left over. Exaggerated as it might seem, the death of a pauper in a city hospital, the birth of an unparented child, were of infinitely more consequence, reaching backwards and looking forward, more mysterious, more significant, than this soon to be forgotten making or losing of fictitious millions.

'Hammering the oils,' were they? The lips of a single unknown girl held more of portent than the neurasthenic intentions of all the money-lenders in the world.

But in the matter of human contact, Gulian, so he told himself, had dismally and finally failed. Failed with himself, failed with all the women he had ever known, failed where Drusilla was concerned, failed even with his father, since, no matter how much he tried, somehow he could not convey to Mr. Eyre the affection and consideration he wished now so much to convey to him.

And he had failed as well in this comparatively simple task of being a business man. He was losing his initial impetus. The role of the bright faced office-boy was becoming tiresome and the prospect of promotion no longer seemed worth while. As a class he still found brokers and bankers insufferable, and secretly he didn't give a snap of his fingers how Beadlestone, Shipman, Endicott & Co., or Eyre & Co., made their money so long as they made it and left him alone. Business success was all very well so long as its ultimate aim was the inner and exterior glorification of beauty and love and the advancement of justice and fine dealing, but now he had no beauty or love to glorify, and he did not see himself any longer as peculiarly fitted to advance either justice or fine dealing. Why should he bore himself for nothing? The original motive of a subtle revenge upon the sneering Perry and the bland Philip seemed to him for the first time utterly childish.

(It always had been childish, but then without childishness where would the world be?)

What a fool he was and had been. Life consisted wholly of temporary sensations, and security consisted of removing yourself as far as possible from the adventitious wounds of fate. For the past few months, after a life carefully devoted—or, so he thought—to the former self-protective philosophy he had been doing nothing but attaching to himself tendrils every one of which would sooner or later cause him sorrow. Some of them already had. Marriage itself was nothing but the creation of death through birth. He would go back to casual climates and casual people and casual happinesses. As long as his father lived he would have to remain near New York, of course, but after that nothing would hold him. Much as he loved 'Hibernia,' the memory of that too would have to be put out of his mind.

He arrived at this decision somewhere around three o'clock and he was much relieved when his mind was made up. He dropped the letters he had finished into a basket for out-going mail and, arranging his other papers carefully and pushing back his chair, stood up and went over to the ground-glass door that separated his room from the private offices of Perry.

The day still hung between sullen heat and storm. From the window at one side of the door, as far as

Gulian could see, across the leaden reaches of the river and the sprawled uncertainty of Jersey City and the smoky wastes beyond, the sky was a uniform gray, pale and depressing. But in the distant west was a faint heaped up purple that promised sooner or later thunder storms. Gulian wished they would come speedily, releasing this unhappy pressure with the swish of rain and the tumult of wind. The hour fitted down upon him like a steel cap.

In answer to his knock, Perry's voice told him to come in.

He opened the door and found himself at the very heart of confusion and exhaustion. Perry's desk was strewn with papers and telegrams and crumpled slips of paper, white and yellow, overflowed onto the floor and bulged from the inadequateness of a single waste-basket. Perry himself was leaning back in a chair, his legs thrust out before him, one thoughtful, nervous hand tapping with a pencil on a rosewood table.

He did not turn his head at Gulian's entrance and for a moment Gulian waited in silence.

"Well?" Still Perry did not turn his head.

"I'm going to quit," said Gulian. "I thought I'd tell you."

Perry turned his head at last and Gulian was astonished at the slow horror that crept for a moment on broken panic wings across the room. Perry's face was ashen colored and rigid.

"Going to quit?" he asked in a hardly audible voice. "Why?"

Gulian laughed. "What's the matter with you, anyway? Your nerves are rotten, aren't they? . . . I'm going to quit, that's all. I'm flattered you take it so hard."

The rigidity of Perry's face relaxed, releasing it into

long slack lines of weariness and self-indulgence. The mask of perpetual youth, sneeringly gay, for an instant dropped, showing a tired man careless of externals.

"Your nerves would be shot to hell too," he commented listlessly, "if you'd been through what I've been through. . . . What do you want to quit for?"

"I'm fed up. Sick of it. I think I'll ship before the mast."

A childish anger, futile and sputtering, shook Perry like a wind. He brought his fist down on the table and half stood up in his chair.

"You damn fool!" he snarled. "What in hell do I care what you do?" He sank back into his chair, his voice suddenly becoming coolly arrogant. "When you've been longer in business, my good friend," he said, "you'll know enough not to bother the head of a firm on a day like this with nonsense. Why don't you hand your resignation in to Clarkson where it belongs?"

His short moustache lifted itself back from his teeth and his eyes, fixed upon Gulian, were bulgingly contemptuous.

"Thank you," said Gulian.

A tingling coldness was running along the back of his neck and up his veins. He took a deep breath. He was filled with a waiting gentleness.

He hoped Perry understood this gentleness. He hoped Perry realized that if he spoke again in that voice he would be thrashed then and there. He wondered if Perry realized the fact that he was talking to a man who hated him more than anyone else in the world; a man who, although to his own regret, a trifle timorous in the face of common grievances, could not stir up much rage against them, turned to ice in the presence of cruelty and effrontery. Pampered fools got through life more easily than they deserved because sensible people found it too much bother, too hopeless a task, to rebuke them; but sometimes retribution struck them like a fist.

Perry did understand; he understood Gulian's eyes better than he understood Gulian's words. His own eyes wavered and lost their arrogance and smiled with a feeble attempt at good-nature.

"Don't lose your hair," he advised. "It's all in the game. I didn't mean anything. You're not used to business yet. When you are, you'll find there isn't much time to waste in amenities. Wait a minute and I'll take you up to the club and give you a cocktail. I need a flock of them myself. And you'd better not quit."

"Yes, I am going to quit," persisted Gulian. "And I'm sorry, but I haven't time for a cocktail. I want to turn things over to Woodruff, and if possible I want to get out to the country tonight."

He turned away from his brother-in-law and passed through the door. He was smiling absent-mindedly as he sat down at his desk again. He had seen an example, sardonic and not very complimentary to human nature, of a truth it takes a kindly, peaceable man half a lifetime to learn. Individual courage is as rare as mass courage is common, and if you keep your temper well in leash but unloose it when necessary with devastating completeness and unexpectedness, your opponent, as a rule, is frightened. Perry was a coward and a bully—most men of bad nerves and self-indulgence are—and from now on, Gulian realized, he had the upper hand of Perry no matter what happened. Some day he would take advantage of that fact.

He spent three hours instructing the patient Woodruff, who was losing the precious moments of his afternoon holiday, and was losing them with the un-complaining humility of the educated but unsuccessful man, in the unfinished problems of his end of the work. It was half-past six before the two arose from the desk and made ready to depart.

Woodruff sighed, snapping elastic bands around various piles of letters.

"And is this all, Mr. Eyre?"

He was a little pale man with a bulbous forehead and dusty hair that looked as if it had been rubbed away by cheap hats seldom removed. He wore spectacles and his clothes were shiny.

"Yes, that's all. Where are you going?"

"Up to the New York Central."

"Where do you live?"

"Hydranga Wood."

The great office building was deserted, and after the crowds and turmoil of the day, had filled itself with shadows and spaciousness. The elevator men in their gray uniforms were official and detached and considerably more dignified than the excited financiers who employed them. They were clothed in the self-containment of impersonal service.

Woodruff chattered lispingly of chickens. Barred Plymouth Rocks. Color came into his pale cheeks and pale eyes. It seems he had always wanted to raise chickens ever since he was a boy. He was Vice-President of the Hydranga Wood Barred Plymouth Rock Association. They had wonderful times—the chicken-men. They met at dinners and shows and visited each other constantly, and all the time they talked about chickens . . . their beautiful strong legs and their lovely barred feathers, and lice, and roup—and their dispositions. . . . Oh yes, Woodruff had a wife and two children. . . . It was hard keeping big chicken-runs on the salary of a broker's clerk. . . . What was Hydranga Wood like? Well, it was a fine place for chickens. There were several chicken-men there. Woodruff found the society congenial.

He and Gulian took a surface car, and at Twentieth Street Gulian left the passionate small man still dreaming about his gray and black paramours. He was hurrying back to them as a lover hurries to an assignation. Once home he would sit and watch them by the hour . . . lovely strong yellow legs; shining barred feathers?

Dusk is not an hour but a metamorphosis in the heart of man, turning him from what he has to do to what he wants to do; from duty to desire; from prison to passion; from being a dull grave creature to a gay uncharted child. And one thing is certain; idle women make poor lovers for the lovers hurrying back to them, since they have nothing else to occupy them but love.

Gulian turned eastward and into the breathless close of Madison Place where the leaves of the maples hung limply in a portentous stillness and the tower of St. Jude's rose like a blunt gray finger petitioning silence. He twisted his latch-key in the door and walking along a hall lit by a single lamp and smelling of baize-covered furniture and the stagnation of summer, ascended to the more generously illumined library.

Under a lamp, lit because of the gathering storm, was a batch of letters arranged by Prescott's careful hand. A letter from Mr. Eyre . . . he hoped Gulian wasn't ill; he had been so silent during dinner. Had anything happened at the Gates' to disturb him? What a night it was—! He was writing an hour after Gulian's departure. A million fireflies! A smell of honeysuckle, of grasses, of green darkness. . . . Three bills—one of them from a club and as is always the case with club bills, twice as large as anticipated and entirely vague . . . and a letter from Vannya—not informative. Finally there was a square white envelope bearing the postmark of Slaton-on-Hudson. Gulian picked this last up curiously and, with a sinking of his heart, recognized Lael's handwriting. What did she want with him now? Further recrimination and further punishment! He was sick of punishment! Lael, like his father, must have posted the letter shortly after he had seen her. Undoubtedly, considering the briefness of time that had elapsed since their quarrel, she had been very angry when she wrote it.

He slit the envelope reluctantly and there unfolded itself before his eyes this astonishing communication.

I do not want to marry you—I do not want to marry anyone. But then I can't have complete freedom and yet have the other things I find I can't get along without. And I can't get along without you—I've tried it and I can't.

I know you love me and I know you hate me. Perhaps you wouldn't hate me so much if I married you. At all events, it seems to me that is the only way to stop us from quarreling. And I'm tired of quarreling with you. I want you to make me stop.

My poor sweet worried Gilly! You're so childish. I don't know whether to laugh or cry over you! . . . You were so funny when you stooped to pick up your hat!

We're both drifters. We have too much brains and not enough outside pressure. We'll drift, and drift, and drift, and die, unless someone does something definite.

I wanted to tell you a lot of things this afternoon but you wouldn't let me. I wanted to tell you first, that the family have finally decided to send mother and myself to Europe for three months. We sail the 14th. I also wanted to tell you that I was leaving here tomorrow afternoon—" (That was today; Monday)—" and would be home late if you wanted to call me up. Will you?

Perhaps this letter will shock you—you are really very conventional; but . . . think it over. I've come to the conclusion that it's our one chance. And since you won't do anything, I have to. I'm reckless and have all the tendencies of badness, but if you make me love you the way you can, these will go into the loving of you.

Anyhow, I don't care. It isn't really important how much you love me now, or I love you. It's how we feel five years from now. Engaged love is a safety-match; it may start a fire or it may go out. It's only a match. . . . That doesn't mean I don't love you.

LAEL.

P. S. Burn this letter up if you hate it. Probably I wouldn't have written it if I hadn't been going abroad. I always feel lonely just before I go abroad.

I don't dare read it over. It's too terrible. I should tear it up if I read it over.

L.

Gulian turned the pages slowly back and began once more from the beginning. It was true, as Lael had predicted—he was shocked; he was experiencing the inevitable male reaction where affection is too bluntly offered. There are fifty thousand years behind the hunter to put him at a loss when the quarry openly surrenders. And yet the wise hunter knows that that is always the case no matter how cleverly disguised.

Besides, he felt hurt for a moment, his dignity offended. Lael had found him funny. He hadn't meant to be funny.

But then what did these things amount to anyway? What about this 'you business' he had been thinking about only yesterday at lunch? This quintessence of personality, the thing a man really loves if he loves at all? This something belonging to the soul of a woman that has little to do with her present words or her actions? The thing that keeps a lover a lover long after the obvious beauty of which he has once been the owner has slipped from between his fingers? What about that?

Swift as wings in the darkness they should be hunted out—beloved women, and found with a fierce quietness. And no words should be said to them to be quarreled over. The mind sits lonely and apart and can abide no disagreement, but the heart and the body are wild unthinking things that flee instinctively, or else seek shelter with their kind, and when, as in the latter case, they are content, the suspicious mind can steal up in the shadow of the contentment and learn its way about. Gulian knew nothing about this girl Lael, he knew less about her than about any woman who had ever attracted his attention; she had the secretiveness, the implicitness of youth, the shy suspiciousness. It would take her years to become articulate, even although she belonged to a frank generation, and yet he knew that she was the only woman he had ever found with whom he could be content.

The house was very still; so still that one seemed to hear the thick soft echoes of the countless feet—some of them feet of other lovers—that through the years had trod the empty rooms. And before Gulian there were only so many years left; not so very many; and each one went faster. Soon the sound of his own feet would also be echoes soft and thick and noiseless. Even the sound of Lael's young feet! . . .

He shook his head with something like a sob and putting the letter in the pocket of his coat, plunged from the library down the dimly lit stairs. At their bottom he called for Prescott. There was no answer and he rang a bell.

Prescott appeared slowly from the tenebrous spaces back of the dining-room. Gulian looked at his watch. It was half past seven.

"I won't be home for dinner," he said; "and don't

wait for me after ten o'clock. Call up Miss **Satori** at once, please, and tell her that I am on my way up to her house."

He hurried along the deserted streets until he found an empty cab and when he had discovered one, drove northward through the adventitious darkness of the approaching storm.

Lael had just finished dinner. She was alone with her mother, a blond flaccid woman who endeavored to preserve a disappearing youth in the face of laziness and a passion for sweets. The little golden drawing-room, usually so gay, was shrouded in summer coverings and had a general air of hasty departure.

Mrs. Satori was not clever but she possessed the acumen of those who themselves have had passionate experiences, and she looked at Gulian with interest, and in a short while made an excuse to go upstairs.

She herself would not have chosen Gulian for a son-in-law. He was too uncertain, too vague, and he was not notoriously rich. Besides, he was much older than Lael, and although Mrs. Satori had always said that Lael 'should marry a man older than herself,' there was a happy moderation in all things. And finally, with her rococo ideas, she did not consider Gulian good-looking. In fact, she thought him rather ugly. She liked blond, plump, blue-eyed men. Gulian had lovely eyes, but they were bad eyes—violet eyes always were; and as for the rest of him, it was horribly sunburned and rather lined and his nose was much too long. Moreover, he said things you didn't understand and you weren't always sure he wasn't laughing at you.

But Lael was an unsatisfactory daughter, and if she didn't get married pretty soon she wouldn't get married at all, and since beggars can't be choosers, any

son-in-law in a storm was better than none . . . and
so on, through numerous mixed metaphors and mixed
conclusions. Mixed metaphors and mixed conclusions
being the especial method of thinking employed by the
female portion of the generation to which Mrs. Satori
belonged. At all events, you could get no better family
socially in New York than the Eyres, and that was
one comfort. . . . She did hope Lael, in the present
crisis, would behave herself.

Gulian waited until Mrs. Satori's footsteps died
away. The moment was voiceless, filled with the beating of his heart: Time seemed to balance itself upon
the thin point of a needle; he heard outside the patter
of rain. He got up and went over to the chair where
Lael was sitting and stooping down pulled her up to
him.

"Shut up!" he said gently. "Shut up! . . . Don't
say a word!"

English speech draws further and further away from
the language of English literature, but it is no less
tender.

* * * * *

An hour later Mrs. Satori, in her upstairs sitting-
room, heard a little bell ring persistently and answered
it and sent a maid down to tell Gulian that his brother
wished to speak to him.

Gulian looked up incredulously. "Mr. Philip Eyre?"

"Yes, sir; Mr. Eyre."

"Where is he speaking from?"

"From your house, I believe."

"Blame it!" exclaimed Gulian dolefully. "That's
because I told Prescott where I was going."

He went out into the hall and found another receiver
and unhooked it. Philip's voice answered him.

"Is that you, Gilly?"

"Yes."

"Busy?"

"Fairly."   Gulian suppressed a chuckle.

"Will you be coming home soon?"

"Why? Anything important?"

"Oh, no! I'm a bit lonely and restless. . . . I want to talk some things over with you."

"Sure nothing is wrong?"

"Perfectly."

"What time is it?"

"About half past nine."

"Then I'll be right down. . . . Certain there's nothing wrong?" The constant fear concerning his father stirred in the depths of Gulian's heart.

Philip's voice was muffled and tired.

"Certain. Nothing at all."

Gulian hung up the receiver. An old grievance against families filled him with a momentary annoyance. How could there ever be such a thing as unalloyed happiness when you were intimately involved with half a dozen persons, each one of whom was likely to call upon you at any time? He went back to the drawing-room where Lael was waiting.

"Philip wants to see me about something," he said. "I'll have to go."

Lael stood up. In the mellow light she looked like a slender flame, ruddy and lambent.

"Tomorrow and the day after," she said, "and then I go away. . . . You must see me each moment you can. I feel so silly and light-hearted."

She went to the door with Gulian and stood bareheaded in the ominous soft night. The rain had ceased, but the wind held promise of more to come.

"Does weather like this make you feel afraid?" she asked. "I'm horribly afraid . . . now that I'm going to marry you. So many things might happen. I'm not going to tell anyone we're engaged until I get back from Europe. I want to hold it in my heart and laugh over it if any of the silly Englishmen or French-men I know try to make love to me. And you mustn't tell anyone, either. And then the minute I get back I'll marry you. We won't drift any more, will we? No; we won't. You'll be a great man; a great banker or a great poet, and I'll help you. We'll have a lovely country-house—perhaps 'Hibernia'—and a little house in town; and then when we get tired of people we'll run away to lonely places. Won't that be fun? . . ."

She was leaning towards him and Gulian caught her to his heart. "The strangest thing about life," he said, releasing her, "is its precise and continued reversal of everything you plan. But it's apparent fortuitousness is uncannily not fortuitous. There's something behind it. This afternoon I was going back to Japan . . . or France . . . or anywhere, and now I have a country-place and 'a little house in town.' I wish Fate would warn you. . . . I gave up a perfectly good job. Perhaps I can get it back. I suppose when you're ready to die you are forced finally to admit that it's all been only about a quarter what you planned yourself, and the rest what's done to you. However, that's no excuse for slackness, is it? Nothing happens to you, unless you put yourself in the way of it and keep in training."

He started down the steps.

"And not so very long ago," reflected Lael in a soft amazed voice, "on these very same steps I received the most terrible of lectures."

CHAPTER III

PHILIP RETIRES

IT WAS nothing that Philip said or did, no obvious sentence or action, that confirmed Gulian in his vague annoyed uneasiness, in the discomfort that arises when you know the person to whom you are talking is preoccupied with some problem he cannot, or will not, put into exact words. Rather it was a large blond opaque silence and repression. Philip had always, spiritually and physically, been an overpowering person. He filled his environment with his person and his mood. Being a religious man, like most religious men he labored under the delusion that he hid all but his more kindly and charitable reactions, but as a matter of fact he did nothing of the kind. When he was gay his surroundings shook invisibly; when he was gloomy they were foggy with apprehension. Tonight he was preempting the library of 15 Madison Place.

Gulian, coming back from Lael's little house far up town and stepping from the comparative darkness of the stairs into the warm light of the occupied room, found Philip reading, one hand shading his eyes. Or whether he was actually reading or not, it was difficult to tell, for he was peering at the pages of the magazine he was holding with a rigid intentness that sometimes means entire inability to make sense out of the print. At the sound of Gulian's entrance he put the magazine down and rose slowly to his magnificent height and smiled, but his eyes did not smile. Perhaps it was the shadows that made them appear a trifle sunken and bewildered.

Gulian suffused at the moment with recaptured youth, discovered this solemnity to be even more irritating than usual. He wished it were possible for him to tell his ponderous brother the secret stirring his own heart. He supposed Margaret had done something more stupid than usual, or that the heat had been devastating Philip, or that a member of the Bible-School class had exhibited a humanity shocking in a member of a Bible-School class. Such things worried Philip. He had had in his life no real tragedy and no real humor and his humor was sad and his sadnesses unconsciously humorous.

Avoiding as much as possible any real contact with this damp dejection, Gulian stepped over to the mantlepiece and helped himself to a cigarette from a large box that stood beside the clock. When he had lit the cigarette, he turned about and smiled down at his brother through a cloud of smoke.

"Well, my friend," he asked, "what in the name of Heaven's the matter with you? . . . Everything gone to pot?"

He regretted Lael's cheerful drawing-room and the sound of her laughter. Why did one have to be withdrawn from such rare happiness to waste time over the imaginary troubles of spoiled relatives?

"Anyway," he continued, "I'm glad you're here. There's something I wanted to ask you."

His glance could not take itself away from Philip's hands, which clung limply to the arms of the chair in which he was sitting; each long fleshy spatulate finger spread out separately.

"You see, I gave up my job with Perry today, and I

think I did it in such a manner that he won't be very anxious to take me back, or if he does, won't be very gracious about future opportunity. What would you advise? Haven't you a place for me in the bank yet?"

Philip, sitting very erect to the left of the fireplace, nodded his head gravely.

"Why, yes," he said. "I suppose so. I'll look into it."

But Gulian was aware that what he was saying was falling upon partially deaf ears. He sighed. "Personally," he said, "I'm going to have a drink. How about you?" He went over to a closet let into the wall and unlocking it, brought out a bottle of Scotch whiskey. "I think Prescott is still here. I'll ring for some soda-water and ice."

Philip raised an automatically protesting hand.

"Nonsense!" said Gulian emphatically. "God made whiskey for just such occasions as this."

He poured a generous drink into a long glass and handed it to Philip, and took his own glass over to a large chair near the reading table. Prescott came and went, bringing the ice and the charged water. Gulian deprecated wistfully the impossibility of asking Prescott to sit down and join them. His presence would have relieved the atmosphere. In his own muffled rambling anecdotal way Prescott was entertaining and philosophic.

"The trouble with all you unco-good people," he said to Philip, when Prescott was gone, "is that you think there's such a thing as absolute good and absolute evil, when there isn't—it's all in the method. Evil is only underdone or over-emphasized good; ugliness is only inchoate or exaggerated beauty. Everything in the world is made out of the same material; what counts is how it is handled. The drunkard is merely a poet who has taken the wrong road towards sublimation, and the prostitute is merely a woman who, realizing the glory and power of her body, hasn't realized the proper way to conserve its glory and its power. Alcohol is a good creature, my son, if used rightly; so's food; so's everything. The dyspeptic who abuses his stomach, or has abused it, is just as much of a criminal as the drunkard who abuses his brain; and just as anti-social, though not so obviously or dramatically? Where do you suppose the sins and suppressions of a family at the mercy of a sour invalid end? And how do you religious people reconcile this idea of absolute evil with the idea of an absolute God, anyway? How can they both exist in the same universe? And if they do exist, which one got in first? If God did, how did He happen to let evil in? A sort of Pandora's box? . . . Drink up your drink. At the present moment it's as holy an act as prayer; you're tired; you need it. And now tell me what's the matter with you."

Philip took a deep swallow of whiskey and got to his feet and crossed the room to one of the windows, where he stood, looking down into the blackness of the garden. "I don't know whether there's any absolute evil or not," he said slowly; and then abruptly; "but it's all talk, anyhow . . . talk!"

His hands, heretofore so limp, gripped the white sill. Gulian watched him with a puzzled frown, and then stood up himself and crossed over to the window and stood beside Philip, his hands in his trouser pockets, his expression tolerantly amused.

"You keep the fountain going, don't you?" said Philip. "That's a good idea. . . . Listen to that thunder."

With the unexpectedness that had characterized all his movements in the past few moments, he turned

about and began to pace up and down the room,
his head lowered doggedly, his shadow, huge and ragged, following him. "When I do die," he burst out
passionately, "I hope to God it's in a storm—I always
did like fighting something tangible—like a football
game. I'd like to kick life once before I go out. I'm
all mixed up; I'm tired." He paused and stared at
the wall before beginning once more his measured
promenade. When he took up again the thread of
his thoughts it was in more subdued tones, as if he
was ashamed of his former feverishness. "I know
that sounds queer coming from me," he apologized,
"but I've held in so blamed long. . . . I had to talk
to somebody."

Gulian did not move from his place near the window.
"That's all right, my son," he said gently. "I'm
glad you're going to talk to me. Go ahead and talk."
He was no longer sorry that his visit to Lael had been
interrupted.

Philip continued his march up and down the room.
"It's nothing," he said; "nothing in particular—
I've had a hard day; it's brought things to a head.
. . . I've been wondering what the sense of it all is.
I don't seem to have gotten anywhere—there're no
rewards; and yet, there's no one who has worked
harder than I have. What have I got? Not one
single minute when I seem to have really had
hold of life, that is—not one since I left college! Not
one minute! It's gone by like a dream—a nightmare
—and it's left me awake and thirsty. I can't get to
grips with happiness. It isn't there for me. It's
eluded me. I reach out; I think I've got it; it isn't
there! I've never had one moment of it—not since
football. Not a moment when I was caught up and
overwhelmed with it. Most men have, even the mean-

est. Some get it fox-hunting. Well, I tried that; it was good fun; but it left no permanent satisfaction. And I tried a country-place—that was nothing but hired men and a big restless house. A few men get it from their wives. My wife doesn't love me. God knows what she does love; I haven't found out; but it isn't me. And yet according to all standards she's a good wife—at least, she's not a bad enough wife to release a man either publicly or from his own conscience. I'm not at liberty to go out and find someone who really does love me. And finally, I thought that at least I'd find it in business. Well, I haven't. Business is dull, dull, dull! What do you do with your money when you make it?"

He paused for the second time and raised his head and stared at Gulian. "I'm bored," he said musingly, with an odd finality and calmness. "I've tried to bluff myself, but now I've made my mind up. I don't even love my son. I've tried to, and I can't. I'm dried to an ash; turned to dust; blown away. I'm a damned failure. I can't even, deep down in my heart, believe any longer in God. I don't believe in Him. If there was a God He wouldn't let a man suffer as much as I do just because he has lost his capacity for suffering; feel so much just because he can't feel any longer. I've hunted God all my life and I can't realize Him. You've never hunted for Him an instant, yet every day you believe in Him more and more. Oh, yes, I can tell that—some sort of a God. And it's the same with everything. You've never done anything but experiment and play and waste your time, and yet you've been happy, and are happy, for all your pessimism and cynicism. . . . I've never been happy at all. You're finding your way towards something; I don't even want to find my way towards

anything. What is it all about? Do you know? . . .
What's it about?"

The wistfulness in his voice had died away with his
final sentences, leaving it resentful and accusing, as if
he was indicting Gulian and some unseen but listening
presence with a monstrous injustice.

"That's what I wanted to see you about," he concluded. "It's nothing . . . of no importance! I'll get
over it, but I had to let go."

Gulian had been following his brother's dejected
figure with unwavering eyes. Now he pointed to a
chair.

"Sit down, Phil," he said.

Poor old Philip! He was suffering from what every
man suffers from sooner or later, but his egocentric
pride prevented him from realizing that his disease
was universal and usually curable. For the first
time in his life Gulian felt older than Philip.

He found his own chair again and the remains of
his drink. "There's nothing the matter with you," he
resumed, "except that you're worn out and all in. I'm
no doctor but I know the symptoms. I thought you
were on the ragged edge when I saw you first in April.
Moreover, you're just beginning to mature. You've
got growing pains. There's not a bit of sense to anything you've been doing. Stop it and get out. Take
a year's rest. The bank will get on without you. As
for Margaret, have a talk with her and instil some
sense into her head. If she won't listen to reason, get
rid of her. That's brutal, but it's plain common sense.
You've as much right to happiness as anyone.
You're still young. I'd take the point of view, if I
were you, that your apprenticeship is now over and
that life had really just begun. The reason why most
people are unhappy, anyway, is because they evade

issues. They won't make or break. They're afraid. That's been my trouble. Just the mere discovery recently that it was my trouble has already begun to bring me some placidity. I never saw a brave man yet who was thoroughly unhappy, did you?"

Philip stared at the empty fireplace before him. "You think it's just tiredness?" he asked, looking up with a curious shining translucent smile, as if for that instant he was infinitely wise and infinitely amused.

"Yes," retorted Gulian; "why not? Why—is there something else?"

"Oh, no; nothing."

Gulian studied the end of his cigarette. He was finding himself not as surprised that Philip should be talking this way as he might have been. He was only vastly interested and touched. After all, this brother of his had not always been the bland person of recent years. In his youth there had been a hint occasionally of berserker rages. One could not have seen him on a muddy November day, his blond head charging above the charging line, without suspecting that. Besides, he and Gulian were brothers; had the same blood; the same quizzical father. How could they be so very different? Well, they weren't. But what a wasteful, indecipherable business the finding out of such primary facts was! To take thirty-five years for it!

The clock on the mantelpiece struck eleven.

"I'm sorry!" said Philip in muffled embarrassment. "I didn't mean to let you in for all this." He seemed to be hunting for a satisfactory excuse. "I've had a hard day at the bank," he repeated. ". . . It's been frightfully hot."

Gulian jumped to his feet and crossed the intervening space between the two chairs. "Phil," he said, stooping down, "what in thunder is a brother for if he isn't for something like this? I'm sorry you're feeling rottenly, but I'm damned glad too, if rather selfishly, for it's given me a new relative."

He waited for some response to this impulsiveness. He heard the clock ticking behind him and felt the mounting of blood to his cheeks. He was not in the habit of showing his emotions so openly. Philip got slowly to his feet. "Good gracious," he exclaimed yawningly, "it's later than I thought it was! Can you put me up for the night, Gilly? It's a long way up to my house."

Gulian's eyes narrowed. "Certainly," he said, stepping back. "I always keep a bed made up in my sitting-room. Let's be going."

The Philip he had seen for a moment had disappeared, leaving the Philip he knew only too well. A very stupid Philip; yet much more understandable. Gulian was wounded and annoyed.

"You weren't mixed up in that petroleum business, were you?" he asked, trying to hide his chagrin.

Philip was completely himself again; slightly patronizing, tolerant.

"Oh, no; but any kind of a break affects everyone else, of course. Shall I turn out the lights?"

"Please."

In the semi-darkness of the one hall lamp, they went up the stairs side by side.

"You can hear that little fountain all the time, can't you?" said Philip.

"That's one of the reasons I keep it running. . . . It's company."

"Sounds like a voice. . . . Funny what a hold the house you were brought up in has over you, isn't it?"

Here was the ingenuous Philip again; the unknown Philip. But Gulian was wary.

"I don't feel much that way about this house," he answered coldly; "I feel that way about 'Hibernia'."

"Yes, I know; but then you were there considerably more than I—father didn't get in the habit of going there for such long stretches until I was fifteen or so. This is my home-place."

When the third story was reached, Gulian led the way into his sitting-room. The square old-fashioned room lay breathless in the heat; there was a faint odor of books and chintz and tobacco. Beside a reading chair a lamp was lit, and on the center table another lamp in a tall green Chinese vase glowed from under a silk shade.

Gulian went into the front room and brought back pajamas and a striped dressing-gown and a pair of fibre sandals.

"This all you want?" he asked.

"Nothing more that I know of . . ." Philip was in a cordial, sleepy, yawning mood. "This is pretty nice, Gilly . . . makes me young again. . . . These were my old rooms, you know. I think I'll take a bath. You haven't got a book to read, have you? Something absorbing?"

"Here's 'A Chair On The Boulevard.' But you'd better go to sleep."

Philip shook his head and smiled. "Too restless."

"Why, you're half asleep already."

"Not really."

He passed through Gulian's room on his way to the bathroom, and Gulian heard him splashing about in the spacious tub. Presently he was back again, his blond hair sleek and wet like that of a small boy and his magnificent bulk shining through the thin dressing-gown.

"Gad, that's refreshing!" he said, pausing by the long mirror, and salving his soul with the euphemistic profanity of the religious man.

Gulian looked him over appraisingly. "You haven't taken on much fat," he said. "You look pretty fit to me, outside of the fact that you're tired."

"I am fit . . . but—well, I'm tired." There was a little complaining laugh in Philip's voice.

"Do you remember that time you made a touch-down on a loose ball?" asked Gulian.

"Perfectly."

"I was at prep-school and hated you."

"We always have rather hated each other, haven't we?" said Philip thoughtfully. "Curious! We haven't in crises, though."

"No, not in crises."

Gulian, as usual, easily mollified, wondered if he hadn't better take advantage of this further lucid affectionate moment on Philip's part to tell Philip about Mr. Eyre and, possibly, about Drusilla. Ask his advice. Then he decided it was too late and that he had better think these confidences over first.

Philip went into his own room but in a second or so was back.

"Gilly," he asked, "asleep?"

"No." Gulian sat up in bed and switched on the light beside him.

"There's something I wanted to ask you, but forgot all about. It's foolish . . . but I feel so blamed rottenly at times."

"What was it?"

"Well, it's this way—if anything should happen to me suddenly I'd like it awfully if you could manage to look after young Philip—Junior, that is—as much as possible. Would you?"

Gulian drew his knees up under the sheet and frowned above puzzled eyes. "Now what in God's name *is* the matter with you?" he asked.

"Nothing; only I thought so long as we were speaking of things I'd mention it to you."

"But I am his legal guardian under your will, aren't I?"

"Yes, I know; but I want it to be more than merely legal. . . . I want you to have him with you as much as you can and away from Margaret. He's my one bid for permanence, you see. And there's another thing as well—inside my breast pocket I carry always a little memorandum book. It will tell you where I keep the key to my desk in my study at home—the room next to my bed-room—and the combination of the secret drawer that has a little safe in it. You will find some papers—do what you think best about them. My latch-key is on my key ring."

Gulian leaned still further forward. "Look here!" he said sharply and in the manner of one whose endurance has been tested to the breaking point, "will you kindly tell me if you are really sick or in trouble?"

Philip's smile was completely reassuring. "Absolutely not!" he repeated. "I'm merely reaching the age where things do happen suddenly to men and so many of them leave their affairs at loose ends."

"You frightened me," said Gulian. "Get to bed. I'll do everything you want, but people like you—especially when they begin to get nervous about themselves —live for years. I'll die young, because I'm not bored and because life, no matter how disillusioning it is, fascinates me. Goodnight, Phil. Tomorrow we'll lay plans to get you out of this sickening hole."

He wanted to be left by himself—he wanted in the darkness to re-assemble his newly discovered, interrupted, dreams; to reconstruct Lael's face and voice and lips and laughter. To see again in his imagination the shining kindness in her young eyes and reflect upon her heretofore only dimly suspected wisdom and intuition.

"I'm sorry I frightened you," said Philip gently.

Hindsight is so horribly discriminating. Afterwards Gulian realized that all the while he had known Philip had wanted to tell him some secret, grave and revealing. That the shadow of this had crossed and recrossed between the actual words of their conversation like the shadow of a bat. He blamed himself for his attitude of slightly wearied condescension—of amused tolerance. His surface mind had done this, pushing back the warnings of the wiser, subtler hidden mind. But then, things like this did not happen—they were the outer fantastic fringes of what might happen but never did. Such things did not happen; not in your own fairly self-restrained, well-in-hand environment. . . . Gulian awoke an hour or so later with the tread of rain and the reverberation of thunder in his ears. A great storm had broken at last over the city and he heard the whispering of the leaves outside his window and the threshing of the boughs. And then he remembered that, coming up from sleep, he had heard another sound—or thought he had heard it—sharper and nearer than thunder. Something close and unusual. He listened wide awake, staring into the windy darkness, his heart beating quickly. Very slowly he got out of bed and reached for an electric torch, and with the round eye of light preceding him, stepped into Philip's room.

The round eye of light found a window and melted into the blackness beyond, rain cutting across it like a flight of silver arrows; and swept a table—there was Philip's watch and a roll of bills and some loose change and his key-ring—and paused for a moment upon a chair on which Philip had hung his clothes—a dwarfed and enervated simulacrum of a man—and finally came to rest upon a spot on the floor. On that spot the light rested an interminable moment.

"Philip!" said Gulian suddenly in a terrible voice. And then again; "Philip!" but more softly.

The name dropped into a sable pool fringed with rain and storm tossed branches, and left no ripples behind it.

With a sort of frozen precision and calmness, making a wide detour as he did so, Gulian went over to the wall and turned on the electric switch, and the room sprang into light. But he did not look back until he had shut both the windows and drawn the water-soaked curtains. He was methodical and thoughtful, and his eyes were expressionless. Finally he faced again the spot on the floor his torch had found and accentuated. . . . Philip, his blond hair shining in the ruddy glow of the lamps, the striped dressing-gown half torn away from one shoulder, lay sprawled out upon his face, a revolver within a few inches of his limp right arm.

Gulian went over to the prostrate figure quietly and getting down on his knees, thrust his hand under the bare, splendidly muscled breast. There was no beating of the heart. It was quite still. Gulian withdrew his hand; blood had turned it a dark brown.

For an instant Gulian stared at his hand sombrely. He was not as yet shocked by the immediate fact; he was stunned, shocked, by the larger mystery, the wider significance. Why had Philip done this? Was it the result of a single unbearable moment, or had he been planning it all the while—during their not especially despairing talk? Had Philip been walking and talking with Death every minute of the time when to outward appearance he had been talking to him, Gulian, his brother? What a ghastly thought! No, it must have been a sudden madness. But now no one would ever know.

The world is full of men and women with just such a question as their hourly companion, and death stands with a finger to its lips.

Gulian regained his feet. A gust of white anger made him tremble. The damned grotesque wickedness of it! The absurdity! The waste! Life was so easy to kill; so impossible to reconstruct! He wanted to compel time to step backwards. Only ten minutes ago—five—and he might have prevented this tragic folly; this one conclusion that has no reversal! If he had only not gone to sleep; if he had only followed his instincts and insisted that Philip tell him what it was that was troubling him!

Why, the time was so short, that Philip was still here! There was no doubt of it; you could feel him, perceive him; almost reach out and detain him. There had not been a sufficient interval for what was really Philip to leave what had been known as Philip. But nevermore would there be any talking to either the real Philip or the everyday Philip lying there on the floor. No more talking! There was a wall between wide as space and mysterious as the stars. . . . Gulian walked over to the telephone and picked it up.

"City 24229!" he demanded.   "And hurry! . . . It's a matter of life and death!"

There was a chiaroscuro interval to be got through

with before anything happened. In Gulian's ears was the soft buzzing of a thousand wires, as if the lines were busy with the ghosts of the day's conversations.

A girl's sleepy disinterested voice recalled the common unimportance of tragedy.

"Your party don't answer," she cooed nasally.

"He's got to—he's a doctor!"

"I'll try again."

A man's voice broke in, annoyed and half-awake.

"Well? . . ."

"Is that you, Doctor McCarter?"

"Yes ——"

"This is Gulian Eyre, 15 Madison Place. . . . Yes, Gulian Eyre. My brother, Philip. . . . Yes, Philip Eyre. . . . has hurt himself. Revolver. Get here as quickly as you can."

There was a second of thoughtfulness.

"I'll be down at once."

"Thank you." Gulian hung up the receiver.

He recrossed the room to a window and pushing aside the curtains, flung the sash open once more and leaned his elbows on the sill. The first rush of the storm had gone by, leaving a steady slanting rain light enough to show through its mist the vague shadows of the buildings beyond the garden. And it had seemed to Gulian as he opened the window that a presence had passed him and vanished into the night.

He wondered if such sensations were absurd or rational. They were very general. Most people experienced them. Why weren't they rational? There was such a small thin edge between life and death—How could something so alive be in an instant so unalive? Or how could it ever be unalive, if by death was meant annihilation? How could the curious small spark, unlike any other spark the world has seen or ever will see, be snuffed out?

The answer was, it couldn't. Out of the slime into the sunlight and from the sunlight into the upper air, that had been the history of man. A million million years of wishing and he had wished himself to where he was. And he was still wishing. The chrysalis and the worm and the great-winged moth. There was no glory nor calm nor beauty beyond the ultimate power of man's wish. The little spark did not snuff out. The sparks flew skyward. Some day their descendants might be suns. Man had lit within himself, or it had been lit for him, a candle no winds could extinguish. . . . No, not even the winds of death.

Gulian turned away from the night and went downstairs to wait for Dr. McCarter, switching on the hall lights as he descended through the dark well of the house. He opened the front door just as a closed car drew up to the curb and a gaunt figure in a raincoat sprang out and ran up the steps.

"That you, Eyre?"

"Yes."

"Your brother?"

"On the third floor."

"How is he?"

"Dead."

"Good God!" said Dr. McCarter and hurried on.

He took the steps three at a time, but on the threshold of Gulian's study he paused, and looked at the sprawled figure on the floor, and closed the door.

"This is just as you found him?" he asked softly, removing his raincoat and opening his instrument case. He turned Philip gently over on his back and drew away still further the already partially torn away pajama coat.

"He pulled at this," he murmured thoughtfully.

His lined, sensitive old face, beneath its close crop-ped gray hair, was alert but immobile like that of a man listening for a footstep; his delicate fingers worked ceaselessly. He got to his feet.

"How did this happen, Gulian?" he asked.

Gulian had lit a cigarette and was sitting in a chair looking up at the ceiling. He lowered his head until his eyes met directly those of Dr. McCarter.

"It was accidental," he said quietly.

"Accidental?"

"Yes. All I know was that I was sitting here watch-ing him; he was showing me this gun—he had bought it on account of his long night rides out to his country-place—and suddenly the thing went off. He was in the best of humors. . . . We were chatting and laughing."

"Don't be a fool," said Dr. McCarter sharply. "You'll get into trouble." His eyes were absent-minded, mortally sad, reminiscent, like those of some ancient priest weighted with sorrows all the more sor-rowful since they were not his own. "The muzzle of this gun was against Philip's chest. Where were you; in the next room asleep?"

Gulian came back from remote reflections to the present. He sprang to his feet. "Is there no escaping life even when a man is dead?" he said. "Yes, I was in the next room. What of it?"

Dr. McCarter's voice was gentle. "Don't worry. I will arrange things. . . . It will not be the first time. There will have to be an inquest, of course; but I will see that there is a verdict of accidental death."

"There's a note-book in Philip's pocket and the keys to his house," said Gulian. "He wanted me to have them. Can I take them?"

"It is irregular," assented Dr. McCarter, "but most intelligent things are irregular. Yes, go ahead."

Gulian went over to the chair where Philip's clothes hung and thrusting his hand into the pocket of the coat pulled out the little red leather note-book; then he picked up the key-ring from the table.

"There are some things you ought to do, aren't there?" asked Dr. McCarter, watching him.

"Yes . . . a great many things."

"Well, do them. Don't hesitate to leave me. I'll take care of all details."

"Leave you alone. . . . Here?"

The shadow of a grave smile flitted across Dr. McCarter's lips.

"I am an old man," he said; "death doesn't frighten me. Most of the people I love are dead. When you are my age, death is an infinitely more familiar and less perplexing thing than life. The dead are the only completely kindly and understandable people there are. . . . Besides, one is not afraid of a man one brought into the world as I brought Philip. . . . Hurry along, Gulian. . . . Get dressed."

CHAPTER IV

DAWN AND NOON

THERE were three telegrams to be sent, couched in the evasive language of disaster, to Mr. Eyre and Margaret and Drusilla, not to be delivered until a decent hour of the morning, and this accomplished, Gulian was free to continue his journey to Philip's house, save for a telephone message to Prescott to join Dr. McCarter at Madison Place immediately.

The storm had passed, leaving the streets full of little shining pools and the sweetness of rain, and from the Brooklyn heights came the fading echo of thunder. In the scented vacuum that follows a summer storm moved, here and there, an isolated policeman in rubber cape and hat still glazed with wet, and an occasional crawling picaresque cab whose eyes searched the dusk audaciously like those of a masked man seeking shabby adventure.

Gulian hailed one of these worn magic carpets and gave Philip's address, and eventually found himself ascending the smooth slopes of Fifth Avenue; past the immense department stores, slumbering behind their walls of plate-glass and narrow columns of gray stone like museum exhibits of the vain and vanished cities of Syria; and past the Public Library, where for a few hours the blind heroic search for knowledge was arrested; and past the first fretted layer of hotels and clubs and little expensive shops that sold flowers and jewels and paintings.

Life was so quiet; so newly washed; it was difficult to realize that back there in Madison Place—one could not realize that back there in Madison Place, the lamplight still focused upon a sprawled inert figure. The vision lapped up to the edges of comprehension and receded. Nor was it entirely apprehensible until the narrow facade of Philip's house was reached. Then its clinging unshakableness grew suddenly burdensome; stifling, close pressing. In the empty house that Philip had built and where he had lived, stiff and impersonal as it was, his presence was more abroad than in the house he had chosen for the final release of himself. This presence, heavy and gravely watchful, as if it had hurried back from some new and important business to finish a task half-remembered and vaguely worrying, seemed to catch up with Gulian in the vestibule and to follow him along the shadowy hall and to stand, looking over his shoulder, when finally he sat before Philip's desk.

Gulian had watched his cab glide along the wet asphalt until it had turned again the corner into Fifth Avenue before he had inserted the latch-key in the door. As he had done so, he had struck a match and glanced at his watch. It was half past two. Beyond the door had been complete darkness and the muffled atmosphere of a house partially closed for the summer, and a switchboard to the right that Gulian remembered and had thrust out a hand to find and press at random one of the little ivory knobs. A warm radiance had flooded wrought-iron balusters and softly tinted walls and Venetian prints in black frames, and had disclosed, further along, the entrance to the elevator. But there were servants somewhere about, and Gulian, wishing to make no more noise than was necessary, had extinguished the lights and chosen the stairs, his

feet sinking into the thickness of a carpet hidden
beneath a crash covering.

Philip's bed-room and sitting room were on the third
floor to the rear, and above the yawning vacancy of
the second floor, with its blind openings that led to
deserted living-rooms, was a faint illumination that
grew stronger as one ascended. Careful preparations
had been made for Philip's return. The electric candles of the landing had been left burning and below
them on a table were an evening paper and a bottle
of water and a silver dish with fruit and sandwiches.

Gulian pushed the closed door to Philip's quarters
open and entered soundlessly. He at least knew that
there was to be no further immediate occupancy—
nothing, save the ghost that follows occupancy; a glint
of the cups Philip had won, the sober richness of his
books, the wistful catalepsis of photographs; a redo-
lence of brushes and leather; the impalpable impress
of the going to and fro of an absent personality, intimate and heartbreaking. Gulian dared not look about
him. This inner place of habitation was still too sen-
sitized; still too quick with the imprint of the dead
man. He walked directly over to the lacquered black
and gold desk, avoiding as he did so a couch covered
with flowered cretonne and the table beside it, on
which were foreign novels in paper covers, and magazines, and a lamp under a shade of orange colored silk,
and pulling out the chair that stood before the open
flap of the desk, sat down and began to consult the red
note-book. A hidden drawer was to be found and in
it a tiny safe. So Philip had said and so the little note-
book made confirmation . . . a knob to be twisted
and pulled forward; a slip of paper under the mina-
ture strong-box that gave its combination.

Gulian turned the knob between careful fingers

and a section of the lacquered wood slid back, disclosing steel walls. And a further turning of another knob,
this time a metal one, brought the secret itself into
view—a small pass-book such as banks use, in which,
Gulian saw at a glance, had been entered with scrupu-
lous care the names of various securities and the sums
of money expended in purchasing them and the names
of the brokerage houses through which the purchases
had been made. Fastened to the book by an elastic
band was an envelope addressed to Gulian in Philip's
handwriting.

That was all; otherwise the tiny safe was empty.
. . . Gulian began to feel rather like the recipient of
a jocose present who unwraps sheet after sheet of
paper and opens box after box in the end to find nothing. And he was still puzzled by the deviousness of
it all; a deviousness that would not have been overly
effective had the red note-book fallen into anyone else's
hands. Why, if you wanted to be mysterious, carry
your mystery around in anything but your own head—
the only secure strong-box, and not very secure at that
unless your tongue is equally padlocked? But then,
he had always heard that when men wished to be especially secret they indulged in such childish mysteries.

He unloosed the envelope from the elastic band
and drew out its contents, a single sheet of paper with
Philip's initials in heavy black relief at the top. The
curt sentences were ominously cryptic.

"I don't know what you are going to do about this.
I don't know what there is to be done—I can't think
any more. My head has stopped functioning. At all
events, do the best you can. Perhaps you will see a
way out. At least you will be able to attack the problem with a clear vision.

Philip."

The frown marking Gulian's forehead grew deeper. Now what did that mean? He supposed the pass-book would explain, but until it did, nothing was clear save the fact that Philip's action had been no temporary vertigo, no scarlet dizziness, but a climax carefully planned and executed. Philip, the heroic physically, the bland optimist, the man who had spent his leisure preaching to others the necessity for faith, had deliberately shot himself . . . or at all events, had been weighing the act in his mind.

Anger at Philip swept Gulian for a moment and was shamefacedly suppressed. You couldn't very well be angry with a dead man. He picked up the note-book and opened it at the first page. He was surprised at the simplicity of the explanation it contained. The motive that had prompted Philip to take his life was one of the motives that had occurred to Gulian but had been rejected as too crude. Hot-bloodedness, oh yes, there were no limits to that. Being thirty-five and fairly experienced, Gulian placed little beyond the realms of possibility where hot-bloodedness was concerned. But it was incredible that a man of Philip's wealth and Philip's traditions should have done just what Philip had. But then it wasn't incredible, because it was done so often. What craving for power, what itch for excitement, what anaesthesia for an unhappy personal life, what madness due to the by now anachronistic bonanzas of the war, had driven him to such insanity?

And how long had it been going on? The little pass-book was dated back only a year. However, none of these questions mattered. What mattered was that this time Philip had been caught between the doors of fate, and was dead, and had left a ruinous debt behind him. . . . Succinctly, he had been buying—mostly on margin—worthless securities with funds that belonged to his banking house, and pocketing the profits, and buying again. And succinctly, on this particular Monday he had pocketed a loss greater than he could bear.

Some love of order—it is almost always the case when men who have been honest steal money; the intention of some day paying back what he had taken; had caused him to put down neatly and precisely every move he had made. Perhaps the very preciseness of the process had salved to some extent his conscience.

Gulian added and subtracted and made duplicate lists of his own. Practically all of the stocks listed had gone down in the recent crash; glittering alchemic promises; dreams of instant and immense wealth, feeding the inherited instinct of the American, still a pioneer, that the earth is an Aladdin's cave that needs only to be struck to yield gigantic fortune.

Gulian noticed that Perry had been the greatest factor in these transactions. Philip, then, had bought mostly on Perry's advice. No wonder Perry had been worried that afternoon. He would continue to be worried, Gulian grimly decided. What was to be done about Perry? Something had to be done. He could not go on forever being a stench in decent men's nostrils.

Gulian recalled his own attitude of a few hours earlier towards Perry's nervousness and the panic in general. He—Gulian—had been so aloof and so condescending. Neither himself nor anyone dear to him were involved, or could be involved, so he had thought. . . . No man is ever uninvolved about anything. The whole world is drowned by the same drop of water and given wings by the same thought. The breeze that stirs the leaves in India has its echoes in Newfoundland,

and the moon sees all things. At the furthest we are all seventeenth cousins. . . .

Gulian stood up from the desk and folding carefully the duplicate slips he had made, placed them and the pass-book in his breast pocket. He shut the tiny safe and slid to the secret drawer and went to the window, holding Philip's letter in his hand. The net curtains hung motionless in the breathless dampness of the night. Gulian pushed them aside and leaned out. There was a hint of dawn in the air. He must have sat before the desk much longer than he had thought. He took a box of matches from his pocket and striking one, held it under the single sheet of white paper. The flame crept up until it almost touched his fingers before he opened them and let the blazing remnant drop through the sallow darkness. Then he turned back towards the room and extinguishing the lights, and the one in the hall, crept downstairs and into the street.

He was no longer angry with Philip. The faint, thoughtful coolness of the approaching dawn; the mysterious fissure it makes between the new day and all the hours that have gone before; prevented anger if nothing else. He was only infinitely pitiful and amazed and wondering; and where he himself was involved, startled. On his shoulders had fallen suddenly and definitely the task of carrying forward unaided an honorable tradition and an honorable name. Odd, when you came to think of it, that only a few weeks before he had been the member of the family most in need of guidance! Curiously enough he was not in the least afraid in the presence of this unexpected conclusion, merely filled with a sort of fierce anticipation.

Later on there would be, he knew, of course, relapses. For one thing, in the corner of his brain lurked the assurance that never again would he be able to trust life completely. From now on incredulity would enter into all his laughter; he had come too close to horror. Between him and horror the layers of his consciousness had been scraped away until now there was stretched only a thin tegument like the red membrane of the brain. He would have to see to it that never by any chance was this tegument pierced, or he and horror would be the same thing. And yet, although he did not realize it at the time, it is only because of such thin teguments that the keenness of life is ever experienced.

He thought he understood more fully why Philip had done what he had. When the devil is weary of trying to tempt the conscientious he uses his last and infallible weapon, the favorite vice of the godly, pride —the gray familiar of the churches. And in a world in which men have such a little time to live and in which they are all engaged in the common adventure of death, pride, although the most dangerous of vices, is also the most childlike and pathetic. Here, Gulian decided, had been no vulgar theft but a desperate attempt to maintain an equilibrium, to keep up a scale of living that had been possible in more prosperous times; to prevent an unsympathetic Margaret, an eyebrow-raising circle of theological and business friends from realizing that the god-like man was not quite so god-like as they thought. Especially perhaps the church. The one thing the church cannot forgive is a loss of money.

Gulian did not hunt for a cab this time. He wanted the interval the walk to Madison Place would give him. Soon it would be day and with the coming of day the hostile forces of life would re-awaken. And there were a great many things to be decided before then, particularly his father to be thought of; he would have to lay immediate plans to prevent Mr. Eyre from suffering too great a shock.

As he walked he became more and more oblivious of his surroundings. Time apparently ascended through planes of decreasing pallor, punctuated by the almost unnoticed streets he passed, until, near Thirtieth Street, a white morning took the sky, and heat struck him, and the glare of the pavements. Through these planes of light he seemed to have followed directly in the wake of time, a disembodied creature absorbed in thought.

On the other side of Thirtieth Street he paused. He knew suddenly exactly what was to be done—the future had clicked into place like the lead slugs of a linotype machine—if he could only do it! Despite his experience in Perry's office he was still an amateur in business; still afraid of the abracadabra, the folk-lore, the tribal taboos of the business world, although he was still sure that in the business world, as in all other worlds, direct action was the only correct form of action. Convinced, that is, that ample men have no time for red tape, but unconvinced that he himself was an ample man.

He turned into a small cheap restaurant and ordered a breakfast that he ate with an absent-minded precision. When he was through, he went over to the telephone booth and asked for a number in the 'Sixties.' He would have a talk immediately with Mr. Oxenard of the law firm that handled his family's affairs. That shouldn't be difficult. Lawyers were up and about earlier than bankers, and in emergencies were more like doctors . . . amenable to out-of-the-way appointments.

A sleepy servant's voice answered him and was shocked at the request to see Mr. Oxenard. 'Mr. Oxenard wasn't awake yet. It was only half-past six.' "I don't give a damn whether he's awake or not," retorted Gulian, with a new accent of command. "Go up to his room and tell him that Mr. Gulian Eyre— E-y-r-e—is on his way to consult him about a matter of utmost importance—a matter that cannot be delayed a moment. I'll be there in about half an hour. Tell Mr. Oxenard to bathe and dress and have breakfast and be ready to see me."

From the other end of the wire an incredulous gasp made a period to these orders.

"Don't gasp," advised Gulian. "Do as I tell you."

He replaced the receiver and paid his bill at the desk. The blonde rosily plump Swedish girl smiled at him. "Nize morning," she observed.

"Yes," he said staring, as if surprised and suddenly overcome by the importance of the statement, "it is. Cooler."

He turned back into Fifth Avenue and caught a 'bus going north, and climbed to the swaying upper platform. At this time of day a 'bus was almost as quick as a cab and considerably more pleasant. He was surprised how much he enjoyed his cigarette and the light breezes that smelled of watering-carts and wet curbs and awnings.

At Sixty-fifth Street he got off the 'bus and turned eastward.

A slightly annoyed, and prepared to be much more annoyed, Mr. Oxenard greeted him over a cantaloupe, the silvery yellow of which, close to the round choleric face, made it appear like a moon about to be swallowed up by the sun. As a younger member of the Eyre family, Gulian was known only slightly to Mr.

Oxenard and that unfavorably. Mr. Oxenard had always heard of him as a wild and itinerant young man and had sent him his monthly checks grudgingly. He supposed now that this unconventional call had to do with some scrape in which a chauffeur or chorus-girl were involved.

"Thank you," said Gulian, sitting down without being asked. "I took a chance of your being in town. . . . I knew you were one of those sensible people who didn't live in the suburbs but sent their families away where they could only join them over week-ends."

He ignored Mr. Oxenard's mounting anger. He had a feeling that after this he would never be bothered again by the mounting anger of any old gentleman, or group of old gentlemen, no matter how important they were. Boiled down, they were merely old people who ate cantaloupes rather greedily; spurted them about.

For three hours he and Mr. Oxenard were closeted together, first in the house on Sixty-fifth Street, and then in Mr. Oxenard's office down town, where there were numerous papers to be gone over. At ten o'clock, accompanied by Mr. Oxenard, Gulian entered the banking house of Eyre & Co. and asking for Mr. Prendegast, went directly back to Philip's room, brushing aside astonished doormen and office-boys. He sat down at the ponderous desk that stood before the portrait of his father. He avoided looking at the portrait of his father.

"Mr. Philip will not be down today," he said to the hovering suspiciousness of the maternal secretary in a tone of cold evasiveness that silenced her questions but agonized her with curiosity. "Please call up my house—15 Madison Place—and ask the butler if my father, or Mrs. Shipman, my sister, have arrived, and if not, tell him I will be back in about an hour." He turned to Mr. Oxenard who was blinking meditatively at the wall opposite. "Do you want me to talk to them, or will you?"

"It is much better that you should."

"All right."

Presently Mr. Prendegast entered, completely at a loss as to why he should be summoned to appear in the senior partner's room by the senior partner's brother. He seemed on the point of becoming vaguely angry. The sucking of his lips and the washing of his osseous hands in imaginary water were more pronounced than usual. He was dressed in an exceedingly ugly suit of sleezy gray silk and wore a flowing tie of shepherd's plaid. Gulian's heart sank at the sight of him.

"Sit down, Mr. Prendegast," he said, finding some difficulty in pronouncing the words, although no one would have suspected his nervousness, "and please don't interrupt me. This is Mr. Oxenard of the firm of Oxenard, Davidson and Firth. He is my attorney; he was also Philip's."

At the use of the past tense, Mr. Prendegast's vague eyes became less vague and he looked at Gulian fixedly. "I know Mr. Oxenard," he murmured.

Gulian proceeded. "Who are the two very best young men this firm has?"

"Well ——"

"The ones with the most imagination and the best records?"

"I should say Hitchcock and Tarbell."

"Will you ring a bell and have them in?"

Mr. Prendegast, still mystified, made a motion to do as he was told, but Gulian checked him, and he resumed his seat, peering at Gulian malevolently, his lips moving up and down.

"Before they come," said Gulian, "I will have to tell you the main facts of my story. My brother Philip has shot himself. Only you, Hitchcock and Tarbell are to know that. Nobody else is to know anything. My brother is lying dead in my house. . . ." He was astonished at the calmness with which he was able to announce these dreadful truths. "He has stolen from this banking house, of which he was senior partner, something near to two million dollars. . . . No; sit down, Mr. Prendegast! . . . Thank you! . . . Unless we move very rapidly and surely this house will fail and Philip's name and all our names—including yours, Mr. Prendegast—and very rightly, too, for your negligence—will be disgraced. Also, it will kill my father. I have gone over everything with Mr. Oxenard. Philip leaves practically no assets; his property is heavily mortgaged, even his life insurance. Incidentally, he has wiped out the entire fortune of my aunt, Mrs. Dorrance, as well. I can imagine no more complete disaster."

Mr. Prendegast looked at him for a long moment.

"What are we going to do?" he asked finally in a helpless voice.

Gulian shook his head as if the ineptitude of such a question puzzled him.

"Do?" he repeated. "Do? Why, what is there to do, of course, but make it good? By selling out nearly everything my father owns . . . and at about one-half its value, naturally, as it will be an enforced sale . . . we will be able to cover the deficit. . . . That is what I have come to tell you."

"You mean to ruin yourself?" asked Mr. Prendegast in awe-stricken accents.

"Yes—if that's what you call ruining yourself." Gulian sat back in his chair. "This bank didn't belong to Philip, Mr. Prendegast, it belongs to his family. It was started by my great-grandfather. That seems to me considerably more of an obligation than if the obligation were merely financial. Besides, I trust the ruin is only for a few years, and it will be by no means absolute. We will not have to sell my father's country-place, and he will still retain his interest in this concern, and there is some other property as well. We won't starve. But that is unimportant—what is important is that we'll have to reorganize and carry on as if nothing had happened. The news of this must not get about. . . . Any more than can be helped, that is. I shall expect and demand a position here, of course, but especially I shall expect you, Mr. Prendegast, to try to recall what banking knowledge you once had. Do you think you can?"

He paused and opened his eyes very wide, for the moment not violet eyes at all, but hard blue eyes, upon the small, gayly untidy man listening to him so intently. He was amazed at the success with which he was carrying through his plans and he was especially amazed at himself. His theory, then, regarding business had been true, and life, in this respect as in all others, was only ferocious at a distance. Like a hill, it looked steeper the further you were away from it. All people were just as much confused as himself, and the majority considerably more so. Big a fool as you knew yourself to be, the percentage of utter fools was greater. Folly was the only profession in which there was any competition. The thought was comforting.

However, he felt almost ashamed of the ease with which he had overcome the first small dragon in his way. Most heroes must have felt a similar shame. The stone with which David killed Goliath was merely the truth, a tiny stone seldom picked up, and David no doubt was mystified at discovering what a huge bundle of straw Goliath was. It was exactly as if you had been told a secret that wasn't really a secret at all, or had joined a mysterious society to find that the masked men who composed it were the most commonplace of neighbors (as they always are, for only the commonplace have any need of masks).

"Do you think you can recall what banking knowledge you once had, Mr. Prendegast?" Gulian repeated gently.

Mr. Prendegast awoke from deep reflection. "I think so," he said.

"Good! You will, however, have to forget almost entirely your collection of beetles, or whatever it is you do collect. . . . You collect beetles, don't you?"

"Chrysanthemums," corrected Mr. Prendegast with some heat.

"Well, chrysanthemums. . . . You'll have to forget them for awhile and concentrate upon the business at hand."

"I'll forget 'em," said Mr. Prendegast testily. He sucked in his lips explosively. "See here—you know I'm liable, too, don't you? This is a partnership. And I'll be able to bear my share. . . . I'm not a poor man."

A Covenanting ancestor suddenly looked out of Gulian's face. "No you won't," he said coldly. "It's not your affair—thank you just the same. My family stole the money and will pay it back. And now, if you'll ring for Mr. Tarbell and Mr. Hitchcock?"

But at the same time he had indulged himself in a grim vision of Sydney and Vida stripped of their resources and had wondered what would become of them if such a thing happened. The gun-man and the courtesan are after all no more than merely half our friends deprived of their incomes.

He had come to like Mr. Oxenard; he liked him even better as the conference proceeded. He and Mr. Oxenard seemed to be fellow conspirators in an honest conspiracy. Beneath his fat and his gray hair and his thick cynical mouth, this attorney possessed a store of facts and a constructive imagination. He did not blanch from the actions of men. He seemed to take it for granted that a man was capable of any virtue or any vice and from that premise went on without wasting further time. This was a relief. The business mind, in distinction to the professional mind, is too exclamatory over sin; too put out about it to be entirely sincere.

But Mr. Oxenard's imagination did not follow Gulian's all the way. There were moments when it failed to keep step. Such a moment occurred when, the conference being over, he and Gulian paused on the classic steps of Eyre & Co. before going their separate ways, and Gulian, looking up at the sky, spoke as follows:

"Undoubtedly," he said thoughtfully, "there is some sort of a God—anthropomorphic or intellectual or gaseous or self-constructed or whatever you want. And undoubtedly He bends to His will whomsoever sets himself up against Him."

He lowered his gaze from the sky and looked at Mr. Oxenard directly. "Only I wish," he added, "the present-day god wasn't so invariably a banker. I would so much rather have been broken to the wheel of piracy or troubadoring or of being a cardinal, wouldn't you?"

He waved his hand and set off towards the subway on his journey to Madison Place.

Fortunately Mr. Oxenard, having trained himself through many years to auricular efficiency, had failed

to hear what had been said, realizing after the first
sentence that the outburst was to be abstract and
philosophic. His recently achieved portrait of Gulian,
therefore, as a brilliant if curious young man remained
unaltered.

Gulian had not as yet had time to piece together the
separate parts of this bewildering day and a half; the
sultry panic, the interview with Perry, the melting
beauty of his discovery concerning Lael, the magic of
his hours with her, the night with its glacial horror
torn by a thunderstorm. Nor did he wish to piece
them together for awhile. There were emergencies to
be met with first and overcome before he dare settle
down to synthetic reflection. The principal emer-
gency was his coming interview with his father. It
was now half past eleven and Mr. Eyre would have
reached Madison Place and would have heard the
carefully guarded account of Dr. McCarter, or the
account of the person Dr. McCarter had left in charge.
But Mr. Eyre would want to know more, and what
was there to tell him? Gulian was sorry not to have
been there himself, but that could not be helped. It
was with a mind, however, uneasy with thoughts of
disaster that he hurried along the cross streets and up
the steps of his house. Even the most circumspect
story might have affected his father seriously. The
fundamental tragedy, whatever its motive, was not
altered.

Prescott opened the door for him. Prescott had
been crying.

"Has Mr. Eyre come yet?" asked Gulian breathlessly.

"Yes, sir. He is waiting for you in the garden."

Gulian went straight out to the garden and saw his
father sitting in a little alcove fashioned from the

wall just beyond the bronze boy of the fountain, where a stone bench had been placed to take advantage of the shade. Mr. Eyre was leaning back, his eyes closed, his chin on his breast, his hands hanging limply between his knees where a cane reposed. Gulian's heart stood still. The sense of disaster rose to a climax. This was to be the final blow, was it? He did not hurry, he walked slowly down the brick path towards the alcove, the sliding lisp of the water making an undercurrent for his thoughts. Water went on. . . . Perpetually. . . . It was eternal.

And then, very quietly, Mr. Eyre stirred and sat upright and reaching for his cane, clasped his fingers over the smooth malacca and brooded upon Gulian.

"Is that you, Gulian?" he said. "Sit down." His old eyes were washed clear of any traces of emotion or rebellion. They were expressionless with knowledge. They had been washed clear decades before. "Sit down," he repeated. "You had better tell me everything. . . . Yes, it's all right. Don't worry—my poor boy!"

CHAPTER V

AND VARIOUS DAYS AFTER

OF THE rest of that period immediately following, the two and a half months from July 11 to October 1, there is very little to tell, save for a few outstanding incidents: an interview with Aunt Virginia; a letter to Lael . . . here was slow torture greater than Gulian had thought possible; a visit from Perry; and then, much later, in the early part of September, the announcement to an astonished circle of friends that Marian Gates was going to marry Vannya. Evidently Vannya had made use of his visits to Mr. Eyre.

Gulian, when he heard the news, was depressed. Added to the natural male jealousy where a companion of the same sex is being married off, was an especial objection in the case of Vannya. Somehow one couldn't think of Vannya domesticated. There would be a subtraction from the already too small fund of general gayety. But Vannya's words on the subject set at rest to some extent any fears that there would be a too subversive change in his attitude towards life.

"She iss the only Ameerican girl I haf met," he informed Gulian, "who does nodt talk too mooch. She iss a splendit wife for an arteest. . . . She does not theenk too mooch, either."

Gulian was interested in Drusilla's reactions to this surprising turn of affairs. There was little, however, to be got out of Drusilla. She was dewily amused and congratulatory. Her wide gray eyes seemed to be storing future resources for humorous reflection.

413

But Aunt Virginia apparently had been stirred to a final desperate effort to set straight a world steadily growing naughtier. At the moment she was staying at 'Hibernia,' and rumor had it that, coming across Marian one morning down in the village of Slaton, she had attempted, as an ancient friend of the family and a woman tried in sorrow and knowledge, to correct what could at worst be only a youthful error of judgment on Marian's part. Marian was supposed to have met this altruism with a stubborn effrontery that confirmed Aunt Virginia's fears concerning the younger generation's lack of decency and common-sense. Ordinarily Marian was a quiet girl, not given to explaining herself, rather blank, in fact, but now her eyes were brilliant and her red lips charmingly voluble. She spoke in aphorisms that would have astonished Vannya—or perhaps they wouldn't have. For, despite his remarks on the subject, Marian wasn't dull and he knew it; she was merely, like most of her contemporaries, willing to take for granted the banalities that had been the staple subjects of conversation amongst her ancestors.

"I am not marrying Vannya's past," she is reported to have said; "I am marrying his present. I am not even marrying his future—that's up to me to take care of. I am marrying just Vannya. . . . How do you know so much about him, anyhow?"

"I don't," Mrs. Dorrance had replied, "but I know Russians, and your fiancée is an intimate friend of my nephew, and although Gulian is a man of excellent impulses (she would not have said even this three months before, but now she was forced to admit it)— he is totally un-American in his attitude towards women."

Marian's red lips looked brutal. "What's American?" she asked harshly. "The way my father treats my mother? That's Turkish, too. If I were an American of your period I would long ago have pointed a dignified virgin finger of scorn at you and have told you to leave this grocery shop. As it is, I am discussing things with you amicably. If I can't prevent Vannya flirting with other women, I'll find out if I'm not getting fat, or something else equally unattractive. And as to pasts, a man you never heard of, Dr. Freud, has shown that even the most innocent young girl has a past whether she knows it or not."

Now what possible chance for a happy marriage was there to be found in such a farrago of immodesty and unmaidenliness? The idea of a young girl even mentioning the word virgin, let alone knowing what it meant!

Gulian had gone up to see Aunt Virginia in her Catskill retreat three or four days after Philip's death, as soon, that is, as he could get away from New York. He had found her surrounded by a subdued but secretly rebellious hotel staff and the usual number of demure sycophants. In this adulation Aunt Virginia, despite her recent bereavement, was taking pleasure. She was dressed in a mourning that made Gulian's arm-band seem callous by contrast.

"I must have a long interview with you after dinner, Aunt Virginia," he had said.

But when the time came he found it difficult to tell her his news, especially as she insisted that Octavia Hiatt remain in the room.

"Octavia is like a sister to me," she said, "—a younger sister."

The heavy-lidded gray eyes and the expressionless green eyes focused upon Gulian and made him even more nervous than he had been to begin with. There

seemed to be no getting away from these two pair of
eyes, no corners left for casualness. He felt like an
executioner called upon to execute two old women.
He stammered through an explanation as simple as he
could make it. He was still irritatingly afraid of Aunt
Virginia. Her silence and her immobility made him
feel that in this matter, somehow, it was he who had
been to blame.

For a while after he had finished, Mrs. Dorrance
had continued to stare at him, her useless beringed
little hands clasped in her lap. At first he thought she
had not understood him!

"And so there's almost nothing left?" she asked
finally.

"Practically nothing. Perhaps we'll be able to save
a thousand a year. . . . I'm so sorry. I . . . "

Aunt Virginia raised a hand.

"And I will have to sell my house, I suppose?"

"I'm afraid so. It will only go part way towards
paying your debts."

There was no increase of expression in the light gray
eyes.

"A thousand a year would get me into some nice
home for old ladies, wouldn't it? . . . I don't know
much about such things. I wouldn't like to leave here
too suddenly. I . . . people might think it queer."

The crises of emotion are odd and reached by queer
means. Gulian had once seen an old woman whose
three sons had been killed at her feet by an enemy
shell but who was dry-eyed and outwardly calm until
she found that the same shell had killed a pet canary.
During the past four agonized days he had felt
no desire to weep, not even when he had first seen his
father, but now something tore at his throat. . . .
Old people were unbearably pathetic unless events

went well with them. They had already gone through too much . . . .

A moment of gorgeous sentimentality, a wave of magnificence that broke upon him like sun-flecked surf, swept over him, and he sprang to his feet and crossed the room to his aunt and put his arm around her plump shoulders.

"You won't have to go into an old ladies' home!" he said in a queer small voice. "I'll be damned if you do. We've got 'Hibernia' left. . . . There's lots of room. Besides, I'll be making money soon."

He remembered the vacant jade eyes of Octavia that no doubt were boring into his back with a sea-green helplessness, and an access of pity was added to the pity he already felt. "And Octavia too!" he added. "Don't you worry about Octavia, either!"

A prospect feudal and domestic and sunnily opulent opened out before him. When you came right down to it, the only way, anyhow, to live was with your entire family about you.

And then Aunt Virginia spoke drily. "Don't be absurd," she said, pushing him away. "You know perfectly well I couldn't live with you or your father for a minute. If you can help Octavia and me out a little. . . . I shall dislike it, of course, but I daresay it is necessary. . . . There, there! I'm grateful even if I don't show it. And there's no need for swearing."

She was quite right, of course; Gulian saw the force of her statement immediately. But he did wish, his heart munificent from tragedy, that a perfect patriarchal family life was still possible. Like socialism, it seemed the easiest thing in the world until you tried it.

And Mrs. Dorrance was more right than she knew as a few weeks showed, for Gulian came nearer to having the beginnings of a patriarchal family than he had anticipated. As a start, he found himself with a ready-made son upon his hands. Philip's desire that he be more than merely a legal guardian for young Philip seemed to be on the point of being literally fulfilled.

Acting upon Philip's request, he had suggested to Margaret that owing to her present financial condition and the confusion of her future, it might be better for young Philip to stay with his grandfather for awhile, and Margaret had acquiesced with an absent-minded eagerness that puzzled him. In fact, Margaret had puzzled him from the moment of Philip's death, and she continued to puzzle him. There was a bright indurate insanity about her that before had been exhibited openly only in her public relationships. She had rented a little cottage down on Long Island and was apparently beginning to live a life of dextrous widowhood. It was doing her good physically. She was beginning to look exceedingly pretty, and the faint traces of avidity that were now appearing openly in her eyes did not detract from her allurement . . . for those that liked that type of allurement. A number of men—younger than herself, or older than herself; never her own age—seemed to like it. No doubt in the first instance they were impressed by the puzzling combination of beauty and efficiency, and no doubt in the second, as older men will, but not middle-aged men, they forgave the efficiency because of the beauty. Found the efficiency not such a very serious matter after all. Gulian foresaw a speedy second marriage. There would be folly undoubtedly, but not scandal. Released as Margaret seemed to be, nevertheless the shadow of the Woman's Party would continue to haunt her with its gaunt chaperonage.

This unofficial adoption of young Philip, an adoption

that threatened to become permanent—and Gulian wanted it to be permanent—had, however, put the final touches to his determination that in no way should Lael share in the grimnesses or possible grimnesses of this new life of his. It was enough to expect a girl like Lael to marry him, let alone expecting her to be an amateur mother to an elderly gentleman and a growing boy. He would have to be content with the elderly gentleman and the growing boy. In fact, for awhile, all the yearning of his heart went out to the elderly gentleman and the growing boy. They were so helpless and dependent. If he could preserve them for himself and have them as the centre of his life, what more would he ask for, save, of course, the success in his work that had now become indispensable.

He had given himself plenty of time to think over the situation that existed between himself and Lael, and every day that passed added to his original conviction. There were no heroics about this, no senseless renunciation, merely, as he saw it, an intelligent fairness and a wise precaution as to future happiness.

In the short while that had intervened between the Tuesday of startled tragedy and the date of Lael's sailing for Europe, he had seen her as little as possible, pleading, as was true, overwhelming work, and the actual day of sailing, he had made it a point to arrive at the steamer so late that any opportunity to be alone with her would be of the briefest description. In all the hurried interviews he had had with her and in her attempts to talk to him over the telephone she had been unaffectedly solicitous and sympathetic, rather pathetically eager to be of help, and this baffled interest had flared up in a final outburst of temper as she was saying good-bye to him.

The moment was a dangerous one for Gulian; he had almost laid his case directly before her.

"What's the matter with you?" she had demanded "What have I done? Why do you keep me in the dark? What makes you so queer?"

The anger in her eyes weakened Gulian even more than tenderness would have done. "I'm not queer," he answered evasively; "I'm just dreadfully shaken and busy."

"Ah, yes, poor soul! . . . Gilly, look at me. . . . No——? Oh, what is the matter with you?" She drew away from him. Had she been older she would have insisted upon an explanation, but she was still shy with him and, being young, still thought all indifference personal. She shrugged her shoulders.

"It doesn't make much matter, I suppose," she said wearily. "No doubt you'll tell me when you want to. You're a person of moods. Only I'm more grown-up than you think, and you can't treat a grown-up woman this way. . . . You'll write me soon, won't you?"

For an instant in the emptiness of the companionway she clung to him with a fierce questioning pressure of her young lips that astonished him and afterwards, when he thought of it, which was constantly, almost broke his heart; most certainly came near to breaking his resolution.

If Lael had only been a little older; if she had only already had her just share of life; if she had tested things and discarded them and found more or less exactly what she wanted! But a man of his age could not continue to ask a girl of her age to take part in what had suddenly become an exceedingly restricted adventure. How could he if he loved her? What kind of love would that be? From the very beginning this difference in their ages had been a cause for humility with Gulian (just as, although he did not know it, it had been a cause for humility in Lael), a something that had made him overly suspicious and at times diffident, and now it seemed to him to have become an insurmountable obstacle. He was no longer able to offer Lael any of the compensations that otherwise would have helped to balance the inequality; nothing now but his own personality. And that, as he told himself, was not enough. There was a certain shining quality about youth that demanded a shining quality in return, and although he had had that shining quality he felt now that, for a while anyhow, perhaps for good, he had lost it. Laughter demands laughter, and he neither wanted to laugh nor to play. Young people should have as their just dower opportunity for glowing incident, for width of choice, for experiment. And only money or freedom can give these things. It was not in him to ask youth to abandon this generous birthright. It was not in him to deny to anyone any of the too short and too rare effulgences of life.

But like all baffled lovers he drew for himself a picture of future reward. Some day, when Lael had grown older, some day when he was his own master—even Lael's marriage to some one else would not prevent this—he would seek her out again. She could get rid of the other person. . . . But meanwhile, it did not please him much to think of the other person.

Lael wrote a couple of weeks later from Deauville, whither a mother with an obsolete notion of gayety had dragged her, and Gulian wrote back a letter that it took him three days to compose. Yet it was only a page and a half long. He found it difficult not to be brutal without at the same time disclosing to Lael his real feelings and motives.

Life had become very complicated, he explained.

Since Philip's death much of the work of reorganizing
the house of Eyre & Co. had fallen upon his shoulders.
He was absorbed and dehumanized. He no longer
thought he could give her what she wanted—if he
ever had been able to do so. At all events, he doubted
himself. He was quite sure he could not make her
happy.

Lael did not answer this letter and he told himself
he was much relieved. As a matter of fact, he was exceedingly bitter. She had accepted his proposal too
readily, indicating that he had been right in the first
place. Anyway, he would now be able to concentrate
upon his work; would be able to turn from a world
of emotion and plunge into the sharp, clear, bracing
unemotional world of men—if there was such a thing.
He doubted it. At all events, he was tired of emotion.
. . . His doubts concerning the lack of emotion in
the world of men were not set at rest by the interview
he had with Perry three days or so after he had given
up all hope of hearing from Lael.

It was a curious little interview and exceedingly
emotional. It took place at five o'clock of an August
afternoon in the library of 15 Madison Place where
Perry had hunted Gulian out, to find him in his shirt-
sleeves, and dirty and hot, checking up, with two burly
packers, the furniture of the house, which had
been sold. At the end of the interview, Gulian
threw the little Artemis that stood in the niche of
the stairway at Perry's head and nearly killed him.
And the worst of it was, that although at first he had
been alarmed and shaken, upon reflection he realized
that this was the only time he had completely enjoyed
himself for over a month. Incidentally, he had been
able as well to accomplish another end long desired.

Briefly, the incident was this.

Amongst Philip's possessions were a hundred thousand shares of something that had been picturesquely called by those who for a short time had loved it, 'Texacania Pete,' for so they had shortened the more ponderous name of Texacania Petroleum Fuel and Gas Company. Philip had bought the shares for a dollar apiece and they were now worth exactly nothing. But Perry, in his debonair, cool, amused fashion, apparently wanted them and was willing to pay twenty-five thousand dollars to satisfy his desire.

"Why?" Gulian's long nose wrinkled.

Perry smiled. "I'm sorry," he answered. "That's a secret."

Gulian reflected. He was standing before the empty fire-place, his hands behind his back, and Perry's supernatural neatness, something that began with raggedrobins in the buttonhole of a blue suit and ended with delightfully radiant shoes, was particularly offensive to a man who knew his own person to be disordered. "Then I'm sorry, too," he retorted, "but I can't sell, either. I never sell or buy anything blindly. A few months ago I might have, but I've learned not to. You taught me that yourself, Perry." He grinned. "I'm getting rather smart about business, aren't I? . . . What's up? 'Texacania Pete' solvent again?"

Perry had been beautifully patient in the face of this insinuation. "Don't be an ass!" he had remonstrated. He got to his feet, one hand on the table. "I suppose twenty-five thousand dollars of real money wouldn't be out of place in Philip's estate, just now, would it?"

"What do you know about Philip's estate?"

"I handled most of his investments for him."

Gulian's eyes were sombre. "Yes, by thunder!" he said suddenly and softly. "You did, didn't you? I had temporarily forgotten that. . . . Well, tell me exactly what you want, and maybe I'll listen."

"I've some information."

"No doubt you have. What is it?"

"I've already told you it would be betraying confidences."

Perry was amazed at the unpleasantness of Gulian's laugh. "Oh, damn confidences! I've an idea they don't mean much to you, anyhow. . . . However, I won't badger you. If you haven't anything really to say, I'll get back to my packing. I'm too busy for mere gossip."

Perry controlled himself with an effort. He was still a master of diplomacy. His smile and voice were embracing. "Oh, very well! You're a business man, so I daresay you'll understand. There's no reason why you shouldn't be told. But it's entirely between ourselves. There's a company I'm interested in that wants the Texacania in order to reorganize it, and with Philip's block of stock and some others I can lay my hands on, we'll have. . . ."

"A controlling interest?"

"Yes, a controlling interest."

"Then Texacania *is* worth something?"

"Not till we get hold of it."

"You mean . . . ?"

Perry shrugged his shoulders and smiled more broadly.

"Oh!" said Gulian thoughtfully. After a little while: "Oh! . . ." he said again. "Nice fellows! . . . Yes, I think I see."

He regarded his brother-in-law with a look of dark amusement. "A few months ago," he continued, "I wouldn't have understood all these nuances of business, but it shows what education will do for you, doesn't it?

As I take it, you mean to get possession of this company —which has real value back of it, untold value, probably, or you wouldn't want it—and then reorganize out of it all the investors you can—the little investors. To the big ones, a few of the big ones, like Philip's estate, you'll have to pay some money. Is that right?" He took a step forward. "Well, I'll tell you, Perry, just what I think of it, I think it's a damned crooked scheme no matter how often it's played, and I wouldn't sell you a single share of this stock if it was the last asset I had in the world. There's been too much. . . ." He stopped short in time; he was going to say more than he intended. Perry did not know that already there had been too much dishonesty in the Eyre family.

"Now once more," began Perry amicably, "don't be an ass. This stock is no good to anyone just at present. If we . . ."

Gulian yawned broadly. "Oh, for God's sake," he interrupted indifferently, as if he were speaking to a tiresome minor official, "get out of here and leave me alone. I won't argue with you."

It was not a tactful conclusion, the diplomat in Perry abruptly succumbed to the man who was not used to being crossed and very surely not used to being spoken to in such a manner. He came up closer to Gulian, his lips drawn back. Afterwards Gulian wondered about this, for he knew that Perry was afraid of him and that Perry was aware of the fear. But then, in Perry's experience, physical fear of another man had probably amounted to little. The people amongst whom he moved were not given to fisticuffs. "And I won't argue with you, either," he said. "I'll just tell you something, . . . I've taken about enough of your insults. I'll give you until Friday to make up your mind. Listen, my friend, I was Philip's broker. Where do you suppose he got all this money to wild-cat with? His own money? Not by a blamed sight! If it had been, why are you selling this house? Why are all his houses being sold—everything; even his cars? What's the matter with Drusilla's income from the family estate? Can you answer me that? Well, I know. So you can keep some of your nastiness to yourself."

He turned on his heel and started for the door, but when he reached it, he paused and looked back. "I do business a certain way," he added; "and when I do it I usually have my facts in advance. Some time you can tell me how Philip came to shoot himself. All this would make a nasty story if it got about." He continued on his way down the stairs.

It was incredibly rash of him; but then, as has been said, he was unused to primitive action of any kind; and he was not aware that recently a further wound— the thought of Drusilla's unhappiness—had been added to Gulian's already wounded mind. However, he must have known that at the best Gulian's nerves were not in the most stable of conditions. Obviously he did not know that, very softly and meditatively, Gulian was following him down the stairs in the semi-dusk of the dismantled house, or that Gulian's brown face was as white as the wall he was touching with one hand.

The meditative eyes, rather terrible in the white face, watched the sleek back in front of them, the curly close-cropped hair, the jaunty assurance of the shoulders.

The rotten little cur of a blackmailer and thief! The damned mincing ghoul! Gulian saw again the room upstairs and the eye of his electric torch search-

ing the pregnant darkness. His hand, scraping along
the wall, touched the slim coolness of the Artemis, and
suddenly the thin membrane that had been stretched
between him and horror drew tight as the cover of a
drum, and he felt the muscles of his chest harden and
a wind touching his hair and, picking up the Artemis,
he hurled it with all his might at Perry's retreating
figure.

The naked little goddess hurtled through the air
and fell with a thud in the hall below, and Perry
wheeled about and looked back with his mouth open,
his eyes wide with fright.

For a moment Gulian could not move; his legs
were like queer empty boots below him; like crumpling
leather. He was a trifle sick and wanted to laugh
grotesquely. He had almost been a murderer! That
would have been, indeed, a fitting climax to all this
tragic comedy. But he controlled himself and looking
down at Perry saw something in Perry's eyes that gave
him a sudden inspiration. There was no debonairness
about Perry now.

Gulian put his hands in his pockets and took each
step slowly until he was standing on the step above
the one on which Perry had halted. He hoped Perry
wouldn't notice that his knees still trembled and that
he had difficulty in preventing his voice from breaking.

"I want to see you a moment, Perry," he said quietly.
"Will you go in there?" He indicated the door to the
drawing-room. Perry obeyed him mechanically. "I
want you to divorce Drusilla."

Perry's eyes had not regained their habitual careless
amusement, and now they stared at Gulian as if their
owner was unable to reconcile this dangerous maniac
with anything he had ever before known about him.
"You see, I'm fed up with things," continued Gulian

in the same quiet tones. "I've reached my limit. . . .
Have a cigarette?" His gentle accents were unpleasantly like those of a considerate executioner who asks
his victim if he wishes a final glass of water. Perry
appreciated the unpleasantness.

"No, thanks," he said hurriedly.

"In other words," Gulian proceeded—he had never
bullied anyone before and he was beginning to enjoy
it hugely, now that the terror over his own action was
passing—"I am pretty near to being a desperate
man." This was not in the least true, but it sounded
convincing. He was on the edge of discovering a
further ancient truth, and that is, that once you have
an enemy thoroughly scared, it is difficult to be too
melodramatic—if you keep your voice down. "I'm
desperate and I don't give a damn what I do. I've
lived in a whole lot of savage countries and I've seen
some pretty savage things."

Perry half rose from his chair and sat down again.

"I . . ." he began and licked his lips. "Look
here, Gulian," he managed to say with a fair show of
nonchalance, "either you're crazy or you think you're
playing some sort of a practical joke. Whatever it is,
I don't like it, and if you're not very careful, I'll swear
out a warrant for your arrest as soon as I get out of
here, and damn scandal. This isn't the South Sea
Islands, or wherever it is you're used to. You can't
threaten people."

"The Artemis wasn't a joke," reflected Gulian.
"And the South Sea Islands are very orderly. Besides,
I haven't threatened you. I merely said I was a
desperate man and that I wanted you to urge Drusilla
to divorce you. I wouldn't think of threatening you
unless you swore out a warrant for my arrest. And I
won't threaten you, only I'll remind you that if one

man wants to hurt another man horribly it is almost impossible to prevent him. Policemen aren't quick enough. And before the thing happens, all you can do is to place a man under bonds to maintain the peace. If he doesn't care about his bonds, what are you going to do about it? . . . That is, unless you want to employ an armed guard."

Perry jumped suddenly to his feet and started towards the door. "You damned fool," he said, "get out of my way. I've had enough of this nonsense." But he halted with his chest against Gulian's chest and realized, with a sinking of the heart, how much taller Gulian was than himself.

"The door's locked," explained Gulian gently, "and there isn't a soul in the house. Also I hate you more than I hate anybody else in the world. . . . In fact, you're the only person at present I do hate. You're a skunk and a coward and a bully and a cad. You're a rotten, smirking little snob. . . . Yes, sit down! Sit down, and take it, and smile. Try to look pleased. Now I *am* threatening you. If you say a word, if you don't give Drusilla a chance to divorce you within a month, if you don't give her a more than generous allowance—more than the courts will grant—if you do one single thing I don't like, I'll beat you within an inch of your life. And don't think you'll get out of here by promising and then go back on your word. I don't want you to promise anything, I don't want you to open your lips, I want you to go like the whipped dog you are. And you know what you'll get if you aren't good. All your life you've run over people— well, you're done. Done for good. Understand?"

He took the key out of his pocket and slipped it in the keyhole and opened the door.

"You can leave any time you want to," he suggested.

As Perry went past him, Gulian could feel the agitation of his useless anger.

He followed Perry to the front door and watched him as he walked away along Madison Place. And then he leaned against the door-jamb and looked at the dusty August trees. The late afternoon was listless and drooping, save where here and there it caught up stray rubbish and whirled it about like some idle and frowsy child playing with the leavings of the slums.

Gulian was sardonically amused and exceedingly sad. He loathed quarrels; they made him physically ill; the occasional necessity for them depressed him for days afterwards. No matter how you looked at it, they were shameful things. Ape-like; indecently stripping. But it was amusing how easily the bully was handled. One thing only, war and the discipline it involved, gave the bully any chance against the man who chose to take matters into his own hands. . . . He wondered what he actually would have done had Perry shown any spirit. It would have been an ugly situation. But Drusilla's future was assured. He was quite certain of that. Funny what a sensation honest ruthlessness seemed to create in an urban and dishonest world!

"My young man," he said to himself, "in all matters of the feelings you are becoming an unstable and dangerous person. From being a peaceable citizen, you are getting the habit of lawlessness. You're proving it again and again." He was thinking now especially of the little Artemis. "It is lucky that from now on your life will probably have a minimum quantity of that sort of stuff in it. . . . Very lucky. . . . You might readily be a criminal." . . . What an absurd person Perry was! All bulging eyes and a moustache and a suit. . . . His eyes sunk into his cheeks like burnt raisins when he was frightened.

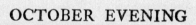

OCTOBER EVENING

OCTOBER EVENING

Gulian walked up through the October dusk towards 'Hibernia.'

Recently he had made it a habit to walk up from the station. It was the only exercise he got and his accustomed muscles were not happy without exercise. Besides, the walk gave him the only real chance he had to think—his own especial kind of thoughts. From early morning until the four o'clock train back to Slaton he was absorbed in the affairs of Eyre & Co., and on the train back he had, as a rule, various problems to turn over in his mind and the evening newspaper to skim through. And when he got home, he was as a rule too tired to do much else but talk or glance through a book in a desultory fashion and go to bed early. Sometimes, when he was stirred by a thought or an incident, he was able to write verse.

But these walks up from the station were his holidays, and he had come to love the way they gave him a growing intimacy with the countryside and enabled him to note from day to day the changes that took place in the gracious sweep of field and woodland. September with its iridescent dust and midges and its sense of fulfilment was over and in the air was the brooding magnificence of October.

October is the American month, as early spring is peculiarly Italian and June peculiarly English. The background of the nation seems to express itself more directly then than at any other time. Perhaps this is because corn, the most typical yield of the land, is so much in evidence. For most Americans when they are homesick there is a dream, not of the pastel blue of May, nor the leafy thicknesses of August, nor the white days of January, nor the sea, nor the mountains, but of corn in shocks filling the misty dip of some folded valley. And the vision touches them more than anything else, and makes them for a moment what they too seldom are, deep lovers of the homely and the aloof and the mysterious soil.

On either side of the winding ribbon of road that Gulian was following, behind narrow strips of rustling dead weeds and fences of rail or whitewashed boards, stretched the corn. Not the great fields of the middle west, but small kindly hillside acres, hemmed in by the flaming scarlet and yellow of the trees. The corn was like the bivouacs of scattered regiments encamped until the spring, only the regiments were asleep or away, for there was a complete stillness and an unbroken gravity.

Gulian drew the sharp sweet smoky air into his lungs and swung along with lengthening steps. A little amber moon took on a brighter yellow, and the blue haze deepened, and here and there the lights of farm houses burned like setting stars.

For the first time in many months—for the first time in years, perhaps—Gulian was finding himself somewhere near the intangible edges of contentment. Not happiness, that was too exultant, but contentment. A contentment, however, that might every now and then under the spur of some stimulus such as a galloping horse, or music, or a book, or a good meal, or a friend, or a landscape vividly seen, turn for a while into happiness.

He was beginning to get his life under control, to direct it instead of having it direct him, and he was beginning to realize the satisfaction that lies in that fact; the satisfaction of the runner of races and the thrower of javelins. He was beginning, moreover, to realize that the train of circumstances that had driven him into his present position had been on the whole fortunate.

Not that he had any illusions about what he had done, or was doing, or was likely to do, or that he felt any more than ever like the youthful hero of commerce—the shining Benjamin Franklin. He did not feel for a moment that he had found his perfect sphere of action or that a kindly fate, knowing more about what he wanted than he did himself, and acting in a typically national fashion, was holding his repentant nose to the grindstone of worthy effort. He knew that he had not found his perfect sphere of action, and that the sphere of action in which he found himself was by no means a perfect one. There were certain ennobling and directing trades, and banking was not one of them. Statesmen (yes, God save the mark, if they really were statesmen!), engineers, explorers, scientists, judges, scholars of all kinds, artists, sea captains, the higher sort of mechanics, farmers, doctors, priests; any man who served something bigger than himself, and especially if he served it with some degree of danger, physical or mental, belonged, so it seemed to him, to these ennobling trades no matter what he himself as an individual might be. But bankers and brokers and merchants, and all but the rarest of actors, and the silly apes of the motion picture world, and the men who sold motor cars, all go-betweens and middle-men, who served, under a great pretense of service, themselves only, were in truth servants and should be treated as such. An older world had assessed their kind properly and a newer world would one day do the same.

However, that wasn't the point. In the imperfect and at present only partially developed state of affairs, a man, unless he had some highly developed talent, was still so little his own master that he had either to allow himself to be caught up by the machinery, trying as best he could to master it, or else step outside it and die of inanition. And this was especially true of the American. There was no other choice for the American. For other nations, yes; but not for the American; not, at least, for ages to come. Tradition, surroundings, his own secret troublement, rightly or wrongly, were stronger than he.

His own secret troublement! Yes, that was the real explanation.

It was a queer business, this being an American. Not a happy job, a lonely job, both as an individual and as a citizen of the world. And it had become infinitely queerer and more complex since the war. A misunderstood, inchoate, grim sort of an undertaking.

Gulian reviewing his own life thought he could see, with it as an example, some sort of an epitome of the whole thing, and in encompassing the epitome could understand more clearly the strange upheavals, the tragedies that had taken place in his family; the unrest of the people about him; the tragedy of Philip and the unrest of Drusilla and Margaret and Vida. Only his father had escaped, and his father belonged to an older generation to which there was no turning again.

As for himself, he had tried to break away from the tradition and had been caught and brought back. He told himself once more that, by and large, he was glad he had been caught and brought back. Whether you were lucky enough to belong to one of the ennobling trades or not, was, as a rule, a mere matter of environmental chance, but to do some sort of work was a tribal necessity. Bred in your blood; part of your bone.

He tried to visualize the vast sprawling country with its feeble attempts here and there towards kemptness, and its great areas of unkemptness, and its sweet hidden wildernesses, nibbled into day by day by the armies of defacement; its millions upon millions of people with their various desires and ambitions. Slow magnificent rivers, and hurrying mountain streams, and fields like the sea with the sun on it! You went across a plain until you came to a blue vaporous mountain range and you crossed this and dropped down upon another plain, and you crawled for eternity across this second plain until you came to another mountain range—this time, a high breathtaking range, sheer and snow-capped,—and beyond this was another plain, only this time it was a desert, and then another mountain range, and then the sea. Everywhere there were cities, curiously similar cities, and everywhere there was talk of trading and buying and selling. . . . A man could not grasp this immensity, it made him feel solitary and afraid. He could not love his land intimately as an Englishman loved his tiny island or a Frenchman loves the ordered smallness of France. The best he could do was to pick out some little part of it and try to love that. And the majority hadn't even the courage or the vision for this. Otherwise, it was like trying to love a gigantic goddess whose feet alone you could see and whose head was lost in the clouds.

And this was the first thing that had happened to the American, the first thing to remember about him . . . he had lost touch, through no fault of his, with his earth. No wonder he talked in catch-words, and went to war with shibboleths on his banners, and had to think in symbols—the corn, October, Democracy; no wonder he seized hold of any passing folly. His environment was still too big for him, he had not adjusted himself to it, or rather, had not adjusted it to himself. He was still a citizen of a fabulous planet and in order to make himself at all comfortable found it necessary to invent myths. Only the Russian would understand what this strange vague yearning meant; this sense of homelessness at home; this feeling of being lord of a great heritage but a heritage still in chancery.

Here, in short, was what had happened. A prodigious continent had been settled by a race of poets . . . oh, yes, there was no doubt about that, the adventurer is always a poet, an inarticulate poet; the solid member of the family stays at home—and was still being settled by poets. And these poets had found more than they had bargained for, they had found a country of magic casual opportunity, a country so far-spreading that imagination had been both aroused and driven in upon itself. The individual had atrophied, as a unit he had expanded. In other words, the poets had sat down to a meal larger than they could digest and they were still suffering from indigestion.

But poets are strange people. They are fiercely individualistic and yet given to universal thinking, and their individualism is, after all, a mental affair. They are willing to forego the outer liberties if they can enjoy the inner. So they are both slave and master in one. They are very gentle on the surface because they can envisage the unpleasant countenance of strife, but they are inflexible underneath because they do not want their secret thoughts to be interfered with. They are sensitive and, like all sensitive persons, cruel when

wounded. They are slow to make war but terrible
when they do because they make it rhapsodically. On
the surface they are quick and sympathetic but fundamentally they are cold and secretive. They are vain
and dissatisfied and, always seeking something beyond,
are never able to content themselves with the beauty
around them. They are bad lovers and worse husbands—not brutally, for, as stated, they dislike quarrels, but in the concrete tendernesses that matter. They
are given to panaceas, to the madness of crusades, to
windy discussions, to a multitude of insanities, but at
the heart of them there is a core of gold, worked or un-
worked, finer than any spiritual metal there is. And
curiously enough, paradoxically enough, they make the
finest executives possible, for they have the imagination
and the nervous energy of the sensitive man. Not the
small, saving, efficient executive, but the executive of
wide dreams that come true.

The emphasis and proportion of all these qualities
depend, of course, upon the atmosphere in which their
possessor finds himself. In an atmosphere tender and
mellow and humane the vices come very near to being
virtues and the virtues are more than virtues, they are
inspirations; in an atmosphere that is alarming and
over-stimulating the vices tend to become specialties.

They are childish people in most ways, these races
of poets, and yet they have a nucleus of thought older
than the hills or the seas. They are born with what
other men can never learn. And above all, and this
must never be forgotten, like all thin-skinned creatures,
like all children, they are superbly Jesuitical; lying to
themselves to save themselves pain, and lying to others
so that in saving others from pain they will save themselves in turn. They rationalize their failings and the
things they cannot help, and they pat themselves on

the back and tell themselves what splendid men they are and what a splendid time they are having doing the things they hate.

And it is not a tender or mellow or humane atmosphere when poets and frontiersmen have to be executives whether they want or not, and it is not a tender or mellow atmosphere when they have to put their thoughts into baskets so large that the kindly small human things drop out. The American was in danger of functioning, as it were, only from the eyebrows up. He was in danger of losing direct connection with the ground. Baffled and driven back upon himself, driven by these overpowering forces which chose him and which he tried to drive, he was in danger of living in his imagination solely. He was in danger, that is, of becoming slightly monstrous.

That was how Gulian saw his fellow-countrymen as he walked up through the dusk, although he was aware that most people, especially his fellow-countrymen, would laugh at him. Let them laugh, he knew it was true. There is no man who so vehemently denies being a poet as the poet who is neither writing nor living poetry, and there is no man who impresses the casual spectator as being less of a poet than the poet who is suppressing his inner desires.

But Gulian added to this portrait—added enormously. In the past three years more had happened than in the fifty years preceding; a revolution and a revelation and a recognition had taken place.

Upon this imaginative cold childlike creature, this youngest and oldest of animals, had fallen the toga and the tragedy and the inspiration of empire. They had come to him without his conscious asking or his conscious knowledge. He had wakened one morning to find them his. And this had happened after a great war had already stripped him of the remaining vestiges of his moral and religious traditions. In this loss, of course, he was not unlike the rest of the world, but in this gain he was utterly unlike the rest of the world. And the rest of the world, besides, had never been as perpetually worried as he had been and had always found infinitely more compensation in the blander pleasures of life.

Added to his strange heredity, then, his disconcerting environment, there had now been added the terror and the amplitude and the responsibility of power. Forced as the American was to think in ships and oil fields and millions of acres of wheat, how could he think in the terms of such personal things as wives or children or God or beauty or sonnets or laughter? He trembled before the smoky djinn he had let loose, worshipped him and hated him.

Was it odd that the always grave American was now grave beyond reason, unamusing, grim, sententious? Was it odd that he was nervous and sharply bitter in what pleasures he had? Was it odd that he tore life to pieces as an ill-controlled child might tear a perplexing toy? He was restless with his preemption, his overwhelming calling. He was driven even more than ever back into the cold refuge of his imagination. He was alternately exalted by the greatness of his destiny and depressed by the smallness of himself; aware, even at his most boastful moments, that he was at best merely humus for the generations to come. And humus is never in itself a very gay or very lovely substance.

This strange, absurd, pathetic, conquering, notable Hamlet of the modern world, with his catch-words and his motor-car; a score of platitudes on his lips and a score of unrealized desires in his heart . . .!

. . . Gulian was not depressed by this picture; to

the contrary he was touched and cheered by it. Whatever the present might be, of such material there could come in the future nothing else but greatness, and a fine, universal greatness at that. Some day the poet would conquer his environment and get his feet back to the ground and laugh again and be happy, because, out of confusion, he had been able to create some degree of beauty and peace and wisdom. Something as beautiful and orderly and tender, perhaps, as these encampments of the corn. . . . As to the rest of it, it was as trite as such truths always are, that only out of sorrow comes sympathy, only out of tragedy understanding, and that you have first to hate the world before you can ever really love it, lose it before you can ever really find it.

Philip had lost it and had not waited to find it again. Probably he never would have found it. It took men and women of sturdier fibre than his to make the search in these days of drifting values. He had mislaid his anthropomorphic god and could find no other. Vida and Margaret did not count, they were drugging themselves with substitutes. But Drusilla would come through. And as for himself, Gulian, he was luckier than most. Lucky not only in the fact that he had been forced to undertake what otherwise he would have wasted much time in making up his mind to undertake, but lucky that he had been left, or rather had been driven back to, certain simple and fundamental possessions—an old house, an old man and a little boy. Most of his countrymen had no such trinity.

He had come now to the entrance of 'Hibernia' and through the elms and maples and firs could see the glimmer of the house, as if it too had watched the inscrutable blue autumn evening and then had lit its lamps and withdrawn into itself.

Gulian walked up the winding carriage-drive. The air was spicy with the scent of chrysanthemums and burning leaves. The little moon was caught in the branches of an elm like a bird's nest built of golden twigs. He came to the front door and laid his hat and stick on a chair in the hall and went along this gracious passageway, with its century-old paper of Dutch ships, high-pooped and high-bowed, breasting a faint green sea, until he turned into the wide, low-ceilinged living-room where his father and Philip Junior were sitting.

"Rhi-o-nascoris!" exclaimed Philip Junior, looking up from the volume he was devouring. ". . . This book tells you all about them. They have horns on their noses."

Mr. Eyre peered over the edge of his newspaper.

"There's a note for you on the mantel, Gulian," he said. "Prescott left it there half an hour ago."

Gulian went over to the hearth and took the small envelope from its place and suddenly his heart stood stock still and he could not see.

The single sheet trembled in his hands.

"Gulian," it said: "I am back again and I am staying again with Marian Gates. Yes, I came here because you were here, just as I came here before because you were here. Will you come over to see me as soon as you get this?

"No, I don't want any explanation and I won't give any. I have become a grim and determined woman. You can divorce me afterwards, but you must marry me first. While I was abroad I heard practically all that was happening to you, and since I have been home—only two days—I have seen Drusilla. Do you think lack of money frightens me, my dear?—I am clever about lack of money.

"I used to think that nowadays people didn't love the way they used to. Now I know they love infinitely more. They have less to keep them back. There are only a few things that seem really important any longer. . . . At all events, we can't help ourselves. I've known that from the beginning. So have you. We have to take our chances. It is depressingly inevitable.

"I am writing this because when I see you I will be shy and can't tell you. Perhaps, too, I may be disagreeable. People are often that way.

. . . "Possibly if you come straight from your house through the garden to the Gates' you will find me. I am restless. I shall leave this note with Prescott. You will be back soon."

Gulian slipped the letter into his pocket.

"I am going out for a moment," he said, and stepped through one of the long windows that gave upon the terrace, back again into the limpid night he had just left.

Below him the garden lay like the pooled smoke of an evening fire, blue and vaporous, and above it, over the dark masses of poplars, was an emerald sky. There was a sense of something eternal, a recurrent beauty, the substance of which was never the same but the effect of which altered but little; a something tremulous but quiet. And then, coming towards him through the garden, at the foot of the steps, he saw the white figure of Lael.

He hurried down to her. "I was restless," she sighed. ". . . Do you mind?"

"Mind?" He wanted to cry.

It seemed an age that he stood there looking at her,

although it was only an instant before he took her in his arms. But he did not want to break that blue evening moment, filled with the first sight of her. He knew that it was the most important and at the same time the least important moment of his life. Merely a beginning— And he was by no means sure of the road. He was asking a great deal of this girl; she would have to give him a great deal. She was young, untried, impatient— But he was sure of the end of the road. About Lael he had no longer any doubts whatsoever. Underneath she was as fundamentally direct and dependable as the first born mother of her sex. Something new had come to womanhood, or rather, something old had been re-found. He would quarrel with Lael a great deal—he knew that—but with her each quarrel would mean merely a further welding.

She shook the lapels of his coat.

"Oh, Gilly!" she said. "Oh, my blessed one! Oh, my dear! You're such a damned fool!"